The flare continued well out of sight, coming to rest amidst the stars. But it did not rest long for a voice came from all over the heavens softly addressing the flare, "Vrenessbith, it is time to wake.

Vrenessbith - a tear which gave birth to a whisper, a whisper which became a breeze growing into a wind that exploded into the greatest legend of Scotland. A story of tenderness, compassion, conflict, enduring strength, and undying love.   Vrenessbith!

Vrenessbith
Awakening

by
E. Gale Buck

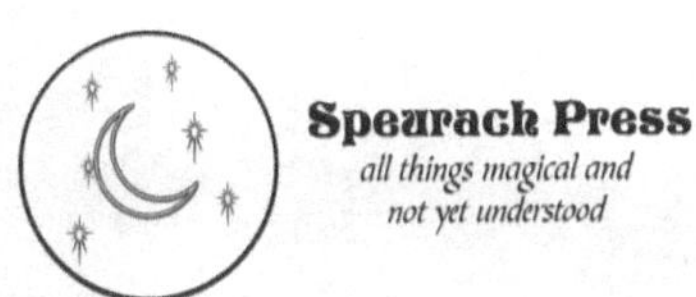

Spearach Press
*all things magical and
not yet understood*

ISBN: 978-1-7321681-0-7 (paperback)
         978-1-7321681-1-4 (e-book)

This is a work of fiction.
   Magical Realism; Historical Fantasy; Action & Adventure
   Suitable for Young Adult - Adult

Published June, 2018 by
Speurach Press
all things magical but not yet understood
an imprint of
The Silver Wreath
Raleigh, North Carolina
www.woodsmanstories.com

Printed in United States of America by Ingram Lightning Source

Dedication and Acknowledgment

I dedicate this story to my wife, Christy, and my daughters, Felicity, Jordan, and Noel, and my son Brock. They are my inspiration and my joy and, like Iain, I would do all within my power to see that they were cared for.

I also acknowledge this story could not have been written without considerable help and thank the writers at Storyteller's Book Store, Wake Forest, NC. They endured this story, helped me clean and polish it. They also were a major force in my learning how to write. So, to Drew, Lauren, Leslie, Kelly, and Michael - Thank You. And finally, those intrepid travelers who dared to venture into this story bringing reviews out the other end, Kaki, Barbara, Betty, Shirley, James, Drew, and Ross - thank you all for your efforts and comments.

Now I invite you into a land that never was but has always stood with a proud heritage and inspiration. Journey to this land of mystical magic and a time of long ago and always. Journey into a realm rich with adventure steeped in your own passion and experience. Reach into the mystic wonder of The Highlands with *Vrenessbith*.

E. Gale Buck

The North Side of the Great Loch

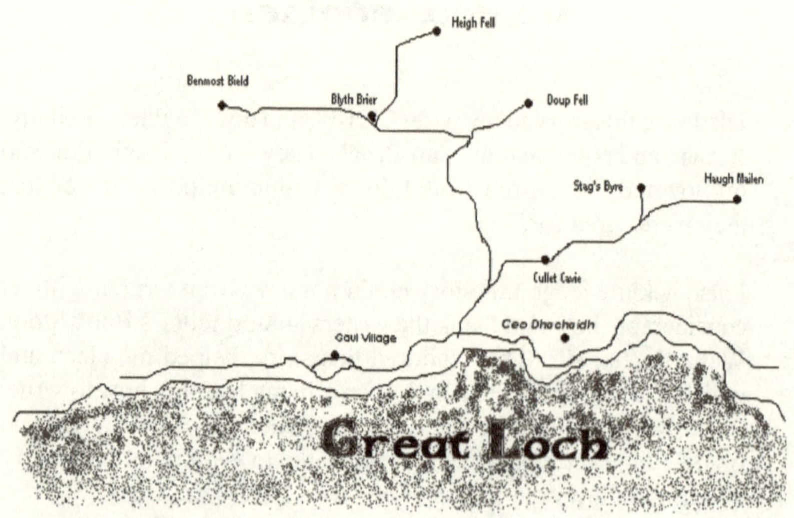

The Village Names and what they mean

Ceo Dhachaidh	Home in the Mist
(kyo GHaCHy)	
Cullet Cavie	Brother's Home
Stag's Byre	Stag's (deer's) Bed
Haugh Mailen	Journey's End
Doup Fell	Hidden Valley
Blyth Brier	Cheerful Briar
Benmost Bield	Farthest Shelter
Heigh Fell	Mountain Top

Glossary follows on page viii.
Cast of key characters at end

Welcome

Many stories have come from the Highlands of Scotland. These tales carry a relentless spirit and rugged sense of freedom. The Highlands by spirit offer all the necessary elements of a good tale - hills, mountains, caves, memories of rugged Scots struggling to survive, and a magical mist. An enchanting shroud of mist itself leads one's mind into its magic. This is the land where elves, faeries and witches were born. But despite the mystery and magic of highland tales, legends have always had a foundation in fact. The mist is real, the mountains are rugged, and the people are strong individuals who cherish their heritage and freedom.

Please note, some of the words in this manuscript may be odd to you. Footnotes are at the bottom of pages and a glossary follows, on page viii.

Welcome to a land rich in heritage and strong in character, where life itself guides the way.

<u>**Glossary of Celtic and Gaelic Terms**</u>
Note: proper Gaelic phonetics is difficult to interpret and there is no single standard. To aid you, the reader, with the beauty of this language pronunciations have been adapted for easier understanding. '~' separates syllables. Emphasis is on the capitalized letters. A few words are simple enough as written.
Some definitions and pronunciations may be found on internet at:
    Am Faclair Beag, www.faclair.com
    LearnGaelic, learngaelic.scot

athair - ah~HED - father, old Gaelic
bairn - bear n - children
ban-ridir - ban RI~jed - wife of a knight or nobleman
Bana-Bhuidseach - bana VUD~jach - ancient sisterhood of women
    dwelling within the mountains of the Highlands.
beanag - benag - wife, term of endearment
bean an taighe - ben an TIYA - goodwife
bean-usual - ben USAL - gentle-woman
byre - bire - cowshed, barn
cavie - CA~vee - a faerie community, often hidden in old trees or
    rocks
ceilidh - KAY~lee - social gathering, a party with music, dancing,
    and often storytelling
Comleidh - COM~lee - an elder faerie who oversees the well-being
    of the community. Teacher, guide, counselor.
coo - cow
creathall - CRE~hal - a cradle
ell - early Celts used a measure of ell, the distance from the tip of the
    finger to the elbow, termed the "ell", a measure of about a yard,
    37 inches
faerie - fairy - small inhabitant of forest. Their wings often reflect
    light giving the appearance that the faerie itself is a source of
    light. They generally appear human-like, with arms, legs, head
    and torso but can change forms as needed. Faeries' primary job is
    to assist nature and they tend to grow round with age.
fridgin - FRIG~in - young faerie
gobhain - go~iN - blacksmith
gré - grEE- natural essence of the world
hag - common name for member of Bana-Bhuidseach

léige - EL~ega - a league or three miles (predates Roman measure)

màithrean - MAH~ren - aunt, mother's sister

nighean - NEE~an - daughter

noigean - NOK~ean - noggin or head

patan - PAh~dan - youngster

peiteag - *PAY~jak* - jackets

plaid - PLAde - originally the end of the kilt taken from the waist on the right side, up the back and pinned with broach on the left shoulder.

seanair - SHEN~ed - grandfather

seanmhair - SHEN~e~ved - grandmother

siabhrach - SEE~vrak - male faerie

siabraichean - SEE~vrak~en - plural, group of male faeries

slat or *slat-uilne* - SWATH UL~nay - Gaelic term for Celtic measure of *ell*, which translates as "measure to elbow", a measure of about a yard, 37 inches.

sonnaidh - SON~agh - fort or garrison

Cast of key characters can be found at the end.

Ancient Rubble

Angus Gregson and his wife Lillian walked across the hillside toward an ancient oak tree nestled down the hill at the edge of the forest. Their three grandchildren ran about enjoying fresh air, sunshine, and this unusual hillside. Stopping short of a pile of rock, Angus gazed across to the loch below.

"I am going to see Belinda," Lillian told her husband. Kissing his cheek gently, she continued down an old worn trail toward the majestic oak which dominated the tree line.

Angus nodded and looked to the three children. Liam, an eight-year-old boy with more energy than six lads his age, picked up a stone from the pile and pulled his arm back for a mighty throw.

"STOP!" Angus commanded. "Whit are ye doin' there lad?"

"I was gonna see if I could reach the loch from here," the boy beamed with pride.

"Dinna ever take a stone from this place! Any of ye!" the old man scolded.

"Why, Seanair?[1]" Alex asked, picking up a stone and examining it. At eleven years, he was the oldest of the three.

"These stones once formed the seat of power in these mountains, back when these Hielands were first settled by Celts," Angus replied with pride. "Dae ye see that great black streak on the edge of those two large stones? Dae ye see how they fit together, those two? This was once one massive rock, split by lightening to make two chairs of glorious importance. Decisions were made upon and around these stone seats that shaped our Hielands to be as we know them today."

Lillian returned to her husband, telling him, "Belinda said the herbs I need are still growing in the old thicket of morning grain."

"Who is Belinda?" ten-year-old Marian asked.

"Belinda is Comleidh of the cavie[2] in the old oak tree," Lillian replied. "The cavie is home to Hieland Faeries, and Belinda is thair leader, teacher, counselor. Kind of a wise old seanmhair[3]."

Alex slowly rolled the stone in his hand, forming a question in his mind. His grandparents talked of stone splitting lightning and faeries as though they were common, yet, looking around the hillside he felt

---

[1] *seanair* - SHEN~ed - grandfather

[2] *cavie* - CA~vee - a faerie community, often hidden in old trees or rocks

[3] *seanmhair* - SHEN~e~ved - grandmother

something very uncommon had happened there. "Seanair, when did this happen? This lightning and seat of power you talked about."

"Ye might want to get comfortable, this tale will take a bit of time to tell ye," Angus replied, leaning on his walking stick. Lillian arranged the children on the hillside above the old storyteller and looked at him with anticipation. Looking to the faces of his bride and grandchildren, his heart began to swell, pounding with excitement. Angus was a storyteller of rare quality. Within each of his tales he shared not only a story but his heart, drawing his audience into other worlds. His love of this particular story gave him more passion than any other legend for this was his story. A story he inherited by birth and tradition, a legend handed down from his grandfather with this same fervor. The air around him became charged with his subtle excitement. Controlling his breathing and words, Angus carefully opened doors to an exciting new world as he began his story, the birth of his great Highlands.

Many years ago, before these mountains were appreciated by man, regions of Britannia and Western Europe were ruled by a powerful people, the Celts. Their origin is a mystery of lost history, however it is believed that these roaming warriors were cousins of ancient Norse Vikings. The trail of their existence begins in the mists of northeastern Europe from whence they emerged fearlessly with sword in hand. Many Celtic groups made the lands they captured their home. Settling among those they conquered, they would draw what they fancied from the land, the people, the people's traditions. Whatever they wanted they would take and make their own. They also left their mark behind when they eventually moved on, for they were craftsmen and masters of metals and stone. Captives were trained in the commanding art of Celtic warfare. Then, as their armies moved on some Celts would remain in their new homes while trained captives marched off as new warriors.

Angus looked at his grandchildren and saw Marian was barely listening but the boys were drawn to his voice. He continued.

There was, however, a troop of Celts who wandered in search of battle, seeking only conquest. These warriors, the fiercest of the Celtic nations, traveled throughout Europe conquering and taking only the richest, most valuable spoils of war. Their families followed behind them but these warriors never stayed any place longer than it took to restock and revitalize. Because they had families in their company, these Celts adhered to a stronger code of honor in warfare. They never attacked any unarmed man, never struck down a woman or child, and never burned homes. Their conquest was military. They had no use for unnecessary death or waste.

After a time the size of their families grew cumbersome, slowing the army's pursuit of conquest. There were many discussions about how to manage the ever increasing numbers. Some of the strongest warriors wanted to simply leave wives and bairn[4] behind and continue alone. Others wanted to send their families to a land safe from enemy retaliation. A land where they could build a home village. A place warriors could rest between campaigns.

Marian had tilted her head and tuned in when Angus told about the families. He now prepared to hook the boys, permanently. His voice deep, soft, and silken, the gifted storyteller released his words with a mesmerizing cadence.

Iain Gregor was a respected leader of these wandering warriors. His personal magnetism called people to join and fight beside him. A warrior of great honor, Iain's reputation as a victor and leader spread far ahead of him. When it was decided to send the families to build a village, Iain was selected to protect them. He chose a brother and cousin to stand beside him. They in turn chose twenty additional men. This guard of twenty-three seasoned and tested warriors was charged with the task of moving one hundred nine families to mountains in the northern region of Britannia.

Another of Iain's brothers rose as leader of the wandering troops. Their plan was to continue their campaign for two or three years and then find their families. At that time, when warriors, wives and bairn were reunited, they would discuss their future.

Journeying west toward Britannia, Iain's numbers grew. A village facing starvation joined these Celts on their quest, swelling their number to nearly one hundred fifty families.

Arriving in the mountains of Britannia, Iain and his families found a landscape of mountains reaching skyward and endless hills rolling one into another. While breathtaking in its beauty, it was not a welcome land for such a large population. A single settlement had been planned

---

[4]*bairn* - bear n - children

but difficult terrain did not offer enough space for one large village. After exploring the region, eight smaller villages were born, tucked into glens and glades of the vast mountains. Many months were exhausted settling families into workable pockets of this new land. Each village required a source of water, room to grow crops and space to build huts. Some villages began with a small group of twelve families and only two protectors. The largest group with forty-two families had nine trained warriors. One group found welcome within an established village. Two scribes, who recorded travel and battles of the Celts, kept a roster of which families went to what villages so their warriors could join them when they arrived.

═══════════

"Seanair, was our family on one of those lists?" Marian asked, her eyes dancing in reflected sunlight.

Aye, we were with Iain's group. Ye see Iain attracted the largest group, settling here, on the shores of that great loch ye see in front of ye. Water in this loch was sweet and crystal clear.

"Seanair, the water in our loch is not 'crystal clear,' it is black," Liam interrupted.

"Aye, ye are right, lad. Today, it is black but when the Celts arrived it was clear, and ye will not find out whence the black came from if ye keep interuptin' me story."

Now, if ye look around, ye can see how this hill rises sharply from the banks of the loch, to where a great boulder once rested, where those broken stone sit now. This boulder measured three ells[5] long and nearly two across. Standing on this great stone one could look out across the loch below, and the clearings and forests to either side. This area to my right, yer left, was thin forest and ye can see its gentle slope, good for building huts. To the other side of the boulder, the hill slopes downward toward dense forest. Behind ye, rests that expanse of flat, briar-filled meadow before the rise to the hill beyond. This stretch of wasteland was once spongy, made so by a stream meandering to the loch below. Liam, ye wanted to throw a stone? Well, few men could throw a rock across those briars to the other side. Look how the hill then rises once more toward the clouds. Angus looked thoughtfully up the hill in front of him for several seconds before turning and pointing

---

[5] *ell* - early Celts used a measure of ell, the distance from the tip of the finger to the elbow, termed the "ell", a measure of about a yard, 37 inches

toward the loch. Down below, that narrow strip of trees along the bank of the loch was wide enough, then, to hide this hillside and the village that grew up here.

A mist covered the village area most mornings, as it did earlier this day, giving rise to the name Ceo Dhachaidh, which means Home in the Mist. What they dinna know when they first settled here was they also had friends ready to help them with struggles they were about to face. Great and powerful companions living at the edge of thair village in yon ancient oak tree.

Angus pointed to the tree Lillian had been visiting.

"The faeries lived here then, Seanair?" Marian asked, her face scrunched up in a puzzle.

Aye, lass, the faeries were here then, as now. A great colony, or cavie as they call it. Today, Belinda is thair Comleidh, but then it was Resbith who led the faeries. That old oak tree [Angus pointed to an ancient oak tree] was home to great wee spirits who saved the hielanders many a time, especially a special faerie born of pure love, called by the name of Vrenessbith.

Unseen Shroud

Angus *surveyed his audience, seeing each was hooked on his story, he asked a question.*

"Now, as ye might imagine, Celts brought new things to these mountains but they also brought something they dinna even know they were carrying. Can ye imagine whit that might be?"

The children and Lillian looked at Angus with puzzlement filling each face. Delighted with their response, the old Scot resumed his tale.

One day, Resbith flew slowly to the top of a great oak tree which hid her home, the home of those faeries in her charge, their cavie. As Comleidh of this cavie she was responsible for its well being and safety, the welfare of all who lived within its branches and beyond, within this region. Her task had become much more difficult since the arrival of strangers on the hillside. Men and women unlike any she had ever seen had nearly destroyed the peace of her community. More than one hundred people had planted a village near her tree.

Arriving at the topmost branch, Resbith settled and looked across to the valley. She often watched these people. "How am I to learn about them?" she once remarked to another elderly faerie. Morning sunlight streamed across a mountain ridge, filling the village with promise of a grande day. Mist, which normally hid this village was uncommonly light and served only to soften these first rays of morning. Beginning a stretch and search for greater comfort, Resbith abruptly stopped all motion and stared into the village.

Watching men, women, and children begin their day, the Comleidh saw something normally not visible through heavier morning mist. Nearly every man and woman bore a shapeless shroud of grey. Darker on some than others, this shroud clung to each person in a different fashion. Some carried it lightly flowing down their back, as though a faint wisp had dropped to rest and would quickly move on. Others lumbered under its dark weight, stooped in posture and struggling to move about.

Curious as to the nature of this anomaly, Resbith flew straight to a woman carrying a darker version which poured off her shoulders enveloping most of her body in its heavy vapor. The wee faerie stopped suddenly on her approach due to a frigid reeking about this woman. Air about this woman was unbearably cold and choked all senses of this faerie who lived by her sensitivity to nature. Trying to clear her head, Resbith realized it was not truly an odor or cold but an absolute sense of total dismay. Feeling its freezing anxiety reaching to wrap around her, the wise Comleidh understood what she had encountered. With the heavy shroud encasing her own being, Resbith burst free and rose to a safe distance. An arm of the shroud, which had stretched briefly to include the inquisitive faerie, faded into nothing. Resbith sighed softly with regret, "*Gleò ar ùspairn cùlaigean*, you are the suffocating struggle of survival. I have heard legend of you but never before witnessed your presence. Had I returned to *gré*[6] without this day I would have been happier."

Not knowing what to do, the disheartened faerie returned to her oak tree. Looking back, she could not see any *gleo* for the sun was no longer filtered by the light mist. Reaching her cavie, she sought the warmth, love, and support of her family.

<center>~~~~~~~~~~~~~~~~~~~~~~~~~~~~~</center>

"Seanair do we have gleo around us?" Marian asked, interrupting her grandfather.

"Aye, I imagine we have a bit though I cannae say I hae felt it of late. Ye see, we canna see it with our eyes. Ye feel it in yer soul. When life is difficult, old gleo becomes dark and heavy, making things worse, but when we celebrate all that we have, we cannae feel its presence at all." Angus looked at his granddaughter and smiled. "Are ye ready for a bit more of this story?"

All three grandchildren nodded with expectation.

"Good. Where were we? Ah, yes. . . .

None of the people of this young village knew their days were made difficult by the *gleò ar ùspairn cùlaigean*, they just knew their lives were difficult. Also, Resbith was the only faerie who could see this weighty shroud worn by the people. Few of the other faeries had enough life experience to allow them to see what was hidden from our sight. She did ask other elder faeries and while some had heard of the *gleo*, as she called it, none had ever actually seen it. As Comleidh of her cavie, Resbith woke early each day in hopes of checking on the *gleo*, ready to do whatever was needed to keep it out of her oak tree.

---

[6] *gré* - grEE - natural essence of the world

Slowly these strange settlers became accustomed to life in the mountains and their struggles became less severe, more like daily challenges. Years rolled past peacefully, until the time their wandering warriors were expected to arrive.

Unfortunately, it was not the husbands and sons of the Celtic settlers who found *Ceo Dhachaidh* but a group of Roman soldiers. Early one morning, these unexpected Romans surrounded the village and waited until most of its men left to hunt. Finding a brief period where they had an advantage of numbers as well as surprise in their favor, the Romans launched a swift and devastating attack. A Roman captain, who had hunted and slaughtered many Celtic warriors, led a ruthless charge on women and children. Families of the Celts were being destroyed.

Hearing anguished cries of attack, hunters immediately turned and ran with all their strength back to *Ceo Dhachaidh*. Emerging from the edge of the wood Iain saw a Roman Captain pursuing his own children. Iain's older son, twelve years of age, struggled to defend his younger brother against the merciless attack, blocking blows with his dirk[7]. He was no match for the Roman Captain.

Summoning every ounce of his legendary strength, made even greater by his raging fury and boundless love, Iain launched his spear. Time stopped for this Celtic father as his spear sped across the village toward the soldier. Passing slain and maimed women and children, the instrument of rescue sailed through the bloodied village and burning huts, gaining power from its purpose. As the scream of time resumed, the spear impaled the captain, lifting him and pinning him, still alive, to a tree more than six feet from where he had plunged his sword through both boys less than a second before the spear's arrival. Iain's heart exploded at the sight of his children being slaughtered; he fought with unbridled passion, an erupting fury, that could not be matched by the Romans. Only two Roman soldiers survived their attack, a young lieutenant and the captain pinned to a tree. Iain forced the lieutenant to his knees in front of his captain.

Turning to the Captain, Iain declared with a voice that caused all to stop what they were doing and turn toward him, "Yeu have done a disgraceful act! Ye are not worthy of yer rank. Yeu have used your sword against innocence! Yeu have led your men in a battle against

____

[7] Dirk - the Celtic dirk was approximately eighteen inches long, including the handle of bone or dense wood. It is a one-handed thrusting weapon.

nature!" With one blow of his mighty sword, Iain beheaded the captain then turned to the Roman lieutenant. His voice filled with anguish, sending icy chills down backbones of all within its reach, Iain asked, "Ye have destroyed our village . . . murdered our families! . . . WHY?!"

Struggling to find his voice the lieutenant replied weakly, "Our emperor wants all Celts killed, no matter where they live."

"WHY?!" Iain growled, his anguish changing to anger.

"We conquered your armies," the lieutenant replied, finding courage in his response. "But it was costly. We lost legions. Yet, even as Celts were being executed, they sang 'Iain Gregor will avenge us.' Over and over. It became their song of death. Our Emperor wants the head of Iain Gregor presented to him on a spike."

Without hesitation Iain responded with conviction, "Yeu return to yer people and tell yer emperor that if I ever see another Roman soldier in this land, I will cut them down. Then I will find him and personally destroy his family as he watches. Dogs and crows will devour their carcasses." When he finished, Iain stood tall and surveyed the death which filled his village. "Show this soldier the road home and burn these worthless bodies."

Surviving villagers gathered the bodies of their loved ones and neighbors, laying them carefully on a funeral pyre. They then gathered Roman bodies, throwing them into a pit of fire. Iain wept that night as he lit the flame that carried his bairn, brothers, and sisters to their afterlives. All surviving Celtic warriors joined in a promise to never leave their village unprotected and to unite with other villages in defense against the Roman insanity.

Roman patrols continued to litter the mountains. Communications between patrols was almost nonexistent as these small groups hunting Celts wandered aimlessly. Whenever a patrol stumbled into a village, Celtic warriors answered their presence with death. Iain grew weary of their frequent intrusions and sought to keep the Romans out of his village. Entrances to *Ceo Dhachaidh* were hidden with bushes and other natural plants. Traps were laid to announce the arrival of unwanted visitors.

Marian stood and looked down the hillside toward the loch.

Lillian reached a hand out to her husband who gently helped her to her feet. She then stood behind Marian placing her hands on the girl's shoulders, asking "Whit troubles ye, wee one?"

"I see the hillside and trees, or bushes, at the edge of the loch but I don't see any traps."

"Aye, and ye would nae hae seen them then, either," Angus replied with gentle confidence. "Those bushes are gone now for this was many years ago. But even then, Iain and his Celtic warriors knew well how to hide thair village." Angus smiled at his wife, acknowledging the pain, love, and excitement in her eyes. "Tell ye bairn whit. Why don't we return to our lodge and I will continue the story a bit later. Ye will all want to be fresh for the Great Battle for The Hielands."

Lillian nudged up close to her husband, kissing his cheek as she quietly scolded him, "Ye dinna hae to be so graphic wi' the violence."

Angus smirked with satisfaction as he and Lillian collected their grandchildren, herding them back toward home.

Both boys groaned disappointment. They were not ready for Angus to stop.

"Dinna moan so, lads, we can continue back at the hoose," Angus encouraged with a hand on each of the boys' heads. "I might even show ye 'the book'."

"WHAT!" Liam exclaimed, reeling around in disgust. "You got this story from a book?!"

"No, lad, I dinna. No exactly. I will show ye when we get home," Angus replied with a gleam in his eye.

"Wait," Lillian cried out as they left the hillside. "I forgot my herbs. Come children, ye can help. Comleidh Belinda said they were along the briar thicket so be careful of thorns."

The boys grumbled as they followed their grandmother to a meadow across the hillside. Marian took Lillian's hand, skipping along beside her. Angus looked out across his beloved hillside, across the loch and to the mountains beyond. Breathing a deep sigh of contentment, he followed the others to a small glen overgrown with briars which hid several desirable plants beneath their thorny cover.

The Book

Lillian gently washed her herbs in a wooden bowl filled with cool water. Marian watched with interest, then asked, "Why do you use a wooden bowl and not rinse our herbs in the sink?"

"Ah, lass, because these are fresh wild herbs. They are traumatized from when we gathered them and now I want to soothe them so they will release thair flavors more fully. Like when I stroke yer head to awaken ye in the morning."

Just then Liam called out through the house, "SEANAIR!"

"Marian, go tell yer brother to look in the library and not call out so loudly," Lillian requested, gently shaking water from her herbs.

Marian found Liam standing at the base of the steps to the bedrooms.

"What is the shouting all about?" Alex asked from the top of the stairs.

"I want to see the book! Seanair said he would show us the book!" Liam insisted.

"In the library," Marian said, shaking her head.

Alex tripped down the stairs and all three went in search of their grandfather, who was napping in his library. Alex poked Angus in the shoulder, not so gently.

"Whit?" Angus growled, not pleased about being awakened from his afternoon ritual.

"You said you would show us 'The Book'!" Liam demanded with all the authority an eight-year-old could muster.

"Aye, I did that," Angus acknowledged, rising from his favorite resting chair. After stretching a wee bit, he crossed the room to the book shelves. Pulling a step-stool to a section near the rightmost side, he turned back to the children. "Now, ye must understand. These books are rare, the only copies anywhere, and they are old. Dinna pull them down without yer seanmhair or myself here to read with ye." Seeing agreement and wonder on their faces, Angus climbed the steps to the next highest shelf, removing one of two matched leather volumes. Crossing to a nearby table he reverently placed the book down and opened it to a page near the front.

"Ohhhhhh," the children cooed in wonder. The pages were yellowed with age, but more impressive was the exquisite handwriting.

"Did you write this book, Seanair?" Marian asked with awe.

"Nae, I dinna write this one. I am trying to complete its story in a second volume." Angus moved his head toward the upper shelves where the book had rested. All three children looked up and saw a twin to the book Angus held.

"If you did not write it who did?" Alex asked, his face glowing with curiosity and anticipation.

"Ye will not believe whit I am about to tell ye. Ye will want to see for yerself. Alex, climb up on that stool and retrieve the wooden box next where I got this book," Angus instructed.

"No, I will get it," Lillian interrupted. "I am sure ye could manage it Alex, but if ye were to fall, yer parents would never let ye come again."

Angus stood behind his wife as she ascended the steps of the stool and reached for the box. Holding it close to her chest with one hand, she put the other out to Angus for balance. Lillian then placed the polished oak box, measuring about fifteen inches long by ten inches wide and eight inches deep on the table beside "The Book."

Angus retrieved a key from his desk and returned to the box which was secured by a small but solid lock. Placing one hand on the box, he turned to his grandchildren.

"When I was about Marian's age my seanair found an old leather bag filled with even older parchments. Believing them to be of some value, he had a friend help him treat them so he could unfold and unroll them. Make them so he could read them." Angus then unlocked the box and removed one rolled up golden parchment. Unrolling it with extreme care, he lay the ancient document out so the children could see it, blocking Liam's hand when it came too near. "These parchments bear no author's name, but after years of study Seanair believed they were written by two women of Ceo Dhachaidh, Sarah and her daughter Erial, possibly even Erial's daughter-in-law, Rachel. Not having any schools, they developed thair own language, a written representation of how they spoke, which was mostly a mix of ancient Norse, Celtic, and Gaelic languages. Very few could read or write then and it was unheard of for women to read. Using legends he had heard about our hillside, Seanair spent years just learning thair language."

"Where we were this morning?" Liam asked with excitement.

"Aye, that very hillside," Angus continued. "Seanair then began to translate each of these parchments into our language. He wrote thair story in this book. About ten years before he died, Seanair realized he would not be able to finish this task so he taught me to read the *parchments. As yet, I have not quite finished, but hope to within a few months."*

"Why did they write these stories?" Alex challenged. "People did not write anything back then."

"Oh, but they did," Lillian replied. "Paper, or parchment, was difficult to come by and was expensive. Part of whit makes these scrolls so valuable is many of them are hand made from grasses of our hillside. I think Sarah saw the way listeners became entranced when warriors told thair stories and knew the stories might not survive if they were not recorded. On one scroll she talks about having seen her father write on a parchment; a talent he learned as a sailor."

"There are not so many parkments in that box, Seanair," Liam observed.

"Parchments," Angus corrected. "And ye are correct. These are those I am working on now. We have many many more stored away for safety."

"So, how did Sarah and Erial learn these stories?" Alex asked, honestly curious. "Did they hear them around campfires or what?"

"Mostly they lived them. Every day," Angus replied, locking the box.

"I believe they also talked with the faeries," Lillian added. "Sarah talked with Resbith, the Comleidh of that day, and Erial and Vrenessbith were friends."

"Other parts may have come from Ingrid, Seumas' wife and yer great so many times grand. Then from Vidar, Erial's husband, and some may have come on the wind," Angus confirmed. "As Iain once said, if ye listen to the wind ye can even hear how yer enemy is tossing sleeplessly with worry about facing ye in battle the next day." Angus looked at the entranced faces of his grandchildren. Assuming a smile he lifted the first book, offering "Would ye like to hear the next chapter of thair story?"

Three grandchildren quickly sat on the floor in front of Angus' chair. Angus carefully stepped over his audience to his seat of honor and Lillian took her chair opposite her storyteller. Laying the book across his lap, Angus turned over a few pages at the beginning and began reading as he told the story from the book.

Coming of Purpose

About five years after the Romans attacked *Ceo Dhachaidh,* an early blanket of white covered the mountains. Snow didn't usually fall until much later, but this year leaves on the trees were still golden when the landscape changed unexpectedly. All the world seemed to become still and quiet as the sun silently disappeared. A full moon reflected off freshly fallen snow casting a ghostly glow across the land. Still burdened with half their foliage, trees cast shadows resembling spirits from another world. Tree trunks appeared thin and dark with huge heads that changed shapes as wind blew through the forest crown.

Returning from a rare journey to a village beyond his mountains, Iain Gregor welcomed the soft light as he trudged through familiar forests made strange by eerie vestiges of dark shapes. A slight cape of deer skin covered his broad shoulders and his brown woolen kilt caught an occasional burst of wind. He carried a small pack over one shoulder. His own shadow stretched ahead of him, climbing over rocks and wrapping around trees as he moved.

The unexpected snowfall slowed his journey but he was determined to reach home without further delay. He had traveled this land countless times so unseasonable changes in terrain did not confuse his direction but the uncommon stillness did distract him. Pausing often, he listened to the mountains and trees. Nature had something to tell him, but he could not yet hear her secret. He was still too far away. Pushing onward, Iain listened intently for the concealed message.

A thrashing sound coming from a thicket about thirty-five ells off his trail, broke the unnatural silence. Thinking this was not the message he had been expecting he knew he must still check it. A young stag wrestled beneath a pile of briar and bramble. Its hind leg broken and tied by a rope to a big tree. Iain looked around, reasoning that someone had set a trap, a poor trap. The young stag had been caught but its weight was too much for the limb that was to have held him. Apparently the limb had fallen on his leg, breaking it and crippling the stag. Thrashing about in pain the creature had become tangled in every bush and growth within reach. Iain knelt beside the terrified animal, speaking softly. His powerful yet tender voice calmed the panicked animal. Gently, he put his right hand on the stags' face, stroking its neck with his left hand.

There was a conversation of sorts, an exchange of information. The young stag asked to be released from its pain, and if Iain would release him he would be rewarded with a valuable message. Iain understood. Carefully and gently he continued to stroke the stag. With one definite but gentle movement Iain broke the creature's neck.

Iain knelt in the snow holding the stag's head until its body was quiet. There was no more pain or suffering. The animal was free. Once its body had stopped quivering and was still Iain began to untangle him from the snare rope. He could take the stag home for food and there was always need of good rope. As he untied the line from the big tree, he found the promised message. Scattered debris from setting the snare was not only the mark of an inexperienced hunter, it was the mark of a Roman soldier. Carefully Iain examined marks on the tree and signs on the ground. He determined that the snare had been set after the snow had begun, earlier that day. It had been five years since the attack on *Ceo Dhachaidh* yet Romans still infested this land. Signs of clumsy movements in brush around the back of the tree led Iain to reason that there had been two, maybe three, soldiers. A small patrol to be sure. Was it large enough to be detached, moving on their own? Was it a routine scouting party from some new Roman outpost? Were they lost deserters trying to survive in these forests?

Finding no other signs of the clumsy hunters Iain lifted the stag to his broad shoulders and resumed his journey. Home was another hour distant but with the added weight and snow, maybe two.

The lodge of *Ceo Dhachaidh* was warm and dry. It was long, with animal skins hung on walls to help block the wind. It was dark except for light from a long trench fire burning in the middle of the floor. Remains of a small wild boar, which had provided dinner, continued to roast over a smoldering end of the fire. Women worked together to collect left over food for coming meals. Many feared food would be scarce in months ahead. This was not an every day gathering but the unexpected weather had caught many people unprepared. Collectively the community could survive, individually it would be difficult.

Young children ran around laughing and playing together. Men gathered about a large cask, enjoying a beverage similar to ale but more like mead. Their bellies were full and they were not worried about the cold or food. Elizabeth, Iain's wife, reached out to carve some meat from the boar. Her husband would be hungry when he returned. One of the men, who had been drinking for some time, reached across the fire toward Elizabeth.

"A woman should not be using such a large knife," he called. Retrieving the knife he knocked Elizabeth off balance, toward the flames. Iain's cousin, Seumas, caught her but the other man continued his ranting. Seumas tried to move him away from the fire and take the knife from his hand. With a quick dance step the man rolled away from Seumas, dropped the knife, and wrapped his arm around Elizabeth. Taking advantage of the lodge door bursting open she twisted away from the unsteady man. Cold wind knocked him to the floor.

A tall and powerful silhouette filled the doorway. Shoulders so broad they could not fit through the door. Its head reached above the frame so that it had to bend over to enter. Snow and ice covered fur-wrapped feet. Seumas stepped away from the fire allowing light to fall on the intruder; it was Iain. Quietly the Celtic leader dropped a deer carcass on the floor as he reached for the man who had assaulted his wife. In a single motion Iain tossed the man outside the lodge and closed the door.

"Cork the casket," Iain ordered. "Save it for celebration or survival. Tonight is neither. Yeu two skin this stag and prepare it for roasting."

Two young men quickly tugged at the carcass, dragging it out to a slaughter pen.

"Welcome home, cousin," offered Seumas as he retrieved Elizabeth's knife and finished carving a piece of meat from the boar.

"It is about time ye came home," taunted Elizabeth. "I was beginning to think ye had settled in another village."

"Quiet," replied Iain, as he wrapped his arms around his wife, delivering a great kiss as though it had been ordered by all the gods of war and nature. Others stood quietly until they were finished for this was not unusual. Homecomings were a grand time for Iain and Elizabeth and nobody interrupted them. "I missed yeu," Iain said quietly, "and this time I have a surprise for ye."

Elizabeth smiled at her warrior, stepping aside as Seumas handed him a large chunk of hot meat. The mood inside the lodge returned to normal. Everyone knew Iain was home and all was as it should be.

Iain removed his cape and pack, taking a seat near the fire. Elizabeth joined him, sitting at his side. Seumas and other warriors sat nearby asking of news about the mountains. Iain related events of his most recent journey and shared good news.

"There was a traveler, a seller of goods, who happened by a village to the east while I was there. He came from the south and had a most wonderful display of rare goods and items from other lands." At this point Iain looked over to Elizabeth and winked. She replied with an enticing hint of a smile and a gleam in her eye. "This man travels the land buying and selling goods. Recently he was in a Roman camp. He says the Romans have been ordered out of the mountains. It seems the 'barbarians' who live up in these mountains are too unruly to waste further resources on. The Romans are leaving, those who dared venture up here. We can now return to our lives in peace. But we must be on our guard, for I found evidence that they are yet in the forests. That stag I carried in was victim of a sloppy Roman trap. A few troops remain in the forests and we must be aware if they approach."

The two young men returned from skinning the stag and began to question Iain, "Did ye kill that stag or just find it on the trail?"

"I killed it to ease its pain," replied Iain. "It was the stag that showed me Romans are still in our forest."

"There was not a mark on the deer's body. It had a broken leg and a broken neck. How did ye kill it?"

"The Roman snare broke its leg. I broke its neck."

"I told ye so," charged one of the young men. "It is the power of the Deer Stone."

"No," answered Iain, "it is not the power of the Deer Stone. That stone is an honor that any of ye can win. I talked with the stag and eased his pain. If ye would slow yer actions and open yer hearts, yeu too could hear whit the forest has to tell ye. The forest will not talk to a sword but it will speak with a heart. Be still and listen."

"When do we get a chance at the Deer Stone?" the youth asked, boldly raising his posture.

"I see a challenge," Iain laughed with delight. "As is our custom, when the snow clears we will have a celebration. Celebrations require meat. Whoever returns with the largest stag gets the Deer Stone. Remember, it must be a stag; no doe or fawn. It must not bear any marks of knife, sword or spear. In keeping with yer challenge, and our custom, I hang the Deer Stone on this pole."

Iain removed a talisman he was wearing around his neck and hung it on a lodge pole behind him. A leather lace with an oval bone as long as Iain's thumb, showing detail of a deer's head in its grain. Antlers curved up within the lines of the bone at holes where a strap was secured and chips of a shiny mineral were embedded in the eye sockets. Some said it gave Iain his strength and ability to talk with animals. Iain enjoyed the myth, for no one had ever been able to better him in this contest.

While he was standing, Iain took Elizabeth's hand and started for the door. "If yeu fine people will excuse me, I am tired."

Iain picked up his cape and pack as he and Elizabeth left the lodge. Stepping over the unconscious man who had assaulted Elizabeth earlier that evening, Iain grimaced, shaking his head. The two departed for their hut.

<center>~~~~~~~~~~~~~~~~~~~~~~~~</center>

"Okay, children, ye can all help me finish preparing our supper," Lillian interrupted. She assigned each one to a job. "Marian, ye can help me with the herbs and the boys can clear thair things from the table and set it so we can all enjoy a pleasant meal. Come now, each of ye." Lillian then bent over to kiss her husband, whispering in his ear. "I think they may be a bit young for this next part. Ye enjoy it, me love."

Angus looked at his departing wife with amazement. Left alone in his library, the old storyteller read the next part to himself, silently.

Entering their small home, Elizabeth lit a single candle on a shelf above their bed. Flickering light cast dancing shadows. At the far end of the small room dying coals glowed faintly beneath an iron pot hanging in the fireplace. Iain removed the pot and placed two logs in the stone cavity, hoping to chase the cold out of the hut. He blew gently on the embers causing the logs to burst into flame. A small table with four log benches stood near the fireplace. Next to the bed a set of shelves held a small but serviceable assortment of clothes. In another corner Iain's brother's sword hung from the rafters; this brother killed when Romans attacked their village. An unused bed hid in the rafters where their sons once slept.

Iain dropped his pack on the bed and began to open it but was distracted by Elizabeth's movements behind him. She removed her outer dress, leaving the coarse undergarment, and was releasing her hair from its bun. Iain sat on the bed, watching. Hair cascaded over her shoulders, falling nearly to her waist. She was a solid woman, neither heavy nor slight, a good stock to survive the harsh life of these mountains. Iain admired her smooth and muscular legs.

"Whit are ye doing?" Elizabeth asked as she caught Iain watching her.

"Admiring great beauty," he replied softly, getting down on one knee, "let me help ye."

After removing her footwear, he rubbed each calf gently. Standing behind her, he held her arms, just below the shoulders, ever so gently.

"I have a gift for ye, if ye care to remove that coarse dress," Iain smiled. Their eyes locked briefly. He then went back to unwrapping his pack.

"And will this gift of yers keep me warm against the night?" taunted Elizabeth.

Iain pulled out a soft cotton undergarment to replace her coarse woolen dress. In the candlelight Iain saw her red and inflamed skin as she removed the scratchy wool. She flinched as he gently ran his hand over the irritation.

"I have something else for ye," Iain smiled as he produced a flask from his pack. He poured a generous amount of creamy liquid from the flask into his hands, warming it, and then began working the substance into Elizabeth's reddened skin. Her dry and tender flesh pulled the sweet-smelling creme off his hands, instantly soaking up every drop.

Elizabeth and Iain were more than husband and wife. They were best friends, each incomplete without the other. Iain's returns were a celebration of their marriage, a celebration of their love; a love so powerful it promised to continue even beyond death.

Angus smiled to himself, thinking of his wife and their life together. He then laid a silk ribbon across the page to mark his place and put the book on his desk. Whistling softly, he joined the family in the kitchen where he poured two glasses of wine for himself and Lillian.

Gentle rain spattered against the windows of Angus' library while he sorted through the morning mail. Advertisements went directly into a trash bin while bills were stacked neatly in his right-hand drawer, to be opened later. He had no sooner finished sorting when three eager faces appeared before him.

"Have ye finished cleaning up from breakfast already?" the smiling grandfather asked. He knew what they wanted.

"Yes, sir," *they replied in unison.*

"Well, outside with ye then. Don't waste a day lollying around the hoose."

"It is RAINING," *Marian moaned.*

"Won't you read a bit more from your book, Seanair?" *Alex asked politely.*

Angus was both surprised and pleased that the request had come from the oldest of the three. Standing behind his desk, Angus stretched then picked up the book. "I suppose, since it is RAINING outside." Sitting in his chair, he opened the book to its silk marker. The children sat on the floor in front of him as Lillian placed a cup of tea on the table beside his chair. The two grandparents exchanged a wink as Lillian sat in her chair and raised her own tea to her lips for a sip.

"Okay, now where were we?" Angus sighed as he ran his finger to the beginning of the next section of their story.

The next morning found everyone in good spirits except the one gentleman who had too much to drink from the keg. Sunshine warmed the land as the weather returned to a more seasonal character. Snow melted quickly and by afternoon wet ground was visible.

"Cousin, the snow has faded away," Seumas called to Iain across the village, "doesn't that mean we get a chance at yer Deer Stone tomorrow?"

"The deer run is usually a spring adventure but I will agree," Iain called back. "Ye lads had better not splash any water about ye this night. Yer sweet smell will definitely ward off any stag for twenty léiges.[8]"

Elizabeth poked Iain in the ribs and smiled, whispering "Right enough for yeu to say, after last night ye are smelling like a bouquet of spring flowers."

That night the village gathered to make arrangements for the Deer Run. Celtic warriors circled Iain sniffing. "Who is it that will chase off the stags?" they taunted. Iain only smiled.

Finally, Iain gave last minute instructions, "If ye hae a mind to join the run, and anybody can run if they wish, be here at the lodge before first light. Deer begin to move as light breaks and we want them to clear their nests before we scare them to death. Be sure to carry yer dirk to

---

[8]*léige* - EL~ega - a league or three miles (predates Roman measure)

guard against wolves and Romans, but no blade is to be used on any stag. We also need six men to stay with the village."

There were many chuckles as Iain delivered his instructions. Eight men volunteered to stay with the village, one commenting, "Let the *patan*[9] hae thair run. I hae done it already." Runners all rubbed past the hide of the deer Iain had delivered the day before. A touch of bad odor for good luck.

Morning found some runners barely awake for their event while others were eager to get started. Four warriors stood ready, including Iain, plus six young men, and one young woman, Rachel. Several men objected to having a woman on the run.

Iain stepped in front of her, looking down in judgement. She appeared very small next to his large muscular frame. "I dinna know," Iain defended her, "she seems a bit small, but she's dressed for the run and she's carrying a dirk. I think we should let her join the fun. Maybe she can teach ye lads a thing or two about jumping briars."

Dress was important, because much of the run would be through briars and brush. Most of the runners wore kilts, a length of woolen cloth wrapped around their waist and tied over the shoulder, and various sorts of leggings to protect against sharp branches. Iain, champion of this event, wore a deer skin wrapped around his waist, as a vest, and on his legs and forearms. These hides had been cured in a special way to make them supple but they still carried earthy scents of forest and deer.

After a vote of confidence by the runners, everyone, including Rachel, started into the forest. There was a deer herd believed to be near feeding grounds just over a léige to the north. No one spoke a word after they left the village.

First light created eerie changes in the forest. Black of night yielded to deep purples giving trees a ghostly appearance as though looming menacingly overhead. Shrubs and ground cover melted into dark shadows making it impossible to distinguish a deer from a bush, until it moved. Breathy clouds loomed in front of each of the hunters as they huffed out full volumes of air trying to keep their lungs primed for the fast start that would be required when a deer crossed their path. Deep colours of dawn slowly yielded to daylight.

The hunters had traveled less than one-half léige in total silence when a deer jumped across their path. One of the younger men, Eric,

---

[9] *patan* - PAh~dan - youngster

started to run after it but Iain grabbed him, patting his own head indicating there were no antlers. This was a stag only event. Just then Rachel raced past Eric; a stag followed the doe. The young man slipped Iain's grip like a wet eel and the run was on. Others joined the chase.

Younger runners left the path in full pursuit of the stag through the forest. They beat through bushes and small trees, keeping eyes on their quarry but always trailing. When the stag crested a hill and dropped into a small ravine Rachel and Eric took off to the right. These two young runners were running hard, side by side. Iain followed the two, more out of curiosity than pursuit. Cresting a hill, Iain saw Rachel and Eric draw close to the stag. They had flanked it, one on each side.

Other runners quit the chase, rejoining the group on a small hill. Panting spectators marveled with growing interest as stag and pursuers continued across a broad field. The stag leapt over bushes, logs, and a stream. Eric and Rachel matched him leap for leap. In desperation the stag ran into some briars. Coming out of the briar thicket Rachel was even with the stag's hind legs. Eric's kilt hung on a bush but he spun around freeing himself. He lost his kilt but never lost his pace.

Adrenalin continued to fuel the two runners as their quarry began to tire. Rachel was now just behind the stag's shoulders and the half-naked Eric was even with its hind legs. Eric saw the path turning to the left ahead, into Rachel. Quickly, as though set to music, Eric doubled his stride, launched himself off a fallen log and wrapped himself around the stag's upper neck, just behind its antlers. Eric and his prize came down on top of Rachel who had wrapped herself around the stag's lower neck. Tumbling into a stand of brush the captured stag struggled briefly then lay still, breathing heavily. Rachel and Eric looked at one another, neither had ever been in this position before. Neither knew how to kill a deer without the use of a knife. They soon began to laugh and their laughter caused them to loose their grip. In the blink of an eye the stag was back on his feet and gone. Rachel and Eric were left on the ground trying to figure out what had happened to their prize.

With the stag gone, Eric and Rachel decided to find their group but they were too tired to walk alone. When they emerged from the brush, the group saw them walking with their arms wrapped around each other, their laughter dripping with tears of exhaustion. Upon seeing Rachel holding up half-naked Eric, the group began pointing and giggling. Seeing the group's reaction, Eric realized his state and turned into the bush with a giant leap that would have made any stag envious. Watching Eric's bare behind fly into the bushes, Rachel's face glowed crimson as she turned away from the others, doing her best to subdue her own laughter. Giggles of other hunters erupted into fits of hysterics.

Iain did his best to calm the group and had almost succeeded when Eric returned, with his kilt. Looking down at Eric's red face Iain began laughing uncontrollably. It was nearly twenty minutes before the Deer Run could continue. Once all were composed and quiet, the hunters resumed their journey to the grazing ground. Approaching a meadow they sighted a giant stag standing on the trail. Iain signaled everyone to stop and remain still. He then cautiously walked up to the old deer.

Motionless, the stag sniffed the air constantly and did not bolt or run away. Standing nose to nose, Iain and the stag seemed to have a conversation. Iain looked at the side of the stag's neck and began stroking a large scar. Then a most strange ritual took place as Iain butted the stag in the neck with his head. The stag knocked Iain with the side of his head and Iain grabbed the stag's antlers. There was a short wrestle and the stag withdrew.

Iain stood in place but signaled the other runners to hold still. After a few minutes a younger stag appeared and approached Iain. Snorting, pounding the ground with his hooves, this full-grown buck lowered his antlers as challenge to Iain for ownership of the herd. Casting his eyes to the hillside behind where the stag had come from, Iain saw about twelve does and six to eight younger males. Iain stood still, snorting at the stag. Accepting the challenge the stag slammed his head into Iain's head. Iain went down on the ground; as he rose, the challenger lowered his head for a charge. Stepping sideways quickly, Iain avoided powerful antlers and reached for the stag's neck, barely getting a grip on it. Over a period of fifteen to twenty minutes Iain and the stag slammed at each other with the sides of their heads. Avoiding head-on charges, Iain caught an antler only twice. Both combatants stumbled with fatigue. Rearing on its hind legs, the stag launched a final attack against his rival. Using the deer's own weight, Iain caught the stag beneath its front legs. Rising under the great animal, Iain toppled him sideways. He then grabbed the antlers and placing his knee on the stag's neck, twisted its head with all his strength. Death was instant.

The old stag had circled behind the hunters during the battle and now called to his herd. All the deer on the hillside came down, walking quietly past Iain, the slain stag, and around the group of hunters. Runners were stunned to witness and experience such an event. Except for the silent movement of the herd all of creation was motionless, as though time had stopped.

"Seanair, that did not really happen, did it?" Liam asked. His eight-year-old face was glowing with excitement.

Angus could see he wanted to believe. "I am only readin' to ye whit is in the book. I admit that I hae never wrestled wi' a stag such as this but I hae fed many a doe wi' me hand. Maybe I can teach ye how to do that while yer here this summer." Watching his grandson's eyes almost expand beyond his face, Angus asked, "But that will be on a day without rain. Now, may I continue?"

Rachel and Eric looked at each other as another young stag came into a meadow less than twenty feet away. Barely disturbing the calm of the air, they gave pursuit. Sensing the runners' motion the deer started to leap but it was too late. Rachel and Eric grabbed the animal as it took flight, rolling it to the ground where they could wrestle with it. Their quick actions startled other deer which quickly disappeared. Liam, who had been a warrior with Iain, came over to help Eric and Rachel. Placing his knee on the stag's shoulders he held the stag still as Rachel and Eric together broke its neck.

It had been a successful run; two stags killed for the coming feast. While runners cut carry poles to transport the stags, everyone talked about what had happened. Iain, who had been very quiet, finally shared a short story.

"On one my treks through these woods I found that old stag trapped in a briar thicket. He was much younger then and I thought he would be an easy kill. I wrestled with that beast for more than an hour. He gored me four times and I was bleeding badly, but he was nearly lame as well. We stood nose to nose and slapped each other with our noigeans[10]. Finally, we had to quit from exhaustion but we have been respectful and friends with one another ever since. I see him often and always try to spend a minute or two remembering that old battle. It is a strange relationship, but a truer friend I have never known. That stag I killed this day was a marauder and had tried to steal the herd without a challenge. The old buck was trying to call his herd back. I just gave a friend a hand."

Everyone looked at Iain with astonishment and disbelief. They had all seen their leader battle a stag, and win. Yet, not one could fully

---

[10] noigean - NOK~ean - noggin or head

believe what they had witnessed. Iain's tale of friendship with the old stag did not make the battle easier to accept.

"Let's go," Liam called out. "We have two stags to dress for supper."

<center>~~~~~~~~~~~~~~~~~~~~~~</center>

The day of the deer hunt began early for Elizabeth, Seumas, and others. Standing together in the predawn hour they watched hunters leave their village in pursuit of meat for a celebration. Roman intruders had been a dark shadow over the village for many years, and news that the shadow was lifting was indeed reason to celebrate.

As morning progressed, soft clouds floated across a deep blue sky. A brilliant sun restored seasonal warmth, melting remnants of an early snow. *Ceo Dhachaidh* was busy, alive with folks in relaxed pursuit of daily tasks and preparations for ceilidh[11]. Older children began the process of gathering food from storage bins. Women prepared great pots for cooking. Men gathered wood to the village common and built fires. There would be a feast tonight if runners brought home some meat. The small deer Iain delivered two nights before was ready to roast but would not feed the entire village. Conversation was lively and the mood was festive.

Raising its snout into the air, a piglet boar wandered about the village unnoticed. Sniffing and looking from here to there, this small intruder seemed to be in search of something. Its body showed signs of new dark brown hair, almost black, but still had the light brown stripes common to the young. Nearly eighteen inches long, it weighed about sixty pounds.

While the small intruder meandered around one of the huts, a young girl, Mary, spotted it and followed. With all the available curiosity of a three-year-old, Mary watched the piglet push through rubbish piles and continue its wandering around the huts. After following for some time, Mary decided to practice her herding skills. Picking up a stick, she prodded the piglet with a sharp whack on its back side. Startled, the piglet leapt straight up several inches, turned toward its assailant and snorted. Mary responded by whacking the piglet on its snout as she had seen her big brother do many times.

The piglet decided the party was over and he was ready to return home to the wood. Squealing briefly, piglet ran back in the direction it had come. Mary followed, swatting at its backside as they ran. It was

---

[11] ceilidh - KAY~lee - party, celebration

difficult to tell who was making the most noise, the piglet squealing as he tried to escape or Mary laughing in pursuit.

They ran around several huts and then back to the village common. The common had become quite busy and a pair of running bairn was not exactly in keeping with the order of things. Mary and piglet were now running around people instead of huts. Startled villagers tried to get out of the way as the chase wove in and out of busy workers. Soon all the young folk of the village were involved in the chase, screaming and laughing with delight. All the bairn except the piglet.

Seumas put an end to the chase by grabbing the animal. Suspended by its hind legs the piglet let out a squeal that chilled the Celt's blood. Holding onto the animal, the old warrior turned toward the boar pen to deposit his catch for later. Seumas had not taken many steps when he heard a loud snort behind him. He stopped in his tracks as the deeper tone of the snort commanded his attention. Turning carefully, Seumas saw a very large boar challenging his movement; its massive body covered with dense wiry black fur stretched nearly a full ell in length, weighing over two hundred-fifty pounds. Its long round snout protruded from a deep sloping triangular wedge-shaped head, raising clouds of dust with each snort. Slowly the experienced warrior crouched down and put the piglet on the ground. Mary did not understand what Seumas had done and quickly resumed her chase of the piglet. The large boar took chase of Mary.

Elizabeth had been watching the spectacle unfold while she kneaded bread dough. Without hesitation she jumped to her feet, charging toward Mary. Mary continued to try to turn the piglet back into the common. Reaching out to grab Mary, Elizabeth was tripped by the piglet. Now at full charge the large boar, a furious mother, had Mary as her target. Elizabeth stumbled to regain her balance while grabbing at Mary. The boar slammed its massive head into Elizabeth's leg, knocking her into the child. Elizabeth and Mary grabbed onto each other as the boar turned to charge again. Rolling over to protect Mary, Elizabeth heard a loud, deep, bloodcurdling squeal. Two spears had stopped the large boar's charge. Seumas ran toward the boar and Mary's father ran toward Elizabeth.

"Where is my piglet?" Mary cried as Elizabeth let her go.

The piglet was not to be seen. Several older boys began to drag the large boar to the slaughter pen. It would make a fine addition to the feast. Mary's mother brushed dirt from the child's dress, scolding her for playing with the piglet. Seumas helped Elizabeth back to her hut where she cleaned herself off. Preparation for the feast resumed with Mary and her piglet being the main topic of conversation.

―――――――

"I saw a piglet in the forest two days ago!" Marian exclaimed with delight.

"Aye, they are out there but don't ye go trying to herd them," Lillian warned. *"Where there are young there is a watchful mother."*

Just outside the village, deer runners returning from a successful hunt heard a strange rustling in the bushes. Iain quietly picked up a stick and stuck it into the bush. Immediately, a young piglet boar ran out of the bush, squealing and making a ferocious noise. Recognizing a valuable resource, Iain signaled Eric and Rachel to catch the beast.

The piglet ran in circles about and between the group of hunters. Understanding that it was Eric and Rachel's task to capture the piglet, older hunters did their best to get out of the way whenever the piglet came near them. Eric and Rachel, both fast enough to run down a deer, could not outmaneuver this wildly meandering piglet. Pursuit ended abruptly as the piglet shot under the two deer being carried on poles. Eric darted around the right. Rachel darted around to the left. They met each other on the other side, colliding with such force that they knocked down one of the trussed deer which fell into the second, creating a pile of man and beasts. Piglet stopped about ten feet away from the pile, turned to gaze at the mess he had caused and snorted as he trotted off . . . very satisfied with himself.

Those men who were still standing laughed until tears flowed from their eyes, their faces glowing with delight. Eric and Rachel glared at each other, each blaming the other for letting the piglet escape. As the piglet disappeared into the bush even Eric and Rachel laughed, helping each other up. Everyone needed help and it was some time before the hunters could make their entrance into *Ceo Dhachaidh.*

The runners' triumphant arrival stopped abruptly; a scene of absolute havoc lay before them. Cook pots were overturned, food and wood piles scattered throughout the common. Everyone was busy cleaning up as though from battle. Iain saw Elizabeth outside their hut, nursing her wounds. Without hesitation he raced to her side.

"Whit happened here?" he asked as he took the rag from her hands and began soothing her cuts and bruises.

"We were attacked . . . "

"Who? Yeu were attacked by who?" interrupted Iain, not allowing Elizabeth to finish.

"It is done . . . relax! We will eat our enemy this night, unless ye have something better." Elizabeth pointed to the slaughter pen where men were dressing a large boar.

Iain looked at the boar with amazement. Before turning back to Elizabeth he asked, "There wasn't a young piglet involved in this battle by chance?"

"Yes there was," Elizabeth replied. "How did ye know?"

Iain began laughing again, loud and hearty. This time he laughed so hard he hurt himself, or rather he hurt where his stag had caught him in the chest.

Elizabeth and Iain tended to each other's injuries. The rest of the village spent the day dressing game and preparing for a feast. Topics of the day followed two events, the piglet chase and the run of Rachel and Eric.

All of *Ceo Dhachaidh* celebrated Rachel and Eric as their story was relived and retold over and over - including the comedy of Eric's lost kilt. These two were the youngest and smallest runners to ever bring down a deer. Together they had accomplished what others only dreamed of. And Rachel, never before had a woman gained respect as a runner. The celebration that night would be one to remember. Iain having the larger kill kept his Deer Stone.

It was late in the evening, long after dark, before dinner was ready to be served. A common table was spread with breads, kale, carrots, turnips, venison and pork. This was a hearty feast and well deserved. Following the meal there was dancing around a crackling fire as sounds of clapping hands and song filled the air. Never, in the history of *Ceo Dhachaidh* had there been such a day as this.

At the peak of the evening Iain got up to salute the runners, as was custom. He called Eric and Rachel to stand before him. Before Iain could begin his toast there was a loud high-pitched whistle and crack. These unusual sounds came from the sizzling carcass of their small stag. Drawing his dirk, Iain walked over to the half-eaten deer. With a single powerful blow, Iain severed its neck from its shoulders. He then reached into the cavity beneath the shoulders and withdrew a bone. The bone was roundish in shape with steam hissing from a crack. Iain carefully pushed his dirk into the crack. After checking that it was secure he placed the bone into the coals of the fire for just a few seconds. Holding the dirk upright in front of him, Iain returned to where Eric and Rachel stood, waiting. Removing the bone from his dirk he shook it . . . it rattled.

Iain looked at Rachel and Eric squarely as he told them, "Only if a stag is killed cleanly and honestly, as a first kill, will it present ye with this." Iain then crushed the bone in his hands and revealed two identical deer stones, oval shaped bones where the grain strongly resembles the head of a stag. Each stone about half the size of the one Iain wore. He presented one to each of the runners as a tribute from the stag to them.

"What happened to the deer stone?" Alex asked. His face alive with the possibility of holding such an enchanted talisman.

"Iain's stone was passed down over the years as different men wrestled with larger deer. But these other two, even more special than Iain's . . . well, ye will have to wait to find out just where they are today." Angus winked with delight at his eldest grandson.

Many weeks passed with weather randomly changing from stormy and cold to warm and pleasant, and back again. Finally, weather settled into a warming trend and rituals of preparing for Spring commenced. Villagers began the torturous work of turning hard-frozen soil and planting seeds carefully saved from last year's crop. Hunters laid traps in a more careful manner so as not to hurt their catch. Female animals heavy with young would be released to ensure future generations. Free from fear of Roman invasion, men and women of the mountains looked forward to new opportunities and adventures.

The village of *Ceo Dhachaidh* saw spring budding in Rachel and Eric as well. These two young people had once been solitary but were now close friends.

Rachel's mother had died in childbirth. The infant Rachel was raised by her mother's sister, Gudrun. Gudrun had wed her childhood sweetheart at an early age but was widowed shortly after the ceremony. Her brave young husband went to battle beside Rachel's father. Only his sword came home. Gudrun blamed Rachel's father for her loneliness because he returned and her husband did not. Because of her anger, she did little more than feed and clothe her niece. Rachel's father was a Celtic warrior. He fought hard. He drank hard. He had little use for a daughter. The only toys this young lass knew were her father's swords and knives. She watched her father prepare for battle and would imitate him while he was gone. When he was home, she stayed out of his way and out of sight. At age eleven Rachel witnessed her father's dying battle when *Ceo Dhachaidh* was attacked by Romans. All she could remember of him was how hard he fought, and that became her inspiration as she grew up. Young men of the village were afraid of her and grown men respected her from a distance.

Rachel blossomed at an early age. Acknowledging her arrival to womanhood, one of the farmers of *Ceo Dhachaidh* tried to take her after his wife died. The man grabbed Rachel by the arm and dragged her off as his prize. They had not gone ten steps before Rachel, with the cunning and agility of a trained warrior, pulled her father's blade from its concealed carrying place and put it to her attacker's throat. Speaking with absolute confidence and the manner of a warrior she swore, "Ye touch me again and I will remove all yer misery and loneliness at yer shoulders!"

The villagers were pleased to see Rachel finally accepting her womanhood when in the presence of a young man. Her manner became more restrained in the company of Eric.

Eric was the youngest in his family, with two older sisters. His father was a farmer. He learned from his father the value of hard work and how to make the land produce. He was good at it. Eric took great pleasure in a beautiful sunrise or sunset, and could talk his way out of almost any situation. Most other young men wanted to learn to fight and become Celtic warriors like their late fathers but Eric always found greater pleasure in a bountiful harvest and a full table. He was a better than average trapper but had never taken part in a deer run until he ran beside Rachel.

Rachel and Eric became good friends and companions, respecting each other tremendously. The Deer Run had awakened both of them, making them aware of their maturing lives, which they enjoyed sharing with one another. *Ceo Dhachaidh* looked at the growing relationship as a promise that Rachel would be tamed. Young men of the village who had teased Eric for not picking up the sword were in awe of his courage with this lass.

<hr>

Springtime also revealed effects of winter on aging members of the community, though few took notice. One old woman, Magnhild, had lost her husband and one son before migrating to these forbidding mountains. Living alone, she struggled from day to day but seemed to always find a smile to encourage others. As this changing winter faded into spring Magnhild's bones moaned with weary despair.

Resbith watched as the old woman struggled with pails of water, carrying them from a spring above *Ceo Dhachaidh* back to her hut. Seeing this valiant woman weighed down with *gleo*, the faerie flew to her, hovering just ahead of Magnhild. Sunlight reflected through Resbith's wings creating a sparkle to Magnhild's eyes. Raising her head, Magnhild saw a sky filled with puffy white clouds. She felt sunlight bathing her face and much of the weight of her *gleo* slid away. Feeling revived by nature Magnhild stood just a bit taller and carried her water with less pain.

Resbith smiled and took encouragement from Magnhild's small victory.

Mountain villages were often isolated during harsh months of winter. More hospitable weather of spring brought new growth and new challenges. A springtime sun approached its peak as a group of travelers approached *Ceo Dhachaidh*. Asking for Iain, they were directed to where the Celtic leader worked the soil. Iain embraced several men warmly as old friends. Men who had once been comrades in arms. Others were introduced as leaders from different villages. The men engaged in a deep conversation. Now and then Iain would look up and point toward other men around the field. He even signaled for several to join this peculiar meeting. All business completed, Iain and the men he had called into conference went to their individual huts. Visitors moved up to the lodge.

Iain strolled over to Elizabeth. Wrapping his arms around her, he spoke with deep concern. "The Romans are back and these men believe that they are planning to burn all villages in our mountains. We must find them and see what business they are about. I will take three others and we will join these men searching for the Romans. I do not know how long we will be gone. Seumas and others will stay close to watch over our village."

"We will go, too" offered Eric and Rachel in unison. They and others had gathered to hear the news.

"No," Iain declared. "Eric, ye can join with us for I may need yer speed and agility. Rachel, ye need to stay and help Seumas watch over the village. Ye show great courage but are impetuous, which would be dangerous on a journey such as this. If we are not successful or discover a greater Roman force than we can handle ye will be needed to help train others and prepare for battle."

Rachel tried to argue but lost to the silent command of Seumas' strong hand on her shoulder. The sun had barely passed its peak when a growing group of battle-proven warriors and men of the soil left *Ceo Dhachaidh*. Iain kept company with their leader, a man named Seth, who advised Iain of his concerns from what he knew personally and also had been told by a friend who traveled the mountains and lowlands beyond.

All day the group marched in search of Romans, resting only briefly that night. Sunrise found them on the move again. Members of this unusual troop made sure each had enough to eat, none hoarding provisions. Taking a path that led out of the mountains they found a clearing where Romans had stayed the night before. Fire beds were still warm. Iain and Seth recognized signs of military encampment as they studied the ground and bushes around the clearing. Calling to their band, Iain struck a new direction at an increased pace. Dusk was settling over the mountains when a ribbon of smoke was sighted in the distance. Nearing a Roman encampment, Iain told the others to hold back. He entered alone.

"Do ye hae a bit o' meat to spare?" Iain asked as he approached the fire, his large frame silhouetted by a bright moon rising early over mountains behind him.

Roman guards snapped to attention quickly, bringing spears to bear on Iain in their surprise. Iain casually pushed them aside as he advanced cautiously.

"I'm na here to do battle," Iain soothed his way into the fire light. "I am only looking for a bit of warmth away from the night chill, and possibly a bit o' meat to chew."

A Roman officer and an old hag of a woman, or at least she had the face of an old woman, sat across the fire. She wore a combination of robes and scraps of tattered cloth that made her almost indistinguishable from the rags she wore. Had she not been sitting beside the officer Iain would not have seen her at all. The officer introduced himself as Junious Augustus, an Officer in the Emperor's Army. He then introduced the old woman as Hester, his guide through the mountains.

"I have traveled these mountains often," commented Iain, "how is it I have never met ye before?" His eyes locked onto Hester and her eyes bore into him.

"I am not of this land," replied Hester, "I know of it by my ancestors. My family has traveled this region for generations and I know every rise of these mountains by reference."

Iain agreed to this possibility but was very uneasy with this woman. Hester also became restless as their conversation continued. Each challenged the other with references to different land marks. This contest might have continued for days had a strange event not interrupted them.

A young Roman soldier picked up a Mediterranean bagpipe and began to play. Attempting to get the large bulbous thing under his arm, he gave up and hugged it to his body as he blew into it. Sounds wailed from the bag like cries of a sick she-cat. The soldier had brought this obnoxious beast with him from his previous post but had not yet learned to control it. He blew and squeezed and wailed until Iain could stand it no longer.

"I know not whit ye seek in these mountains," yelled Iain, "but ye'll never catch it with that thing wailing. Even a dying Celt would flee from that sound."

"Do you know of Celts in this region?" Junious inquired.

"Aye," affirmed Iain, "the Celts have settled throughout these mountains."

"And of a Celtic warrior named Iain Gregor?" continued the general, "Have you ever seen his village, a place called Kyo Gotcha?"

Sensing a shift in Hestor's posture Iain paused before answering. This Roman patrol was after him and by recent reports, they were willing to burn the mountains to find him. "Iain Gregor, ye say?" Iain countered, "I heard he died last winter, gored by a stag."

Immediately the old hag stood and cast off her heavy outer robe. "You say you died last winter?" she challenged. "You are very healthy indeed for a corpse."

Iain jumped to his feet trying to counter her advance. Hester grabbed a vine from around her waist and snapped it around Iain's arm. Crying out in pain he fell back into the darkness. Without hesitation the small band of Celts charged to his rescue.

Junious Augustus grabbed at the old woman roaring, "Come on witch! Get me back to safety!" Quickly and silently the old woman and

Roman officer disappeared into the dark. A brief battle raged as Celts slew all remaining Roman soldiers.

Seth was the first to return to Iain's side. Iain did not move nor did he respond to shakes and calls from his fellow Celts. No one could find any signs of life in his powerful body. The men of Iain's village discussed how they were to break the news to Elizabeth when a strange light shimmered around Iain's head.

"Iain can't be dead!" Liam cried out. "He is the hero of this book!"

"It may seem so, lad, but ye must wait and see. Even heros die," *Angus warned, a twinkle in his eye.*

"WHIT HAS HAPPENED HERE?" Iain cried out to his sleeping friends. Alarmed men stumbled to their feet. "Whit has happened?" Iain repeated.

Seth and others told Iain all that they knew, admitting they understood very little of what had happened to him. "When the fight was over and ye were on the ground. A light began to dance around yer head! A voice came from the light and said ye were not dead, only sleeping. We were told to rest right here and that ye would be guarded and would rejoin us in the morning. I dinna know whit was in the light but ye are here again."

"Hester is a mountain hag," Iain explained. "Only a hag could move like that. She is the first I have seen but I have heard of her kind before. This light ye describe can only be the presence of Faeries of the Myst. I have heard of them as well, maybe even seen them in the distance but I have never actually talked with one."

"We have been watching over you since you came to our hillside," a small voice called from a nearby branch. Everyone looked quickly toward the branch seeing four small creatures. Each seemed to glow as morning sunlight gathered in their delicate wings. They appeared as an impression of goodness incarnate, light and friendly. Then they were gone as though they had not been there at all. The entire group of men stood motionless in disbelief and wonder.

After some time had passed without sightings of wee faeries or Roman soldiers, Iain proposed that they return home and prepare for battle. Everyone quietly gathered their gear and prepared for a long march. Entranced by the beast the soldier had been squeezing, Eric grabbed the bulbous bagpipes. Wrapping the wooden pipes and leather bag with a rope, he slung the bundle over his shoulder.

Silence governed the journey home. Each man relived the battle over and over in his own mind. A few considered what they were all now facing - uncertainty, battle, fighting an enemy in their new home. An invading army had been ordered to destroy all Celts and they could not return to their homes and families until they completed their mission. Shrouded in quiet the journey seemed longer than it was.

Just before midday Iain began to sweat and stumble. Seth tried to help him stand, but Iain was too large. His body went limp and collapsed. Companions washed his face with cool water, trying to revive him. After several minutes Iain opened his eyes. He shook uncontrollably with a freezing chill and then lay motionless.

"It is the effect of the hag's poison," a small voice told them.

Turning quickly the men saw Iain's great stag approaching, with two faeries riding on its antlers. The faeries now appeared as wee men with great wings. Morning sunlight seemed to make their bodies glow. Each appeared slightly smaller than the length of a joint in a man's finger.

"This man will be weak for several days from the effects of that poison," continued one of the faeries. "It would be better if he did not walk. The stag will carry his friend."

The great stag walked over to Iain and pushed Iain's arm with his nose. Iain feebly looked at the stag and took hold of an antler. As the stag raised its head Iain fell back to the ground, unable to hold on. Standing steadfast as a guardian, the stag waited. Several men lifted Iain onto the stag's back where he slumped forward, arms above his head, cradled in the powerful antlers with his head resting near the top of the stag's neck. The small band of warriors continued their journey into the night. As they approached the woods of *Ceo Dhachaidh,* Iain revived enough to climb down from the stag. He thanked his friend for the assistance and bade him farewell. Seth took Iain's arm over his own shoulder to steady him as they entered the village. Overhead two faeries kept watch, moonlight shimmering in their wings.

<hr>

Seeing Liam fidgeting with a question, Angus confirmed what his grandson wanted to ask, "Yes, Liam, this was the same great stag Iain had wrestled earlier." Liam settled back with a huge smile of satisfaction filling his face. Angus resumed his reading, smiling himself with great pleasure.

Leaders from other villages who had come in search of Romans stayed in *Ceo Dhachaidh* until Iain fully recovered from the effect of Hester's poison. For two days he would fall into a cold sweat every time he attempted to resume his chores and duties. It took four men to make up his loss and even then work was left undone.

On the fourth day after the encounter Iain called all village leaders together. Their conference lasted hours as they discussed the situation. All agreed that something must be done to prepare unprotected villages for the inevitable battle that was to come. Runners were sent to summon leaders from each settlement not represented in the current conference. The plan was to assemble a council representing all eight villages who would then create a strategy for preparation. Realizing these men would be staying in *Ceo Dhachaidh,* possibly for several months, temporary housing was constructed in the soft meadow above the hill. This field had not been used before because it became soggy in heavy rains. One long hut, large enough to sleep up to ten men, was constructed of grass and straw.

The first leaders arrived late on the second day following the runners' departure. Small groups continued to arrive for five more days. Many residents of *Ceo Dhachaidh* spent time with these visitors. Rachel was intrigued by their stories and spent hours sitting at their fires. One young man, named Bryan, found Rachel to be enchanting as she wove stories of a deer stone, a rampaging piglet, and other tales of excitement retold from her father's travels; all of which kept him spellbound. Bryan was captivated, possibly more by the lilt of her voice and her charm than her stories of action. Rachel enjoyed Bryan's company as well.

Once all villages were represented, their leaders met in council. Some had no idea that the Romans posed a threat to their freedom. Celts knew from experience that the Romans would raid the mountains until they had achieved their goal, whatever it might be. Those will little or no fighting experience struggled to understand how they could stand against such an invading army. Every leader had questions, many which could not be answered at this time.

Late on the evening of the tenth day after the Roman encounter, after a full day of meeting in council, Iain stood at the top of the hill at the edge of *Ceo Dhachaidh*. Looking out across their hillside, across tree tops below, his gaze continued to waters of the nearby loch which reflected moonlight with a mystic shimmering. The evening sky was cool and pleasant, filling with thousands of twinkling stars.

Seeing her husband lost in thought, Elizabeth wrapped her arms around him asking, "Whit troubles my husband?"

"I am not troubled," Iain responded, "rather I am enriched. This land is special. I feel as though we have been brought here for a purpose. Look out there. Ye can see the greatest creation of all the world. We lived in many lands as we traveled but nowhere did the land have a soul such as this."

Iain's words took on a life of their own, drifting on the evening breeze, touching others' hearts. Soon, visitors came to the hillside, men and women from *Ceo Dhachaidh* and those from other villages who had come seeking answers about Romans. Everyone looked out across the hillside, over the trees, beyond the loch, even beyond the mountains across the loch. There was a reverent sense of oneness with all who stood there. Along the lower edge of the hillside meadow deer began to emerge and other small creatures took positions as though a great miracle were about to occur. Nobody, man or creature, wanted to miss this miracle as Iain continued.

"We are standing on this hill as though we are on top of the world. All of creation is at our feet. This land is calling us to protect it and to establish a new order within our world. We are being summoned to assure that no one, neither those who live here nor those who would come, damage this land or injure her soul. Romans and hags would do great harm to this land and we must protect her. Her soul is crying out for us to stand at her defense and stop their raping and ravaging of her beauty and innocence. We must stand together, now and tomorrow, to answer a higher calling from this special place. These mountains, these high lands must be protected."

The sky seemed to respond to Iain's words. First one shooting star streaked across the sky and then another. Soon the sky was filled with a spectacle of shooting stars. Faerie lights, moonlight captured in their wings, filled the woods and all creatures came to the meadow to experience the birth of a new world.

"We," continued Iain, "the people of these high lands must unite with one another and with our mother earth. She will enrich us with her bounty, giving us great purpose of life . . . reason to live. As we have become trustees of this great land . . . hielanders . . . our children also will become trustees . . . they will be the hielanders of tomorrow. Our souls, Mother Earth, these great hielands, and we as men are undeniably bound together. We must work together for the survival of each of us . . . man, woman, child, creature, and earth."

A roar went up from the crowd that had gathered around Iain and Elizabeth. Voices called out in unison, "HIELANDERS!" confirming Iain's call. Suddenly a tremendous bolt of lightning ripped from the heavens striking a large boulder in front of Iain. The air roared, rumbling as a thunderous crack split the boulder into the shape of two great chairs. The ground shook violently causing some people to fall as these two stone chairs rolled apart and then back to one another. Each came to an immovable rest, one on the edge of the other, side by side facing the waters of the loch below. All present accepted these great stone chairs as a gift of the gods of sky and earth now united in agreement with Iain. A gift which now provided a place for the new order of highlanders to begin.

━━━━━━━━━

"Seanair, is that where that pile of stones came from?" Alex interrupted.

"Aye," Angus replied. "This entire hillside shook and rolled when those seats were created. Many who stood there shook with fear but they dinna run. No, they knew something exciting was happening and they wanted to be part of it. I will tell ye how it went if ye wish."

Four faces looked to Angus, holding their own excited anticipation inside, begging him to continue.

The splendor of that special evening continued for some time and the spirit of the people seemed to reach a feverish pitch. It was as though the lightning which split the huge stone also charged the hill with energy and excitement. Men felt stronger, women felt an unparalleled confidence in their community. Everyone called for action, an end to the Roman threat. As the calls of people on the hillside rose to a roar, Iain climbed onto of one of the stone chairs and called to the visiting leaders.

"Go back to yer villages," Iain instructed, "and call out yer wisest and yer strongest. Return to this meadow in eight days with six leaders from each village. These men will become the defenders of these high lands . . . Our Hielands! We will train them in the Celtic ways of defense and study the wisdom of these mountains. These leaders will then return to yer villages and build an army of warriors in the Celtic tradition. We will defend our Hielands, this land that has become our home."

<hr>

"Angus," Lillian called softly as her storyteller paused his narration. "What about some lunch?" She then turned her head toward the window behind Angus' desk, commenting, "An it appears that the rain has stopped."

Defending the Highlands

Sensing the presence of young children invading his quiet, Angus lowered his morning newspaper. Seeing three young people with eager faces, he asked, "Yes?"

"We want you to finish the story," Marian replied.

"Shouldn't ye be playing outside?" Angus argued, trying to be a crusty old grandfather.

"It is raining again and I do not want them outside in this weather. It appears we are in for several days of wet," Lillian replied. "Yeu children settle down in front of the fireplace and I bet Seanair will gladly tell ye more about how early Hielanders became protectors of these wonderful mountains."

Angus tried not to smile with anticipation, but it was difficult. A low fire crackled with warmth in the large room, he had built it earlier to chase the dampness away. Three faces looked up at him, their appetite for adventure growing. Lillian, his wife sat across from him in her chair, her face also filled with anticipation.

"All right, where were we?" Angus asked.

"A great bolt of lightning spilt a huge rock into two chairs and Iain told everyone to go home and bring men back to train in the old Celtic way," Liam answered eagerly. "They are going to wipe the Romans out of our Highlands."

Opening the book to the silk ribbon, Angus scanned the page in front of him. Looking to the children he asked, "Do ye remember that Eric had collected the broken pieces of Mediterranean bagpipes?"

Everyone nodded. Angus resumed his tale. . . .

Eric set his mind to repairing the Mediterranean Bagpipes captured from the Roman patrol. More to the point, Eric was bewitched by this strange beast and spent the majority of his time trying to understand it and become its master. The bag, made from the skin of a goat tied at its legs, was supposed to act as a great reservoir of air. It had been cut during battle with the Romans. Unwilling to sacrifice a goat, Eric fashioned a similar design, though smaller, from a large piece of deer hide.

———

"Excuse me, Seanair?" Alex interrupted politely. He was intrigued by the story.

"Yes, Alex?"

"You said this book was from the diaries of women, how did they know all about the bagpipes?"

"The Book is indeed the product of ancient diaries, however my seanair and I have filled in some gaps to make the story more interesting. As I recall from the one time I saw the parchment about these pipes, it was not flattering at all. Whomever wrote the first passage did not appreciate this important development. They did add an entry later which Seanair included in this text. This book is not a direct translation but a compilation, a story. Otherwise, ye would all be spinning in confusion."

Seeing his grandson was satisfied with his answer, Angus resumed his reading.

Eric recalled seeing the soldier attempt to get the great bulbous bag under his arm, finally resigning himself to hold it more in front of his chest. Eric's smaller bag tucked easily under his own arm. There was also a problem with the drones. Three harmonious pipes coming from a single stock lay across the Roman's arm and seemed unmanageable. Eric separated the single drone stock into three smaller ones, fashioning them so that they lay individually, spread across his shoulder. He kept the blowpipe used to fill the bag with air and chanter arranged much the same as they had been on the old pipes. A chanter where the melody was played, was attached to the end of the bag. The blowpipe was inserted into the neck closer to the main reservoir which now fit under his arm. This remodeled bagpipe was very different from what the Roman had suffered. Eric quickly learned to tame this new beast.

The deerskin bag on Eric's pipes leaked air and was difficult to keep filled. Iain recommended that Eric use fat to preserve and seal the hide. Rachel helped Eric prepare a fat and herbal substance, which she had seen her father prepare for treating leather. They then melted the mixture so it could be poured into the bag. Herbs helped cut the pungent odor of the fat. This mixture seemed to seal the bag.

Eric had seen bagpipes played only once and then from a distance, so he had to learn to play these new pipes by experimentation. The beastly contraption made strange sounds. Sometimes its sounds would scare livestock. Coos[12] stopped giving milk and game disappeared from the forest for days at a time. Occasionally the music lilted pleasantly

---

[12] *coo* - Highland cow

through the trees giving a haunting peace to man and animals alike. Determined to master this new instrument, Eric continued his trials. Growing weary of constant skirls, villagers conjured their own ideas. Suspecting multiple threats to his treasure, Eric took to "hiding" in the forest to play. But he was easy to find because the sound of his pipes pierced through the trees, continuing nearly half a léige.

Faeries in the woods began to plot against the squawking noise of the pipes. One faerie, Seebtin, decided to explore them and see if he could help. While Eric "played," Seebtin circled the drones and chanter. At one point he flew up the chanter, stopping its air flow and sound. Like Eric, Seebtin was convinced there was a way to make these pipes more musical and would not be dissuaded from his search. He found that with his wings outspread he could lower himself into the drone and spin in the escaping air. The result was a pulsing sound, and a tickling sensation for Seebtin. Other faeries joined Seebtin by spinning in separate drones. Their games did not improve the overall sound but proved very entertaining and ticklish to the wee creatures.

Late one afternoon three traveling musicians happened upon one of Eric's practice sessions. These visitors carried musical instruments from different lands; another set of Mediterranean bagpipes, a small harp and a drum. The drummer also played a set of reeds, a pan flute. Jason, the piper, was very curious about the pulsating sound he heard from Eric's drones but the faeries hid when the musicians arrived so Eric could not reproduce or explain the sound. Jason played Eric's pipes, finding them to be much easier to manage than his own. Eager to have help with his pipes, Eric invited the travelers to sit with him at supper. They gratefully accepted.

After supper Eric and the musicians retired to the great stone chairs. Eager to meet these visitors, villagers of *Ceo Dhachaidh* joined them, asking the musicians many questions about their travels and what they were doing in the mountains.

"The lot of us have been traveling around Britannia for nearly two years, looking for small villages and learning their melodies and songs," Jason explained. "We plan to collect music from around the world and present it at royal courts, for a small fee or gratuity of course."

As the moon rose above distant mountains, the musicians demonstrated some melodies they had learned, explaining backgrounds for each one.

"Yer music was nice. I haven't heard the like of it since, oh . . . when Eric found those blasted squawkers. I heard yer names earlier, I am Ian Gregor. Tell me, have ye come across any Roman patrols or wandering soldiers in yer travels?"

Marc, the drummer, and Shane, the harpist and singer, appeared very nervous with Iain's question but Jason calmly replied, "Romans are not much for good music, especially songs of local villages. You must first fill them with wine and then fit music to their raucous mood. They once broke my pipes and cut Shane's harp strings because they had a bad day. I would prefer to avoid Romans, if possible."

After villagers departed Jason taught Eric what he had learned on the pipes. He also showed Eric how he could adjust reeds within the pipes and adjust the length of drones for a softer, gentler sound. As the pipes mellowed, many villagers returned to the musical circle. They offered songs from their fighting days and Seumas even sang a love ballad to his wife, Ingrid. Rachel showed a strong interest in Shane's harp. He obliged her interest with a smile and a very friendly lesson. To promote his relationship with the red-haired lass, Shane helped Rachel begin making her own harp.

Iain and Elizabeth sat in the great stone chairs. Seven days had passed since Iain sent visiting warriors to recruit others from their villages. The couple quietly watched wispy clouds floating high in a painted sky, close to the setting sun. Textures across the sky reflected brilliant red hues with streaks of orange and yellow flowing between them. The air was dry and unseasonably cool. Another day was coming to its end, but an elaborate heaven seemed to beckon the beginning of a new age.

Elizabeth's mind filled with thoughts of potential dangers for the struggling new communities as villages joined forces against Roman intruders. Iain recalled the sacrifice they had already paid. Memories of past struggles of reaching *Ceo Dhachaidh* and images of his brother filled his mind stumbling over visions of his sons playing on this hillside.

Memories gave way to a growing strength within Iain. A strength of purpose and vision now confirmed by a deity in the sky. Pondering new thoughts and treasured memories he sought inspiration from the

changing sky as it rolled a calm darkness over them, "Whit am I goin'
to say to these men? These farmers about to become warriors?" He
knew their purpose, to protect their new home - these Highlands and all
they encompassed - but what words could he use to convey this
importance to them?

Several young boys jousted on the hillside below Iain and Elizabeth,
playing at being warriors. Their lances were short but their courage and
intent soared.

---

*Liam jabbed at Alex, his older brother. The younger was very much
in the spirit of his grandfather's story.*

"Stop it!" Alex blurted out.

*Angus looked down at both boys with warning in his eyes. Both
quickly settled and Angus resumed his story as Lillian added a log to
their fire.*

One lad left the mock battle and walked up to Iain. Standing so
small in front of Iain's massive form, the boy asked, "How do ye speak
with the deer and why are ye guarded by faeries?" His partner in battle
joined him and posed another question, "Me da' says ye know whit yer
enemies are doin', even when ye canna see them. Is that true?"

Iain looked down at the young men, memories of his two sons
racing through his mind. "We are all protected by the faeries," Iain
replied. "For as long as ye protect and defend this land that is their
home, the faeries will be at yer side. As for yer other questions, I invite
ye to this spot at sunset tomorrow." Iain smiled with a great sense of
relief as he shook the hand of the first young man. The lads assured Iain
that they would be there and returned to their jousting.

Iain looked at Elizabeth, "Those young men gave me the answer I
needed in their questions. These wee lads knew my conundrum and
presented it to me so that I could see it at last." His face was gleaming
and his smile broader than the emerging heavens. He talked for a great
time. Elizabeth listened contentedly, enraptured by his excitement. The
shimmering night sky would have faded in his flourishing energy had
she not taken him to their hut.

Morning came early the next day and a rising sun found Iain
preparing for this most important of days. He awakened Seumas,
dragging him from a deep sleep. The cousins worked together all
morning cutting down a strong straight tree, just greater across than the

spread of Iain's hand. This tree trunk was to be planted near the stone chairs. Placement was critical to Iain who searched diligently for the perfect spot. Standing on the stone chair he would swing his arms over his head, bringing a large stick down on Seumas' head - gently at first. When the stick stuck Seumas on the shoulder or ear Ian asked him move him to the side where he was struck. This strange routine was repeated over and over. Seumas was not beyond complaining, "I dinna know wha' ye are looking for but I would like to keep my ears, if ye please." He generally moved at least half the width of his body, not fully understanding the subtle movements Iain was seeking.

Martin, another older Celt, came to Seumas' rescue nudging Seumas so he would move only a little at a time. Many men had gathered to watch this demonstration, chuckling at Seumas' complaints and not-so-subtle movements. All laughed uncontrollably when Seumas grabbed Iain's stick, using it to whop Iain on his leg.

Finally the stick landed in the center of Seumas' head three times in succession. They planted the tree trunk precisely where Seumas stood. Together the two Celts dug a narrow hole as deep as from the ground to their knee. Finally finished, the pole stood unwavering and vertical with its top nearly as high as Iain's shoulder when he stood on the stone chair.

As midday approached, many visitors began filling the village of *Ceo Dhachaidh*. These were representatives from other villages. Most were farmers coming to be trained as highland warriors in the Celtic tradition. Few had Celtic blood coursing through their veins but all embodied the Celtic spirit. Iain and Seumas welcomed new arrivals, asking each of them to be on the hillside in front of the stone chairs at sunset. They then helped them find a place in the village expansion to set their camp. Visitors knew they would be here for a time, but had no idea what they were truly committing themselves to.

<hr>

Villagers and visitors gathered in the hillside meadow of the great stone chairs as the sun began to set. Sheep and coos were moved to the byre[13]. Locals redirected folks who might have unknowingly trampled crops planted along the bottom of the hillside. Overhead the sky put on another brilliant display. A large body of clouds blocked direct rays of sunlight. Great fingers climbed out from a central palm-like body hovering overhead, each brightly illuminated by the setting sun. Above

---

[13] *byre* - bire - cowshed, barn

and beyond this great hand in the sky, the heavens glowed a rich red with orange and yellow trim. Iain squeezed Elizabeth's hand as he looked to the heavens finding confirmation of his purpose. Eric played a gentle melody on his bagpipes. Rachel accompanied Eric on the harp, guided by Shane. The music was rough, but still a delight to all, or most, assembled.

Elizabeth saw the young boys who had inspired Iain coming toward them. Several men attempted to turn the wee warriors back, but Elizabeth called to them and sat them down beside the great chairs. Iain greeted each of them personally, thanking them again for their questions.

Soon the crowd settled and anxiously looked to their Celtic leader for his presentation. Iain climbed onto the chairs, towering above the crowd. He carried a battle axe and broad sword. Seumas stood nearby with sword and spear. These two great Celts were impressive in their battle dress, very impressive indeed. Excited murmurs raced through the crowd; most echoed "This is why we came!"

"Last night," Iain began, "a young lad asked me if I talked to animals. He also asked me about faeries and a friend of his asked me how I knew whit my enemies were doing. Celts have long looked to the land for their strength, but whit I am about to reveal to ye goes beyond that. These great mountains give us shelter and food. They have become a home, OUR home, and we have sworn to protect this land against thoughtless invaders who would destroy it. That is why ye are here, to learn how to protect this land, these Hielands of our tomorrows and of our children. Throughout the ages we Celts have plundered lands and cultures taking whit we wanted, often by force. This powerful past is why invaders are hunting us. I tell ye now that the Celts are yesterday and the Hielanders are today." Iain pointed toward the Celtic warriors standing near him, several looked back at him with concern. Iain smiled at them with confidence and put his hand on Seumas' shoulder. "We are no longer plunderers of the land. We are now defenders of this sanctuary.

"In the days and weeks ahead, ye will learn to throw the spear, swing the battle axe, and defend yerself with stave and sword. These skills will not defend our land, indeed they will probably barely keep ye alive in battle. A talent for battle does not win wars. Ye will also learn to walk with the deer, and listen to the owl; ye will learn to feel the true strength of this earth and be lifted by faeries." Iain brushed his hand across the top of the pole he had planted, gently sweeping several faeries off their perch. "The true power of conquest does not come with an ability to throw the axe . . . " Iain threw his heavy battle axe spinning high into the air. "It comes from being able to catch it!" As the battle axe came down Iain caught it by the handle and in a single motion brought the axe down into the pole, splitting it into the ground. Watchers gasped with astonishment.

Young Liam gasped as he witnessed the huge axe spinning through the air then splitting the log. Angus smiled, commenting "Aye, as ye just did, Liam. Only their gasp was from more than one hundred Hielanders." Seeing that everyone was truly following his story. Angus resumed his story commenting, "Iain did not miss a beat of his heart as he continued inspiring his new kinfolk. . . ."

"If ye will surrender yer fears, we will replace them with confidence. Confidence does not come from carrying a big sword or swinging a bigger axe. Confidence comes from believing in yer purpose, a purpose greater than yerself. From knowing there is a faerie on yer shoulder ready to assist ye as ye protect his home. Confidence comes from listening as owl and deer tell ye how yer enemy could not sleep, worried about facing *YEU*! Confidence comes from feeling the boundless spirit and strength of the earth climb through yer feet and legs . . . filling yer heart with purpose. Ye will defeat yer enemy by standing before him with a confidence greater than his sword or axe and filling HIM with fear. His fear will defeat him before ye draw yer sword! Ye will undoubtedly have to raise yer sword against our enemy, but it will be yer oneness with this land that will give ye the strength to ward off his blows and deliver yer own. *YEUR* confidence will empower ye in all that ye pursue.

"Many lessons in the time ahead will wear ye down and ye may even cry out for rest and mercy. Some of these lessons will give ye peace, hope and enlightenment. Ye will gain the power of the sword and an understanding of faeries, deer and this land. We have begun a new age and *YEU* are the defenders of this land . . . the Hielands . . . our home. We are Hielanders, and we will set a new course for all others to follow. Not the Celtic way but the Hielander's Way!"

Iain stepped down from the stone chair and immediately left the meadow with Elizabeth at his side. Men, women, visitors and villagers all looked where Iain had been standing, each trying to understand how they were to meet this challenge laid before them.

Silently the sun disappeared, softening the sky, and the highlands settled into an easy slumber. Would-be warriors gathered around fires and in the lodge. There were few words. Most were filled with apprehension of the near future. Iain had given them a challenge. Each heart on that hillside, every Highland soul's concern was living up to that challenge.

At the edge of the hillside, sitting high above her cavie, Resbith stared with awe and concern. *Gleo* shimmered in the moonlight, falling thinly from shoulders of men who were excited about this new challenge. Women seemed to be collecting their husband's *gleo*, increasing their own with apprehension and worry.

〜〜〜〜〜〜〜〜〜〜〜〜〜

At sunrise a new order began to appear within this new community. A food line was established near the village lodge and all those training to become warriors came to be fed. There were forty-seven visitors and eleven villagers from *Ceo Dhachaidh*. They were tall and short, hefty and slender, loud and quiet, but there was only one woman. Rachel. All were more vocal than they had been the night before and most conversations had to do with the training they were about to receive.

One visitor, Shaun, boasted of how he would excel in the training. A large man, both tall and hefty, he claimed "War is ma special talent. These old Celts will have to learn from ME! I will show them things they don't know they don't know!" Iain heard the boasting and took Rachel and Eric outside for some advance training.

After breakfast, Iain called all students to the meadow. He had the Celts stand to his right with Rachel and Eric to his left, in prominent positions. There were only six Celts, including Iain, to train fifty-two farmers. Iain began his address telling everyone that they must first demonstrate their skills.

Shaun pushed his way to the front of the group, challenging the positions of Eric and Rachel, "Are ye expecting us to need nursing?"

"Please explain yer question," Iain replied, trying to hide a grin.

Shaun grunted, "These two runts, are they to tend our injuries?"

"No," Iain countered, "they are yer first test." Iain picked up two staves, each as long as a man's height, throwing one to Shaun and one toward Eric and Rachel. Rachel, being slightly faster, easily snatched the wooden pole from the air before Eric could reach it, grasping it firmly in her hand. "The test, sir," explained Iain, "is to see if ye can knock young Rachel down with yer stave."

"I'll not attack a lass!" argued Shaun.

"Don't worry," Iain assured him, "I won't let her hurt ye."

Outraged by the insult, Shaun struck out at Rachel with his stave. Rachel easily deflected the attack. Shaun swung again with greater force. Rachel again deflected the attack, stepping aside. Now senseless with rage, Shaun made a fatal mistake; he lunged at Rachel. Rachel hit Shaun solidly across his chest with her stave. While he was off balance, she brought her stave around low, scooping his feet out from under him. She then placed her stave on his forehead. He had been vanquished. A roar of approval came up from the crowd. Iain helped the fallen giant to his feet.

"This exercise was not intended to embarrass Shaun," Iain explained as the big man, his head bent low, returned to his friends, "but to show whit a little training can do. I gave Rachel and Eric a bit of special training earlier this morning."

Rachel and Eric then demonstrated with each other what they had learned. The spirit of training had been validated. Iain called upon the Celts to take eight or nine farmers each to test their understanding of how to use a stave.

Each group was very much the same. In an agricultural sense everyone was quite adequate. They knew how to use their staves to push each other away and a few could even stop an attack. None knew how to use it as an assault weapon. Training to change these farmers into warriors commenced.

<hr>

Angus looked up and saw a twinkle in Alex's eye, but Marian was glowing with Rachel's victory. Liam appeared to be enraptured with this adventure. Seeing Lillian's smile, Angus continued.

That first day of training passed slowly as strong men, who had considered themselves protectors of their homes, discovered how inadequate they were as warriors. These proud and powerful men could till soil and harvest crops to feed their families and defend against wild animals but were unprepared for the realities of battle. By the time the sun shone strongly in the midday sky everyone could defend themselves with staves. The Celts assaulted with varying degrees of tenacity as their students blocked attacks and managed to fend them off.

Self defense was only a beginning however, for they now had to learn to launch an assault and become aggressors. Iain's words from the night before rang in their ears. *"Many of the lessons ye take in the time ahead will wear ye down and ye may even cry out for rest and mercy."* Before day's end they were indeed weary beyond expectation and ready to rest.

During one of their infrequent rest periods Bryan, one of the visitors favored by Rachel, approached her. He was exhausted from the day's activities but was strong enough to seek her. They had little time to talk before the next training session began and Iain called on the two of them for a demonstration. Bryan was instructed to attack Rachel and she was to counter or defend herself. As directed, Bryan used his training, landing a few light blows before going for his main stab, as he had seen Rachel do earlier that morning. Rachel used his lunge to disorient his balance and then simply tripped him with her foot. Iain beamed with approval at his favorite student's moves.

Rachel reached down to help Bryan up. He was embarrassed, but not too embarrassed to use her posture against her. Taking her hand, he quickly spun her around so that he had her in his arms, her back to his chest and his stave on her chest. Rachel, stunned at Bryan's maneuver, responded in kind. Quickly tucking her head she rolled, carrying Bryan head over heals with her. Both sat on the ground laughing as Iain applauded the quick thinking on both sides. "If all of ye will learn to think and react like that," Iain told the crowd, "we will vanquish all who would invade our Hielands!" Real lessons of how to attack more effectively then began, with Bryan and Rachel opposite each other.

The sun set on the exhausted farmers with agonizingly slow speed. Many wanted to forgo the pleasures of an evening meal in favor of sleep, but Seumas took the challenge of getting everyone fed. One weary young lad found himself across Seumas' great shoulders and being carried to the lodge. A meal of venison and turnips awaited them. All ate their fill and settled down quickly, even Shaun.

Visiting musicians joined Eric at the meal. They were impressed by lessons of the day, showing some sores on their hands from where they had taken part. Jason, the piper, offered Eric a new tune. This melody was soft and slow, helping to soothe tired souls of student warriors. Seebtin rested on Eric's shoulder as Eric quickly picked up the tune, adding some embellishments of his own. The encampment slipped peacefully into silence as the pipes came to rest.

Trainees did not rouse easily with the next sunrise, most moaning about aching muscles and weary souls. Celts walked the camp shaking tents, kicking protruding motionless feet and forcibly dragging a few from their covers. All were tired and most ached from abuse and battering of the previous day. Slowly, they found themselves once again gathering at the lodge in hopes of a warm and nourishing meal. What they received was warm and it was nourishing but lacked a great deal in taste. The meal was something like oatmeal, mostly gruel, with little flavor. Men did not complain but ate quite a lot. The day ahead was going to be demanding.

Everyone gathered at the meadow just as they had the day before, however Iain launched into a tirade, "WHERE ARE YER STAVES? Ye had them yesterday and ye should NEVER be without them! Ye must carry them at all times. LOOK AT YEU! Most of ye have come to fight but neglected to bring yer weapon. Are ye going to stand around all day and shake each other by the hand or are ye going to go and get yer stave that will one day save yer life? . . . GO!!" Everyone without a stave ran with embarrassment to camp to retrieve their weapons. When students returned, properly equipped, lessons resumed.

The musicians, who had been standing to the side, expressed gratitude for hospitality and friendship shared with them but excused themselves from lessons. After packing their belongings they spoke briefly with Eric and left. Returning to the group, Eric held up his hands displaying sores he had earned the day before, explaining that Jason and the other musicians did not want to add to their own collection of blisters and aching muscles.

By the end of day two, fifty-two farmers knew many different ways to use a stave to defend themselves. They had learned how to attack an enemy and most importantly to never leave their stave behind. These same fifty-two farmers collapsed without energy to seek food. Celts prodded the weary into food lines. Eric, however, found enough strength to end the day with his pipes. Seebtin sat on Eric's shoulder singing ancient faerie melodies which Eric found on his pipes. Melodies flowed freely, lingering on the hillside, meadow, and camp with a haunting memory long after Eric rested. A brilliant heavenly display filled the skies, commending the well-spent day.

Troops rose the next morning with a surprising energy. Many had compliments for Eric, expressing gratitude for a peaceful end to a trying day. As they sat together enjoying a repeat of gruel from the day before, several began to sing Eric's melodies. Numerous people joined in, each lending his own rendition of a melody. There were "brrras" and "ddrrums" and "frumshus" and "tachems." Seebtin listened with delight as these humans tried their voices at old faerie strains. Their renditions became as haunting as the melody until Iain interrupted by calling everyone to arms.

Training the third day began with another surprise. Iain raised his battle axe and with three short strokes along the end of a stave gave the stave a point changing it into a spear, which he then thrust through the air. All heads turned, following its flight across the field. Few onlookers dared to breathe as their eyes focused on the spear with sky and trees blurring in the background. Silently the new weapon soared until it plunged squarely into a small bladder filled with water hung near the field's edge. "Yer stave can also land an attack from a distance," Iain explained.

Using iron axes, students carefully put points on their staves which now served as two weapons. Clouds dotted a bright morning sky, rolling about slowly across as farmers became proficient with their spears. Celts worked patiently with these men of the earth, teaching them how to hold and throw with increasing accuracy. Bryan showed great natural mastery for his new weapon. Taking Bryan aside, Iain showed him how to add power to his throw. Together the two men worked diligently on every move and every posture. Bryan continued to gain power without losing accuracy, challenging the skill of his tutor.

About midday Iain announced a break in training. "Ye are eating this village out of all stores," he called. "Now, ye must feed the village. With bow and spear go find game in these woods. Ye don't eat until meat lockers are replenished."

Everyone was weary and weak but understood the task at hand. Small groups ventured into the wood that surrounded *Ceo Dhachaidh*. Hunters soon discovered that noise from training sessions had driven larger game from the region. Hunting parties returned to the village with a total of only ten squirrels and three rabbits.

Women who had been working diligently to feed this army were exhausted. Many had to fight their own temptation to send all to bed without food. Elizabeth convinced them to serve gruel, again.

That night as the village settled to melodies from Eric's pipes, Elizabeth went to Iain and Seumas. "I believe in whit ye are doing," she began, "but the village cannot support this training camp. Ye have taken our own men away from their work and added forty mouths to feed. The game is gone, which has never happened before. Ye may be saving our Hielands but ye are starving *Ceo Dhachaidh* and exhausting our women who would support ye."

Iain looked at Elizabeth with distress and asked, "How many more days can ye feed them?"

"Three," replied Elizabeth, "only two if they fill their bellies." She shifted her shoulders under an enormous weight of unseen *gleo*.

Iain thought for a moment, drawing circles in the dirt with a small stick. He knew he could not send these men home without further training, but he could not cripple his village either. "Here is a plan," he began very slowly. "They know the basics. Tomorrow we work with iron, both battle axe and broadsword. We will have to divide them into groups because we don't have enough weapons."

"Whit of those with bows?" Seumas interrupted.

"Aye, more than half brought bows with them. Tomorrow night before supper, we will have a contest of the bow, just to evaluate their skill. Seumas and I will get meat tonight so we can fill their bellies full. We will move camp on the second day. Training of how to survive and how to move efficiently will be taught on the march. We will keep them out for three or four days. I will ask a few to stay here to replenish stores and watch over our village."

"Iain, they are tired and worn" Seumas appealed. "They will not be able to survive a forced march."

"We won't move them hard," Iain argued. "Just enough to give them a taste of whit a campaign is like. I also need to know that they will be ready to move when the intruders return."

"And whit of when *ye* return?" asked Elizabeth. She was greatly concerned about the march and its results.

Iain looked into her face, into her fears and doubts. He could see fatigue replacing dedication. Taking a deep breath, he replied, "Then we enter our next stage of training. Everyone will return to their own village. Seumas, I, and a few others who can train effectively will travel to their villages. These men, who are being trained now, can help us train their neighbors. Surely other villages will be able to feed four or five instructors for a few days."

Seumas agreed. The sky was overcast that night with a threat of rainfall looming over the next day. Elizabeth kissed Iain gently and watched as he and Seumas collected their hunting gear. Her eyes and heart followed as they disappeared into the dark woods. Turning toward her hut Elizabeth struggled with an unseen weight on her shoulders, knowing the burden of responsibility Iain and Seumas carried was much greater.

Sunshine did not greet warriors when they awoke the next morning. A light drizzle of rain was their master, confronting weary folk as they rose to their next challenge. They gathered slowly at the big lodge. Dressed carcasses of three deer hung in the slaughter pen and two small boars roasted on a spit over a fire in the lodge. Gruel was not so objectionable with hot roast pork beside it. Portions were small but bellies were grateful.

Conversations that morning centered on the boar and deer. Everyone knew it had to be from Iain, but such a haul had to have taxed even his talents. There was even jesting with suggested reasons why Seumas and Iain were not eating with them as they normally did. One grateful warrior laughed, "I wager Seumas ran the game from deep in the forest and Iain killed it as it took flight." "No," bettered another, "Iain stood at the edge of the wood and called out 'I am hungry, feed me lest I come and grab yer young!' Then every animal for three mountains came and fell dead at his feet." All conversation ceased when sounds of Eric's pipes broke though the rain. These were not lilting melodies but hard rhythms demanding action, a return to the meadow.

Troops quickly gathered at the meadow, finding Iain and Seumas in full battle gear. "Whit is the reason for this garb?" Shaun asked. They had not been dressed like this since the first day. Iain pulled his broad sword from its sheaf on his back and Seumas swung his battle axe into a defensive position.

"Most of ye will fight battles with stave or spear," Iain explained. "But today ye will be introduced to more destructive weapons of war. Any of ye who have iron weapons, bring them out. Now!"

Nearly half of the men cheered as they slipped in the mud, running to get their "real weapons." *Ceo Dhachaidh's gobhainn*[14] inspected iron broadswords, claymores, battle axes, and other assorted devices brought by students. He took several to his forge to be sharpened or make other repairs. Iain and two other Celts began instructing students in proper defensive maneuvers and offensive moves with the broadsword. Seumas and another Celt worked with battle axes. Very few warriors could handle this massive device efficiently. Constant rain made it difficult to handle these heavy iron weapons. Untrained hands

---

[14]*gobhain* - go~iN - blacksmith

frequently lost control as water interfered with a firm grip. Only quick reactions of competent instructors averted precarious, potentially deadly situations as axes spun off in unexpected directions.

Rain subsided that afternoon and an aroma of roasting venison floated across the hillside. Hungry for roast meat and to be the best, thirty-one men displayed a wide span of skills with their bows. First prize in this contest was first position in line for roast venison. Women of *Ceo Dhachaidh* brought oats and barley in from their community stores and bread was plentiful. Shaun, who was eliminated in the second round of the shooting contest, boasted from the group, "This will be our graduation meal. We hae completed our training in one week. We should all be proud and intruders had better be wary!"

As promised, the best archer was allowed the honor of first cuts from the roast meat. Others filed into the lodge in somewhat the order which they had finished in the contest. Once all were served Iain stood and addressed his students, "As Shaun said, ye should be proud, and aye, intruders might better be aware, at the least. But this is not yer 'graduation meal.' Tomorrow at sunrise ye are to pack yer gear and be ready to move. Yer training will now be on the march. While ye are out ye will move quickly and collect yer food stores when we camp. When the intruders return I expect that ye will be called to a fast assembly. Tomorrow begins yer advanced training."

Iain joined Elizabeth, Seumas, and Ingrid as everyone listened to the uneasy quiet that followed his announcement. Rain continued to pound on the thatch roof creating a dull roar punctuated by crackling of the fire. After several minutes without anyone speaking Shaun announced, "Well, It doesn't look like we will be eating for a while. I guess I should have some more!" The silent gathering erupted with laughter as the big man reached for more pork and conversations took on new life.

<hr>

Rain continued all night, hammering tents and shelters heavily at times. Many sleepless warriors listened to night noises and restless wanderers sloshing through deepening puddles.

Neither Bryan nor Rachel could sleep. They spent predawn hours walking together in the morning mist that replaced the nightlong rain, sharing concerns about coming days.

Iain, Seumas, and the Celts gathered at the stone chairs before others were rousted. Each had come prepared, dressed in full battle gear and ready to move. These men were older than their students, but their strength was still much greater than the average man's. Anxious Celts engaged in quiet conversation, shifting to admit Bryan and Rachel into their circle. Greetings exchanged, battle-trained men went to work. Stomping through mud they rousted trainees from their uneasy rest, gathering these would-be-warriors into marching ranks. Each had his gear about him and a stave in his hand. A few had swords and other devices, but none had food. Women of *Ceo Dhachaidh* had been told they could rest this morning; there was no breakfast waiting at the lodge.

Few villagers were awake to see the spectacle of fifty-four departing warriors. Martin, an older Celt who had injured his arm while training a new warrior, and three trainees stayed behind to tend to safety of the community. Elizabeth and Ingrid stood quietly, watching their husbands march away from them. They had lived this scene many times, but never in *Ceo Dhachaidh*. There was a new pain with this leaving. Both women shifted their shoulders as the last of the men disappeared. A great weight had settled upon these women, a weight that could only be lifted by their husband's return.

The procession began slowly. Not wanting to march and haunted by their unfed stomachs, would-be warriors plodded through mud. Iain found Eric and brought him to the front of the line, "Play a mighty tune so these men can find their strength." Eric raised his pipes and began to play. Fumbling with a melody, skirls added to the misery of a rain-soaked trail. Seebtin joined Eric at his shoulder. This wee faerie hummed a melody which found its way to Eric's fingers. Sluggish steps quickened as music of the pipes gained a pulsing momentum, ringing through the morning. Even though their stumbling became a reluctant march, men still found their stomachs empty.

It was mid-afternoon before the march stopped. Happening upon a clearing by a brook where signs of game were plentiful, the small army made camp. Hunters secured two deer and a small boar from the forest, bringing hope to hungry warriors. While the game cooked, lessons resumed. Iain and Seumas showed how to defend against the sword and battle axe using the familiar wooden stave. During the meal and later around the fires everyone discussed ideas about how to survive a forced march. Commonly shared advice was to save some food from supper for the next morning. Many requested Eric slow his tempo on the bagpipes. Stars slowly claimed the night sky and would-be-warriors slept peacefully, most under blankets, a few under heavier cloths that could be used for tenting but were not this night.

Iain woke Eric early and called upon him to wake the troops. Eric's cold fingers fumbled across his chanter until he stumbled upon a melody to roust a sleeping camp. Wailing bagpipes destroyed warriors' sleep the second morning. Everyone assembled quickly and the march resumed. Routine continued much the same as the previous day, but spirits were higher and the pace more lively. Every man had saved a bit of meat from the night before which kept stomachs from rumbling.

Early in the afternoon Iain called a halt to their march, commanding "Make camp!" Lessons began before anyone could get settled or comfortable. Seumas provoked the farmers to fight, staging a mock battle, testing each man and what they had learned. What training had succeeded? Members of different villages defended their encampment, their land, from other invading villagers. There were a few minor injuries as some became a bit over zealous. Losers had to go in search of game which was not plentiful. Three boars served the company well enough.

Eric's pipes, which had driven men's steps for two days, provided a settling peace as darkness fell and fires rose. Iain made rounds to the several fires. Trainees were predominantly quiet, however one young man rose as Iain began to leave.

"Sir, will ye be teaching us to talk with the owl and deer?" the young man asked nervously. "How do ye find game where there is none?"

These questions echoed through the camp and before Iain could answer, a crowd had gathered. Farmer-warriors stood waiting. Faeries hovered near Iain's head as though urging him to respond.

"These mountains, *our* mountains," Iain began, "have a life all their own. Within that life are the lives of all creatures who live here - deer, owls, boar, faeries [Iain smiled up at his elusive friends], even the land itself. Ye must first come to a peace within yerself, know yerself, have confidence in every step. This peace and confidence will open yer heart to the tremendous possibilities that surround ye – including the deer, owl and hundreds of other natural wonders. I talk with the world around me because I first listen to whit it is saying to me. When ye wake in the morning, before ye utter a word or a groan, listen. Listen to the wind. Listen to the silence. Listen to the grass rise from being stepped on by deer that walked among ye whilst ye slept. When ye hear the wonders of these majestic mountains, then ye will have peace and yer confidence will grow. Ye will find a tremendous energy searching for a place to be unleashed. Reach out and accept that energy and the grace of these mountains and gifts of the many inhabitants here. Do not fight to win over or defeat whit is around ye. Accept the grace and power tha is given freely."

"I do not understand whit ye say," the young man argued.

"That is because ye have not yet slept or listened." Iain smiled as he walked away from the crowd.

"I sleep with my window open, Seanair. Will I hear the deer if I listen?" Alex interrupted.

"No, silly, you have to be sleeping where the deer are walking," Marian replied with disdain.

"Actually, tha is an excellent question," Angus countered, resting the book in his lap. "It is not just the deer ye wish to hear but whispers of our mountains. They are soft and can only be heard by those who are truly worthy of their secrets."

"How do you become worthy, Seanair?" Liam asked. His face alive with earnest curiosity.

"Ye must first accept whit ye canna see. Allow all of yer senses to guide ye. Surrender yer guard, but keep yer whits about ye. Only then will ye be able to hear the true voice of our Hielands."

"Does the city have a voice as well?" Liam pursued.

"Aye, I suppose it does but I hae not ever heard it. All creation has a voice, many voices. Ye must surrender yer natural guards to learn whit creation has to teach."

"Would this be a good place to stop for lunch?" Lillian asked.

Angus looked at his book, flipping forward a few pages. "Nae, we hae an important event rising. A few more pages then we can rest the story."

Seeing his wife's smile, Angus continued.

Many men tried to listen to nature the next morning, but most groaned and stretched as their third day of marching dawned. A few heard silence, but most just grumbled about pains of the coming day.

While walking in the morning mist Seumas discovered tracks of Roman soldiers. A company of unknown size had come through this area during the rain, a day or so before. Iain wanted to take a handful of warriors to find the Romans but Seumas convinced him to keep everyone together. Pipes and men's voices remained quiet as they followed tracks left by the Roman patrol. Rains had softened the ground and their trail was easy to follow, but there was no way to accurately count the number of soldiers making them. Late in the morning they came upon remains of an encampment. Abundant signs indicated the Romans had spent a day here, possibly drying out, moving on earlier this day.

Seumas studied the encampment and estimated the company size to be about 50, maybe slightly larger. "They are only hours ahead of us and moving slowly," the experienced Celt told his men. Visions of an encounter swept through everyone's minds, filling Celts and students with an uneasy tightness. Quickening their pace, they moved on in pursuit.

The sun was sliding toward surrounding mountain tops when a column of smoke appeared in the sky, more smoke than campfires would create. Not far away one of the trainees pointed out two coos and a dozen sheep lying on the ground, slaughtered but not for meat. Iain, Seumas and two Celtic trainers instinctively broke into a battle run, swift but not fast, conserving energy for what lay ahead. Silently and powerfully four experienced warriors sliced through brush which pushed quietly aside as these men moved swiftly ahead. Trees passed unseen as their eyes focused on the smoke. Their fighting experience linked each of them as one body. These warriors who had fought side-by-side on many battlefields slipped into a single pace, four sets of feet landing on the ground as one, four strides matched in perfect unison. Their breathing was as one breath, not heavy but deliberate, as though each of them was breathing not only for himself but for all of them.

Trees gave way to a large clearing where healthy rows of crops and a small village had been earlier that day. Romans lingered around smoldering huts and devastated fields. Seasoned soldiers congratulated themselves on their victory while officers tortured village residents for information.

Without a signal or a word, Celtic arms rose together, pulling swords from sheaths on their backs. There was not a sound between them, not a crackle in the grass, not a bead of sweat. Four perfectly matched warriors.

Students followed, more than fifty yards behind, working hard to keep pace and not make noise. Faeries formed a guard in front of these inexperienced warriors. Invisible wings and bodies reflected the afternoon sun creating a radiance which encouraged the men, feeding their confidence and giving them strength.

Roman invaders were not expecting intrusion and did not see the Highlanders, seasoned Celts and their students, charging across the furrowed field. Highlanders swept into the village.

"FOR THE HIELANDS!" A bone-chilling call sliced through still air dragging the breeze with it as Highlanders rushed past unsuspecting Roman guards. Without hesitation or thought experienced warriors cut through to the Roman officers. Torture of residents quickly changed to slaughter of Romans as trained farmers became warriors engaging stunned soldiers who were supposed to be guarding their conquest. There was a fever in the attack that none could explain, but it was short lived. Celts dispatched the Roman officers quickly and without hesitation. Students engaged soldiers, catching them off balance. Training with staves paid off as these simple pieces of wood took the life of soldier after trained soldier. Sword play was mercifully short as attackers disarmed and dispatched Roman after Roman. Surprise and fury in equal measure carried these farmers-turned-warriors to their first victory.

Minutes after the Highlanders entered the village all Romans were dead. Iain checked to make sure that no Roman survived while Seumas and the other Celts tended to injured warriors and villagers who had been confined by their Roman captures. Completing his survey, Iain returned to the few surviving residents. Two men and a woman provided sparse information.

"We are a small village as you can see," one of the men stammered, "only five families. We are all Gaelic, born of this land. These Roman soldiers marched into our village and called for an elder. My father stepped forward and he was slaughtered, as if for sport!"

"They beat our children and ravaged us. Every one of us!" the woman cried out, her choking voice filled with horror.

"One of our men, Angus, tried to stop them when they attacked his wife," the second man contributed. "He was murdered before he could strike a blow!"

"Soldiers began burning the village and they pounded us with questions about some village training warriors. When we could not answer they cut off my brother's fingers and tortured him until you arrived," the first man added. "When the soldier saw you coming, he drove his sword through my brother's heart!" The man looked at Iain, Seumas, and other warriors walking about his smoldering village. Filled with rage, he cried out "Are you who they were looking for?"

"I fear so," Iain replied in a soft, apologetic voice. "Yeu, yer village, are innocent victims. We have tried to build an army to stop the atrocities of this Roman invasion. It is tragic that they found ye first."

Gauls witnessing Iain's confession cried. Men wanted to attack these warriors who had come to their rescue, but knew they were not their enemy. Still, pain of loss burned within them with no way to ease the blaze.

A faerie sat on the right shoulder of each survivor and wounded, and on the forehead of each of the Gaelic dead. Iain surveyed the Roman party again, looking for a familiar face or someone not of Roman ancestry. He found no one.

Quiet filled the evening as Celts took care of the Gauls, comforting frightened children, women, and men. Slaughtered livestock were brought in to feed everyone and injuries were redressed. This first encounter of real war had stunned the new warriors who now called themselves "true" Highlanders.

A rising sun found the Highlanders preparing the dead for burial. Iain ordered construction of pyre stands but the Gauls requested burial according to their own tradition. Weary warriors dug pits so they could bury these men, women, and children with honor and send them to their next life with respect. Slain Gauls rested gently and honorably in their earthen graves. Weeping family members of each of the deceased laid a memory token next to their loved one so they, the living, would not be forgotten in death's journey.

Recognizing they were a weakened village without protection, Gaelic leaders consented to joining with these men who had cared for them. At sunrise of the second day after the battle Highlanders helped Gaelic villagers collect what was left of their belongings and together they struck a new direction, toward *Ceo Dhachaidh*. Iain had been leading his army in a circle and they were only one day's journey from home. They arrived just before sunset but the march had been hard on the villagers. After a brief explanation of the attack, people of *Ceo Dhachaidh* quickly took the Gauls into their homes and all settled in search of a peaceful night.

Iain stood at the stone chairs staring off into the darkness. How had the Romans heard of their training? Reading his thoughts, Elizabeth came out to him and tried to soothe his tortured mind. "Could they have been a company wandering the hills before the training began?" she asked.

Iain looked down at her; he had considered this possibility. The training was planned only weeks ago. Could any traveler have picked up the news and carried it on?

"The Romans were looking for *Ceo Dhachaidh*," Iain responded with great distress.

"They dinna find us," Elizabeth tried to reassure her husband.

Iain was not reassured; instead he stared back across the trees and off into the night sky. Elizabeth stayed with him until he faltered as he stood; she then guided him to bed.

〰〰〰〰〰〰〰〰〰〰〰〰〰〰

Angus carefully pulled the silk ribbon to the page where he was reading and reverently closed the book. With a solemn face he looked to his grandchildren. They in turn looked back with awe and silent wonder. Looking to his wife, Angus winked then announced "Lunch!"

Lunch consisted of cold-cuts, mostly ham, on homemade whole wheat bread slathered with mayonnaise. This was not Lillian's choice but what the children had at home. Lillian and Angus both enjoyed a slice of toast next to a robust salad made with fresh greens from the garden just outside their door.

After lunch the three youngsters went outside for a bit of fleeting sunshine and fresh air. They had been outside only a few minutes, less than an hour, when Liam came running into the kitchen.

"Seanmhair, we are going to the hillside. Alex and I want to train to be Highlanders!" the energetic eight-year-old called before bounding for the door again.

"WAIT! Take Seanair!" Lillian called, putting the last of their lunch dishes away.

Liam turned in mid-stride, racing through the old stone house toward his grandfather's study. Moments later Lillian heard Angus calling out, "Going to the hillside with the bairn."

Marian hung back from her brothers, walking beside her grandfather. Reaching the hillside, Angus pulled out an old meerschaum pipe and packed it with his favorite tobacco. Sitting on the ground where his audience had rested days before, he watched the boys jousting with sticks as though they were real staves. Marian sat quietly, pulling a flower apart as she looked out across the loch and mountains beyond.

Angus relit his pipe for the third time as the sky opened up, pouring buckets of rain on everyone unfortunate enough to be outside at the time. Angus and his grandchildren were soaked to the skin long before sloshing into the kitchen back home.

"Get a bit wet?" Lillian chortled.

"Aye, a wee bit," Angus returned with a grin. "Yeu three get some dry clothes on and join me in my study. I believe we have a village of Gauls to care for."

〜〜〜〜〜〜〜〜〜〜〜〜〜

There was no rousing reveille the next morning. Uneasy minds awoke within *Ceo Dhachaidh* early and silently. Highlanders quietly set to work taking care of survivors of the Roman attack. Lodging had to be built and lives rekindled. With no time to dwell on the past, these Gauls who had lost much now had new friends and an opportunity to build a new home.

Iain spent time talking with David and Robert, the two surviving men of the devastated village. He was seeking an answer to how Romans knew of their activity. Neither had any more answers to yield. With David's help, Iain met with those women who were strong enough to talk. Physically and emotionally exhausted from their ordeals, no one could tell Iain anything of value. Fighting to not lose their identity, Gauls did find hope in the support of their new neighbors.

Warriors returned to their agricultural roles and collected materials to build lodging. Four homes had to be built for five families. A young bride named Sarah, who was widowed when Romans murdered her husband, took lodging with her sister's family. Huts were arranged in a corner of the village giving them the comfort of familiarity and yet a sense of belonging to their new community.

Throwing himself into the effort of building new huts, Bryan labored silently, gathering straw into bundles needed to construct new homes. Rachel joined him as he laid straw on a roof, tying it to the frame with vines. Looking at her, he smiled, but it was not a smile of pleasantry. Rather, his eyes offered acknowledgment and welcome to the presence and efforts of this extraordinary young woman. Rachel returned the same smile. As she helped him fasten a bundle she said, "They will be all right." Bryan said nothing, but put even more energy into his work.

Bryan and Rachel did not talk about the battle that day, but it was evident that a change had come over them. Working side by side, they grew beyond the masks of warriors; a new spirit was born between them. Working side by side, they silently filled the needs of each other, tying bundles of straw to the frame for the first layer and tacking bundles on a second roof layer. Together, each provided needed straw, vines, and straps without request. Each filled a much deeper spiritual need for one another as well.

Together, Rachel and Bryan silently roofed one hut. As they were finishing their labor Bryan slipped, sliding off the roof and knocking into Rachel as he fell. Landing on his feet, Bryan turned in time to catch Rachel in his arms as she fell toward him. Her arms on his shoulders, he slowly put her to her feet but their eyes never parted. Hearts racing, an uncommon heat rose between the two. Bryan held Rachel at her waist, something no man had ever done. Staring into her eyes he became entranced by the expanse of green, hypnotized by their flecks of gold, sliding deeper into regions he never knew existed.

Rachel found herself on the same journey. Whenever she had looked into a man's eyes it had been only to see the intent behind them. Now, she too, was lost in an endless blue of forever. Behind this miraculous world of wonder she became absorbed in a vision of what tomorrow might hold. Resting her hands at Bryan's shoulders, Rachel gently pressed against him. Their eyes never parted.

"If the two of ye are still willing, we could use help finishing this hut before dark," someone called. Both took a deep breath and quickly joined the others who were completing the walls of a third hut.

Seeing construction of new homes well underway, Iain called the council of chiefs together late in the morning. This "governing" group represented each village in the training program. "We are being hunted and while I know who the hunter is, I also know he canna read the signs of our Hielands," Iain began. He spoke calmly with resolve and conviction, not seeking to excite or rally but to share a plan. "Somehow the Romans are being told of our training. We must return to our homes and daily activities, but we cannot cease preparation. I am certain that news of our battle will reach a Roman *sonnaidh*[15] soon enough and more vermin will come to resume and strengthen their search. *Ceo Dhachaidh* cannot continue to support our training. We must now share this burden. We will also set up a runner alert whereby all villages can be notified when Romans invade our Hielands again. Seumas and I discussed this plan before we discovered the intruders, but I think we must begin it now to protect ourselves.

"This is how we propose to continue. Seumas, I, and a few others will visit each village. We will stay for a period of four days before we move on. During those four days we will train all in yer village who are

---

[15] *sonnaidh* - SON~agh - fort or garrison

able bodied and willing to do battle. We will begin with the basics and go on from there. Those who have been trained these past weeks will continue working under the direction of an experienced Celt in their own villages. It will take many months to build a Hieland army but this is the way it must be done.

"Each village must also find runners to serve as a first call to arms. When intruders are discovered again, two runners will be sent to spread the word. When they reach yer village, ye will send two runners to the next village. Never allow a runner to travel alone, for their own safety as well as the safety of the message they will carry. Ye must have all of yer villagers who would defend the Hielands ready to respond when runners arrive. Runners will carry information about where and when to assemble. We may not have time to develop a plan to give to the runners, so if they bring ye only a call to arms then ye must assemble here, in *Ceo Dhachaidh*. *Ceo Dhachaidh* is the gateway to all other villages and strategic to the Romans. We stop them before they get here and they will nae bother yer families.

"Right now we need everyone to help finish building huts for the Gauls and get them settled. We should be able to finish these tomorrow, then we will move training to one of the villages. The future of the Hielands is now in yer hands; yer leadership will decide whether we will be subjects of a foreign power or if we are to be independent of any sovereignty."

There were no questions and little conversation as the council broke up and members returned to their own fires. Seumas and Iain remained in the lodge, each staring into the fire, each deep in contemplation. Emerging from his private thoughts, Iain asked, "Where is young Bryan from?"

Seumas thought for a moment before replying, "I believe he would be from Blyth Brier. Whit are ye thinking?" Seumas knew his cousin well enough to know that Iain had a reason behind every question.

"Have ye noticed how Rachel and Bryan work together?" Iain replied. "I was thinking we could take Rachel with us and start training in Bryan's village. We could then watch them in his home village and see whit develops."

"Playing matchmaker?" queried Seumas, his face starting to glow with a smile.

"I prefer to think of it as being more of a big brother to the lass. I would hate to see her hurt and I would love nothing more than to see her begin a family with the right young man."

"Well," agreed Seumas, "I guess we need to finish getting our new villagers settled. Then . . . we head to Blyth Brier."

Seeing uncommon activity around the village, Resbith found a breeze to carry her on a tour. Caring shown between people, especially for newcomers she had not seen before, brought warmth to her being. Believing they could use some help, Resbith called upon the Spirit of the Highlands to make tree limbs bend more easily for hut frames, stiff stalks used to bind straw more supple and easier to work, bales of straw plumped out a bit covering a greater space.

As she watched one couple, a young man and a familiar red-haired lass, they began to roll down the roof they were working on. Acting quickly Resbith used her command of nature, enabling the young man to land upright and slowed the lass' fall until he was ready to catch her. Both reached the ground safely though they lingered in one another's arms for a long time. Their delay brought a bright smile to the Comleidh's spirit.

When sunlight no longer shone from overhead but reached out from the horizon, Resbith caught her breath with dismay. Mounds of *gleo* were now visible, growing in size and weighing so many people down. Some struggled to stand, yet found the strength to help others. Knowing she could not help everyone the wee faerie captured a bit of fading sunlight, creating private rainbows for a few who carried heaviest burdens. Seeing the colors before them these select few stood a little taller, shedding a bit of *gleo* as they reached out for the glimmer of color before them.

As sunlight faded behind the mountains, Resbith wept for huge mounds on so many shoulders. Great darkness weighing down so many spirits.

A frenzy of activity and work intent on clearing the remainder of the training camp filled morning of the next day. Materials previously used in the training encampment were moved to the new part of the village to aid the Gauls. Stores were gathered and men of *Ceo Dhachaidh* returned to hunting, bringing home enough game for a village seeking to recover a normal life. By midday life buzzed with activity typically found in a Highland community. Most of the Highlanders who had rescued the Gauls carried a burden of apprehension but pushed on in spite, or because, of it.

Several groups decided to leave right away; they missed their families. Warriors from northern settlements of Blyth Brier, Heigh Fell and Benmost Bield talked about traveling together, deciding to wait until next sunrise. Rachel was helping Bryan and men from his village prepare to leave when Iain approached the leader of this group.

"I would like to propose that we begin training in Blyth Brier," Iain began. Everyone nodded in agreement. "Would ye have objection to Rachel being part of our training team?" No one objected. Iain noticed that Bryan gave Rachel's hand a strong squeeze and that she smiled. Pleased with what he witnessed, Iain excused himself, "We will join ye at sunrise."

Seumas asked a group of trainers and students for volunteers to help with training in other villages. Martin had healed enough from his previous accident and was willing. After some discussion, it was decided that Martin would go and Seumas would watch over *Ceo Dhachaidh*. A young man named Peter who had shown great skill and power during the battle with the Romans also volunteered. They were instructed to gather their arms and equipment, and to be ready to leave with men of the north in the morning.

A bit of chill filled the air as the sun rose the next day. Martin, Peter and Rachel were ready to travel, but Iain was not to be seen. This was somewhat unusual, for Iain was always ready to march, hunt, fight, or play. Seumas went looking for him and found him standing in his doorway, in Elizabeth's arms. She was accustomed to saying goodbye, but this time there was a great difficulty on both sides. Releasing his grip with a final embrace, Iain turned toward the group. "Please take care of him," Elizabeth pleaded to their friends. Several men lifted Iain's spirits with good natured teasing as they left *Ceo Dhachaidh*.

Amidst remarks from his "friends" Iain turned and looked back; again, something he rarely did. Seumas and Ingrid stood beside Elizabeth. Iain smiled and set a quick pace toward Blyth Brier.

Iain was accustomed to moving through forests and hills at a rather brisk step. He claimed that such pace helped him to think. Northern men found Iain's speed challenging, but they did what was necessary to keep up.

The journey to Blyth Brier would normally have taken a day and a half. Iain and his traveling companions walked into the unsuspecting village as dark settled about it's quiet. Exhausted from keeping pace with Iain on their journey home, men of Blyth Brier silently slipped into their huts. Iain, Martin, Rachel, Peter and Bryan could hear cries of welcome as each husband and father embraced his family. Bryan showed trainers and men of other villages to the lodge and then returned to his own hut where his mother, Roslyn, greeted him with welcome arms.

Men of Benmost Bield and Heigh Fell continued their journey before sunrise. Men of Blyth Brier, weary from training, worked hard at straightening out their backs and necks as they stretched and twisted around. Friends from the village waking to the news of the men's return came quickly to welcome their friends and neighbors home. A celebration erupted in the center of the village whereupon Rob, an elder who had been part of the training, raised his hands to quiet his joyous community.

"Aye, we are home again but we still have a heavy labor in front o' us," Rob began. "Most of ye do not know our guests. The lass is Rachel, there with her are Martin and Peter. The big ox of a man ye all know by reputation is Iain Gregor. They have come to Blyth Brier to help us train more men for battle. Our mountains, our Hielands, are under siege by Romans and they mean no good. These Celtic Warriors are here to train all of us to keep these intruders out of our villages and our homes." There was an uproar from several men; Rob held his hands up to stop their deluge of questions. "We have seen them. Each of us that went through training engaged our enemy in battle, and we won!"

There was no stopping questions at that point. Everyone wanted details about the battle with Romans. Iain and Rachel stepped away from the crowd. Bryan joined them seeking an escape from memories of battle. As the crowd became more subdued Martin was able to join with village leaders and explain the training program that was about to begin. Local men listened with great interest and were eager to get started. Bryan's uncle, who shared his name, came over to the quiet trio.

"I don't see any scars on ye, Little Bryan," the uncle taunted.

"I was there," Bryan replied.

"Yeah? I guess ye were guarding the back o' the troop," continued the badgering uncle. "Ye never were much for fightin'."

"Well, Uncle Bryan," Bryan began, staring in his uncle's eyes, "after having been in the front ranks and killing one soldier in sword fight and another in hand to hand combat, I still don't care much for fighting. But ye know, there are times when we must do it."

Rachel took young Bryan by the hand and they walked away from his uncle and the crowd. Uncle Bryan watched them walk away, a bit insulted by their coldness. Turning to Iain, he asked, with a bit of malice in his voice, "Who's the lass?".

"One of my trainers," Iain answered. "She will teach ye how to use a stave in battle." Iain then joined the elders and helped to lay out the training schedule. Uncle Bryan rubbed the back of his neck as he strolled over to a group of his friends.

"Ye hae better be wary of that one," a voice warned Iain from behind him.

Turning, Iain found Rob approaching him. "Bryan's uncle?" Iain asked.

"Bloigh Bryan. He is trouble, ye kin count on it," Rob explained, his voice heavy with warning.

"'Bloigh Bryan'?" Iain chuckled.

"Sort of a nickname. He doesn't like it but whit do ye call a big man with a big mouth who causes big trouble?"

After a light morning meal, would-be warriors gathered at the edge of the village to begin training. Iain began to instruct their new students, explaining what they were about to learn and why. While he spoke, Martin, Peter and several trained villagers stood together to one side. Rachel and Bryan stood together to the other side, their backs to the forest.

Iain raised his stave and began to demonstrate how to hold it. At that same moment Bloigh Bryan and a friend sneaked quietly from the forest and jabbed Bryan from behind, poking him in the back below his right shoulder. Before they could jab Rachel, both targeted victims reacted as they had been trained. As if in a finely choreographed dance they turned, smoothly sweeping staves through their attacker's knees. Bloigh Bryan and his friend found themselves on their backsides, laid out like a couple of bear waiting to be skinned. Without hesitation Rachel and Bryan disarmed them. As Bryan and Rachel raised their staves for a killing blow through their assailant's necks, Iain reacted just as quickly grabbing both staves and preventing a deadly finish.

"As ye can see," explained Iain, "ye will learn to stop an attack and repel the assault, even killing yer attacker if necessary. If ye are good, this will become as natural as breathing. If ye are not good, ye could become dead." Martin and Peter helped the fallen pranksters to their feet, whereupon Bloigh Bryan and his friend quietly joined the students for training.

That surprise attack turned out to be a good thing. Many of the village had been victims of Bloigh Bryan's antics and they now saw a way to stop him. Each watched attentively as warriors previously trained in *Ceo Dhachaidh* now assumed roles of instructors. Lessons with the stave went well. Toward the end of the first day of lessons Iain told everyone to bring their best weapons to the lodge that night. Everyone had been trained in the use of stave, however trainers needed to know what other skills and advantages were available.

Blythe Brier offered twenty-nine potential warriors, including a small group of Gauls. This village had been built by native Gauls. Celts settled with these agricultural people and the community grew with a new vitality.

During the evening meal volunteers brought eighteen slings, four swords and three iron-tipped spears to the lodge. Several also brought an abundant supply of heavy rope. Iain allowed that the rope was excellent for building lodges but how was it to be used in battle? A local man named Robbie invited Iain and the trainers outside. He then asked Peter to run toward the well, about sixty meters away. As Peter ran, Robbie pulled a short piece of rope from his belt and hurled it at Peter. The rope flew faster than Peter was running and in seconds wrapped around Peter's legs, tripping him and sending him rolling across the village commons.

Peter began to unwind the rope from around his legs and discovered that it could be bent into shapes and it also had small blocks of wood at each end. He stood upright and tossed the rope gently into the air. As the rope fell, he grabbed it stiffly with his hand. The rope wrapped tightly around his arm.

"How do ye use these ropes?" Peter asked as he walked back toward the group.

"We hunt with them," Robbie replied. "As ye can see, it can bring down a stag. With experience a young man can reach 25 to 30 meters accurately. Further if he is strong enough and lucky."

"These ropes could slow an advancing line," suggested Martin.

"Yes," agreed Iain, as he took the rope from Peter, "but how long would the advantage last?"

"It could give advantage and any advantage would be good," Martin replied earnestly.

Slowly the group returned to the lodge, Iain still examining and contemplating the rope as they walked. Plans for the next day were set after a final review of available equipment. Everyone retired for the evening, except Iain and Martin. They had fought many battles together and both were fixated on trying to figure out how best to use this unusual rope.

Rachel and Bryan retired by way of a hillside near the edge of the village. They said little, rather they watched stars twinkle in a clear sky. Bryan's hand found Rachel's; she moved closer. It was a clear night and the two warriors enjoyed a private interlude with the night sky growing ablaze with stars. Finally, both exhausted from the day's activities, they walked to Bryan's mother's hut where Roslyn took Rachel in, sending Bryan to his uncle's hut. Their quiet farewell glances confirmed that they both desired more evenings such as this.

A mystic halo encircled the sun as it rose on the second day, a ghostly stillness shrouding the entire land. An eerie quiet lay across the mountains with mist clinging to arms and legs of everyone as Iain called on each person to pick up his weapons and form groups. Six younger men had nothing so Iain retrieved slings from the sword bearers, giving them to two of the young men. The remaining four continued practice with staves. All men spent the morning practicing new skills with old weapons. These villagers, farmers becoming warriors, were quick to learn and by midday were ready to move to new weapons. Everyone moved to a different weapon and training continued until darkness fell. This order of training was repeated the morning of the third day.

At midday Iain called all together and assigned them to weapons instructors considered to be their strongest. Some villagers were disgruntled because they did not get their swords or spears back. Martin explained that they should carry the weapon of their greatest strength and ensured all were armed.

Mock battles, one on one, filled the afternoon schedule. Each man did his part to overcome an opponent, without maiming or injuring this man who was his neighbor. Safely positioned at the top of a hillside, visiting trainers watched pretend battles. Iain continued to handle and examine Robbie's rope with his hands.

Toward the end of the day small groups formed to challenge one another and Bloigh Bryan attempted one of his practical jokes. Running from group to group Bryan poked one man in the back with his stave and then ran away, stopping briefly to poke another man. His targets were random. Tired from strenuous training and enraged by the big man's senseless antics six men took chase, running Bryan off the training field into a thicket of nettles. Spines of the bushes pushed into Bloigh Bryan's legs; he fell to the ground as he climbed from the bushes on the opposite side. His legs became cold and hard around nettles sticking into his skin. "Don't worry," volunteered one of his pursuers, "ye'll be all right by day break."

Peter carefully picked several spines from the nettle bush and examined them. Not familiar with nettles, he made numerous inquiries. After supper Peter and two villagers returned to the bush to collect spines. Quietly, they retreated from the group for the evening.

Training began on the final day with an exercise to make sure each warrior was using his strongest weapon. They had been "battle tested" but today they were to run a gamut, a series of exercises employing available weaponry. Artificial enemies had been set up at several stations with a weapon waiting for the test. Every student was to run the gamut and display their skill. Testing took most of the morning but was successful. Each defender was confident that he knew how to defend and attack with stave, sling and many with sword or spear as well. Iain congratulated each on his development and asked if any would like to continue with him to the next village to provide training there.

Bloigh Bryan stepped forward quickly, although still somewhat stiffly. "Iain, ye and yer team have demonstrated yer skills as trainers," Bryan challenged. "I would like to take yeu on in battle."

"Why not?" agreed Iain. "Whit sort of battle do ye propose?"

"There are four of ye, each proven in battle. I know that Little Bryan would like to join beside Rachel so that makes five. Five of ye, proven warriors against nine of us whom ye have just trained." Bloigh Bryan smiled as he found eight good friends gathering around him.

"I would like to play, too," called a tenth man who joined Bloigh Bryan's team.

Iain looked to the other four who were challenged. Each had been tested by Bloigh Bryan and had revenge dancing in their eyes. "Aye," Iain began, "I agree to yer terms providing we all use the stave."

"To the field then!" Bryan cried as he directed his force to the field of battle.

Iain and the trainers strode to the far side of the field. Iain cautioned the group as they walked, "I fear Bryan is up to no good here. Watch yerselves and the edge of the wood." The Celts had not yet reached their position when they heard Bloigh Bryan's battle cry.

Turning apprehensively, the trainers saw their opposing force coming toward them at full run. Iain shouted at his team to clear away from the wood and to spread out. They had little time to comply before first contact. There seemed to be more on their minds than an exercise in skill by the way Bloigh Bryan's team attacked. They did not hold back on blows nor respect any etiquette of practice. They were at war and determined to win; even more, to prove themselves. Repeatedly Iain and Martin called out to hold back blows, which the trainers did.

After several minutes of painful defensive maneuvers one of the villagers landed a solid blow to the side of Iain's head. Iain stumbled from its force, allowing another villager opportunity to attack from his rear. Regaining his stance Iain witnessed a similar attack on Martin. "END IT!" Iain called out with a rage. Trainers no longer held back but now came with a force matching their attackers. Quickly the villager's numbers dropped from ten to seven to five, then to three as they suffered severe and disabling blows. Bloigh Bryan led those three who had positioned themselves for an assault against Rachel. She was cut off from the other trainers for they had been drawn to other parts of the field.

A bold attacker came toward Rachel with a lunge. A voice from deep within Rachel stopped her from returning his offensive; she took an uncommon defensive action. From across the field Peter saw four men converging on Rachel. Releasing a throwing rope from his side, he hurled it toward the attacker closest to him, but the rope did not reach its target before Bloigh Bryan's three converged on Rachel.

Instead of addressing her assailant Rachel planted her stave and lifted herself high into the air. She was directly over her stave, as though it were a part of her, when all three attackers brought their staves to bear on her location. Blows meant to cripple Rachel found only her stave which was cut in half by the combined forces of attack. Rachel fell straight down, stopping abruptly when her broken stave jammed into the ground. She took the force of the fall into her left shoulder. Meanwhile, the rope Peter had thrown when he saw the assault begin found its target. Unbalanced from his attack then wrapped by a rope, the attacker spun into the splintering stave pushing Rachel onto Bloigh Bryan. The big man stumbled backwards twisting his back as he fell to the ground. The third assailant stumbled over his friend who was tangled in Peter's rope.

Iain and Martin arrived together at the muddle of warriors. Little Bryan helped Rachel to her feet, but she could not move her left arm or shoulder. The third villager tried to help his friend out of the rope, but found the rope was full of nettle spines and his friend could not move. Martin helped Bloigh Bryan to his feet, but Bryan was unable to walk due to pain in his back.

Several villagers, who had been observing, built stretchers and carried Bloigh Bryan and his friend to their huts. Bryan's mother checked Rachel's shoulder. It was dislocated, not broken. Iain had Rachel lie down and bite on a stick. With a great jerk he restored her shoulder to its proper position. Roslyn stood by Rachel as she fought back pain and tears which swelled up but never fell. She slowly resumed breathing more normally. Roslyn then took Rachel back to her hut where she could care for her.

Watching the ladies walk away, Iain turned to Peter, "Whit is with this rope?"

"I saw how those nettle spines disabled Bloigh Bryan when he ran through them," Peter replied, smiling with pride. "I realized that rope could be a disabling force if it carried spines that paralyzed. Several of us have been weaving nettles into ropes, waiting to try it out. According to villagers he should be all right in a day or so."

Iain smiled at Peter, "We should check on Rachel and Bloigh Bryan." They walked toward the huts together. Martin was already working on Bryan's back and announced that there was no permanent damage.

As they entered Roslyn's hut she looked up from tending Rachel proclaiming, "What were yeu thinking! I thought this was supposed to be practice. We have ten men hurt, Rachel's shoulder is crippled and yeu, Iain Gregor, are bleeding from yer skull." Without pause she rinsed a cloth in water and put it to the big man's head.

"Elizabeth won't let ye play anymore if ye keep gettin' hurt," Rachel taunted, holding back her laughter.

Taking the cloth from Roslyn's hand Iain scoffed, "Don't mind my head; how is yer shoulder?"

"She won't be playin' anymore of yer games or even travllin' for several days, maybe a week or more," Roslyn scolded.

Iain's concern for Rachel showed on his face but not nearly so strong as Bryan's stare. "Yeu, Young Bryan," ordered Iain, "are going to take Rachel's place as we move on to train the next village. Elizabeth would have my hide if I left ye here with Rachel . . . and yeu are a good trainer."

It was settled and there was no argument. Blyth Brier had completed and survived its training. Trainers would move on to Benmost Bield at sunrise.

Residents of *Ceo Dhachaidh* resumed typical daily chores, tending crops and hunting game. Everyone knew that a great battle was coming, but until it arrived life had to continue. New villagers also assisted in their own resettlement. Robert and David, who were the only surviving men of the Gaul village, wasted no time in joining other men in field work. They spoke little but worked diligently.

Eric saw the strain they were under working together to care for all four families plus Sarah and asked if he could help. Robert did not say anything; he only smiled at Eric and continued working. Eric took this response to be a quiet acceptance of his gesture and worked side by side with Robert. Eric's efforts made it possible for these men to spend a bit more time with their families, easing their adjustment to this new village. Other families of *Ceo Dhachaidh* followed Eric's example and adopted the other two families who had no man to work on their behalf. Everyone yearned to resume a normal life and generous spirits made transition much easier.

Eric spent evenings working on his bagpipes. He would experiment with movements and note combinations until he found melodies. Occasionally someone would whistle a tune as they worked or just for Eric to copy. It became a game to see if Eric could find the tune on his pipes. Whistlers would frequently stop blowing when they changed notes. Eric could not pause blowing so he learned to insert short notes to accentuate his melody. He would occasionally have to shift the scale of the melody to fit his limited nine note range. This did not always work.

Seebtin, Eric's faerie nemesis, found great delight in disrupting the airflow of the drones while Eric played. One otherwise quiet afternoon, Seebtin tired of playing with the drones and began singing new tunes in Eric's ear while he tried to play. The young piper found himself switching tunes uncontrollably as Seebtin played his tricks. This trick turned to Eric's advantage on at least one occasion. He was trying to pipe and some children began to dance. Seebtin inspired a tune change and the dancers quickly changed steps as well. Several adults joined in and a great party started. Eric practiced the quick changes and villagers called the dancing a *rant*, because it was always boisterous and practically uncontrollable. Disgruntled that his prank had gone awry, Seebtin settled on a nearby tree limb while the village *ranted*. Sulking, the frisky faerie dreamt up new ways to bring mischief into the lives of Highlanders.

"Do faeries still play tricks?" Alex interrupted.

"Aye," Angus replied with a delightful smile. "There are two who have an eye fer yer seanmhair. Ye should ask her about Benigh and Fru at supper time. But donna do it when she ha food in her mouth!"

About two weeks after bringing the Gauls to *Ceo Dhachaidh*, Eric went to the great stone chairs to pipe for the evening sky. He found Sarah, the young Gaelic widow, sitting there, watching the sun slide away. "Would ye fancy a tune?" Eric asked with a smile.

"No," Sarah replied, "play what you wish . . . I do not mind."

Eric hoisted his pipes and as he began to play his gaze fell upon Sarah. She was still watching the last rays of the sun and her profile glowed in its light. Eric lost himself in the view of a beautiful young woman. His pipes sang from his heart. Rhythm of the music was slow and comforting. The melody was restful and uplifting. Seebtin was about to begin his antics but settled instead to the stone beside Sarah. Villagers stopped their activities and listened. Couples came together in embraces and a tear rolled from Sarah's eye, sliding slowly down her cheek. A brilliant pink hue filled the sky as Eric released his pipes, letting the melody rest. Without truly looking at him, Sarah gave Eric a soft kiss on his cheek and said "Thank You." She then ran back to her hut. Eric tried to watch her leave but was too stunned to turn his head. He, and the village, listened to the quiet memory of his melody slip peacefully across the loch.

Morning sun had not yet risen and mist hung heavy over the Highlands when Iain, Peter, and Martin called Bryan to join them. Roslyn and Rachel watched the small group disappear as though swallowed by the mountain. Iain's voice called back to the ladies, sounding like the voice of many ghosts that had passed through these mountains before, "I'll be back to pick ye up in five days. Be ready."

"He'll be back before ye know it," Roslyn assured a subdued Rachel with a motherly hug around her shoulders.

"Not soon enough," countered Rachel, "and yet I am afraid too soon."

"Are ye speaking of Bryan or Iain?" Roslyn asked with concern.

"I fear I'm not the one to continue the training with Iain," Rachel confessed, "for I already feel Bryan's absence."

Together Rachel and Roslyn walked quietly back to Roslyn's hut where she tended the sling around Rachel's shoulder. The day passed slowly for Rachel. While she took care of all her daily chores, she was now a warrior used to being away from home. Conversation between the women was slight, but a chain of thoughts spoken aloud intermixed with work and meals carried over several days. Concerns of their two hearts, questions and answers, shared in confidence.

"He is quite fond of ye," Roslyn offered as they washed clothes.

"We have a bond of spirits," Rachel reflected. "It is as though our souls are linked and we know how to protect or help the other without even seeing whit is happening."

"That spirit could be very good in raising children."

"It is a priceless asset on the battle field. It has already protected us. Bryan blocked a Roman blow to my back, opening himself up to attack. We stopped that one together."

~~~~~

One afternoon as both women walked to the slaughter pen to retrieve a small portion of boar, Rachel asked, "I have only known Bryan as a warrior. How is he around the village?"

"How do ye see him?" Roslyn replied with a warm smile.

"Concerned about other families. Unyielding in working the land. Cunning in trapping and hunting for food. Generous to all who might need him."

"Then why do ye ask?" Roslyn paused in step and thought for a minute, before challenging Rachel. "Bryan has never been much of a fighter. Where does he get his strength?"

"From this land, I believe. He is much like Iain in that way. He feels the strength and spirit of the Hielands and he wants to protect them for those who are to follow."

~~~~~

"How did ye come to be a warrior, my dear?" Roslyn asked, preparing vegetables for stew. Their conversation was now becoming more personal.

"I started as a runner. Eric and I ran a deer together. I found it exhilarating and wonderful to be treated as an equal by the men. Actually I was better than many of them and they knew it. I think becoming a warrior was expected of me."

"Do ye enjoy being their equal?"

"I could not enjoy being any brutish man's property."

"Whit about the fighting, do ye enjoy that?"

"I don't know that I ever 'enjoyed it.' There is a feeling of power when I face an opponent with a stave or sword in my hand. But whit is more wonderful is the strength I feel when I have Bryan's hand in mine. Strength is better than power."

~~~~~

"He is quite fond of ye, ye know." Roslyn thought out loud, relaxing at the end of the day.

Rachel would smile when she spoke of Bryan. Not a big smile, but revealing a new peace in her heart and soul. Assisting Roslyn helped shorten the days and Rachel also became acquainted with other women of the village. She even enjoyed tending to Bloigh Bryan's wounds. He ached for several days and Rachel was more than willing to remind him how he received those aches and pains. The entire village seemed to embrace this young lady who gave definition to Highland elegance, grace, and strength. Roslyn kept her close, for the warmth of having a daughter and as a reminder of her son.

Training at Benmost Bield went much like it had at Blyth Brier, except that nobody challenged the instructors. Students worked hard and did their best to learn. Every day ended with a tribute, a verbal salute to the Celts who had gone before them and a pledge of honor to their Highlands.

Peter continued to work on his rope with nettles. It was a good weapon, but had very little range. Throwing the rope through a crowd, as in battle, would be difficult. Rope requires a wide path for travel and the thrower had to be dangerously close to make effective use of it. The thrower also had to learn to handle the rope lest he become a victim of the sharp, poisonous nettles. Martin joined Peter in his efforts. One evening both men joined Sean, a local villager, beneath an apple tree. All enjoyed fresh apples. Sean loaded a half-eaten apple into a sling and flung it across the field to the edge of the woods. As the sunset faded into dusk several deer appeared from the forest and began eating apples that had been thrown across the field by the villagers. All of a sudden Martin stood up and yelled "THAT IS IT!"
~~~~~

Filled with excitement, Martin borrowed the sling from Sean and another from Peter. Cradling an apple in each sling, he tied them tightly to the lighter blocks of wood on each end of a nettle rope. The apple increased the weight on each end by more than double. Folding the rope almost in half, the old Celt grabbed it at the fold, raised the rope over his head, and began spinning it in a circular fashion like a sling. The apples and wood blocks began to hum as they gained speed. Martin then let the rope go, and go it did. Spinning rapidly, the blocks spread apart as they flew across the field. Lunging with surprise when the rope wrapped around its neck, a small stag wobbled a few steps before falling from the attack of the nettles' sting.

Quickly, the three warriors ran across the field to the downed stag. It was not paralyzed, only stunned from the nettles themselves for the force of the blow did little more than scratch its tough hide. Carefully the warriors removed the rope from around the animal's neck, making sure no nettles stuck, and helped it to its feet. Slowly, it stumbled into the dark wood.

"If that had been a man . . . " Martin offered with satisfaction. Peter, Sean and Martin smiled at their accomplishment.

Martin was eager to demonstrate their improved weapon the next morning. A target was set up across the field, a log with a large squash set upon it. Martin tried several throws but failed miserably with every attempt. Peter, too, had very little success in impressing any onlookers. Iain was beginning to enjoy the humour of this event when Sean made an attempt. With casual skill Sean raised the rope over his head, twirling it for several seconds as though it were a sling, then releasing the awkward device when it felt right. Flying with deadly accuracy the rope wrapped around the squash, smashing it as the apples collided on opposite sides. Sean quickly launched a second rope and the force of its blow sent the log rolling into the woods.

"Very well done, lad," Iain congratulated. "Would ye be willing to travel with us to the next village so ye three can finish developing skills with this new weapon?"

Sean agreed and everyone immediately began building and working with the new device. Even Iain made a few attempts with success equal to Martin's. Several men found the device ungainly, clubbing themselves in the head with its weights.

～～～～～～～～～～～～～～～～

Sunset welcomed the trainers back to Blyth Brier. Bryan and Iain immediately went to check on Rachel. Roslyn met them outside her hut, casually walking Iain back toward the other trainers, explaining "Ye will find Rachel quite strong. Strong enough to return to *Ceo Dhachaidh*."

Bryan took advantage of his mother's maneuver, slipping into her hut to see Rachel. The two paused as they saw each other. Letting all reservations fall they embraced. Their arms wrapped around each other with a strength and intent that could not be denied. Neither wanted to let go. With full trust and contentment Rachel turned her head and tucked it into Bryan's chest. Bryan laid a gentle kiss on her exposed neck.

"I hate to disturb this moment," Iain, who had escaped Roslyn's diversion, interrupted, "but, Rachel, how do ye fare?"

"I'll join ye outside," Rachel replied without looking at Iain. Releasing her embrace, she took Bryan's face gently in her hands. Staring deeply into his eyes she firmly, resolutely, told him "I am ready to live and fight at yer side, even die if I must. Now go see to yer mother while I see to Iain."

Martin and Peter were heading to the lodge where they had slept during time of training. Sean went with them, trusting in their experience. Iain was talking with Bloigh Bryan a short distance from Roslyn's hut when Rachel joined them.

"Will ye be ready to leave with us at sunrise?" Iain asked.

"Aye," Rachel agreed. "I do not want to leave Roslyn and Bryan, but there are things I must take care of in *Ceo Dhachaidh*."

"We are not going home, lass," Iain said with surprise. "We will be moving on to Heigh Fell for further training."

Rachel stared at Iain, painfully recalling their plan to visit all villages. Now eager to return home she was not sure what to say nor how to respond. It was not unusual for Iain to be gone for weeks at a time, but he had Peter and Martin with him. They also had families who needed them. After a brief pause she asked the only question she felt Iain might understand, "Iain, whit about Elizabeth?"

"She knows whit our job is. She understands why we have to be gone. We will train Heigh Fell and be home in a week."

"Whit is yer rush to train these villages?"

"Our Hielands are being invaded by Romans. They are killing our people because we are not trained to protect ourselves. We must arm ourselves and be ready for the next battle . . . it may be our last."

"And if that battle comes tomorrow, who will care for Elizabeth? Ye are pushing everyone to exhaustion. Tired soldiers canna fight; they can only die."

"Untrained soldiers die whether they are tired or not. Rachel, I am counting on ye! I am counting on ye and Bryan and Martin and Peter and Sean to teach others whit ye know. To share whit ye have learned. If ye do not pass on yer skills whit chance do these people have? Elizabeth does not like the separation any more or less than yeu do, but this is the price we must pay today to ensure tomorrow. We leave for Heigh Fell at sunrise. Will ye be with us?"

"Roslyn needs Bryan's help. I will stay with him and help him tend to her needs. Then we will both join ye. We should be less than a day behind."

Another sunset lingered over *Ceo Dhachaidh* with melodies from Eric's pipes echoing softly across the Highlands and the long loch below. He was tiring and felt he should stop for the evening, but looking into Sarah's eyes gave him a new strength. He could have piped for hours if only she would sit with him.

"YO! ERIC! You are a savior." It was Jason, accompanied by his musicians, stumbling out of the wood and up the path. They were tired and out of breath. "Your pipes led us through the darkening woods to your village. This place is so well hidden I don't believe anyone could find it on their own! Thank you for the musical escort. You have done quite well with your pipes." While they renewed acquaintances, Jason introduced a new member of their group, Rodney, a singer of some talent who had heard about Eric's pipes. Jason's description of the pipes had made him curious and Rodney wanted to see them for himself.

Eric looked across to Sarah, who was growing tired. "I would be more than happy to show my pipes," he explained, "but it is late and I was about to retire. If ye are here tomorrow, I will talk with ye then." Eric then walked with Sarah back toward the village.

"Will yer bairn be a piper?" Rodney asked as they began to follow Eric and Sarah.

Eric turned his head toward Rodney with a snap, looking quite puzzled.

"Is yer *ban-ridir*[16] not carrying?"

"No, she is not my wife," Eric replied. "Her village was plundered by Romans who tortured and killed her husband."

The musicians stopped and watched the two continue toward the huts, disappearing in the shadows.

Sunlight had just begun to creep into the village as Eric and Robert went into the fields to tend crops. The air was crisp and clean and it was a good day to labor. Eric finished his work midmorning and was filled with an unusual sense of energy. As he finished his work, Sarah joined him and they walked together to see if Elizabeth needed assistance.

Elizabeth smiled as the two came toward her hut. "Yer piping was delightful last night."

"I had great inspiration," Eric replied, smiling at Sarah.

"Ye have done quite well with yer pipes," Elizabeth continued.

"That is just whit Jason told me," Eric added. As he spoke his face lost its smile, becoming very puzzled and concerned.

"Why the shriveled brow, young Eric?" It was Seumas, coming to see if Elizabeth had any needs.

"Last night, as I finished piping," Eric explained, "the musicians came back into the village. They wanted to talk but I could see that Sarah was tiring so I told them I would talk with them today."

"I haven't seen the musicians," Seumas commented, a bit perplexed.

"That is whit puzzles me," Eric agreed. "There was also a singer with them. A man called Rodney."

"Whit did ye speak about?"

"They wanted to know if my baby was going to be a piper," Sarah said with a smile.

"A baby?" Seumas smiled. "Well, is he?"

"I told them she was not my wife," Eric replied. "I told them her husband was killed by the Romans."

Seumas thought for a moment before asking, "Ye say the musicians were here last night but ye have not seen them this morning?"

"Yes, that is correct," Eric affirmed.

"And ye told them Sarah's husband was killed by the Romans," Seumas said more to himself than anyone present. He thought for a few seconds. Suddenly all colour drained from his face. Seumas' voice echoed across the valley in a tremendous cry, "RUNNERS!"

Within minutes two young men stood in front of Seumas, each carried a food sac over his shoulder and a stave. His command was

---

[16] ban-ridir - ban RI~jed - wife of a knight or nobleman

simple, "Find Iain and tell him the musicians have come and gone and they know of the Gauls. Go to Blyth Brier and ask them which way he has gone. Go now and do not relay this message. Ye carry it yerself." The two young men looked at Seumas in disbelief. Seeing fear in their eyes, Seumas continued, "Ye must find the courage in yer heart, for then the Hielands will give ye the strength to run. GO!" Matched in step and stride, two young men took to the wood, their legs stretching across the land racing for tomorrow. "For the future of the Hielands, run and don't stop," Seumas said in a soft voice. Fobothom, an eager young faerie, followed the runners.

Rachel and Bryan watched Iain and other trainers leave Blyth Brier. Rachel's emotions were running hot. It was painful to see them leave without her once again, but she knew Roslyn needed her help. She feared for their safety, indeed the safety of all the Highlands, but she knew that the only way to bring an end to fighting was for this journey to be completed. Turning to Bryan, Rachel wrapped her arms around him and held him tightly. He held her close, but suddenly she pushed away from him. "We have work to do," she said, tears rolling down her cheeks.

Bryan looked at his mother. His face must have shown great confusion for she simply turned him toward the fields and put him to work. Rachel and Bryan worked throughout the morning without break; by early afternoon they had Roslyn's larder well stocked. All chores done, they left for Heigh Fell.

Watching the sun fading below the forest crown, Rachel and Bryan knew they would have to stop for the night. A breeze brought them a faint smell of roasting venison. They knew Iain would not have stopped half way, but a tasty aroma filled the air. Cautiously they continued up the trail, coming upon a camp. Five Roman soldiers sat around a fire, roasting a young deer.

"Hello in the camp! May we join ye?" Bryan called out.

"If you care for burned meat come ahead."

Rachel and Bryan joined the soldiers around their fire. All five were footmen, not one wore the mark of an officer. "What brings you to these wretched mountains at night?" one soldier asked.

The two travelers stepped into the light of the Romans' fire. At least two of the soldiers studied their clothing. Their attire showed no sign of Celtic origin and was like that commonly found in villages about the mountains. Romans therefor considered them Gauls, natives and not a threat.

"I am returning my cousin to her mother's house," Bryan replied. "She helped to tend my mother while she was ill. And ye? Whit are soldiers doing this far back in the mountains?"

"Getting lost, maimed and killed answering the orders of a mad man," replied a second soldier. "Have some meat." A soldier offered a piece of meat to Rachel, but his reach was short, drawing her into the light of the fire.

"This is tough but I guess you mountain women are accustomed to chewing tough meat," he sniggered.

Rachel accepted the offering, pulling away from the fire. She found a rock several yards back to sit upon where she could easily watch everyone. Bryan stepped next to the fire and drew his dirk, boldly cutting a piece of meat for himself, then sitting with the soldiers.

"Ye don't like our mountains?" Bryan asked as he chewed the charred venison.

"These mountains are possessed by demons. Only a mad man would want to fight up here. Our sergeant speared this young deer earlier today. When he went to retrieve the kill, a huge deer came out of nowhere and gored him to death. These mountains will kill you rather than give up their secrets."

"Whit secrets are ye trying to find?" Bryan continued.

"Six patrols have been sent into these mountains to find a village called Kyo Gotchy and some giant spirit man called Iain Gregor."

"Iain Gregor is a legend," Rachel interrupted. "He and that village are a fable. My grandmother told me of this man who stood taller than two men together. He could pass through the woods at night without a sound and the mountains gave up deer and boar to feed him. They even say he talked to faeries. It is all nonsense. Iain Gregor doesn't exist."

"I wish you would come tell my captain that," laughed one of the soldiers. "My captain says he sat across a fire from Gregor. Captain says they were ambushed by him and had it not been for an old hag he kept with him, he would have been killed."

"Our captain met your legend when he was but a foot soldier," offered another. "He has a debt to settle with your legend. Captain Royce was the only survivor of a Celtic ambush. A troop of soldiers was traveling through these mountains and happened upon this village. Without cause Iain Gregor killed all but one foot soldier. He mutilated the troop captain just to scare one real man and then ran him out of the mountains, warning him to never return. That soldier was told to lead a battalion of men back into these mountains and to rid this land of all Celtic vermin. He is Captain now and it is his personal desire to see Iain Gregor die before his very eyes."

"You both have over active imaginations," interrupted a third soldier. "The general wants all Celts destroyed. This village called Kio Gotcha is the last Celtic fortress. We destroy the village and we get to go home. If Iain Gregor is there, he will die. We have a full battalion to see to it!"

"As my cousin told ye," laughed Bryan. "*Ceo Dhachaidh* and Iain Gregor are mountain legends. Stories told by grandparents to entertain children around a fire."

The Romans continued to eat and laugh. The soldier who had given a cut of meat to Rachel looked toward her with growing frequency. At one point he began to stand, eyeing her hungrily. Rising quickly, Bryan put his hand on the soldier's shoulder and whispered into his ear. Looking at Bryan with surprise, the soldier sat down. Soon the Romans fell asleep where they sat. Bryan and Rachel took advantage of their lack of order and disappeared up the trail toward Heigh Fell. It was not safe to travel the Highlands in the dark, but this journey had to be made.

Hidden by a dense mist, the sun rose stealthily, prolonging predawn hours. Iain, Martin, Peter and Sean gathered with leaders of Heigh Fell to discuss plans for the day. Villagers stumbled to their appointed training ground and Iain began his introduction.

Iain had just finished when Bryan and Rachel joined them. Rachel asked Martin to take over the training while they talked with Iain. Speaking privately they told him what they had heard around the fire the night before. Seeing that they were exhausted from their nighttime travel, Iain asked a village elder to get them some food and a place to rest. He then consulted with Martin and village leaders. All agreed that training would continue that day but that the emphasis would be only on the most vital skills of battle. Runners were sent to other villages. Their message was "the battle for the Hielands is near, prepare and be ready for the call."

That evening Iain and Bryan stood at the edge of a field staring at the sky. The sun was setting, painting the heavens blood red. There were no brilliant streams of crimson, just an ominous blanket of red growing darker as they watched. Rachel walked up and stood between them. When Iain realized she was there he put his arm around her shoulder. "The sky says the end is near. I know ye fear whit is ahead but ye will be all right. You and Bryan will have children and they will continue to protect our Highlands . . . but only if ye do whit is necessary now."

Rachel did not reply, she simply stood between Iain and Bryan in silence. Darkness draped across Heigh Fell with an eerie foreboding that night; morning came quickly. Iain's last words to the village leaders were exhortations to continue training as they had been taught and to be ready for the runners' call. Silently the team of six trainers left for *Ceo Dhachaidh*.

<div style="text-align:center">~~~~~~~~~~~~~~~~~~~~~~~~~</div>

It was a full day's journey from Heigh Fell to Blyth Brier; that is for an average man on a normal day. Iain and the trainers left Heigh Fell before dawn, before the first rays of sunlight pierced the mist pushing the dark out of the Highland forest. Their pace was hard, fast, and relentless, slipping around the edge of Blyth Brier as the sun passed its peak. Without rest, as though they were on a Celtic war march, they continued their drive through the afternoon.

Darkness quickly engulfed the forest as the sun set. Iain stopped his team at a grove of large trees. Searching the forest crown, he instructed his companions, "Find a place to rest in the limbs of these trees. Tie yerselves to the branches so ye don't fall from a sweet dream."

With the other five secure, Iain climbed a tree and stood guard. He climbed high, so he could see all below him and view stars peeking through the dense crown above. It was mid-autumn and leaves of these majestic trees were changing colours. Leaves which reflected brilliant reds and glowing golds in sunshine now offered muted shades under light of the moon as it passed overhead. Still dazzling, leaves danced lazily in moon light, changing to dark shadows as they came loose on a gentle breeze, floating silently downward. Conscientiously, Iain's watchful eyes passed from one friend to another, then scanned the ground below them before returning to the heavens. Iain's thoughts went out to Elizabeth with his love for her, to their sons who had been killed by the Romans, and to his Highlands. His communion with the heavens did not tire him, rather it filled his soul with power and new sense of purpose. He continued his watch until he saw the first hint of light float across leaves above his head. He had not slept but he was rested and ready to move on.

Iain gently woke each of his friends from their tree-borne slumber, catching Bryan as he awoke startled. He motioned to each to remain silent but return to the ground quickly. Martin was the last to be awakened. When he reached the forest floor they resumed their intense journey to *Ceo Dhachaidh*. Only one of four deer sleeping nearby raised its head to watch them leave. The sun was still climbing across the sky when Iain left the path and led his trainers down a deer trail that passed through dense undergrowth. They were home by midday.

Rachel and Bryan went to Rachel's aunt's hut. Martin and Peter returned to the embracing arms of their families. Iain met Elizabeth at the stone chairs where she had been waiting. Sean was welcomed by Seumas and other villagers as he made his way into the village. It was a warm homecoming for all the trainers who did not know whether to rest or eat first for they had little of either for two days. There was also urgent news to share!

Sitting outside their hut, Iain kept one hand in Elizabeth's hand as he ate while talking with Seumas. He began telling Seumas of the Roman patrol and his fears. Seumas' face grew very puzzled. He was about to interrupt Iain and ask a question that was weighing heavily on his heart when Fobothom brought news to them, news that answered Seumas' unasked question.

"Your runners did not finish their run," Fobothom exclaimed excitedly. Seumas had not talked with faeries before and did not know what to make of this small creature flying in his face, nor did he understand its message.

"Whit runners?" Iain asked, recognizing the faerie and hearing his message.

"I sent two runners to tell ye of the musicians," replied Seumas. "They came in late one evening and were gone the next morning."

"Young faerie," called Iain, "whit do ye mean 'they did not finish the run'?"

"They met others on the trail," Fobothom began. "One runner was beaten and rolled into the bushes. The other was bound with rope and taken with the strangers. I followed them until they passed near here. Then I came to tell Seumas of his runners."

"Whit of the runner thrown off the trail," Iain asked. "Did he get up or stay there?"

"They poked him with their sticks before they threw him down the hill. He did not move. I believe he no longer lives."

Seumas filled with confusion and disbelief as he watched Iain conversing with the wee faerie. He could barely hear the faerie and did not understand Iain's questions. Iain continued to ask Fobothom for information, "Whit direction were they going when ye left them?"

"They are taking the same path you took when you did battle in the small village. Many faeries followed you on your journey. But these men do not travel as fast, nor as wisely."

Iain smiled at the young faerie and thought for a moment. "Whit is yer name brave faerie?"

"I am Fobothom."

"Fobothom, ye have done well and we all thank ye. Go rest now. Seumas and I will bring our runner home."

Seumas understood these words and quickly retrieved his fighting gear; Iain had not yet put his away. Iain kissed Elizabeth and looked deeply into her eyes; he could see she also heard the faerie. Not a word was said as Iain and Seumas began to run down the trail.

The Romans were near and the Celtic cousins had a good chance of catching them if they moved quickly. They ran silently through the woods. Their pace was quick but not taxing. Their breathing was steady but not labored. They knew they had to be ready to fight when they caught up with the Roman patrol. First, and more importantly, they had to catch them.

Overhead, the sun had begun its downward slide as Seumas and Iain heard voices ahead of them. Silently the Celts drew their swords and dirks, each drawing a deep breath as well. The Romans saw little as Seumas and Iain descended upon them with a horror from years of battle experience. Without a word from any mouth, without a call from a single voice it was over. Seumas released Robie, his runner, while Iain checked the five bodies for life. The three Highlanders then moved the bodies away from the trail and removed all signs of scuffle. Iain did not want to be away from Elizabeth for another night so they did not delay. Seumas questioned Robie as they returned to *Ceo Dhachaidh*.

"Robie, whit can ye tell us about yer hosts?" Seumas asked the runner.

"Romans talk quite a bit," Robie laughed nervously. "They are building a force to hunt Celts and kill them. They are especially interested in Iain Gregor and his village but they cannot find either. Iain, they called ye an 'overblown butcher.' They told stories of how ye ambushed a small patrol with fifty Celtic warriors and butchered all but one of them. Roman generals have sworn to destroy all Celts throughout the Roman Empire."

"We will see whit we can do to stop their plans," Iain replied resolutely, moving ever more intently toward home.

The trail that leads to *Ceo Dhachaidh* was not marked, by design. A stranger to the area would pass it by as a rain wash or maybe a deer trail. Iain turned onto the trail without a thought, and Seumas was close behind him. Robie stopped before turning onto the trail and stared at the forest. "Seumas! Iain!" he called. "Come back, something is not right here!"

Seumas and Iain returned to the main trail and looked at their private gateway. Fading rays of sunlight filled the forest with an effervescent hue. "He is right," agreed Iain, "but whit is it?" The three continued to look at the gateway, the cluster of trees hiding their village, and into the surrounding forest. Something was different but they could not tell what it was.

Robie stood inside the trail and looked back at the main trail. Casually he rested his hand on a limb hanging down from the tree above. Seumas stared back at Robie. After nearly a minute Seumas asked, "Robie, whit do ye have in yer hand?" Robie looked at the limb he was holding. It was about eight feet long, four to six inches around and had no twigs or leaves on it, yet this limb was lodged in the branch above. Looking at the limb, Iain realized it did not come from that tree but was a small fir tree stripped to look like a branch. The addition hung upside down, its roots lodged in the fork of a branch above. It took both Seumas and Iain pulling together to remove the marker. Seumas carried it home with them.

<hr>

The sun came up slowly and a mystical haze hung over the Highlands. *Ceo Dhachaidh* awoke from its dream state and villagers began to work. Women gathered in the common area and men went into the fields. This village showed no signs of concern or trouble, for to these people this was a new day and each new day was just that, new.

Bryan visited with the residents from the Gaul village. Sean worked with Peter for a while and then sought out Martin, who was reacquainting himself with his granddaughter. He marveled at the magic of a new generation, and promised himself to make her life better than his had been.

Rachel spent time assessing her life in *Ceo Dhachaidh*. She watched Bryan visiting the Gauls and other residents. This had been her home for as long as she could remember. Her thoughts went back to her father and life with her aunt. Casting her eyes around the village, Rachel saw

Eric laboring in the fields. Without thinking what she was doing she reached for the deer-stone hanging around her neck, a match to one Eric wore. She smiled as she remembered the deer run and how she had run side by side with Eric and a full-grown deer. Her soul was warmed further by recent memories of Blyth Brier and working with Roslyn. Bryan's laugh echoed across the village as he playfully lifted small children over his head. "There is my future," Rachel thought, "but is this village only in my past?"

Iain and Seumas met at the stone chairs, discussing what to do next. Iain's thoughts returned to his treetop communion reflecting on the new purpose he had found and accepted as his, to protect the Highlands. He always had a clear understanding of what to do, but this time he would not hold his picture up for Seumas to see. "Maybe we should get other village leaders to help decide our course," Iain suggested.

Seumas stared deeply into his cousin's eyes; they had changed. He had always seen a fire in Iain's eyes, a fire that reflected the energy of his soul. Often this fire had been fueled by only a base of flame, a sign of Iain's dedication to his people. Today, for the first time, his eyes were filled with a flame of rage. An all consuming spirit that could not be squelched. "Aye," Seumas agreed, "we should call the village elders together for counsel."

Seumas called to a young boy running up the hill, "Thomas, would ye please run to the village elders? Tell each one to come here at once." Young Thomas did as he was asked, but apparently told half the village as well.

<hr>

"How did Iain know Thomas' name?" Liam asked.

"Iain cared greatly for all who lived in Ceo Dhachaidh, especially the bairn. He maked it his business to know each person and their families. And not just those who arrived with him but travelers who came later as well."

"What do you mean 'travelers'?" Alex asked. His face showing surprise and confusion.

"As the Romans moved up Britannia, those who could nae or would nae be enslaved by their emperor sought freedom in the mountains. Some found refuge and safety in Ceo Dhachaidh and the other villages as well. Iain took time to get to know each family as they arrived, or when he returned from traipsing through the forests."

Seeing his grandsons were satisfied for the moment, Angus continued.

Within a few minutes elders circled the stone chairs and half the village surrounded them. Seumas looked at his cousin's face again and knew that it was up to him, Seumas, to start the meeting.

"Much has happened in the past few days," Seumas began. "We have learned that the Romans are building an army to hunt out and kill all Celts in these mountains. Romans may have killed Michael, one of our runners. They have tried to mark their way to our village and may be hunting for the other seven villages in our community. Iain has suggested that we, village elders, decide whit is to be done next."

The elders turned toward Iain, looking for guidance. Iain stood tall and silent. Everyone waited expectantly. No one spoke.

Martin broke the tense silence asking, "Iain Gregor, ye have dealt with situations of war, whit do ye think?"

Iain hesitated slightly before replying, "These mountains, these Hielands, are our home. We left our warring behind us to settle here. We made this our home, a home for our children and for their children. Romans have apparently destroyed Celtic domains held by our brothers and cousins. They now want to destroy us. I will not stand by and wait for them to bring their butchers' swords into my village and slaughter those whom I love. Leaves have begun to signal the coming of winter, and winters here are harsh. Travel into and out of the Hielands will become more difficult with each sunset. I do not know if the Romans will wait for Spring or come tomorrow. I do know that we have the body of a brave warrior somewhere in these woods and we have two strong warriors who need to be returned to their families. Beyond that I must trust in yer judgement and direction."

For the first time in the living memory of all gathered, Iain had addressed his people without a call to action. Instead he had made a suggestion, a call to direction and asked for the other elders to make the call to action. Seumas and Martin looked at each other, then to the other elders. Seumas read the face of each man in the circle carefully, then he made a decision.

"Tomorrow," Seumas began, "with the dawn, Martin, Robie, myself and one volunteer will return Sean and Bryan to their homes. We will find the body of Michael and bring him home. While we are gone, Iain will continue to train our villagers during early morning hours only. If ye must leave the protection of our village, go in groups of four or five and carry yer arms as well as yer tools with ye. Everyone must continue with yer duties and responsibilities. Trust in the strength of the Hielands, these mountains, and our people to keep us all safe."

Bewildered villagers shook their heads as they returned to their waiting tasks and chores, however the elders lingered briefly. Iain looked at Seumas as he put his hand on his shoulder. With a twinkle in his eye, he softly told Seumas, "Ye hae done well, cousin. Ye hae shown that ye can lead our people into a brighter tomorrow . . . but I would hae left within the hour."

Eric's pipes sang melodies of strength and determination that evening. Many of the villagers came to the hillside to listen; their spirits were high. As evening grew late, Iain suggested that it might be time for Eric to change his piping habits.

"Whit do ye mean?" Eric asked with serious concern.

"Yer pipes can be heard throughout the region," Iain explained. "In the stillness of the evening even the birds and animals stop their sounds to listen to ye. Maybe ye should play in the daylight so visitors might be seen following yer melodies to our hillside."

Eric remembered Jason's words and how he had followed the music of the pipes into the village. He knew Iain was right and agreed that this was a good suggestion.

That evening Eric sat close to Sarah; they spoke in quiet tones. Eric reached out and took Sarah's hand; she squeezed his gently. Bryan and Rachel also sat on the hillside. They did not speak, but watched the symphony of stars as they held each other close. Iain and Elizabeth stood beside the stone seats. Iain stood behind Elizabeth with his arms wrapped around her; together they watched the other couples. "Here is the mystical magic of our Hielands," Iain said softly. He then took Elizabeth by the hand and they retired for the evening.

Resbith paused high in her oak tree, she too was retiring for the evening. Looking at the couples on the hillside she marveled at how shrouds of *gleo* could not hold to their shoulders when they held another close.

<center>~~~~~~~~~~~~~~~~~~~~~~</center>

"Wait a moment, what just happened?" Alex cried out. "Did Iain just give up? It didn't sound like he gave up?"

"Aye, ye are as confused now as the elders of Ceo Dhachaidh were back then," Angus replied. Do ye recall the time Iain spent in the top o' the trees?"

"Yes," Alex replied, not sure what this had to do with the situation.

"Well, Iain, as a warrior, came to know his duty at tha moment, up in the trees. He saw it was time to prepare his cousin for a role o leadership."

"WHY?" Liam called. "Why should Seumas be the leader? Iain is the leader of Ceo Dhachaidh and ALL the Highlands."

"Aye, and a good leader knows there are times to let others make decisions and then to own them," Angus counseled. "Whit do ye say we take a break and see to suipear? We can continue tomorrow."

Marian got up and ran to find her grandmother, who was indeed preparing supper.

〰〰〰〰〰〰〰〰〰〰

Friday morning, the day after Highland showers, Angus went into town for a meeting. His old Rover disappeared into the heavy Highland mist long before the rumble of its engine and shifting gears faded.

"Why don't ye play cards or a board game?" Lillian suggested.

"No, I want to find out if they find Michael," Alex replied. He then sat in his grandfather's chair, opened the leather bound book to its silk maker and began reading aloud. Liam and Marian settled quickly in front of him. Lillian smiled, listed for a moment, then returned to her kitchen.

The morning mist faded quickly as Seumas, Martin, Robie, and Victor set out on their journey to take Bryan and Sean home and to find Michael's body. High in the great oak tree, Resbith watched, her heart heavy as she saw these men encased in a seemingly suffocating *gleo*. Each man wore this unseen burden like a great fur cape, yet each marched proudly with determined spirit to fulfill their task.

Lifting from her branch, Comleidh drifted across the small village, growing more distressed by struggles of each person as they shifted under an accumulating and darkening *gleo*. "I can aid a few, but I cannot lift this burden from all," the faerie sighed to herself. Turning back to her cavie, Resbith came upon Rachel. This young woman had just bid farewell to Bryan. Passing an elderly woman struggling with pails of water, this incredible young woman lifted the pails. As they walked back to the elder's hut, the old woman's *gleo* lost both mass and darkness. Rachel's *gleo* dwindled until it resembled a light woolen wrap.

"Why do ye smile so at a time like this?" the old woman asked her young companion.

"I know there are troubles ahead, but I see promise and a future with Bryan," Rachel replied confidently.

"Bryan? Is that the young man who just left with big Seumas and the others?"

"Aye," Rachel confirmed, sighing with anticipation of their reunion. Bryan had been reluctant to leave Rachel, but both had matters and responsibilities to attend to. Their lengthy goodbye was painful but left both with a deep warmth within their souls.

<center>~~~~~~~~~~~~~~~~~~~~~~~~~~~~~~</center>

Seumas stopped his group on the way to Blyth Brier to help Robie identify the location where he and Michael had met the Roman patrol. Many places along the trail looked familiar, but they did not find Michael. Their search took considerable time, without success and delaying their arrival in Blyth Brier until noon on the second day. Knowing it was a full day's journey to Benmost Bield, Sean's home, they decided to wait until the next morning before continuing.

Seumas and the travelers filled the evening talking with friends and telling village leaders of the latest developments. Bryan was glad to be home and looked forward to a few days of simple, quiet labor. Bloigh Bryan asked if he could journey to Benmost Bield with the group and Seumas agreed. When Martin told young Bryan of the arrangement, Bryan changed his plans and joined the group for the two-day journey.

Dawn found the group on the trail, with Bloigh Bryan among their members. Morning travel would have been filled with quiet had Bloigh Bryan not been taunting Bryan about Rachel, his fighting experience, farming and any other thoughts that popped into his head. Bryan refused to answer most of the jabs until Bloigh Bryan quipped about the pace, "Ye men have complained about these training journeys. I see nothing difficult in this walk. My friends and I walk faster than this when we are checking on our snares."

"Uncle Bryan," Little Bryan retorted finally, "yer snare lines cover less than one side of the hill opposite the village and ye do it with a tankard of ale in yer hand. Seumas has been holding back so ye will not fall over. Iain would not hold back for anyone."

Following Bryan's lead, Seumas picked up the pace. Bloigh Bryan's comments ceased. They arrived in Benmost Bield mid-afternoon, several hours earlier than first anticipated. Bloigh Bryan collapsed to his hands and knees when they stopped.

"Uncle, ye must weigh ten stones more than a full keg of ale," Bryan complained as he helped his uncle back to his feet and into a hut where he could rest. The journey was good for both Bryans for they came to know each other in a new world and were now less combative. Bloigh Bryan showed his nephew that he would stand up to fight, whether he was physically able or not. Little Bryan acquainted his uncle with his more quiet and forceful side; a side to be reckoned with.

Sean was glad to be home and made sure everyone was cared for with proper lodging and food. Again, Seumas spent time with village leaders preparing them for the inevitable future.

A scene of growing familiarity repeated the next morning as the group left before first light. They were traveling fast and without conversation when they heard loud voices ahead of them. Martin and Seumas signaled the others to wait while they checked ahead. Cautiously, they moved down the trail and found another Roman patrol standing at what appeared to be a secondary trail. Six soldiers argued about which way to go. Four of the six were barely old enough to carry a sword; the other two had a manner of some experience but showed no leadership in their arguments. One older man, broad-shouldered and assertive in his movements, stomped up and down the trails looking for some sign of a direction. Realizing this young and inexperienced patrol was lost, Martin and Seumas returned to their group and told the others what they had seen. Bloigh Bryan wanted to attack them at once, but young Bryan said he had a better idea.

"These patrols have been told stories about our mountains and Iain," Bryan explained. "Why don't we see just how lost they are and see if we can get them going the wrong way? If they present trouble we can fight, but it would be better if we dinna."

Everyone in the group agreed, except Bloigh Bryan, but he was persuaded to cooperate. The group of Highlanders confidently continued down the trail, confronting the loud and confused Romans. Young Bryan approached a younger soldier of no rank and asked what was wrong. A burly sergeant, the only soldier with more than a blush of beard, pushed his way forward announcing, "We are mapping local villages. This area is now under Roman protection and will be taxed for it." The sergeant looked at the men on the trail, examining their attire and apparent lack of weaponry. Martin and Seumas stood behind the other four, trying to conceal their Celtic arms.

"Oh," replied Bryan, hiding a grin. "Will ye be able to protect us from the bear we are tracking?"

"You are tracking a bear?" asked one of the soldiers, his face growing more pale with each breath.

"Aye," Seumas replied from behind the group. He had heard this tale in Blyth Brier. "A very large bear attacked our village and stole two of our bairn."

"He stood taller than this high," joined Martin as he held his hand over his head.

The Roman patrol grew visibly uneasy thinking about the bear. "Why would he steal your children?" asked one of the younger soldiers.

"He will eat the younger boy and then breed with the girl," Bloigh Bryan inserted, with great seriousness.

"What?" asked the sergeant, his attention turning from the men to their story.

"Aye," added young Bryan. "When mountain bears eat human flesh they become human for a period of one day. During that day they breed with a girl who will bear them a monster just like themselves."

"Well," Martin interrupted, "will ye help us to find our bear and protect us from his attack? Rescue our bairn?"

The sergeant felt the story was absurd but he remembered warnings of evil magic that lived in these mountains. Looking deep into the face of each of the Highlanders, he could see that each firmly believed in the tale they had just told. Raising his hands he offered his apologies, "No, our job at this time is to locate the villages and return to our general with that information. We are not to engage in battles of any kind, unless attacked. Our commander will dispatch an armed guard to this area to deal with your bear. But tell me, which trail leads to the nearest village?"

Young Bryan looked at the trails and pointed them in the direction of a small trail going down the hill. The soldiers thanked him and moved quickly down the trail, stumbling as they went.

Bloigh Bryan was the first to attack Bryan for his actions, "Whit are ye doing? Do ye know where that trail goes?"

Young Bryan laughed, "Aye, I believe it goes to a bear's den. Ye can see bear tracks and claw marks on the trees down near the thicket. I don't think we have anything to fear from that patrol."

With smiles and chuckles of delight the Highlanders resumed their journey and enjoyed a warm dinner in Blyth Brier. Village leaders promised Seumas and Martin that they would keep an eye out for the lost Roman patrol and would deal with them accordingly. "We may just teach them how to plow the land and protect them from themselves," one leader offered.

On the last leg of the journey the group, now four Highlanders, resumed their search for Michael, the missing runner. Often the group would stop to look down the hill for signs of a scuffle, or Michael. They were about to give up their search when Seumas caught the reflection of a friend, Fobothom. The brave young faerie was sitting on a tree limb, waiting for the group. Fobothom led Seumas down the hill and along a deer trail. Seumas could not hear the directions he was being given but he could follow the faerie. Some distance down the deer trail they found Michael, barely alive.

Martin washed Michael's face with cool water which revived him. Seumas then propped the runner against his knee and gave him water to drink. When he was able to speak, Michael described how he had been found by a deer and cared for by faeries. All were astonished at his story. "Iain is right," Michael told them, "give yerself to the Hielands and they will protect ye and give ye life."

Robie and Victor made a litter from their shirts and staves and carried Michael back to *Ceo Dhachaidh*. Elizabeth had considerable experience in caring for wounds such as Michael's and joined his family in tending to his recovery.

Martin and Seumas took great delight in telling of the exploits of the two Bryans and the Roman patrol. Iain was not pleased that they left the patrol in the mountains, but agreed that they would probably never find their way out. He laughed softly as the story of the two Bryans unfolded, not sure which was more tragic, the stories or the gullibility of the soldiers.

Ceo Dhachaidh rested easy that night. Warriors were home, the night was peaceful, and the stories were delightful. Faeries had proven themselves to be great allies and were welcomed into hearts and homes of all villagers. A peace settled over the mountains that night for the spirit of the Highlands was healthy.

Waiting in *Ceo Dhachaidh*, Iain expected something to happen. He continued training villagers for two to three hours each day, and waiting. His battle gear stood in the corner of his hut ready to go, and waiting. After six days he could wait no longer; he called the Celts together.

"We still have four villages that have not been trained and probably know nothing of whit is going on. We dinna know what is happening wi' them. They could have already been visited by a Roman patrol and even seen battle. I want to renew training in two locations. First we get villages Cullet Cavie, and Haugh Mailen together in Stag's Byre. We can do an intensive four day course with all three villages together and be close to them all at one time. Then we go to Doup Fell and take some of the trained folks from Blyth Brier with us. We can do basic training in two or three days and have Blyth Brier complete their training. We will be gone ten days. All of our community will then have basic skills and we will be better able to defend our Hielands in less than two weeks. I will need Rachel, Martin and Peter to go with me."

There was no argument as the Celts blessed Iain's plan with approving nods. Rachel and Peter were asked to rejoin the training team and make ready to travel, which they did. Rain filled the skies the next morning as Highland instructors left on their next mission. Elizabeth felt a strange chill as Iain said goodbye but she remained silent. Seumas and other leaders were doing their best to stay alert and not alarm other villagers. Now, with some of their greatest power away from the village, they had to increase their watch while keeping everyone calm and resolute.

〜〜〜〜〜〜〜〜〜〜〜〜〜

Cullet Cavie was all but deserted when trainers arrived late in the afternoon. Only three families were there, waiting for guests from the big village to arrive. While the travelers ate, villagers explained what they had done.

"One of our men saw a Roman patrol when he was out hunting. We sent runners to Stag's Byre and Haugh Mailen to warn them to keep alert. The next day both runners came back and said old Dru, in Stag's Byre, wanted everyone up there for training right way."

Iain smiled at Martin and nodded with approval. He then looked back to the man telling him what they had done.

"Well, we dinna want to leave our homes unguarded, so the three of us volunteered to stay here. Keep watch and stay out 'o sight. Each of us was with ye for training and that wee battle." His wife then sat next to him. He wrapped an arm around her, squeezing her affectionately. "Besides, my *beanag*[17] dinna want me fighting any more, unless it be with her."

"Whit is yer name?" Iain asked.

"Thom."

"He and Michael showed incredible power with their staves," Martin remarked. Pointing toward a younger man in their company. He then added "And Rabbie, there, would be lethal wi a sword if he owned one."

---

[17] *beanag* - benag - wife, term of endearment

"Ye have all done well," Iain confirmed. "When did this training begin?"

"Six days back?" Michael replied with uncertainty.

"Aye, that would be about right," Rabbie confirmed.

Iain nodded again with approval. Turning to the youngest of the three, he offered, "Rabbie, we will have to see whit we can do about getting ye a sword. But it is late, do ye have a place we can bed for the night?"

Early the next morning, before daylight, the four instructors left for Stag's Byre. Trails were wet and slippery from rain but they made good time. Shortly after midday they reached Stag's Byre, finding villagers actively training. Dru and another local Celt had organized this effort and directed exercises with help from others who had been trained at *Ceo Dhachaidh.* Essential training for all three villages was almost complete.

Iain showed an initial concern about the depth of training and asked to test some of the students. A mock battle was organized between villagers and trainers, including Rachel, Peter and Martin. Students came out strong and proved themselves worthy opponents, matching instructors blow for blow. Some students tested new moves which caught trainers off guard, temporarily giving students an upper hand. As trainers fell, Peter and Martin produced their nettle-laden ropes. Peter had prepared special ropes for training. These ropes were packed with fewer nettles and had a less severe impact on the victim. Ropes flew through the air with deadly accuracy. Students froze at the strange whirring noise which preceded ropes wrapping around their arms, legs and even chests. Like ghosts from the forest, ropes confounded villagers and the battle turned to favor the trainers.

That evening Martin and Peter taught several eager villagers how to make and throw the new rope weapon. Iain spent time with leaders of all three villages, advising them of events in other communities. He left them on alert for a call to arms.

Morning once again found the four trainers following deer paths over mountains. Training at Stag's Byre would continue as it had begun and their efforts were needed in Doup Fell, which was located west of Stag's Byre across two mountain ridges. There were no foot trails but Iain had made this journey using deer paths once before. The group had to negotiate several difficult rock formations but they made the crossing in one day rather than two.

Entering the village from the back, trainers heard a great commotion. Two Roman patrols had taken over the village. Battle-trained villagers had quickly taken defensive action but they were out numbered. Other villagers came to their aid but several were wounded in their attempts. Seeing friends bleeding, untrained farmers ceased their defense. Soldiers were not trying to kill the villagers, however those Highlanders who showed signs of training or experience were bound. "You will be tried for treason," an officer proclaimed.

Silently, experienced instructors moved unseen toward the front of the village. Reaching the invading soldiers, all four quietly drew arms and reignited the subdued defense. Seeing Iain, Martin, Peter and Rachel attacking with force, the tide of battle changed quickly. Strengthened, and now more confident, villagers released their bound warriors and Highlanders took control. Two Roman soldiers were killed and all others were disarmed. One villager was killed and six were wounded.

Officers were identified and questioned. They had nothing to add to what Iain already knew. The problem then became what to do with unwelcome guests. Most of the villagers wanted to kill them and be done with it, but Martin and Iain did not favor this course of action.

"We are not butchers," Martin explained. "If we kill them outright, we will be no better than they are. The Hielands, Our Hielands, cannot prosper when soaked with blood."

Argument and discussion continued without resolution until an older man of the village stood up. "Show them our training and send them back to their general with fair warning."

Iain liked what the old man said. "He is right. Allow them to watch some, but not all of our training. Show them the basics, let them see where we start. They will have a false image of our abilities. Then, we can send them on their way without any weapons or defenses. It will be up to their own training to get them back to their general."

Everyone agreed with the proposal and training began. Lessons were conducted according to the standard four day program. Roman soldiers were allowed to watch only the first two hours each day. Soldiers saw villagers grow from clumsy farmers to defenders of their homes with wooden staves. Training with spear, flying rope, sword and other battle techniques was not open for Roman review. Nor were the soldiers told what fate awaited them.

When the sun rose high on the last day of training, students and trainers staged a mock battle. Toward the end of the day, captured

Romans were brought to the training area. Highlanders, armed only with staves, encircled their prisoners. A village elder stood directly in front of ten Romans, informing them, "Yeu attacked our village, but ye did not strike to kill. For this ye have been granted mercy and release. These people, in this and all other villages, seek only to live in peace and harmony with these mountains. Yeu are free to leave this village and return to yer general. If ye attack us again, we will defend against yer attack and ye will forfeit yer lives."

One of the officers raised a question, "What of our weapons? How will we defend ourselves in these hostile mountains?"

"Ye will survive or die in these hielands by yer wits. If ye are smart, ye will survive, otherwise yer bones will enrich our lands."

Highlanders opened their circle, revealing the trail out of the village. Soldiers turned slowly and began to walk down the trail. Soon they were out of sight, but not out of mind for two armed villagers followed at a discreet distance.

The mood in Doup Fell was festive that night. Three deer had been roasted and a keg of mead was tapped. Training had been completed. Romans had been defeated. It was a good night to be alive in the Highlands. Celts, elders and visiting trainers watched with guarded joy, for while there was not a blade of steel among the Roman soldiers, they now knew where Doup Fell was located. If they made their way back to their general, he would most certainly send them back for revenge. Iain assured everyone, "They may get lost and wander back, but they are not armed for assault. If they do return, yeu are ready."

Late in the evening, villagers who had followed the soldiers returned sharing tales of the Romans' confusion and inability to navigate through the mountains. "They found the main trail, but then turned toward Blyth Brier. One officer kept yelling that he had already been up that trail and there was nothing up there. Finally they turned toward the loch. We followed them to the pass before we returned. I am not sure they will find their way out, nor could they find their way back to Doup Fell."

A great cheer went up from the crowd and festivities continued. Rachel stood silently apart from the others. Iain joined her, "Something is heavy on yer heart."

"I was hoping to meet with Bryan during the training."

"Ye miss him . . . had ye said something earlier I would have had some men take ye to Blyth Brier this morning."

"No, I need to return to *Ceo Dhachaidh*. I must finish some matters with my aunt before I meet with Bryan again."

"Ye will meet with yer aunt tomorrow, and I will personally take ye to Blyth Brier any time ye wish."

Rachel smiled at Iain, giving him a tremendous hug. He was indeed both father and the big brother she never had.

Instructors returned to *Ceo Dhachaidh* two days earlier than expected. Families were indeed pleased to have fathers home and all spent the evening relating stories of their journey. Old Celtic warriors were pleased to hear of the progress in Cullet Cavie, Stag's Byre and Haugh Mailen. "A proper Celt will not wait to be told to take action," an older man remarked. Stories of Roman patrols caused mixed feelings, that is until the story of their departure from Doup Fell was told. A common comment became, "leave a Roman in the mountains and he will confuse himself to death." Iain smiled when he heard the comment, but he knew it was not true. The Roman army did not dominate much of the civilized world by getting lost in mountains. This was a force to be regarded with respect.

During the days that followed, Celts and village leaders discussed tactics for continuing preparation. No one wanted to wait and be taken by surprise. They needed to take some action to find out what the Romans were doing. Iain convinced them to wait seven days, using this time to rest and prepare themselves to battle for their Highlands. In seven days they would make plans to find their enemy.

Pleasantly, six days passed without incident. Days filled with farming, hunting, and other domestic work. *Ceo Dhachaidh* was blessed by the Highlands with abundant autumn crops and game returned to surrounding hillsides not long after the training camp dispersed. A peaceful sense of escape settled across the village, but it was crushed on the seventh day.

Late that afternoon Eric played his bagpipes on the hilltop near the stone chairs, as had become his habit. A group of hunters had just returned, loaded with game. At the edge of the woods, below the hill, a Roman soldier appeared from the shadows, and then another.

Eric stopped piping, calling loudly "I-AIN!!"

"WHAM!!! Those Romans are going to get it now!" Liam exclaimed with delight. "Keep reading, Alex! I want them to get theirs! Iain will handle this!"

Liam chuckled a bit and continued.

Eric stopped piping, calling loudly "I-AIN!!"

The two soldiers climbed the hill with their arms outstretched. They were armed but made no motion toward their weapons, indeed quite the opposite. Six more soldiers appeared but waited at the edge of the trees at the bottom of the hill. A dozen men carrying farm tools stood above this line of men with other villagers surrounding the two ascending the hill. Stopping at the top of the hill in front of Eric, they stated their purpose. "We wish to speak with your village leaders."

Before Eric could respond, nearly every man of *Ceo Dhachaidh* joined him on the hilltop. Many carried farm tools, some had dropped their tools to grab staves. Every man on the hill held a powerful defensive posture, ready to defend home and community. Experienced Celts took positions at the bottom of the hill, their hands ready on sheathed swords, attentively watching both groups of Romans.

Witnessing the speed with which the crowd gathered, the Romans grew uneasy but continued to hold their arms outstretched. Carefully one of the men searched the crowd, repeating his statement, "We have come to speak with your village leaders."

Seumas and Iain pushed through the wall of Highland warriors. Reaching the soldiers, Iain announced, "I am Iain Gregor."

Both soldiers spontaneously reached for their swords but stopped before touching their grips. Resuming his non-combative posture the leader offered, "Our general has asked us to call upon leaders of all the villages in this region. He invites you to a conference. This meeting is to take place on the hillside near the village where our Roman patrol was killed. I believe you are a leader of many villages; how long will it take to assemble all of your leaders?"

Iain thought for a moment, looking at the sky. "We will meet ye there in six days, as the sun peaks."

"We will convey your agreement." The soldiers turned to leave.

"Why do ye come with an invitation? A small patrol and not an army?" Iain asked.

"Our two patrols made it out of your mountains and reported your treatment of them. Our general would like to meet you and your leaders before deciding how to proceed. Maybe we can reach an accord."

Iain thought briefly before replying, "We will see ye in six days."

The Roman soldiers left, walking down the hill much as they came with their arms still out from their sides. As Seumas and Iain turned back toward the village both muttered in unison, "It is an ambush."

Iain quietly put out a call for six runners and all village leaders. Runners stepped forward from the crowd as the call left Iain's lips and leaders answered with a rousing cheer. Smiling, Iain looked to his runners. "Ye need to go to the villages at daybreak. Tell them that they are to immediately do two things. First, assign half their fighting forces to defend their village. All women, children and elderly are to hide a safe distance to the north of their village. They should set up small shelters for warmth and protection, well hidden in the forest. The defensive force is to go with them. They should avoid conflict but do not allow any to suffer at the hands of Romans. Second, bring all remaining forces to the clearing *BELOW Ceo Dhachaidh*, by the loch. No one is to come to *Ceo Dhachaidh*. All must arrive at the clearing by sunset four days from now. This will be difficult for our farthest villages but they must make it. Avoid use of common trails whenever possible, and do not engage Roman forces unless it cannot be avoided. Do ye understand?"

Iain looked deeply into the eyes of each of the runners. Each face reflected understanding, but there was an objection from one of the village leaders.

"Whit can ye hope to do with only half a fighting force?"

"I expect Romans to attack our villages while we prepare to meet with them. They do not want us to suspect them so they will send small groups of two or three patrols to each village. I will not let them destroy our families while we are attending a 'peace conference'."

"But HALF? Iain, have ye lost yer mind? Ye won't have enough men to defeat an army in their sleep!"

Turning to the runners Iain amended his order, "Agreed. Tell each of the village chiefs that we need one man more than half. That will give us enough advantage."

Several leaders shook their heads in disbelief. Experienced Celtic warriors stood strong and silent. Iain then turned toward the leaders, "I need Seumas, Martin, and Peter to go to the Gaul village. Take David with ye, he knows the area and can help scout it out. We need to know where these Romans are preparing to stand, where they are encamped and whit the land is like. Watch for placement of traps. Ye might want to take one or two others with ye to help watch yer backs."

Slipping slowly below the horizon the sun stole the warmth of the day, leaving a gray sky quickly turning to black. Nights were cool, almost cold now. No one saw any point to standing in the presence of their inevitable dilemma. All retired to their huts for solitude, warmth, and preparation.

<hr>

"That sounds like a good place to stop reading for now," Lillian interrupted. "I have lunch ready for ye and I know Angus would nae want to miss the great battle."

Alex smiled and carefully laid the silk bookmark across the page. He then returned the book to his grandfather's desk, where he had found it.

Liam groaned with disappointment. "I wanted Iain to clobber those Romans on the hillside."

All three children followed their grandmother into the kitchen where a hot lunch waited.

Angus returned from his meeting as the children were finishing their lunch. "Am I too late?" he asked as he kissed Lillian on the cheek.

"No, sit down," Lillian replied as she began making a sandwich for her husband. "How did it go?"

"Not so good. The yank has won over two more councilmen. Fortunately, I still hold the deciding vote and title to the land."

"Can they just take our land?" Lillian asked with concern, looking to her husband as she held a spatula in her hand.

"We hold the hillside in trust. It is not truly ours. If the community decides they want touristy condominiums instead of a quiet heritage . . . I just dinna know. I am thinking I would like to go to the tree and speak with Belinda. She has the most to lose and maybe she will have an idea."

Lillian placed a sandwich and glass of cool water in front of her husband. After swallowing a bite, he asked, "How are the bairn? Any troubles this morning?"

"Oh, no. Liam read the book aloud . . . quite nicely, too. But I stopped them, for he was coming to the battle on the hillside and I know ye do enjoy that chapter."

Angus smiled and finished his lunch in quiet. As Lillian lifted his empty plate, he called to the grandchildren, "Who would like to go to the hillside? I need to speak with Belinda."

It sounded like a herd of wild beasts as all three pounded down the steps. "May I meet Belinda?" Marian asked, her face glowing with anticipation.

"I dinna see why not," Angus replied, tapping his hat onto his head.

"I can't believe it," Marian cooed as they returned home later that afternoon. "Belinda actually talked with me! I talked with a faerie! And Wavtho, did you see how he danced in my ear? He has such a beautiful song."

"Be wary of Wavtho," Lillian warned lovingly. "He loves to lure young ones into the hills and leave them there. I canna tell ye how many times we have had to search into the dark for victims of his pranks. He says he never leaves them in danger but I'm nae so sure. Wee ones have all been scared, just the same."

"Okay, I am told ye are ready for a great battle between Hielanders and Romans," Angus exclaimed, clapping his hands and rubbing them together. He opened the book to the silken ribbon and reviewed the text before him.

All three children dropped to their seats eagerly as their grandfather opened the book. Lillian kissed her husband on his forehead, saying, "I'll see to supper."

Angus resumed reading.

Light frost covered the ground as runners began their journey north. Each kept his load light, carrying only essential weapons and enough food for their run. They were alert and ready. Predawn darkness shrouded familiar trails. Seumas, Martin, Peter and David had decided that four were enough for their expedition to survey the Gaul village. They slipped out of the village unnoticed and were gone as *Ceo Dhachaidh* stirred from its slumber. Iain stood atop of the hill, at the edge of their village, watching groups depart on their separate missions and waiting for the sun to rise. His thoughts focused on those who had just left. Heavy mist provided good cover for all.

It seemed an eternity passed as he waited for the sun to rise. Iain's thoughts had left the travelers and were now focused on his village, *Ceo Dhachaidh*. He needed to take special precautions as their location had been discovered too easily. He would set up blinds, just as he had instructed others, but there had to be something more. When should he evacuate the village? Today? In four days? As soon as he could, that was the answer. But what was the missing piece?

Iain pondered the problem as first rays of sunlight began to pierce the mist, looking from his village to the forest, then to the loch. Shrugging his shoulders as though shifting a great weight, he slowly turned from the loch and looked again toward the growing number of huts. Their shapes were barely recognizable through the morning mist. He recalled this mist was what gave *Ceo Dhachaidh* its name, "home in the mist."

Continuing to scan the village, his eyes were drawn to the area of the Gauls where the mist was unusually thick. Curious, Iain walked slowly up the hill toward the Gauls' huts. They had fire pits and a dense acrid smoke rose from these pits. Smoke hung close to the ground, rising only to a height just above his head.

Iain found a stick and began poking into a fire hole. He saw nothing unusual, just some wet bog similar to peat. It gave off very little heat, but a lot of dense smoke. He picked up a handful of the bog stacked nearby and was examining it when Sarah came out of her hut.

"Whit is this bog ye put on yer fire?" Iain asked.

"We add 'bog' on to slow the fire at night," Sarah replied. "There was a wet land near our home village that provided a good peat that would last all night without flaming up. My sister, Ester, found a similar wet land not far from here yesterday, but this stuff smokes horribly."

"Yes," smiled Iain, "and a most beautiful smoke it is. Please tell Ester that I would appreciate her showing me where this wet land is."

Later that morning, Iain put Eric and several other men to work building blinds. They found a protected area nearly half a léige from the village that would support the entire community. He then recruited several other men to go with Ester and bring back a large supply of peat.

That evening the village gathered at the common lodge and Iain explained his plan. "Tomorrow ye are to gather necessities, blankets and food. Ye will move to blinds that have been built for ye. Ye may be in these shelters for several days. As soon as all are moved, men will build smoke pots all over the village using this wonderful peat our Gaelic brothers have found for us. "

Some of the villagers were beginning to think Iain was suffering from the strain of too much worry. Their village had been safe for years; why go to all this trouble now? But no one voiced objection to his plan so it was done. As the sun set on the second day, *Ceo Dhachaidh* began to disappear into a cloud of smoke.

Morning of the third day was spent settling into the temporary village of blinds. Iain left one half of his local force with the villagers. Others he took toward the loch to wait for men from other villages. They quietly moved around the edge of the huts for extended exposure to the peat smoke caused a great burning in their eyes and throats. When they reached the hilltop, near the stone chairs, Eric stopped to look back. He saw a force of Roman soldiers, numbering fifteen or more, disappearing into the smoke.

Eric signaled to Iain who turned in time to see the last few Romans enter the smoke. Iain directed Eric to circle around and alert the defenders in the safety blinds. "Tell them to enter from the north but to be cautious about whom they attack." He then signaled his warriors to draw their weapons and prepare for battle. Like cats stalking their prey, Highlanders followed Romans into the smoke.

Shadows had all but disappeared under a high sun as the Highland scouting party approached the burned-out Gaelic village. David was not sure that he wanted to join this journey, but he did know the area and was ready to do what he could to stop this Roman invasion. Arriving at their destination mid-afternoon, Seumas and Martin worried about walking straight into the village. Seumas stopped his group a quarter-liege from their destination and counseled with David about different approaches. Finally, they moved off the trail deep into woods above the village. Finding a place where they could watch without being seen, all rested.

Martin and Seumas had both learned patience through many years of battle. Patience had given them the experience to survive. David and Peter had not yet learned patience and grew more uneasy with each passing moment. The younger men were about to give up watching and move in for a closer look when a Roman patrol came into view. They walked slowly through the village remains, checking something in the grass. Having completed their inspection, the Romans did not linger but moved on. As soon as they were out of sight Seumas whispered to David and Peter, "Wait here. Martin and I will take a look."

Both younger men sat quietly without argument as battle experienced Celts slipped down the hillside and into the village. They sought the same marks Romans were inspecting and found reason for concern. Romans had set numerous traps. Each involved some type of spike and was intended to cause death. They left the area undisturbed.

After a brief conversation, all four men moved around the fields toward the hillside where the meeting was to take place. Romans were freely moving up and down the hill without any concerns. Highlanders quietly watched several patrols setting traps throughout the woods on either side of the hill.

"We need to map these traps they have set," Martin thought out loud.

"I had some animal hides that could do," David replied softly. "But I would have to go back into the village to get them."

They waited until dark before retrieving the hides. Powerful emotions consumed David as he walked cautiously between the burned out huts, studiously avoiding Roman traps. Slipping into his former home, he dug under a pile of charred furs. With little effort he pulled out three supple rabbit hides clean enough to be used for their maps. Martin found several burned sticks suitable for drawing and the scouts retreated to the forest for a safe sleep.

Highlanders divided into two teams the next day. David and Martin sketched locations of major traps around the village and safe entries. Seumas and Peter drew maps of known Roman encampments on the clean sides of their rabbit pelts. David remembered a meadow suitable for supporting a large force a short distance away, beyond the crest of the hill. Working their way stealthily to this meadow, the Highlanders found it in full bloom with Roman soldiers, much like clusters of mushrooms appearing after a summer thunderstorm. To one side of center of the meadow was the general's camp; they saw no reason to get any closer. Peter estimated the force to number over three hundred soldiers. Seumas and Martin felt it was more like five hundred. Rather than discuss the issue, or take a second count, the men sought refuge for the night.

Confident in their dominance, Romans continued to sleep until sunrise, even as Highlanders stole through the woods toward *Ceo Dhachaidh*. The Highlanders had made good maps and their only dispute was on the number of soldiers. Dispute was pointless because the Highland force could number only one hundred, if they were lucky. What did it matter whether the odds were five to one or three to one? Highlanders were seriously out numbered.

They were nearly home when the scouting party smelled something foul in the air. Seumas and Martin began to run the final distance;

David and Peter worked to keep up with them. Turning into the woods below *Ceo Dhachaidh,* the scouting party found five Roman soldiers waiting to stop anyone moving up or down the trail.

Seumas and Martin both had weapons in their hands and were not willing to stop for a few Romans. Each man used a familiar move; they each ran over one soldier, deflecting another with their broad sword. They were not interested in fighting, only in returning home to their families. Their forceful maneuver was effective. Three soldiers were dead and one other was seriously wounded. Peter and David engaged the fifth guard quickly dispatching him to his afterlife with his comrades.

The four men stopped at the top of the hill, looking at smoke surrounding their village. They were ready to plunge into it, not knowing what to expect, when their neighbors began to emerge. Most were coughing and gagging from the smoke, all carried bloody swords or staves.

Iain emerged behind everyone else, his arms full of Roman swords. He dumped his load on the ground next to the stone chairs and told several men to go find more. "Be careful," he called, "there may be more still alive." A final count gave the Highlanders twenty additional swords, spears and shields. The first skirmish for the Highlands had gone to the Highlanders. There were no Highland casualties and there were no prisoners.

"Ye men in the village guard, return to the blinds and stay alert," Iain called. "Eric, pipe us a tune to let the others know we are coming to the loch."

"Iain," Eric asked as he began to raise his pipes, "how did ye know the Romans would attack the villages?"

"Many years ago, on one of my first campaigns," Iain explained, "we had been struggling to break the defenses of the region we were in, but the residents would not yield. The commander of our forces called leaders from all the villages involved to a peace meeting. On the day of the meeting, groups of ten to twelve warriors were sent to each village. We thought we were to escort leaders to the meeting. Seumas, my brother and I were in one of the escort groups. When we got to the village, their leaders, and most of their warriors, had left for the gathering. The remaining men attacked our group, but we were stronger and killed them all. Our group leader then started killing women and children. We called at him to stop, but he dinna. When he ran his sword through a four-year-old boy, I lost control. Before he could drop the child, I had taken my captain's head. Our group then turned on me, but Seumas and my brother defended me. We were told that our orders were to kill everyone in the village. The three of us refused to kill women and children and stood to their defense. The others left the village and returned to camp. A young woman, the murdered boy's sister, came and thanked me for defending them. I told them to leave the village before an army returned to finish the job."

"Whit happened when ye returned to camp?"

"They had ambushed the village leaders and killed them all. My Uncle Sean, Seumas' father, began to argue with the commander about his war tactics. The commander lost and Uncle Sean took over. He made all Celtic warriors swear to a code of honor: to never execute helpless women, children or men. Even war must be honorable if society is to survive it. We spent many months in that region rebuilding it. I also found the young woman who had thanked me for stopping the slaughter. Her name is Elizabeth. Now, where is that music?"

Eric raised his pipes and proudly piped warriors to the loch. His bold melody reverberated across the cove, fading as it skimmed across waters of the loch. Three of the seven villages had already arrived and it was a grand entrance. Eric continued to play his pipes, bringing two more villages to the gathering later that day. As the sun sank below the mountain tops, warriors of Heigh Fell and Benmost Bield arrived. Their leaders quickly sought Iain for there had been trouble on the trail.

An old Celt named Angus . . .

"Seanair, was that you?" Liam interrupted excitedly.

"No, lad. 'Angus' was a common name but I carry it proudly as it was my seanair's name, too."

An old Celt named Angus told assembled elders what they had encountered. "Heigh Fell and Benmost Bield met in Blyth Brier. As we passed through the village, we saw what seemed to me to be about four Roman patrols coming into the lower side. We could see no others in the village, so we took to the wood. The soldiers gave chase. We lost three of our brothers and two have injuries that might keep them from the gathering."

"Whit of the Romans?" Iain asked.

"We left their bones for the wolves and the bear," Angus boasted. "Every one of them."

"And Doup Fell?" Iain again asked with deep concern.

"These Romans do not know how to move through the forest; they leave a wide path of footprints. We examined the trail from Doup Fell and while we did see where Highlanders had come out, we could see no signs of Romans going in," Angus reported confidently.

Iain turned to address the leaders and others who had come to hear news. "Roman leaders have no honor. They are here to kill us and our families. Seumas and Martin have told me that the Gaul village is set with traps, and the sides of the hill where we are to meet are as well. We need to arrive at the Gaul village late tomorrow, after dusk, and set up camp. We will send a few men ahead to clear the traps. I want the Romans to wake and find us camped on their field, knowing we could have cut their throats as easily as building our fires. I also need about thirty men to move onto the hillside. There is an area that may have no traps, but ye will have to sleep in trees. I expect our leaders will be ambushed by Romans and I want some support to get us to safety. Everyone should now relax and get a good rest tonight. Tomorrow will be a big day and we will need all of our strength."

Highland warriors broke into small groups to talk and rest. Iain consulted with leaders for some time, answering questions and making suggestions. The camp by the loch was preparing for battle the only way they knew how. They bolstered their spirits with knowledge of their own strengths and renewed confidence in each other.

<hr>

Heavy mist engulfed the mountains and sleepless Highlanders as they awoke from an uneasy rest. Visibility was limited to little farther than a man could reach with his stave. Everyone expected the mist to burn off as the sun rose, but it did not. Blindly, Highlanders marched through the mist all day becoming disoriented several times. Determined to see Iain's plan through the small army pushed on, even as mist changed from gray to black.

"If ye go about sixty more paces and bear to the left, ye can eat with the Romans."

A haunting, but familiar voice pierced the mist, followed by two most welcome figures. Seumas and Martin, who had led a group sent ahead to disarm traps in the village, greeted leaders of the marching army with a smile and a handshake. "These Romans don't know much about traps," Martin said. "We have searched the entire village and removed all of them. It is safe. We even have several deer roasting for yer pleasure."

There was venison enough for all to eat. After the meal, Martin led a group of twenty-six Highlanders to the hillside. They had problems navigating between and disarming traps along the way but reached the trees with little noise. More importantly, they were not detected. After climbing to the upper branches everyone lashed themselves to tree limbs for security and settled for a chilling night.

Sunlight flooded the hillside the next morning but could not diminish the bitter cold. Encamped highlanders kept several fires blazing for warmth. Iain stood by a large fire near the center of the village warming himself, but his thoughts were with his friends in the trees. How were they doing? Had they been captured? Would they be able to provide rescue when the time came? Possible resolution came to Iain's pondering when two faeries settled on his shoulder. Iain asked the faeries to go to the trees and check on his warriors. They left at once. Iain's mind continued to reel with questions when camp erupted in a loud clamor followed by an eerie silence.

Uneasy Highlanders jumped to arms, calling their brothers to their sides as a Roman patrol arrived. Led by the young officer who had invited Iain to the meeting, the soldiers marched through the encampment. Highland warriors quickly surrounded uninvited Romans; all ready to defend against any aggression. The young officer was accompanied by a captain at his side and six armed soldiers behind him. "I am glad you have arrived safely and your men are comfortable," welcomed the captain. "Won't you come talk with our general?"

"No," replied Iain.

"Wh . . . What!?" questioned the Roman officer, stuttering somewhat with surprise.

"I told ye at the time of yer invitation that I would meet yer general on the hill when the sun is directly overhead. I will meet with him as agreed and not any sooner."

"As you wish," agreed the captain. The Romans turned and left.

Cold enveloped everyone that day, sinking into their bones, as the sun climbed with an agonizing slowness toward the anticipated overhead position. A thick layer of frost covered the ground. Fires helped warm men in camp, but those in the trees had no warmth or protection from the cold. Faeries did their best to bolster the men's confidence, but could not give them warmth.

As the sun crept toward its peak, Iain and Seumas began their walk to the hill. Two leaders from each of the villages accompanied them. A faerie rode on the right shoulder of each leader. Iain looked for the faeries he sent to check the trees, but they were not among their escort. Seumas turned to the Highland warriors who followed their leaders, telling them to stop at the base of the hill. He and other leaders stopped halfway to the top. A Roman guard, including the young officer and captain who visited earlier, stood at the top of the hill as only Iain climbed to meet them. "The General will be here shortly," greeted the captain.

Iain stood on the hilltop with his arms crossed in front of his chest. Minutes passed as the sun peaked, then began its trek toward the distant horizon. Iain looked at the sky. Without a word he turned and began to walk down the hill, back to his camp.

"Wait," the General called. "I must apologize for keeping you waiting."

Iain turned and looked at the man coming toward him. It was the same soldier he had met many months before, across a night fire. At his side was the old hag.

"I invited the leaders of your villages to a peace meeting," the General began. "I am told that you have over one hundred men with your company."

"They are Hielanders," Iain replied. "Anything ye have to say will affect them just as their chiefs. And whit of the three hundred troops ye have beyond those trees?"

"You have been spying on me," the General laughed.

Iain did not laugh. "Ye called us here to talk about peace. Whit do ye have to say?"

"These mountains, or 'Highlands' as you call them, are now part of the Roman empire. As Roman subjects you will receive our protection and you must pay taxes to our Emperor. We need to decide what protection you need and how you are to pay your taxes."

"We are free men, children of the Hielands. We are not subjects of yer emperor and owe him no taxes. I suggest ye save yer treasury the expense of protecting us and return yer soldiers to thair families."

"You do not seem to understand. This arrangement is not optional. You may not wish our protection, but you will pay the tax for having us here."

"Yeu, General, can offer us no protection and we will pay no tax."

"The penalty for failure to comply with this order is death."

"Then draw yer sword and begin with me. We are Hielanders. Free men and we owe yeu nothing."

Iain put his hands to his hips, exposing his chest. He stared straight into the general's eyes. It was an open challenge. A challenge the general could not refuse. Before anyone could draw a breath, the general drew his sword and put it to Iain's throat. Romans appeared out of the woods and stood ready to fight, swords drawn.

Iain stared at the general as a nettle laden rope came out of nowhere, wrapping around the general's arm. The sword that had been at Iain's throat fell to the ground and every Highlander's sword was now drawn, ready for battle. Iain reached out to grab the general, but he and his hag were gone. The captain charged Iain. Soldiers around the hillside charged the other Highland chiefs.

Martin and his men threw a volley of nettle ropes and spears from their trees. They then climbed down and attacked surprised Roman soldiers lining the hillside. The first skirmish was a Highland victory as all Romans were dealt with and all Highlanders escaped unharmed.

Their victory, however, was short lived. A vast force of Romans appeared across the top of the hill, charging down into the Highlanders. Both sides suffered heavy losses. Highlanders fought valiantly and appeared to overcome the odds. Faeries provided distraction by flying into the faces and ears of Roman soldiers, giving some advantage to Highlanders. Soldiers kept coming. Every time a Roman soldier entered the battle another stood ready to replace him. Then, they stopped coming.

Iain looked around at his men. Over half of the Highlanders were dead or seriously wounded. Each of these fallen heros had a faerie resting on his right shoulder, providing a clear and complete release of their spirit into the soul of The Highlands. Faeries also comforted the more seriously wounded, pulling energy and a peaceful healing from the earth. Iain did not know if they could survive another attack of so many waves. He turned his attention to Roman patrols filling the hillside and their general at the top. The general and his old hag were talking, perhaps battle plans. Moments later the general brought up a line of archers, placing them along the crest of the hill.

Elizabeth sat on the stone chairs of *Ceo Dhachaidh* . . .

"WAIT!" Liam and Alex cried out in unison.
"The battle is not over!" Liam exclaimed.

"No, it is not," Angus replied, a patient smile caressing his face. "May I continue?"

Both boys looked at Angus with increasing despair, their minds in confused turmoil. Hearing no further comments, Angus resumed his story.

Elizabeth sat on the stone chairs of *Ceo Dhachaidh* watching the pathway disappear into the forest. She had been doing this for weeks, sitting and waiting. Since Iain left to train the other villages and now for battle, she waited, watching for his return. Today, she felt, would be different. It was different. A sudden cold grabbed the countryside in a relentless grip, now changing to snow. The trail up the hillside was barely visible through the mounting blanket of white, but she knew where it lay.

Her cape could not shield her from the elements this day. Mounting discomfort from cold and wet was about to force her back to the warmth of her hut when she heard a voice from the forest. Eagerly she strained to see who was coming. It was the men of the Highlands. Elizabeth tried to stand and run to them, to find her husband, but cold had weakened her legs; they could not carry her.

Thinking only of Iain, Elizabeth stumbled down the road toward the advancing army. Seumas picked her up, carrying her back to the stone chairs. "Where is Iain?" she asked Seumas, her voice weak and confused. "Why isn't he leading the army as he did when ye left?"

Seamus looked down at the frozen white ground, afraid to speak. Slowly, he raised his eyes until he found Elizabeth's. "Iain has fallen," he said in a soft, tear-filled voice. "We were beaten," he continued slowly, "our feet frozen, our arms aching, and the Romans just kept coming. Then their general did an unforgivable act. He commanded his archers on the hill to fire on us. They drove arrows into us and into their own men. They murdered their own men, even after we were beaten. Iain could nae stand it. He grabbed the broad sword from a fallen brother and charged up the hill. A sword in each hand and a scream of terror that wrenched every one of us with fear. A few Romans tried to stop him; he cut them down without slowing. When he reached the top of the hill he stood eye to eye with the general and his witch hag. With a single blow he raised the two swords over their heads and buried them into the ground below them, cutting each of them in half. The old hag laughed with her horrible cackle as Iain raised his swords. I hae never seen Iain so wrought with rage. All any of us could hear was her cackling, taunting Iain. As he buried the swords he dropped one and brought the other through both of his tormentors, slicing them through the middle like a fresh cabbage. Iain's courage inspired us, for at that instant the rest of us grabbed whit weapons we could carry and charged to join him. Without their general beating them on the Romans fled, but not before they killed Iain. I tried to get to him and serve his back but I just could nae get up the hill in time." Seumas concluded, "Elizabeth, Iain saved the Hielands from the invaders. If it had nae been for his courage we would all be dead and they would be here to butcher yeu, our families, right now."

Elizabeth looked across the land without expression. The death of her husband ended her life as well. Clouds parted, flooding the hillside and valley with light from the sun as it touched the tops of distant mountains. Staring into the light, Elizabeth saw a sight that cowered most of the men on the hillside. Her Iain came through the blazing beams of light to take her. Dressed in full battle attire, as on the day he left, Iain stood proud and strong. He reached his hand out to his wife. Driven by their love her spirit rose, taking Iain's hand. When Elizabeth died a single tear fell from her eye toward the stone chairs.

═══════════════

Angus saw each of his grandchildren about to explode with reactions to this story. Pausing briefly he held up one finger, and winked. Seeing his audience settling once more, he continued.

Guided by a gentle wind Elizabeth's last tear fell softly, coming to rest on a blossom of frozen heather. The very instant this tear touched the delicate flower a grand explosion of light erupted, sending a vast fountain of sparks into the heavens. Even in the bright setting sun of that early winter afternoon the brilliance of this stream of light was blinding. Seumas and other men covered their eyes with one hand, drawing their broadswords with the other. Some men fell to the ground, covering their heads.

As men drew their breath in the midst of this unexpected spectacle, a flare shot upward through the center of the burst of sparks climbing heavenward. A frozen calm settled instantly across the hillside around the stone chairs. The flare continued well out of sight, coming to rest amidst the stars. But it did not rest long for a voice came from all over the heavens, softly addressing the flare, "Vrenessbith, it is time to wake. You are born of love. Love between a man and a woman, and their love for their friends and homeland. Go now and continue their work in this land. Take with you knowledge of things unknown to man, that you may always be there to protect them from evil. Serve well and share your birthright with all who would share with one another."

The flare exploded once more releasing a small faerie. Reflecting heavenly brilliance, Vrenessbith returned to the stone chairs where she settled on Seumas' right ear. Everyone around Seumas stared in speechless disbelief. Here was a tiny form reflecting light from the setting sun, assuming its crimson brilliance. Speaking to Seumas, directly into his ear, Vrenessbith said, "We are here to serve you."

Startled by all that had just happened Seumas slapped at his ear, forgetting he still held his broadsword. Martin and Peter rushed to his aid, helping him back to his feet.

Vrenessbith decided instantly that it wasn't proper to speak aloud with these large creatures. She must find a way to serve them in a more private manner.

Villagers, alerted by the sudden brilliant light, rushed to welcome their Highlanders home. Martin and Peter released a bewildered Seumas to his wife, Ingrid, then wrapping their arms around their own wives and families.

<hr>

Highland warriors from other villages returned to their training camp in the meadow above *Ceo Dhachaidh*. Bitter cold and snow returned with sunset driving men to the warmth of large fires.

Seumas collected his thoughts and watched others laying a funeral pyre for Elizabeth. His thoughts lingered on the previous evening when by Celtic tradition bodies of warriors who fell in battle were sent to their afterlife on great funeral pyres. Not individually but together. The Gaelic village had become a massive blaze honoring every fallen Highlander.

It was now time to honor Elizabeth. Her pyre was laid beside the stone chairs, where she had waited for Iain.

Their work done, men of *Ceo Dhachaidh* joined around camp fires with other Highland warriors. Conversations varied according to who was seated in their company.

Every village had heros in the battle on the hill. Surviving heroes were congratulated for their actions, departed heroes were remembered with honor and respect as the battle was relived at each fire. Eric was applauded around all fires for his courage in battle and at the Highlanders' funeral when more than half the Highlander force, including Iain Gregor, were sent to the next world with a haunting melody from his pipes.

A group of warriors sought Eric, finding him sitting quietly with Sarah, Rachel, Bryan and others. "Ye should be proud of yer husband," one man told Sarah as he looked into her eyes. "Iain was half way up the hill, cutting the Romans down left and right, when young Eric raised those pipes of his. That wailing brought us all out of the trance whit had held us captive."

"And then he began to climb that hill as well," another warrior began. "Without blade or stave he climbed that hill. But those pipes of his were a powerful weapon, for every man of us followed him. He played his way to the top and continued until that hill belonged again to the Hielands."

"I'll never forget the sight of him standing in front of those other musicians," resumed the first man. "He stood nose to nose with those spies. He never faltered, never showed anything but purest courage. Then the spies ran into the forest and Eric turned his pipes back to the hillside. The sound of his pipes filled each of us with a power and energy we had never known. Next to Iain, Eric owns the victory of this day."

"I thank ye for yer praise," Eric solemnly interrupted, "however this lady is not my wife. But I would be most honored if she would become so."

Joy swelled within Sarah, slowly overwhelming her great sorrow, sorrow which griped every heart that night. Smiling, she began to lean across to Eric. As she moved, her unborn child gave a great leap. It might have been the stress of uncertainty or sudden pride and intense love she felt at that moment for Eric, but her baby was coming. Rachel looked across at Bryan and then helped Eric take Sarah to her sister's hut. Bryan gathered an armful of wood and followed quickly.

After getting Sarah settled into the care of Ester, Sarah's sister, Rachel and Bryan strolled aimlessly until they found themselves back at the stone chairs. Their emotions were running high from the events of recent days. They stood silently in the cold for several minutes, their hands locked onto one another's. Seumas had been visiting with other warriors and passed on his way back to his hut. Placing a hand on the shoulder of each of them he spoke quietly, his voice filled with respect, "Ye were quite a pair on that hillside. Never before hae I seen such dedication to a battle and to one another at the same time." Solemn silence returned as Rachel and Bryan looked at one another, then to Elizabeth's body lying in wait on her pyre.

All three Highlanders regarded Elizabeth differently. Seumas mourned her as a devoted friend, wife to his best friend and cousin. Rachel mourned her as a big sister and mentor. Bryan knew her only as the dedicated wife of a great leader; loyal not only to her husband but his ideals, which made her worthy of the same respect Iain received.

Vrenessbith, who had been searching for Seumas, found him standing with Rachel and Bryan. She wanted to speak with him but could not find the right words. Quietly, she floated ahead of the silent trio, glowing from the warmth of nearby fires. Her glow reflected on the still body of Elizabeth, giving the others a vision of hope for their future. Her warmth lifting the hearts of Bryan and Rachel.

"Rachel," Bryan asked softly, "ye are a powerful warrior and an inspiration to us all. As we watch over Elizabeth, I am reminded of the love and the life that she and Iain shared. Could ye find contentment sharing life with a Hieland farmer?"

Rachel turned to Bryan, replying, "Only if I never have to lift a sword again, and only if yeu are the farmer to have me."

Delighted to have witnessed the proposal, Seumas reached out to hug the two young people. "OH, IAIN WOULD BE GLAD!" Seumas exclaimed with delight. "He would want us all to see the sun rise with promise and the two of ye have just given me that! I hear the laughter of wee Hielanders running all over this mournful meadow."

Feeling the excitement, Vrenessbith began to fly circles around the couple, accidentally slamming into the side of Seumas' head, just behind his right eye . . . where his sword had left a bruise from their earlier conversation.

Seumas quickly raised his hand to his head, stopping short of smashing himself once more. Vrenessbith, alarmed at the trouble she had caused, yet again, shot into the sky, fading into the darkness. Rachel, filled with laughter, asked, "Seumas, who is this faerie causing ye such pain?"

"I dinna know," Seumas moaned in reply, "but I fear I will soon learn."

<div align="center">~~~~~~~~~~~~~~~~~~~~~~~~~~</div>

A cold morning mist surrounded the funeral pyre and all who had gathered to say their final farewell to Elizabeth. Her fire was lit with the first muted rays of sunlight, for hers was a spirit that had brightened everyone's day. As flames rose, a ring of faeries circled the fire, their wings reflecting Elizabeth's perpetual radiance. When her body was consumed, the faeries and morning mist vanished from the hillside.

Unencumbered, the rising sun melted lingering snow and cold changed to a more seasonable crispness. Mourners, with heavy hearts, departed slowly returning to daily chores and their own tasks of living. Warriors, weary from battle and loss of friends, left the funeral embers and resumed their journeys home. Slowly the village of *Ceo Dhachaidh* began to return to a more normal daily routine.

Resbith settled in a tree near Elizabeth's pyre. She had talked with Elizabeth only a little but recognized her spirit as one important to the survival of these people. Looking across the gathered Highlanders, Resbith saw *gleo* fading in the morning sunshine. Though this day was filled with sadness, it was a new day. Fear of the Romans was gone and that *gleo* melted away leaving only the toilsome token of daily struggle. At least for now.

Rachel and Bryan planned a wedding celebration to take place in two weeks. This would provide Bryan time to return home to Blyth Brier and make arrangements. He began his journey with a heart heavy with memories and for leaving Rachel, but light of foot anticipating their upcoming nuptials. Bloigh Bryan grabbed his nephew, throwing him over his shoulder when he heard the news. Young Bryan was a hero and now a bridegroom; Blyth Brier would celebrate!

Seumas reluctantly assumed the leadership role for *Ceo Dhachaidh*. One of his first duties was to welcome a new member, the son of Sarah.

"Whit will ye name this wee bairn?" Seumas asked, grinning from ear to ear.

"I feel we must name him for Iain, as he saved my village and the Highlands," Sarah replied humbly.

"No," Eric interrupted, "this is the son of yer husband, a man who also gave his life for yeu and yer village. Ye must honor him first."

The child was named Christopher William, in honor of his father.

As Seumas began to leave the hut Sarah called him back. "Whit is to be done for a man and woman to marry in this village?"

Seumas' entire face beamed with delight as he turned back to Sarah and Eric. "Normally ye would consent to keep one to the other and begin yer life together. However, I happen to know that there is going to be a grand celebration on the hillside in a fortnight. I do believe that Rachel and Bryan would be most happy to have the two of yeu join them as we all begin new lives with new traditions."

<center>~~~~~~~~~~~~~~~~~~~~~~~~</center>

New life had begun and days were filled with joy and activity. Villagers took it upon themselves to build a new hut for Eric and Sarah.

Suffering the loss of so many men in battle, construction of the hut seemed to require many more hands than even building huts for the Gauls. While friends were missed, those involved felt a lifting of their spirits with a new tomorrow being erected in the walls of this simple hut. Eric worked hard with his neighbors to finish the task, but declared that he would not move in until he could take Sarah and Chris with him.

The day of the great celebration was soon at hand, with a ceremony scheduled to begin as the sun touched the top of the mountain across the loch. Following the nuptials there was to be a great meal, stories, music, and the company of friends and neighbors. It was no small surprise to find families from all seven distant villages attending this grand event. As the sun began to reach down to the great mountain beyond the loch, the hillside below the great stone chairs filled with friends and families of the two couples. All of the Highland villages were present or represented, filling the air with a spirit that truly welcomed the new age that was being celebrated that evening.

Several days before, Ingrid, Seumas' wife, had discovered Vrenessbith trying to speak with her husband. Ingrid helped the young faerie speak with Seumas and convinced him to build a special fire for the celebration. Vrenessbith gave him explicit instructions as to its size, location and wood to be used. Before the ceremony she even reminded him to prepare a torch so he would be able to light it at the proper moment.

Now, standing beside the great stack of wood, Seumas watched the horizon. At the appointed moment he lowered his torch to the faeries' fire. Flames rose with a brilliance borrowed from the sky and setting sun. Overhead, floating clouds appeared as pillows of rose trimmed with gold as the last rays of sunlight changed from golden rays to crimson spikes. The faeries' fire reached high into the sky and touched each of the colours, bringing them back to the hillside.

After lighting the fire, Seumas moved in front of the stone chairs with his wife Ingrid beside him. Looking across the hillside, he knew at once the deepest meaning of being a Highlander, that inner spirit which Iain had spoken of so often. With a spirit-filled voice he began the ceremony.

"HIELANDERS! We have come together this day to remember who we are and more importantly, to celebrate who we have become. Many of our brothers poured out their life-blood into these mountains so that we might gather here as free men. As we open our hearts to one another on this night, keep our fallen heroes in yer spirits. Tonight, we begin a new tradition of unity. For we have two couples who have come together and wish to proclaim to the world that they belong together. Let us now hear from each of these couples their intent. Bryan and Rachel, ye have asked that it be recognized that ye are man and wife from this day forward. Whit say ye?"

Bryan looked at Rachel, staring deeply into her eyes, "Rachel, as ye have become my heart and soul, I pledge now that I will do all in my power to keep ye warm and safe and happy for so long as I live. I pledge my very life to yeu for as long as ye are by my side."

Rachel responded, "Bryan, as I have fought by yer side I now pledge to lay down my sword and stay by yer side always. Where we once defended each other with our swords, now let us plow the land and together build our future. I pledge to give ye my body and my soul for all eternity and to celebrate our lives as a loving adventure each day we are together."

Seumas then turned to Sarah and Eric, "Eric and Sarah, ye also have asked that it be recognized that ye are man and wife from this day forward. Whit say ye?"

Eric's eyes joined the smiling eyes of Sarah. Taking Christopher from her arms he proclaimed, "I pledge my strength and my heart to yeu, Sarah, and to Christopher. I pledge to love ye always and to keep ye safe. I pledge also to raise Christopher William as my own and to tell him of his father's bravery, courage, and sacrifice. I offer both of ye my life for so long as ye will have me."

Sarah took Eric's hand, "Eric, I promise to love you always. To care for you and to keep you warm. I promise to never forsake you and to always be your right hand for as long as you have need of me."

Seumas raised his hands and began to speak, however his words stopped as an explosion erupted within the great fire. Seebtin, Fobothom, and several other faeries had thrown some chips into the fire creating an explosion and a stream of fireworks. Flames blazed heavenward with a fountain of sparks and streaks of light. In quick response, the sky filled with the glory of a shower of shooting stars, a curtain of light blocking the emerging stars behind as it streaked across the heavens. While Seumas, Ingrid, and the two wedding couples watched the celestial show a new couple joined the celebration. Iain and Elizabeth stood behind the fire, their two sons standing with them. Each of them brought their fists to their chests, then waved their open hands outward across the Highlands in salute to the bravery and love of those present and throughout this new land. Joining hands, they vanished.

Gasps of astonishment from the hillside changed to cheers of celebration. Vrenessbith appeared where the legendary couple had been and signaled Seumas to finish.

Seumas raised his hands, waiting for the roar from the hillside to quiet before pronouncing, "As each of ye has consented to give yer life, one to another, and as much as this celebration has been blessed by the spirits of Iain and Elizabeth, I now proclaim that a new age has begun and that each of us will have a part in it." A roar of agreement rose from the hillside and the crowd began to celebrate.

Joyous music, feasting and celebrating went on for hours. As midnight approached Eric and Sarah left to put Chris to bed, their first night in their new home. Shortly afterwards Bryan and Rachel were led to Iain and Elizabeth's hut where they were told to enjoy the accommodations.

〰〰〰〰〰〰〰〰〰〰〰〰〰〰〰

Faint rays of sunlight slipped softly from behind the mountains, the first signs of a new day, a new era, stretching through yielding night as Seumas staggered to his bed. A dark figure waiting between the faeries' fire and the stone chairs stopped the celebration-weary leader of the new age. Standing in his path, a foul stench spread from its presence as it spoke with a malevolent voice, creaking as though rarely used. "Your 'hero' killed our leader. For this atrocity your people will suffer the wrath of our society. Hear these words well, for as the new day dawns, your people will find themselves in a new war. A war that you cannot win!"

Seumas looked at the dark figure In the fading light of the fire, trying to understand her words. Flying to his aid, Vrenessbith magnified the light of the fire, revealing the dark figure to be an old hag, a witch. "A war there will be," agreed Vrenessbith, speaking to the hag on behalf of the Highlanders, "but these people have friends who will fight beside them and WE will claim victory!"

Angus reverently placed the silk book mark across the page and closed the volume. Looking at his grandchildren he had to smile for each of them was awestruck and speechless.

Highlanders - First Generation

Lillian *had prepared a seasonal feast for supper. A chicken roasted golden brown was accompanied by fresh asparagus and lentils. A salad of different lettuces was dotted with fresh strawberries. A bowl filled with strawberries and raspberries enticed the children to eat the rest of their supper. All food came from their own garden or markets which sold local harvests. Angus' eyes sparkled with each bite though the grandchildren ate rather slowly.*

Midway through the meal, Marian looked at her grandmother and asked, "Seanmhair, who are Benigh and Fru?"

Lillian gagged slightly and glared hostilely at Angus. Seeing his wife was not going to answer, Angus volunteered, "I will be glad to tell 'em if ye dinna care to."

"Benigh and Fru are flirtatious impulsive faeries who have a bad habit of creating trouble," Lillian replied. Her short response was meant to close the subject but only caused Angus to laugh and the children to stare.

"Oh come now," Angus prodded. "Tell the bairn how they tried to seduce ye on the hillside."

"They were NOT trying to seduce me. Ye keep saying that and it simply is not true!"

"Whit do ye call it when two lads grope inside of yer clothes?" Angus laughed.

The grandchildren were all now hooked on the possibilities of this story of their grandmother and two faeries. Seeing that Angus was not going to let this go, Lillian told her version of what happened one day on the hillside above the loch.

"Okay, it was a late summer afternoon. Hot and humid for the time of year. Yer seanair and I were picking herbs in the field above the hillside. Without considering whit I was doing was improper, I stood and pulled me shirt away from me skin, it was hot and sticky. I did not lift it, just pulled it away and fluttered it a bit to get some air to my chest for cooling. At this same time, these two mischievous sprites, who had been boppin about the herbs all afternoon, flew about my head and shot down my shirt. There, that was that."

"Oh, no lassie, not by long bit. There was more and ye know or ye wouldna be so red at this moment," Angus taunted. "Tell the bairn whit yer two admirers did whilst inside yer shirt."

"They tickled me," Lillian replied, now blushing Christmas red.

"Tickled, she says," Angus continued the story, knowing Lillian would not. "Why those two romantic imps tickled my bride about her middle and then dove into her brasserie, where they got stuck. But they did not stop their tickling, they made it even worse. Yer seanmhair pulled her shirt off in a flash, and popped her brasserie loose and went to swatting those two rascals with a vengeance. Seeing that gorgeous woman standing there reminded me just whit a beautiful woman she is." Angus winked at Lillian, who blushed yet again. "And to make matters a bit worse, every time those two faeries see my bride on the hillside, they try to take a dip into her blouse."

"THEY DINNA!" Lillian exploded. "Belinda and I have both told them they are not to try that nonsense again."

"Which is why they keep tryin'," Angus chuckled as he enjoyed another bite of delicious chicken.

All three grandchildren looked at their grandmother with astonishment and delight. This woman who was a champion of the faeries was also a target of their pranks.

"Why would they do such a thing?" Marian asked, her face delightfully concerned.

"They told me that she smells sweet as a fresh blossom," Angus replied. Then, with a bright twinkle in his eye he added, "An she does."

Lillian turned crimson.

Later that evening, after the kitchen and dishes were put in order, Lillian brought a bowl of fresh raspberries to the courtyard outside Angus' study. It was a cool evening, just right for continuing the story of the book.

The words of the old hag weighed heavily on Seumas. For many days, he kept his encounter with the witch a secret, even from Ingrid. "Whit would Iain do?" he agonized. This mantle of leadership was new to him and he wrestled with it. Seumas felt more comfortable as second in command and support to his cousin. Iain was gone now, and leadership responsibilities were now his. Standing at the top of the hill a few steps from his hut and thinking again of Iain's death, Seumas rolled his shoulders, as though adjusting to the new weight.

"A beautiful sunset," commented Ingrid as she joined her husband, taking his hand in hers. "T'would be a shame to lose it in a worry."

Seumas looked down at his wife and smiled as he put his arm around her shoulder. "I am not lost in worry," Seumas confided, "I am just lost. I always found it easy and natural to follow my cousin's lead.

Now, I am to be leader of a new people, and my first challenge is unlike any Iain and I ever faced."

"Then ye must look inside yerself for the answer," Ingrid replied. "Yeu have a family who loves ye, and yer friends respect ye. We will stand beside yeu in any endeavor or problem."

"Yes, but I do not understand the words. I am not great with words and those that have been given to me are confusing."

Ingrid stroked her husband's arm, attempting to relax him. "Maybe ye should say them out loud. If ye heard the words in yer own voice, they might be more clear."

"Possibly, but I hate to burden ye with this concern. Maybe I will take the problem to the elders tomorrow."

A whisper floated softly into Seumas' ear. "Tell Ingrid now, she will support you and help you understand."

Seumas looked around quickly, for the last words he heard were not from Ingrid. They came from a small voice, one he was becoming familiar with but still struggled to understand. Revealing herself, Vrenessbith repeated her message, "Tell your wife."

Seumas looked down at Ingrid. His broad shoulders and large build towered over her slender and much shorter body. "The night of the wedding celebration, after all had gone to sleep, I was stopped by an old hag. She told me that her leader had been killed in the battle on the hill and that her society would claim revenge. They are going to war with us. The old hag said this war would begin the next day and we could never win. Then that faerie, Vrenessbith appeared. She told me that we had friends who would be there to fight with us. This faerie said we could claim victory."

"I believe the 'friends' Vrenessbith was speaking of are the faeries and the spirits of the Hielands." Ingrid tried to calm her husband's fears, but the fear in her own voice was unmistakable. "There is nothing stronger than the spirit of this land, and the magic of its faeries will strengthen us. As for when the war is to begin, I have seen no hags or witches in our village. Perhaps they have reconsidered the trouble of a war in our Hielands and changed their plans. Why don't ye tell the elders whit ye told me and see whit they have to say?"

"Yes, perhaps tomorrow," agreed Seumas. What his wife said did make sense, but he wanted to consider her words before approaching the council of elders. Quietly, Seumas and Ingrid turned away from the hill and started toward their hut. Seumas took one last look around to see where Vrenessbith had gone. He did not see her.

Vrenessbith had achieved the tender age of three weeks and was busy learning about this wonderful world of humans, animals, faeries and the Highlands. Elder faeries normally responsible for growth and development of young faeries were exasperated by her curiosity and energy. These elder faeries, Guardians, had asked for help from those younger than they. Seebtin, Fobothom, Estavery, and Brianne kept a very close watch on young Vrenessbith. Adolescents themselves, they had been schooled in the ways of the world and had the energy to keep up with their wee charge. It also gave these faeries, who were becoming couples, a chance to spend time together away from watchful eyes of Guardians.

Vrenessbith filled each day trying to complete some new lesson or adventure. Curious as she was, each new experience generally involved getting out of some situation she should have not been in. Vrenessbith found great pleasure in exploring badger burrows- with badgers in residence - and sailing among the clouds. She learned that baby owls, while adorable in appearance, are always hungry, and faeries should not lie on the bottom of the loch with spotted newts. After four days the young courting faeries asked the Guardians for relief.

Resbith, the most elder Guardian and Comleidh[18] of the faerie cavie[19] just outside of *Ceo Dhachaidh*, caught Vrenessbith by her toe and set her on a limb beneath a solitary golden leaf. With a tone reminiscent of both Celtic commander and loving mother, Resbith counseled Vrenessbith. "The cold months of winter will soon be here. Animals of these mountains are trying to prepare for the trying months ahead and you are getting in their way. It is time you learned of faeries and our place in this world."

"Where are we from?" Vrenessbith's words erupted without thought or hesitation.

Resbith settled at the base of a tree limb, putting an acorn cap behind her back for support. After much shifting and moaning, the plumpish rosy-cheeked faerie answered, "Faeries come into this world in two ways. Most of us are born out of the love of two faeries, just as deer and birds. But there are others, such as yourself, who are born out

---

[18] Comleidh - COM~lee - an elder faerie who oversees the well-being of the community

[19] cavie - CA~vee - a faerie community, often hidden in old trees or rocks

of a miracle. When lightning strikes a faerie stone, sparks will fly in many directions. A few sparks climb back up the lightning path and draw in its energy. These sparks turn this energy into life and become faeries with many magical powers. This is how I came to be."

"Was I born out of lightning?"

"No, wee fridgin[20], you were born of the purest and most powerful love. Never has there been a man so much in love with this earth, his wife, and life itself as Iain Gregor. Never has there been a woman more in love with a man and her community than Elizabeth Gregor. When Elizabeth saw the spirit of Iain come across the valley, she shed but one tear as her heart burst. She willingly left this life to join her husband. You were born of that single tear. Your birth was more miraculous and promising than any bolt of lightning to ever strike these mountains."

"Does that mean that I have magical powers?"

"You are magic. You have the wisdom of the ages and the power of the earth itself."

"If I have such wisdom, why am I so confused?" the young faerie asked, excitement in her eyes beginning to fade.

"Your wisdom needs time to mature. You will increase in understanding as you grow and require it, but the promise of tomorrow is already within you."

"How will I . . ."

"Your wisdom will be revealed as you grow," Resbith assured her. "With each new adventure, your life will reveal its promise and you will understand more. But, you must be careful and considerate of others. You are a special faerie and there are those in this world who will try to capture you and end the promise tomorrow might hold. Guard yourself always and be wary of those who seek you."

"Should I not find a safe refuge until I understand my place?"

"No, for that is not the way of the faeries. It is our way to give what we can to all creatures of the land. We warn the deer of traps, we protect small birds' eggs from hawks and the ferret, and we shield young rabbits from owls. Every faerie, magical or not, has an obligation and the privilege of protecting this land and all who live here in unity with us. Now, go find those two young couples who have been with you. The joining time does not come until after the last snowfall and the renewal of life begins. Remind them to keep proper about themselves."

---

[20] *fridgin* - FRIG~in - young faerie

"There is not much left in these fields," Eric thought aloud, rolling his shoulders under an invisible weight. Seumas, who was walking toward the fields beside him, heard his thoughts.

"Feeding the warriors took a tremendous toll on our supplies," Seumas agreed. "I am not sure how we will make it through the coming winter."

Leigh, Seumas' six-year-old daughter, ran up and took her father's hand. Seumas smiled down at her. Soft auburn hair billowed around her face and the sunlight sparkled in her hazel eyes. Leigh raised her hand to shield her eyes; Seumas took it and as her small hand disappeared in his mighty but gentle palm they continued toward the fields.

===

"Sounds like Leigh has a strong resemblance to Marian," Lillian interrupted.

"Very possible. Leigh is her Great - Great - great so many times Seanmhair," Angus replied.

"We are children of Seumas?" Alex asked.

"Aye," Angus agreed. "That is our family line." He smiled at his grandchildren briefly before resuming the story.

Several elders of *Ceo Dhachaidh* stood at the edge of the field, surveying the land and discussing what needed to be done. Seumas stopped to talk with these men, instructing Leigh to help Eric. Discretely, Seumas signaled two other passing elders to join them. "I had a visitor recently," he began quietly. "An old hag has threatened our villages and these Hielands with war. Revenge for the death of their leader at the great battle."

Silence followed Seumas' words. Not an elder spoke nor challenged their new leader. All looked intently at him as he continued, "I thought ye should know, and that we might warn the other villages to be alert to strange travelers."

Silence again held the group until Martin, who had helped train farmers and fought valiantly beside Iain and Seumas, asked, "Do ye suppose the trees are still golden and crimson in Heigh Fell?"

Another elder looked to the sky, replying, "Can't say, but ye have two, maybe three weeks to make the journey. After that ye can count on Heigh Fell and Benmost Bield being blanketed by snow. Travel will be difficult. Who do ye suppose would care to take such a trip?"

"Martin and I can go, maybe Peter, and . . ." Seumas looked around the village and field. "Young Eric has his hands full with the baby . . . whit about Robert?" Robert was a Gaul whose village had been devastated by Romans. He had fought hard at the last battle, but had never taken part in other village adventures.

"I'll ask him," Martin volunteered. "When do we leave?"

"At daybreak tomorrow," Seumas sighed. Sharing the threat lifted a huge burden from his shoulders, but it was only exchanged for another, reaching all other villages in a short time. This burden was familiar and not so heavy for he had done it several times with his cousin and he would have friends on the journey.

Martin went to speak with Robert. Seumas swept his little girl up in his arms. After a brief conversation with Eric, Seumas carried his daughter back to their hut to talk with Ingrid.

<hr>

Evening settled with a radiant calm. Sunset brought forth a brilliant sky and gentle breeze, signaling cooler weather ahead. Activities around the village seemed to settle much more quickly than usual. Nobody seemed to notice as Eric carried his pipes under his arm down to the hillside. After resting the pipes on his shoulder, he filled the bag with air. Tones from all three drones began to waffle until he methodically adjusted each drone, creating a perfect balance and harmony. Adjusting the bag under his arm, he gave it a firm pat and began to play.

The melodies were retreating at first. Not quite a march and not quite lilting; the music signaled an end to a hard day's work and prelude to a peaceful evening. Several villagers came to the hillside to view the last rays of sunset reflecting from the loch below and to listen to Eric's soothing melodies. Sarah sat on the stone chairs holding Christopher in her arms, watching her new husband with admiration and love. The stone chairs had become an important part of the heritage of *Ceo Dhachaidh*, but never had they held such an important audience for Eric.

"Enough with the lazy music . . . play us a rant!"

Eric did not know who made the request but he was glad to oblige and quickly shifted into a fast and rollicking melody. Several of the men began to dance, kicking the ground with their feet in time with the music. Life was good, surpassing what had been, and the Highlanders were drunk on their spirit of freedom and fortune.

The dancing faerie, Seebtin, enticed Estavery, his sweetheart, to a tree limb near Eric and then flew to Eric's drones. Spreading his wings across the top of one drone, Seebtin twirled in escaping air and put on a show for other faeries. Estavery was very impressed with Seebtin's aerobatics. Brianne and Fobothom joined her and applauded their friend's performance. Brianne then prodded Fobothom to show his skills at dancing in the wind.

"I hae ne'r danc'd o' th' wind!" Fobothom exclaimed, mocking the villagers words. Prodding continued and before long Fobothom flew to Eric's pipes. Seebtin quickly showed Fobothom how to work his wings and use the air flow. Fobothom was reluctant to spread his wings too widely and never quite got the hang of the tricks Seebtin tried to show him. Other faeries laughed and encouraged both dancers to become ever more daring.

One definite problem with bagpipe music, as with any music, is it eventually comes to an end. Eric stopped playing the rant and lowered his pipes, the last rollicking notes dancing into tranquility. Sarah gave him a tankard of ale and a kiss. Seebtin and Fobothom dropped into the depths of their drones.

"Play that tune ye played on the hillside at the battle!" Another request from the growing crowd. Eric thought for a few seconds, then shook his bag so it fell loosely. Seebtin climbed out the top of his drone and joined Estavery. Fobothom held his position inside the top of his drone. Eric raised his pipes, giving the bag a stiff jab as he filled it with air. When the pipes raised, Fobothom once again fell down into the drone, whereupon a sudden rush of air caught the unsuspecting faerie. There was a sudden "PTUSH" as Fobothom shot out of the drone. The abnormal release of air created a force which shot the young faerie into a treetop at the edge of the field. Seebtin laughed so hard that he fell from the tree, landing on a chipmunk who had paused on his way home to see why so many people had gathered in his field. Brianne flew to Fobothom, comforting him with caresses and kisses.

Music sent a hush across the hillside. The rhythm was strong and stirring but as hearts began pounding to Eric's powerful beat, tears of remembrance flowed on every cheek. Eric's eyes swelled as he remembered climbing the hill with his pipes under his arm. His heart beat faster and his melody grew stronger with memories of drawn swords surrounding him and the battle following him up the hillside. He felt undying courage of his fellow Highlanders as he recalled Iain's attack on the hill and ultimate death.

Continuing to play, Eric added new phrases and verses to the melody in response to upturned faces surrounding him. His music changed as memories of each face from the midst of battle washed over him. Slowly the tempo and rhythm relaxed, reflecting the promise carried within each of his friends that evening on this more peaceful hillside.

Melodies of that first great Highland bagpipe filled every soul with remembrance and promise, with resolve and purpose. The spirit of the Highlands was recaptured and shared that night. Stars filled a darkening sky creating a breathtaking panorama. It was an affirmation of purpose and tomorrow, not to be stolen by Romans nor any other invader. These Highlands were home and every man, woman, and child on that hillside was ready to defend their freedom and growing heritage, with their life if needed.

<hr>

Vrenessbith waited quietly for Seumas to wake. With Resbith's guidance she had convinced Fobothom, Truact, Frenzy, Depost, and Enstard to join Seumas on his journey. She now had to explain to Seumas that he had an escort of five faeries to protect him. First rays of sunlight stretched over the village before Seumas began to stir. Carefully, Vrenessbith floated down to Seumas' right eye where she stroked his eyelid with her wings.

Seumas quickly opened his eyes, crying out in agitation and confusion. His right eye was clouded but his left eye was crystal clear. Was this the first attack of the old hag? Was he to go blind and not see his children grow up?

Vrenessbith floated away from Seumas' face. He immediately began to see more clearly. Instinctively he tried to swat at the tiny form in front of his face, but Ingrid grabbed his arm. "The faeries will not help ye if ye kill them as ye wake," she warned him.

"Whit?"

"Can't ye see the wee faerie in front of yer face?"

Seumas looked at his wife in disbelief. Could she see the faeries now? And, more importantly, why were faeries waking him from a sound and much needed sleep?

"Seumas," Vrenessbith called. "SEUMAS!"

Seumas turned his head to find the wee voice. Not seeing anything he shook his head and looked again. It may have been the soft morning light of the hut, his sleepy state of mind, the effects of the music from the night before, or the candle Ingrid lit, but Seumas now saw

Vrenessbith. Her small self floated barely a foot in front of his eyes and her voice was clear as the song of the birds in spring. Seumas stared at Vrenessbith in disbelief.

"Seumas," Vrenessbith repeated. "Faeries will accompany you on your trip. There are five strong young *siabhraichean*[21] who are willing to watch over you and those who will be traveling with you. They will help watch for *bana-bhuidseach* and see that you return home safely."

"Watch for Whit?" Seumas growled.

"*'Bana-bhuidseach*,' the women you call 'hags'," Vrenessbith replied.

"How do ye know this?" Seumas challenged.

"Resbith says you should accept that I know." Seeing Seumas was even more confused, Vrenessbith explained, "Resbith is my teacher."

Seumas shook his head again and stood up. As he prepared for his journey, Ingrid called to Vrenessbith, "Faerie!" Vrenessbith flew to Ingrid, hovering in front of her. "Who are ye?" Ingrid asked.

"I am Vrenessbith. Born of a lover's tear and sent to guard the Highlands."

"Can ye guard my husband as he journeys?"

"I have been told to not leave this area until I learn more of these mountains and the magic that lives here. I have found five more experienced faeries, *siabhraichean*, who are willing to travel with your husband and see that he returns home safely."

"Why do ye do this?"

"I was there when the *bana-bhuidseach* spoke to Seumas." Recalling what her Comleidh had told her, the faerie continued, "I knew at that time it was to be my purpose to protect your people and to help them defeat this evil that would settle around you. These hags would do harm to faeries and all creatures of the forest. We must join our strengths if we are to overcome."

"Thank ye, sweet faerie," Ingrid smiled. "Please guard them well."

Seumas frowned at Ingrid as he walked out the door. His mind was trying to focus on the journey ahead to discuss the hag's threat and Ingrid was talking with a faerie! Immediately upon leaving his hut five waiting faeries flew to his shoulders, ably dodging Seumas' equipment as he slung it in place. He carried a fur cape rolled up and tied across one shoulder, his broad sword slung across his other shoulder. Martin, Peter, and Robert all smiled as Seumas approached.

---

[21] *siabhrach* - SEE~vrak - male faerie. *siabraichean* - SEE~vrak~en - plural, group of male faeries

"Are ye expecting trouble on this journey?" Peter asked.

"None," replied Seumas in a growl. "Why?"

"We see ye are bringing reinforcements," chuckled Martin.

Seumas looked across at his shoulder and let out an exasperated sigh. "They want to travel and we are going on a journey. Now, can we get going?"

"Seumas," a voice behind the big Celt called, "ye had better not leave without this."

Seumas turned as Ingrid wrapped her arms around him, embracing him with passion and regret. "Something to think about while ye are gone." She smiled as she released him.

Smiling at his wife, he replied, "Two, maybe three weeks." The large man then leaned into his wife and gave her a quick peck of a kiss.

Vrenessbith watched this unusual party began their journey that would take them into the highest regions of the Highlands. She noticed how each of the men carried a shroud about his shoulders, some were quite dark and Seumas' appeared to be a different color. She wondered why these men carried such senseless weight as they traveled.

<hr>

Seeing both Liam and Marian beginning to fade, Lillian stopped the reading. "An this would be a good place to rest for the evening. Three young bairn, off to bed with ye."

"I am not a 'bairn'," Marian objected. "I am fridgin!"

"Okay, wee one, off wi' ye," Angus chuckled. He marked his place and closed the book gently. Looking up to evening stars he pondered a weighty problem.

Lillian found her husband still staring into the heavens after she got the children settled in bed. Gently spreading her arms across his shoulders, she whispered, "If ye share the problem it won't be so heavy."

Angus reached up, taking her hands in his. "Aye, ye are right, an I have. I spoke with Belinda, but still I worry."

"If ye hae spoken with the Comleidh then ye hae done all ye can. Ye can speak with her again, but nae this night, so come tae bed." Lillian then tugged gently on Angus' hands until he stood.

Days that followed were filled with church, shopping, and chores for all. Angus journeyed to the hillside on his own late in the third day. After consulting with Comleidh Belinda, he stopped at the pile of stones where he lit his pipe and stared out across the loch below. Aroma of his tobacco wafted through the house ahead of him as he returned.

"So, did Belinda set yer mind at peace?" Lillian asked with a smile.

"Aye, she has the problem well in hand. I will nae worry so much, now. Where are the bairn? Do ye suppose they hae forgotten the book already?"

"Nae, they asked for dinner in the courtyard so ye can resume yer reading."

"Good," Angus replied, slapping his hands and rubbing them together. "I am eager to continue!"

As soon as their dinner disappeared, Angus retrieved The Book, settled into a comfortable chair, and opened to the silk ribbon. After reviewing the page he looked to his captive audience and reminded them, "When we stopped last, Angus and his men were going to the other villages to talk with elders about the old crone's threat. In his company are three other men and five faeries." Seeing all were ready to go, Angus resumed reading.

Nature provided a vast display of autumn splendor for the journey. Trees wore scarlets, brilliant orange, and golden wraps which glowed in the sunlight. Hillsides and valleys dazzled with splashes of vibrant colour. Feeling no sense of urgency, Seumas set a moderate pace. The faerie escort found adventure by rushing ahead looking for unnatural things, anything that appeared to be not as it should be. Each search yielded no result so the faeries would settle on someone's shoulder, until an urge to search ahead returned.

Sunset carried the travelers into Cullet Cavie. Village elders welcomed their friends and spent the evening with them in the common lodge. Seumas told his story of the old hag as all listened. Some were unconcerned; others listened with great intensity. Several elders asked for advice, to which Seumas replied, "We dinna know anything of this new enemy, only that they hae threatened us with another war. We know nothing of thair strengths, thair methods or thair numbers. Ye must be on yer guard and be wary of unknown visitors."

The faeries searched the woods for local faeries to protect the village. Frenzy and Enstard found a cavie, a large community of faeries living in a cave hidden in the rocks and roots of a majestic old tree. As natural guardians of nature, elders of the cavie agreed to watch over and protect Cullet Cavie and to become friends with their larger neighbors. Fobothom and Seumas introduced two senior protectors to the village elders, who were quite surprised at their new allies. As introductions took place amazed villagers realized the specs of reflected sunlight, once taken for granted, were in reality countless faeries ready to support and defend their neighbors.

Sunrise found the men's backs as they continued on to Haugh Mailen. Arriving peacefully after dark, Seumas repeated events of the previous night. Meeting with elders he told his story of the hag, doing his best to assure villagers that there was no immediate danger, and admitting that he was as confused as they were. *Ceo Dhachaidh* Faeries searched the forest around Haugh Mailen, but were unable to find any protectors.

Morning found the travelers on the road again, back down the mountain to Stag's Byre. It was mid-afternoon when they arrived, but they decided to rest and get an early start crossing to Doup Fell in the morning. Truact and Depost found a large faerie cavie near Stag's Byre. Elders of the village and the faeries were most pleased to formally meet one another. Once again amazed villagers were humbled by their lack of awareness about their tiny neighbors and were also delighted when they learned that these faeries had been watching over Stag's Byre for many years, providing anonymous assistance.

Leaving Stag's Byre, most travelers would have continued back down through Cullet Cavie to the western trail. However, Martin and Seumas felt ready for an adventure so they told Peter and Robert that a day of travel could be saved by using deer trails across the mountains to Doup Fell. Peter remembered using these ill-defined pathways when they were in a rush. With some hesitation the younger travelers agreed that they would follow trails of deer.

"Think of the scenery," Martin encouraged.

"Whit scenery?" Peter challenged. "All ye can see is thickets and briar."

Journeying across the mountains did save the travelers a full day, but their backs and legs ached as though they had labored hard for two days. Bent over and climbing across logs they stumbled and climbed their way where deer moved easily.

Sunset had just faded into darkness when they staggered into Doup Fell. A young girl saw them first and ran to her mother, crying, "THEY ARE BACK! THEY ARE BACK!" Villagers came running from their huts ready to do battle with invaders only to fall into fits of laughter at the sight of four nearly broken men. Seumas carried leaves and twigs in his hair and shaggy beard. Both younger men were disheveled, showing multiple cuts on their arms and legs. Only Martin maintained the look of a true Celt. Villagers provided a warm meal and ale which brought life back to the weary travelers.

While they ate Seumas paused long enough to tell his story of the old hag's threat. To his surprise everyone present listened with a keen interest. Not one person in Doup Fell challenged his concerns. When Seumas finished, Martin looked around at the faces of those present.

After a very long moment without any response Martin was overcome, breaking the silence, "Men of other villages have asked many questions when we told them of our concerns. Have ye no challenge to this story?"

"Ye have brought us grave concern," replied one elder. "Shortly after the celebration in *Ceo Dhachaidh*, a woman found her way into our village. She wore tattered clothes and looked as though she had been lost in these mountains for many weeks. We gave her a hut to live in and saw to her needs until she regained her strength. She has already come to be loved by the younger folk, so we have let her stay. She is no old hag, as ye described, but we know nothing of her other than the name she gave us, Brett. She told us this was short for her real name, but that her real name was too long to say easily."

"May we meet with her?" Robert asked. "Will one of ye take the four of us to talk with her?"

Seumas and Martin looked at Robert with surprise but joined him as they went to Brett's hut. A local elder asked permission to visit, which Brett granted. Four travelers and one villager crowded into the woman's hut, gathering around her fire.

Robert assumed control of the meeting as he immediately positioned himself to see her clearly. "We apologize for breakin' in on yer peace like this," Robert began.

"Give it no thought," Brett replied. "I love to have visitors. It helps me get to know the village better." An attractive woman in her mid-thirties, her face showed signs of much hard work in the weather. Her dark eyes sparkled in the glow of the fire.

"Many years ago," Robert began, "shortly after my family came to these mountains, my màithrean[22] disappeared from our village. We searched for many weeks but never found a trace of her. When the village elders told us of yer arrival, I hoped ye might be my màithrean. But ye are far more attractive than she was, and much younger than she would be now. Whit brings ye to these mountains alone?"

---

[22] màithrean - MAH~ren - aunt, mother's sister

"I am sorry I am not your mother's sister," Brett replied, "I know what it is to lose one's family. My family once traveled the land in search of a place to call home. We were attacked by soldiers many months ago and I was left for dead. I do not know how I found this village but I feel they have given me the home my family was seeking."

"Again," excused Robert, "we apologize for intruding on yer privacy. We will leave ye to yer quiet."

"No, please stay. What brings all of you out into the mountains this time of year?"

"The soldiers," Martin said quickly. "Winter is coming and we want to make sure all of our villages are safe and no Roman patrols are wandering these mountains in search of trouble."

"You must be very skilled warriors. There are only four of you."

"We do not seek to do battle," Seumas added. "We seek only peace of mind for the cold months ahead. Please excuse us."

The visitors bid their farewells and left the hut. Seumas stopped abruptly as he stepped away from the door. He was the last one out and no one saw him. Something was wrong, but he could not say what. He was uneasy but could not think why. Turning his head he glanced back into the hut, Brett smiled and nodded her head. Seumas looked intently at Brett for several seconds, but all he saw was an attractive woman with signs of past hardship in her face. Unable to identify the source of his awkward uneasy feeling he deliberately shook it off as though it were a cold wrap and rejoined the others.

While the men paid their visit to Brett, their five faerie companions set to their task of finding protectors in the surrounding forest. Their search, however, was interrupted as they were drawn to a bush covered with small white flowers. The flowers dripped with an autumn nectar that was intoxicating to the faeries. Before realizing they were not alone, all *Ceo Dhachaidh* faeries were inebriated beyond control. As moonlight draped this unusual bush, dozens of faeries danced around it, enjoying its abundant nectar.

"WHOA! The faeries got drunk?" Alex exclaimed with delight.

"Aye, it would seem so," Angus affirmed with a smile. "An if ye will be patient, ye will learn that getting drunk is not a wise thing to do." Seeing all eyes widened with curiosity, Angus continued.

Early morning rays of sunshine warmed the forest floor where faeries lay in their stupor. Frenzy awoke as a gentle breeze from the direction of the village carried a foul stench across their tiny incapacitated bodies. Gasping for air he shook his traveling companions and other faeries, each gagging on the putrid odor as they regained consciousness. One by one weakened faeries stretched, rolled and fluttered their wings. Clumsily, they rose to tree limbs where they could warm themselves in the morning sunshine and breathe cleaner air. Below them an old hag pushed her way through forest undergrowth toward the intoxicating bush, carrying the nauseating stench around her like a rotten cloak.

When his head was clear enough to understand what had happened, Fobothom summoned his team and together they went in search of Seumas to tell him about this vile hag. Fortunately, the village was about fifty meters into the wind and rising sun. When the faeries reached the lodge hall, Seumas was gone. Depost remembered that the men were going to visit Brett and flew in the direction of her hut. Meanwhile Fobothom attempted to get the attention of a village elder; the faerie was almost smashed as the elder tried to swat him, thinking him to be a pest. Frenzy overheard another elder talking about the men from *Ceo Dhachaidh* heading toward Blyth Brier. He relayed this information to his companions as Depost returned gagging and out of breath. Without hesitation five weary faeries went in pursuit of those they had been charged to protect.

Seumas had a quick step this day and a slight smile on his face. After several hours Peter asked what he had on his mind. "Rachel and Bryan," was all he said. After their wedding the couple had moved to Bryan's home in Blyth Brier.

Their pace was tiring to Peter and Robert but Seumas was intent on spending the evening with this young couple brought together by the Roman invasion. Martin brought up the rear, prodding younger men unable to keep pace with Seumas. As though he were a mother bear looking for her lost cubs, Seumas strode into the center of Blyth Brier bellowing, "WHERE IS THAT FIRE HAIRED LASS WHO HUMBLES MEN?!"

Villagers had begun to retire to their huts for the evening, but battle proven men quickly stood ready to defend their homes, circling the loud man from *Ceo Dhachaidh*. Peter, Robert, and Martin pushed through the crowd just in time to see Rachel come up behind Seumas and drop him on his back with her stave. "I'll humble ye if ye ever disturb my supper like that again, Seumas Gregor!"

Bryan welcomed the travelers and helped Seumas to his feet. "I'll help ye with yer supper, if ye have room at yer table for me," Seumas replied, with some humility.

"It just so happens that we have a small boar on the spit, enough for all of ye I think!" This invitation came from Roslyn, Bryan's mother.

"Thank ye, Roslyn," Martin accepted, smiling wide enough to swallow that small boar whole. "We will also need to meet with yer village elders . . . after!" Several elders nodded and said they would come by Roslyn's hut.

The four travelers followed Rosyln when Seumas was unexpectedly assaulted a second time. This time he felt the sharp whack of Rachel's stave across his bottom. Turning to scold his attacker he found Rachel's arms around his neck, "Good to see ye, yeu old Celt." She then placed a large kiss on his cheek.

Angus caught a glimpse of his granddaughter, Marian, in the corner of his eye. She had snuggled against Lillian and was beaming at Rachel's prowess. Marian had found a heroine.

The hut was a bit cramped with seven adults eating a hot meal, but conversation was so lively no one had a chance to complain. All topics had to do with Rachel, Bryan, and updates from *Ceo Dhachaidh*. Their laughter must have carried to all corners of the village for when the first elder arrived he complained, "If ye were going to have a ceilidh why was I not included?" Roslyn shook her head and ran everyone outside to wait for the remaining elders. Seumas encouraged Bryan and Rachel to join them.

The five faeries flew sometimes with the breeze but more often against it as they tried to catch up with their four warriors. Fobothom used every flight maneuver he knew to take advantage of adverse winds. At one point when being blown roughly by a crosswind, Enstard suggested they send their message to a faerie cavie near Blyth Brier.

"None of us has ever been to a cavie near Blyth Brier," Fobothom replied. "And we are charged with watching over these overgrown tree warts. Keep your wits about you because the winds have blown us way off our intended course."

Indeed, they were well west of their desired path in an area none were familiar with. Truact flew high to find a landmark as the others settled into a peaceful clearing. The treetops were magnificent, lush and filled with autumn colour beneath a blue sky. There was a twitch of chill in the air, but that was common this time of year. Truact flew higher until he looked down on all the trees and across at the highest hilltop. The view was mesmerizing and he almost forgot his purpose. Turning slowly in a circle, he spotted the mountain path passing through a clearing just north of his location. Following the path with his eyes he saw signs of the trail to Blyth Brier and then on to Heigh Fell and Benmost Bield beyond. He knew where they were.

Reluctantly, Truact left his peaceful serenity to find the others. He found them in a large clearing beneath a bush with small white flowers, gorging themselves on nectar. Again! They recognized his return but did not care for his news nor his insistence that they continue their journey. In vain, Truact called and tried to persuade Fobothom to follow him into the sky, thinking the clear crisp air would sober the half drunken faerie. Fobothom refused to listen to reason, instead offering a nectar-filled blossom to Truact. Truact reached for a blossom but rather than take the offering he seized Fobothom by his wrist. With all the power he could muster, Truact soared to the heights of the clouds dragging Fobothom behind him. His plan worked for the crispness of the air sobered the intoxicated faerie, flushing the nectar-induced stupor from his mind. The two then returned to the bush and without discussion individually seized Frenzy and Depost, then each grabbed hold of Enstard with their free hand. Straining with their load, they climbed to clean, invigorating air. As the three returned to sobriety, Fobothom made mental notes of where this bush was located. Truact pointed the way and flying just above the treetops they resumed their quest to catch up with their charges.

As elders gathered, conversation with men of *Ceo Dhachaidh* centered on events of Blyth Brier since returning to their regular routines. It was evident everyone had suffered changes in their lives, but life was continuing. There was laughter and it was good to talk about daily activities. The village senior was the last to arrive, with

Bloigh Bryan in tow. Seumas slapped Bryan on the back and welcomed him into the conversation. The group quickly moved into the lodge, for all wanted to retire as soon as possible.

Seumas told everyone of his encounter with the old hag and her words. He then told about his conversations with the elders of *Ceo Dhachaidh* and the purpose of their visit. Questions were few and direct to the point, "Whit are we to do now?"

"Keep yer eyes open to whit does not belong," Seumas replied. "We do not know this new enemy who has threatened our land so we do not know whit to watch."

As the meeting began to break up Robert stopped an elder he had been talking with earlier. "Ye said a single woman had come to the village recently. Would ye take us to meet her?" Robert, Peter, and Martin went with the elder to meet the woman.

Seumas stopped Rachel and Bryan as they began to leave. "Would the two of ye young folks care to trek through the woods with an old Celt for a few days?" Bryan nodded agreement without thought, but Rachel folded her arms in front of her and considered for a moment. After studying Seumas' face she, too, agreed to the trek.

Seumas spread his huge arms in the cool night air. Stretching his muscles relieved mounting stress. Five weary faeries accepted his stretch as an invitation to rest. Seumas laughed when his absent friends made their presence known. "I thought I was missing a gnat today," he chided with a grin. "Where have ye been?"

Fobothom told Seumas of their mishap with the nectar bush and the old hag. As he described the events, Seumas' expression grew quite concerned. "We will return to Doup Fell on our way home," Seumas announced to his small friends.

"We also stumbled onto another great bush, full of nectar, in the forest south of here. There were no villages near this bush, just a great clearing," Fobothom explained.

"That one I would not worry about," Seumas discounted, "But now I know where to look if ye go missing again."

Peter, Martin, and Robert joined Seumas as he announced plans to return to Doup Fell. Seumas explained they needed to look into something the faeries found and asked where the men had been.

"I thought it was odd that another single woman had appeared here just as in Doup Fell," Robert explained. "We went to meet her. She is quite lovely and very friendly. Her given name is Bridgett, but she said that name is too stiff and formal, like her namesake *seanmhair*. She prefers to be called 'Bridg.' Told us that she ran away from home as a young lass and has lived alone most of her adult life. Hearing of the Roman invasion, she felt it would be safer to move into a village where she might find protection."

Seumas considered Robert's report. Was it unusual that another single woman had arrived in a second village? Yes, but travelers frequently sought sanctuary within a village, especially with colder months looming on the horizon. Remembering the foulness of the old hag who had threatened him, Seumas dismissed the woman without further thought. All four travelers found bedding in the main lodge while the faeries settled quietly in the rafters above their charges. The night was calm, peaceful, and quiet . . . except for a snoring serenade from Seumas and Martin.

At daybreak Rachel and Bryan kicked Seumas in his side, gently and lovingly of course. Seumas in turn rousted the others and the next leg of their journey began, in two directions. Seumas, Rachel, and Bryan went east to Benmost Bield. Martin, Peter, and Robert went north to Heigh Fell. Fobothom sent Truact, Frenzy, and Depost with Martin; he and Enstard rode on the shoulders of Seumas. They were to spend a day out and a day back, meeting again in Blyth Brier.

The mood in *Ceo Dhachaidh* was becoming uneasy. Another sudden chill in the air erased the visit of autumn. Winter was close at hand. Standing outside her hut, Ingrid looked into the sky. It was blue, crystal blue with only a few puffy white clouds. She pulled her wrap around her shoulders to shield against the chill and concern she had for her husband. Looking across the village she saw Ester, wife of Robert, the Gaelic leader. Ingrid joined Ester as she visited Gaelic homes.

Regina, David's wife, and his mother, Siùsan, had a disagreement that had grown into a quarrel that was about to engulf half the village. Siùsan, an older woman and very set in her ways, wanted to boil a piglet. This was the way she had been taught to cook by her mother and her mother's mother before that. "Pig is to be boiled!"

Regina wanted to try cooking it over the open fire like others in *Ceo Dhachaidh*. "Let us try to learn from these people who have saved us," Regina pleaded.

"I am of my mother's blood and that will not change!" Siùsan bellowed, getting louder with every retort.

"I am not asking you to change who you are," Regina replied calmly. "I am just trying to learn from these people. If we learn from them, they in turn may learn from us."

"PIG IS TO BE BOILED! With turnips and carrots and peppers! YOU CANNOT PUT TURNIPS AND CARROTS ON A STICK OVER A FIRE!"

"No, but ye can cook them in rocks under the fire," Ingrid offered, trying to help.

"You tell me that you can put a carrot in a rock?" Siùsan challenged.

"No, we put a bed of rocks, then the vegetables, then another layer of rocks. Then we push the coals and the fire on top of them. Would ye like to see my fire?" Ingrid extended her hand with a smile.

Grudgingly Siùsan pushed Ingrid's hand aside, walking in the direction of Ingrid's hut. Inside, Ingrid pushed the fire to one side, revealing a small pit filled with rocks. She scooped out the rocks with a flat wide stick, curved at the end.

"There are no turnips," Siùsan challenged.

"No," Ingrid replied. "Actually, I am making a stew that Ester told me about. Today the turnips are in the pot." Ingrid fished a potato out of a large pot hanging over the fire.

Siùsan tasted the broth, "Needs more pepper."

A scream from the Gaelic huts cut the cooking lesson short. Ingrid emerged from her hut and saw Sean across the way, a large man given to drinking and ill manners. He was trying to force his way into the hut of Regina, one of the Gaelic widows. Turning toward the fields Ingrid saw all the men on the farthest side of the field where they could not hear sounds of the village. Without further hesitation Ingrid ran toward Sean, grabbing a stave as she went. As Sean was pounding on the door, about to break through, Ingrid slipped the stave between his legs and ran around to his other side. Her motion on the stave spun Sean around, flipping him onto his back. His head struck the door then bounced on the hardened earth as he went down. He was out cold. Ingrid asked Ester to grab some rope and told Siùsan to see to Regina. Two other women came to help and together the four women dragged Sean to a tree where they tied his feet to the trunk, nearly four feet above the ground. They left him there.

At midday Sarah and Christopher took a skin of fresh water to Eric. Men of *Ceo Dhachaidh* were busy digging up the last of the carrots, turnips, and other autumn crops. Hosting training to battle invading Romans had devastated supplies and crops through over consumption and inadequate planting. A short harvest and a chill in the air were definite signs that the coming winter would be difficult. Anything and everything edible was collected.

Sarah greeted Eric with a tremendous hug and kiss. Eric took Christopher, Sarah's son, holding him close in his arms. This unlikely young family was quickly becoming the sign of promise for a healthy and prosperous tomorrow. Other men began teasing Eric about being a newlywed and how he was beginning to show signs of not getting enough sleep. Sarah blushed, but Eric snapped back "With my bride's love fortifying my soul I can get along on little enough sleep. Ye codgers need to be worrying about yer own sleep habits and see to it that ye find enough warmth this winter."

The day came to an early close and men laughed when they found Sean tied to the tree. "His face IS a bit red," someone observed. Regina laughed and put a log under his neck to lift his head a bit. Sean pulled the log out, tossing it at the crowd of hecklers. Stepping into the circle to see what was drawing such a crowd, David asked for an explanation. Regina explained the events that led to Sean's situation.

Standing next to the captive so Sean could easily see him, David asked, "As you have not been in the fields nor contributing to the stores of the village, how do you plan to eat this winter?" Sean did not answer but tried to lift himself to untie his legs. He could not. "I believe we have two choices," David continued. "We can leave you here and hope the wolves take care of our problem, or you can beg the forgiveness of young Regina. If she forgives your behavior she can cut you down, otherwise you are here for the wolves to enjoy. I wish you good fortune. Now the rest of you have families to tend to."

The crowd dispersed, all except Regina, Ingrid, and Ester. Sean stared up at Regina. There were no words on his lips but pleading filled his eyes. "I wouldn't want the wolves to get indigestion," she mumbled as she pulled a knife strapped to her calf and cut Sean from the tree. She did not cut the ropes completely, but enough to allow Sean to work himself free. The women then returned to their families, leaving Sean struggling to release himself.

Seumas traveled with a much lighter heart in the company of Rachel and Bryan. Their youthful zest for life kept him smiling and their conversation was more about family and village events than of the task before them, which made Seumas long for Ingrid and her warm embrace. Rachel developed an active relationship with Truact and Fobothom, irritating Seumas a bit for he still had trouble relating to these 'bothersome gnats' as he called them with growing affection. Bryan simply laughed.

Village elders of Benmost Bield welcomed the trio warmly, listening to their story with interest. A middle-aged woman had arrived about two weeks prior but had shown nothing but gratitude and fondness for the village.

"Tell me of this woman," Seumas requested.

"She is pleasant to look at," one man quickly replied, smiling broadly. "And she is a considerable good cook though her dishes are not like ours."

"Did she tell ye a story of her lost family when she arrived?" Seumas asked, wondering if three women of similar description were now more than a coincidence.

"No," another man replied. "She told us she was traveling over the mountain to be with her family and asked if she could winter in our village for safety."

"I would like to meet her. Please send someone to ask her if we may visit," Seumas directed with a stern tone. Rachel and Bryan looked at him with surprise, both wondering about his unusual manner.

Moments later Rachel, Bryan, Seumas, and Thomas, a village elder, strolled to the hut of this woman. "Graclyn," Thomas called at her door. "Graclyn, I hae some friends from *Ceo Dhachaidh* who would like to meet ye."

The door opened and Seumas gasped at the woman who greeted them. She stood just over five feet tall, shapely and beautiful, with a clear complexion void of a single blemish. A blue dress and apron fit snugly and was open at the collar, displaying her ample and attractive figure. She appeared to be about twenty-four years. Rachel jabbed her elbow into Bryan's side, erasing his appreciative smile. Tossing long red hair over her shoulder, Graclyn invited her visitors into her hut. "Please come in, but leave the chill outside."

She stood close to Seumas as he introduced the three of them, stuttering just a bit. "I am . . . hmm, excuse me, Miss Graclyn, I am Seumas Gregor of *Ceo Dhachaidh*; these are friends of mine, Rachel and Bryan. Actually they are newlyweds, friends I recruited to keep me company as I check on remote villages of our Hielands. We are trying to make sure everyone is ready for the winter after a difficult summer."

Graclyn's eyes widened slightly when Seumas introduced himself but replied with a smile and disarming sweetness, "I am pleased to know you care so for your friends in the mountains."

"We are also looking for lost Roman patrols who might suffer in our Hieland winters. I am told ye have family over the mountain and are only stopping for the season?"

"Yes. I enjoy my travels but tarried too long in my last visit. I fear I might get caught in mountain snows if I try to continue my journey at this time. Families of this village have kindly given me shelter. I will move on when the spring thaw arrives."

"Maybe she will find a reason to stay beyond the thaw," Thomas smiled. Graclyn returned his smile but said nothing.

"We must be going," Seumas concluded. "I just wanted to make sure ye are well cared for and Benmost Bield does their part to make ye welcome."

Thomas followed Rachel and Bryan out of the hut but Seumas stopped in the door and looked back at Graclyn. Firelight reflecting in her eyes was cold and dark, sending a chill down his spine.

〰〰〰〰〰〰〰〰〰〰〰〰〰〰〰

While travelers discussed their news with men of Benmost Bield, Truact, and Fobothom searched the nearby forest for a faerie cavie. Just beyond sight of the village they found another delightful bush with intoxicating nectar. Cold, however, had caused the blossoms to fall. Fobothom checked several of the flowers littering the ground beneath the bush but their nectar was bitter.

Continuing their search for a local cavie, they circled through the forest looking for signs of others like themselves. Fobothom spied a possible entrance well hidden in rocks at the base of a old tree. Floating down to investigate they were attacked by a large beast, long in body with short legs, covered in dense fur and led by a powerful snout at the end of a triangular head. The slinky beast came from out of nowhere and launched himself onto the root where the faeries were hovering as they examined the entrance to what appeared to be a cavie. Seeking immediate safety, both darted into the hole. It was a cavie, but there was not a single faerie present.

Truact led the way as they searched deeper and deeper into the dark tunnels. Each brave young faerie growing more apprehensive with the constraining cold gloom. No man would have, could have continued into the blackness of this once thriving community but faeries have it within themselves to see through dense darkness. Reaching the center chambers, they found nothing but more emptiness, a frigidly depressing emptiness that chilled them to their souls. Filling with fear, Fobothom and Truact raced back to the portal where they had entered. Fobothom reached the hole first, stopping suddenly as he realized the beast might still be outside. Truact tried to avoid hitting his friend but managed only to pass around him, clipping Fobothom on the shoulder, knocking both of them to the floor. As they stood each noticed a warning scrawled on the wall, "A great evil has entered the village. It is no longer safe for us here. Our trusted friend, Muestor, will show you to our new cavie."

"Who is Muestor?" Truact and Fobothom asked one another, each struggling with growing fear and confusion.

"I do not know," Truact said after some thought, "but we must assume that the beast is still beyond that entrance. We should leave quickly and fly high to safety."

Almost before their little hearts could beat again both faeries shot out the hole, soaring straight into the sky. Looking back they saw the beast running in circles and bouncing its long body in a frenzy. It then ran a few yards in a single direction and stopped. After pausing to look to the escaping faeries, it bounced up and down again. The beast repeated this action several times, as though it was trying to get the faeries' attention.

"Should we follow him?" Fobothom asked.

"No, there is indeed an evil in this forest and we do not know who or what it is," Truact replied, his voice shaking. "We should tell Seumas."

Satisfied with this safer plan, both bold faeries flew back to the village and safe company of their friends. Seumas, Rachel, and Bryan were sleeping soundly in the great lodge of Benmost Bield when Truact and Fobothom found them. Rachel and Bryan were sleeping close to one another and Seumas slept with his hand on his broadsword. Knowing the dangers of waking Seumas, they decided to wait until morning to talk with him. The faeries took to the rafters of the lodge and settled for the night.

"Hallo to Heigh Fell," Martin called in a loud voice as he, Peter, and Robert entered a village already quiet in the cold and dark of evening. Men bearing swords and staves appeared from nowhere, immediately surrounding the intruders. Realizing who had called to them defenders lowered their weapons and raised their arms in welcome, embracing the weary travelers.

"I have a bit of a boar left next to my fire if ye are hungry," Cynbel, an old Celt, offered.

"Have ye ever known a Celt to not be hungry?" Martin answered with a roar of laughter. "But we need to speak with yer elders while we eat."

"ELDERS! To my home," Cynbel called to men around him.

The hut was crowded as men of the village joined the travelers around a small fire. Mary, the host's wife, fussed as she was pushed to a corner in the back of her own home.

"I apologize for intruding on yer quiet," Martin smiled at Mary. "I will state our business and yield yer home back to yer solitude."

Martin, Peter, and Robert took turns relaying Seumas' story of the hags as they chewed on roast pork. Several of the elders asked questions. "Whit did this 'hag' look like?" "Are old women a threat to our trained Hielanders?" "When will they attack?" "We are a small village; who will help defend our families?" "Whit do we do now?"

Travelers answered all questions as best they could, often not good enough. Martin then asked if any visitors had recently come to the village. Finding that there had been no previous visitors, the travelers asked for bedding in the lodge and retired.

As Cynbel and one other elder left the men at the lodge, Frenzy, Depost, and Enstard appeared with a host of other faeries. Hundreds of wee creatures floated in the air before the men, their wings reflecting light from a torch the elder carried. Cynbel stopped suddenly at the appearance of such a host of small guests, calling out to the travelers, "MARTIN, ye had better come out here!"

"I see ye have found guardians," Robert laughed, raising a hand for Enstard to light on.

Depost proceeded to introduce elders of the local faerie cavie to elders of the village. "Men of the village Heigh Fell, these souls of the forest have consented to watch over your village and act as your guardians. It is their wish that you learn to work with each other and together protect our forests and mountains."

The old Celt looked at Martin, laughing gently, "Ye are telling me that these wee gnats are going to protect us? Against whit?"

"Old friend," Martin began, "we do not know who our enemy is in the coming campaign. We do not know thair numbers or thair abilities. We do know that these generous wee souls of the Hieland forests helped us claim victory against the Romans and are the most powerful ally we have. Learn to hear them and always trust them."

Seumas awakened hours before sunlight appeared and shook Bryan and Rachel. Meat saved from the night before took an edge off their hunger as they made ready to return to Blyth Brier. No one made any sound as they left Benmost Bield. Ten kilometers down the trail Seumas broke the silence, "Will Roslyn hae a roast pig when we return?"

"Not if we arrive at midday," Bryan laughed.

"Too bad," Seumas moaned. "I need a meal prepared by a good woman."

"Ye can prepare yer own meals, big man," Rachel scolded.

"Ye know I meant no disrespect. Roslyn is a good cook. Her roast pig is far better than that dry meat we had last night."

Bryan chuckled, shaking his head. Quiet once again filled the forest, with only the sounds of their feet on the hardened trail greeting the travelers' ears. Daylight was slow to arrive, revealing a sky sealed with heavy clouds. Without sunshine, the air grew colder. About midmorning Seumas unrolled his cape and threw it around his shoulders.

"I wish I had a furry cape," Rachel commented.

Seumas stopped abruptly and turned around. Looking down at the young lady in his presence he pulled the cape from his shoulders and draped it gently around Rachel. "Better?" he asked.

Rachel smiled, to which Seumas replied "Good, now we will move faster so Bryan and I can keep warm."

Arriving at Blyth Brier shortly after noon, Seumas turned and looked at Rachel. The fur cape was barely clinging to her sweaty shoulders; her face was red. Exhausted by the pace and the weight of the cape she pulled the oversized drape off and struggled to hand it back to Seumas, "Here take yer animal back."

Seumas laughed.

Roslyn, who had been speaking with Bridg, strolled down to meet the travelers; she carried a branch of leaves. "Ye are back sooner than I expected. No fun in the mountains this time of year?"

"Whit do ye have there?" Seumas asked.

"I found this bush just inside the forest this morning. I went looking for berries before cold ruined what was left of the autumn fruit. The ground under this bush was covered with blossoms that had fallen off. I thought Bridg might know something since she has been through the mountains but she said she has never seen anything like this."

"Mother, do ye have any pork near the fire?" Bryan asked, unconcerned about the bush or flowers.

"No. We finished the pork that night before ye went wandering about the mountains." Roslyn replied, looking to her son with a scowl.

"Hmpf, I like yer pork," Seumas frowned.

Snow began to fall as the travelers stood talking. Looking across the sky, Seumas frowned again, "I hope Martin arrives soon. I don't like traveling in snow."

"How would ye know it is snowing with that beast about yer shoulders?" Rachel laughed. "I think I will go rest. Bryan?"

As Rachel and Bryan left, Seumas picked one of the flowers from Roslyn's hand. "The faeries were telling me about flowers like this. They said they got drunk from the nectar inside." Seumas tried touching the flower to his tongue, spitting quickly after he tasted the bitterness. "Where are those gnats?" Seumas looked around quickly and called out, "Rachel! Bryan! Have ye seen our gnats?"

"Faeries, Seumas. FAERIES!" Rachel replied.

"No," Bryan added. "I hae not seen them since we arrived at Benmost Bield."

Seumas looked around at the sky and falling snow. "Well, they hae been lost before and found us. Roslyn, do ye hae anything for an old Celt to eat?"

"No," she replied, "but I believe we could find ye something somewhere in this village."

Roslyn led Seumas toward the common lodge. Seumas frequently looked back over his shoulder toward the trail they had just come down.

Seumas did find roast pork and conversation in the lodge. An hour passed with villagers coming in for warmth and leaving to prepare their own fires when Martin, Robert, and Peter arrived. Before sitting, Martin opened a leather pouch he had tied over his shoulder. Frenzy, Depost, and Enstard flew out of the bag, coming to rest on a beam over the fire. "They canna fly in the snow," Martin commented. Seumas looked up at the three faeries, releasing a concerned sigh.

Enjoying hospitality of the village the four men exchanged news and comments about their journeys. When they were finished Seumas got up and stepped outside. Others from *Ceo Dhachaidh* followed.

"Well," Seumas moaned, "do we wait til morning and hope the snow stops or make for home now?"

"Whit about Doup Fell?" Peter asked. "We were going to check on a bush and talk with Brett again."

"Peter, if yer worries about that bush and that woman are stronger than yer concern for yer own safety, ye can go to Doup Fell. It is not safe to travel these mountains in snow," Seumas warned. "I will never understand how my cousin did it. Snow has just begun to collect but the trail as far as the loch is well marked. It will be easy enough to travel if we can get ahead of this snowfall. I don't know that it will get much darker, so if we leave now we might be home in *Ceo Dhachaidh* by midmorning. Whit say ye?"

"I will get the faeries and we can go," Martin decided without further discussion. After collecting his passengers in their leather pouch, he put his hand on Seumas' shoulder and asked, "Where are yer faeries?"

"I dinna know. The gnats were not with us this morning." Again Seumas looked toward the trail to Benmost Bield before calling to the others, "Let's move. It is going to be a long night." Stepping forward he mumbled aloud to himself, "The gnats will have to hold up somewhere 'till the snow stops. We need to get home."

Sunset carried harsh, frigid air, possibly ushering the first snowfall of the season. Choking from the cold, the last intoxicating white blossoms fell from their bush as an old hag waddled up to it and looked down. Hags do not usually smile but this wretched creature sneered as she crouched and scooped up faeries sleeping off their stupor. With a bony hand the hag scooped up three, four, sometimes five unfortunate faeries at a time, dumping them into a leather bag hanging from her waist.

Two faeries on the far side of the bush gagged on the stench of the old hag. One stumbled under the bush, the other tried to fly to tree branches overhead. A long fingered hand, powered by reflexes faster than the ailing faerie, snatched the wavering creature from midair and popped the unsuspecting victim into the foul hag's mouth.

"WHAT?! No-o-o-o!" Marian cried out loud.

"Whit is that, my dear?" Angus asked calmly, his right eyebrow raised mischievously.

"She can't eat them . . . the faeries!"

"And why not?" Angus teased.

"Angus!" Lillian interceded. "READ!"

"Aye, but it will nae get any better for the wee creatures."

Lillian put her arm around her granddaughter, comforting her. When the boys began to giggle, Angus shifted in his chair and glared at them sternly and resumed reading.

Chuckling slightly, she . . . *the old hag* . . . stomped about looking for the last mystical creature who was hiding in the branches of the hag's bush. With increasing frustration she grabbed the bush, shaking it, gently at first then violently. The wee faerie, called Vancint, formed his body around a branch and held on with all his meager strength.

Stepping back from the bush the old hag looked toward the sky, then down toward the village of Doup Fell, and then back to the bush, "You might have escaped me this time, you disgusting little gosnarl, but I will get you!"

Bending over one last time the old hag collected a handful of blossoms, tossing them into her collecting bag which she closed with a firm yank. Waddling as quickly as she could, she returned to her hut where she slammed her treasure bag onto the table. Humming softly, she pulled a ladle of oatmeal from a pot hanging at the edge of her fire. Smiling once again, she stirred the oatmeal two, three, four times around with her spoon. "Spices for my breakfast," she cackled softly as she slapped the bag against the table one more time.

Opening the bag carefully, she dumped the entire contents into her oatmeal and watched each little treasure sink out of sight. "Sweet and spicy for my breakfast this day," she said out loud and cleaned the bowl, down to the very last morsel licking her lips between each and every spoonful.

Angus paused as all three grandchildren shifted uneasily in their seats.

"Did ye hear that?" Rachel asked.

"Whit?" Bryan replied, "The snow falling?"

"No. Listen!" Rachel stood motionless and listened with every bit of her being. "I have to go. I will return as soon as I can."

Before Bryan could object, ask a question, or even offer to go with her, Rachel pulled a cape from the wall, grabbed her stave from its resting place by the door, and disappeared into the snowfall. Filled with apprehension she ran up the road toward Benmost Bield without caution. The only sound in the forest was that of snowflakes landing upon one another, soft and indistinguishable. Controlling her breathing and her footsteps so she could hear through the quiet, Rachel continued to listen with a growing intensity. After running about two kilometers she stopped and stood motionless, as though she had been frozen in ice. Not breathing, not even letting her eyelids close, she listened. Turning her head slowly she searched the sea of white, looking for the one thing that was not supposed to be there.

"Seumas said he missed yeu gnats," Rachel smiled as she approached a branch sheltered by the limb just above it. Reaching out, she lifted Truact and Fobothom, protecting them with her cape.

"We cannot fly in a heavy snow like this," Truact explained. "We need to speak with Seumas."

"We have important news for Seumas," Fobothom repeated.

"Seumas has already left for *Ceo Dhachaidh*," Rachel explained. "I suggest ye come back to my hut and get warmed. Then we can figure out how to get ye to Seumas." Rachel tucked her arm inside her cape so the faeries would be protected from the cold elements. Walking briskly back to her hut, she listened to news about a discovery in Benmost Bield.

"Look who I found on the trail," Rachel called to her husband as she returned to the warmth of their hut. "They have important news for Seumas."

Bryan looked at her in total disbelief, then stepped outside their hut, roaring, "RUNNERS!" Within a minute two runners, three elders, two elderly women and a boy about twelve years old stood in front of Bryan. Clearing his throat, he looked to the two runners and announced, "We have two faeries that need to catch up with Seumas Gregor. He and his men are on the trail to *Ceo Dhachaidh*. Are ye ready to travel?"

"Faeries?" one of the runners questioned, filled with doubt.

"They have important information for Seumas and canna fly in the snow," Bryan stated without any emotion.

One runner looked to the other, then back to Bryan. "We can leave in three minutes."

Bryan nodded, "They will be ready."

The system of runners devised when preparing for the battle with Romans as a way to pass critical information between villages was still available. Because faeries often flew with runners, even saving their lives, these runners did not object to this uncommon duty.

Rachel placed some dry moss in the bottom of a leather bag and then pressed a forked twig into the bag to keep it open. Holding the pouch she helped Fobothom and Truact into their *creathall*[23] and handed them to a runner who slipped the pouch over his shoulder, covering it with his cape. Without a word both runners disappeared into the snowfall.

"Do ye want to know the news that is so important?" Rachel asked Bryan as they returned to the warmth of their hut.

Turning to his bride Bryan replied, "No. For if it is indeed important I would be bound by my conscience to act on it. Right now I am exhausted and wish only to rest for an hour or two."

Rachel wrapped her arms around her young husband. Holding him close, she whispered into his ear, "It is important, but it can wait an hour or two."

Shortly after leaving Blyth Brier Seumas realized the snow was blowing to their backs, becoming less intense with each hilltop they passed. "Martin, should we get home before the snow arrives?" Seumas smiled.

Martin nodded and the two men began to run. After about two hundred strides they dropped to a brisk walk, then back to their run after another hundred strides. Alternating their pace and breathing deeply they covered a great distance quickly. Robert and Peter tried to stop and catch their wind whenever the much older men slowed, only to watch their leaders disappear in snowfall ahead of them. Passing through a clearing about two-thirds the distance home Seumas stopped and laughed.

"Whit brings such a hearty laugh?" Martin asked looking behind them for the two younger men.

"Look up, we have outrun the snowfall."

---

[23]*creathall* - CRE~hal - a cradle, in this case a protected cradle

Overhead, stars filled a crystal clear sky. Around them, trees were visible only as skeletal shadows, surrounded by autumn leaves covering the ground. Behind them the edge of snow clouds appeared as a shadow, dividing two worlds.

Martin loosed the bag tied under his cape, releasing three faeries, "I think ye can fly now without harm." Immediately Frenzy, Depost, and Enstard soared to the treetops and floated gently back to the men they were accompanying. "Maybe we should let the boys rest," Martin laughed as Peter and Robert wearily joined the two men.

"No, my arms ache to wrap around Ingrid," Seumas declared. "But we can walk the last bit, enjoy the beauty of the forest at night."

Robert took a deep breath to ease his panting then raised his arm toward home. Martin and Seumas chuckled as they allowed the younger men to proceed ahead of them.

Seumas heaved a huge sigh of relief when he saw tendrils of smoke rising toward the heavens. Increasing his stride to reach home and his wife, he stopped abruptly when he heard his name echo from behind him.

"Seumas! SEUMAS GREGOR!"

Turning quickly Seumas assumed a defensive stance, his sword drawn and his cape dropped to the ground. "Aye," he replied.

"Bryan of Blyth Brier sent us with an urgent delivery," one of the runners reported as he released a bag from his belt, handing it to Seumas.

Seumas relaxed his posture, handing his sword to Martin who relaxed his battle stance as well. Carefully opening the bag, Seumas peered in. Fobothom and Truact shot out of the bag narrowly missing Seumas' right eye. "It is the gnats!" Seumas laughed loudly. "I was afraid I was going to have to return to Benmost Bield to find the two of ye."

"They carry news of great importance," the second runner announced.

"So, whit news do ye have to report?" Seumas asked, placing his hands on his hips and thrusting his chest out with great authority.

"Benmost Bield has been attacked," Fobothom reported.

"No, we were just there and there was no attack," Seumas challenged.

"Not the village, the faerie cavie," Truact corrected. "There is a large cavie outside the village and not a single soul in its safety. A message on the wall said a great evil had entered the village and it was no longer safe for them. Only a loyal friend known as 'Muestor' knows where they now rest."

"When we found the cavie, we were attacked by a beast of the forest such as I have never seen," Fobothom added frantically.

"We saw no evil in the village," Seumas challenged.

"Whit of that woman ye told us about?" Peter asked.

"Graclyn? Many of the wives may consider her an evil but I know of no way she could be a threat to the faeries," Seumas pondered. "We are close to home; ye men rest for a day and then return to Blyth Brier." Seumas then held his position while everyone journeyed ahead of him except the five faeries who lingered above his head. "Faeries, we will talk again after I rest and my mind is more clear." Speaking these words, Seumas felt a massive weight crawl across his shoulders.

〜〜〜〜〜〜〜〜〜〜〜〜〜〜〜〜〜〜

After a full night's rest in Ingrid's arms, Seumas joined men in the fields. Snow had changed to a gentle rain before reaching *Ceo Dhachaidh*, leaving the fields soft and a bit muddy as it passed by. Stomping around the soft ground, Seumas reluctantly agreed with other men of *Ceo Dhachaidh*, "Alright, I canna see anything more to pull from this dirt. Hosting the villages depleted our stores and interfered with our planting. We will have to portion out what we have. Nobody will be gettin' fat this winter." Turning back toward the village, Seumas began to swat at a pest near his left ear.

"SEUMAS!" a small voice yelled. Truact barely escaped Seumas' hand sweeping above his head.

"I told you he would strike you if you did not speak first," Fobothom laughed.

"Whit do ye gnats want of me today?" Seumas scolded.

"We need to talk about our cavie in the high mountains," Truact explained.

"High mountains?" Seumas puzzled. "Oh, Benmost Bield, where ye got lost . . . the second time. Whit do we need to talk about?"

"That village is not safe! We need to go back!" Fobothom explained impatiently.

"This village here, my home, does not have enough food to get through the coming winter and yeu want me to go search for some beast in the village farthest up in the mountains?" Seumas took a deep breath.

"An entire faerie cavie has disappeared," Truact exclaimed, flaring up as he addressed Seumas. "Your people could be next, if they are not gone already!"

Seumas looked at the two faeries; as their anger grew they took on a bright purple hue and their wings flashed wildly, giving them an appearance of much larger and more fierce beings. Casting his eyes to the ground Seumas pondered the problems before him, then lifting his head called to the villagers, "ELDERS! Elders we need a conference!"

Minutes later elders of *Ceo Dhachaidh* gathered around the stone chairs at the top of the hill. Ingrid and several other villagers came to listen as well.

Taking a deep breath Seumas addressed those gathered. "On our journey to the high country, our faerie escorts discovered a hag in one of the villages . . ."

"Two villages!" Fobothom interrupted.

"Excuse me, TWO! Mister Fobothom says . . . two of our communities have hags. They say the hags are in Benmost Bield and . . . where is the second?"

"With Rachel and Bryan," Fobothom replied.

"With Rachel and Bryan?" Seumas questioned. "Oh, in Blyth Brier, he says. None of us larger men saw any hags but the faeries say they are there. Further, in Benmost Bield an entire cavie of faeries has gone missing and a friend we know just by name is the only one who knows thair current whereabouts. At home we have no hags nor do we have enough food to get us through the winter. The problems are now before ye, do any of ye have something to offer?"

"If we keep chasing hags we will surely starve," Martin chuckled.

"Why is it yeu men did not see these hags? Are they not foul enough that thair smell announces thair presence?" an elder asked.

"The one hag I have seen, on this hillside, was indeed a foul creature," Seumas assured the group. "We did meet several women who recently came to other villages but not one of them was foul. In fact they were actually quite pleasing to the eye." Seumas stopped and thought for a moment. Turning to Ingrid he cast his gaze toward several of the women standing in the gathering.

"Whit are ye thinking, Seumas?" Ingrid asked, recognizing the pondering in his face.

"Both of the women that I met, as I left thair huts, I looked back at them. In the firelight thair eyes were dark. Dark like a night without stars, as though there was nothing behind them at all," Seumas thought out loud. "It could have been the way the fire reflected on thair faces, but the both of them had a great emptiness behind thair eyes."

"Seumas, we cannot risk going back to Benmost Bield before the end of the snows. We nearly got lost coming home this trip; ye would be a fool to go back now," Martin offered.

"Besides," another elder laughed, "every village has trained and experienced warriors. Whit is one woman, or hag, going to do against a group of Hieland warriors?"

Pausing to consider what had been offered, Seumas looked to Fobothom and Truact. Shrugging both shoulders to relieve a growing strain the big man replied, "I am sorry my friends, we will have to wait until the change in season to investigate yer missing cavie. Ye said they have a protector and the snows will hide them as well. As soon as the weather turns and trees begin to bud, we will go to Benmost Bield and search for the faeries."

═══════════

Angus paused and looked at the attentive faces of his grandchildren, then to Lillian. "Are we good to continue or should we take a bit of a break?"

"I have some cake that needs to be eaten," Lillian offered.

"Aye, that sounds delightful," Angus agreed as he laid the silk ribbon marking their place in the book. Standing he stretched and looked to the children who had barely moved, "Well, whit are ye waiting for? The cake will nae come to yeu!"

All three scrambled to the kitchen followed by Lillian and Angus with their arms wrapped around one another. She reached up and kissed him on the cheek.

"Whit was that for?" Angus asked, smiling from ear to ear.

Lillian lifted her eyebrows, replying "Just because." Hearing dishes knocking together, she hurried into the kitchen.

"Are we all settled now?" Angus asked, opening the book in his lap. Seeing his audience settling before him once again, he offered, "Thank ye for my tea, dear." With a wink, he resumed his reading.

Faeries gathered deep within the heart of a great oak tree at the edge of the forest near *Ceo Dhachaidh.*

"The bush was tall and covered with blooms from the ground to its peak," Fobothom repeated. "It looked like a huge ball of snow in the middle of a lush green field."

"No, the bush was small, barely larger than a fawn on its first run with its mother," Truact argued. "It was near a perfect ball in shape, never touching the ground but it was covered with small white blossoms. The field was not green but brown like leaves of the forest."

"Are you certain the two of you saw the same bush?" an elder faerie asked.

"Fobothom and the others were drunk on the nectar of the bush but his head cleared when I pulled him above the trees," Truact replied.

Depost, Frenzy, and Enstard looked at each other with confusion. Not one of them remembered being drunk at a bush as Truact described, in a clearing in the middle of the forest.

All the elder faeries who had gathered to hear the report of the Highlander's journey began to talk at once. "Quiet," Comleidh Resbith called to the gathering. "Do you think the five of you might find this bush and bring us a twig with leaves and blossom?"

"WE WILL DO IT!" Truact and Fobothom exclaimed together and they left, racing from their protective oak and through bare branches of surrounding trees until they reached the open sky. Frenzy and Depost followed close behind them. Enstard sat at the gathering and watched the other four leave on their quest. Free of any obstruction four mighty faerie warriors soared toward the bush out in the forest.

Vrenessbith had not been at the gathering of faeries for she had found another distraction more enticing to her curiosity. Sitting on a branch of an old tree, far removed from both village and cavie, she watched a martryn building a new nest. The weasel-like creature had been nesting in the fork of a tree where it had split in recent bad weather. Determined to find a new home, the martryn scurried up and down each branch until he found a hole in the trunk just below where his old nest had been hidden. Powerful claws dug at the tree, enlarging a hole left by another creature and then carving out the heart of the tree. His long slender body curled up and down, in and out of the hole as he watched for hawks and other predators who might enjoy him for dinner. Vrenessbith studied his movements, seeking to understand the reason for each bit of force. Her study of the animal gave way when she saw four bold faeries fly over her with incredible speed. Recognizing her friends, Vrenessbith could not resist the temptation and immediately gave chase.

Truact and Fobothom arrived at the clearing first and called to Depost and Frenzy to stop. In the clearing below, hags gathered around a bush to one side of the clearing. A light dusting of snow had already begun to disappear. Four anxious faeries landed on a tree branch and watched. They were to investigate the bush but were not going to challenge the hags.

Thirteen hags formed a circle around the bush. Depost became excited when he recognized the hag from Doup Fell. One by one, each hag called out and removed a talisman from around her neck. Three hags had revealed their talismans when Vrenessbith raced past the hidden faeries, racing toward the bush in pursuit of her friends. Fobothom shot off his branch, grabbing Vrenessbith before shooting straight into the heavens as the fourth hag called out and began to reveal her talisman.

With her hands on a thin leather cord, the old hag stopped, looked toward the trees, then toward the full moon coming over the clearing. Sniffing the still air, she cocked her head to one side and listened. It seemed an eternity to Fobothom as he held Vrenessbith tightly, trying to vanish in bright moonlight. Smelling nothing, hearing nothing, the hag finally continued removing her talisman. Still holding Vrenessbith, Fobothom eased through bare tree limbs, staying in shadows as they worked their way to other faeries who breathed a sigh of relief on their return.

After the last hag had removed her talisman she called out, "The night of enduring darkness has begun. Hang your tributes and bring forth the source of life." Immediately each of the hags hung her talisman on the bush and one brought forth a large rock. Chanting filled the air and the hag placed her rock under the bush. All at once the hags began to dance around their bush. Chanting grew louder and more intense. With each circling of the bush the dancing became more animated and dramatic. Thirteen times the hags circled the bush, then the ground rumbled and the night sky roared in response. Suddenly the rock placed beneath the bush exploded, sending pieces in every direction. In its place was an infant. Mottled in coloring and twisted in features the infant resembled a hag, in miniature. The hag closest to the infant bent over to pick it up but as she did the ground once more shook violently and again the sky roared in reply. A large chunk of the rock exploded, leaving only shards and another infant, somewhat more normal in appearance.

The old hag that was about to pick up the first infant lifted the second, tossing it toward the woods, then retrieved the first. Cradling it in her arms she took her talisman from the bush and touched it to the infant's head. Standing proudly she handed the infant to the hag on her left who also retrieved her talisman and touched it to the infant's chest. One by one every hag took the infant, retrieved her talisman from the bush and touched it to the infant on the foot, hand, arm, leg, somewhere that had not yet been touched by another talisman. The last hag to hold the infant wrapped it in her shawl and left, followed by the others. One hag waddled over to the infant tossed aside and wrapped a cloth around it as she left the clearing, taking the infant with her.

"I tell ye we will have to go over the hill to search for game," Seumas explained for the third time. "We have taken too much from this region. It will take two years, probably more, to recover to the point where it will feed us again. If we do not hunt another region, we will starve this winter and through the coming years!"

"I will go with ye," Eric volunteered.

"If ye will not take yer pipes, I will go as well," another man laughed. "Ye might be able to charm the animals of *Ceo Dhachaidh*, but I dinna think animals of the wild would receive ye so well."

Eric smiled at the jest and shook the man's hand vigorously.

"I will go," another man volunteered.

"Count me," Martin joined.

After a moment of silence Seumas called, "Are there no others who wish to prove thair manhood in the cold?"

"I will wait for the deer run to prove my manhood," a young man replied with a chuckle.

"Aye, well if we dinna eat this winter, ye won't be runnin' anywhere when the trees come to bud," Martin replied.

"Alright, my brother and I will join ye," the young man conceded grudgingly, nudging his brother into agreement as well.

"We meet here at the lodge when the sun first lights the sky tomorrow," Seumas announced. "This is NOT a deer run so bring yer weapons and rope if ye have any; we may set traps."

The gathering of men broke quickly. Stomping across the village toward his hut, Seumas mumbled to himself about needing to find food where there was none. Not enough men volunteered for the hunt, and how was he to feed a village on a few bins of grain? When he opened the door to his hut he took a deep breath and turning his head bellowed, "ERIC, would ye like to have yer *bean an taighe*[24] to warm yer bed?"

Eric turned in mid-step, hurrying to Seumas' hut. Sarah and Chris were visiting with Ingrid and Leigh. Seven-year-old Leigh enjoyed caring for Chris and reluctantly gave the infant back to his mother.

"Sunrise," Seumas grunted as he watched the young family return to their own hut nestled into the Gauls' community.

Early the next morning, before first rays of light showed on the horizon, four of the volunteers waited in the cold outside the lodge, stomping their feet and flapping their arms for warmth. "I said first light," Seumas grumbled as he and Martin arrived. Chewing on a piece of dried meat, Seumas looked at the waiting men. Satisfied that all volunteers had arrived, he turned into the village. Proceeding past Gauls' huts, the hunters took a little-used trail leading out the back of the community.

No one talked as they climbed hills and passed through glens for almost two hours. The trail had long since disappeared before Seumas stopped at the edge of a glen sparsely populated with laurel bushes. "Eric, yeu and Thomas scout around to the right. Matthew, ye have not been with us before, yeu and Mark go to the left. Watch the ground for signs of deer or other animals. We will gather again on the far side."

Stopping frequently to look at evidence of a large population of deer, hare, and fox, Martin commented, "I hope ye know where we are; this glen could feed us all winter."

"Aye, but do ye notice that none of the piles is fresh? Everythin' is at least a day or two old." Seumas replied with concern.

Martin and Seumas joined Matthew and Mark on the far side of the glen. "We saw a lot of signs but no game," Mark reported.

"Same," Martin agreed.

Suddenly a whirring sound passed by the men, followed by a stumbling in the bush. Eric and Thomas ran past them, calling as they passed, "Would ye men care to help us?" A medium sized male deer lay on the ground about five meters behind the waiting men, twitching from the sting of nettles and the crash of a rock into the side of his head as he fell. Eric drew his dirk and completed the job his nettle rope, now loaded with a rock on each end for weight, had started.

"Ye have gotten pretty good with that rope," Martin complimented.

"Yes, but he could have easily hit one of us," Seumas complained.

---

[24] *bean an taighe* - ben an TIYA - *goodwife, pronounced ben an ta-ee*

Eric said nothing but began to truss the deer for travel. As he and Matthew finished tying its legs and prepared to slip a stave between them a young doe sprang from a bush barely seven meters away. Thomas and Martin were quick with their staves, hurling them as spears with incredible accuracy. The doe toppled in defeat.

While Martin and Thomas prepared the second deer for travel, Seumas turned to the others. "Eric, Matthew, yeu two circle to the right around this thicket. Mark and I will go left. Try to not kill one another."

Staves and ropes ready, the four men crept around the thicket. A fine snow began to fall around them; only Martin and Thomas stopped to take notice of it. Each of the other four men was deeply involved in studying the bushes, sparse undergrowth, and ground, looking for signs of deer travel - hoof prints, broken twigs, anything to guide them to another meal. Slowly and cautiously they stepped and studied. When the men had nearly come back together all stopped and stared. Two nests of deer were between them, a doe and yearling fawn standing in each nest. Throwing spears would be dangerous because of the possibility of hitting one of the men if they missed the deer. Seumas picked up a large rock and prepared to toss it between the two nests when they heard a loud grunt. Slowly turning only their heads the four men saw the guardian of this thicket. A hart, carrying a rack of at least fourteen points. The powerful animal stood motionless but his eyes, level with Seumas' eyes, flitted back and forth from one group of men to the other. His neck was covered in a full mane and his body showed scars from numerous battles. Fearing attack, Seumas threw the rock, missing the hart but drawing his charge.

As quickly as Seumas heaved the rock the large deer responded, leaping toward the nervous man. Seumas tried to pull his broadsword but the leather line which releases the scabbard got snagged, slowing retrieval. Mark stepped back drawing his dirk and inserting it squarely below the hart's shoulder as it lunged into Seumas. Seumas brought his sword over his head as quickly as he could but the hart's antler gored his shoulder. Seumas and hart fell together.

Three doe sprang from the thicket with two yearlings between them. Eric and Matthew heaved spears at them but only Matthew's hit its mark.

Seumas screamed in agony as the large hart fell on him. Martin ran to his aid but could not resist laughing, "There are easier ways to subdue a deer." Seumas was not amused and was barely cooperative as three men removed the deer without inflicting further injury to Seumas' shoulder. Martin tended to the injury as others trussed the deer, making preparations to return home.

Matthew and Thomas cut down a small tree to carry the hart but the other deer were small enough to carry on the warriors' staves. With the deer hoisted to their shoulders the men looked for their path home only to find the glen covered in white. After crossing the glen Martin looked for their tracks from earlier that day. The blanket of white was just enough to cover their entrance into the glen. Looking into the forest each of the six men had a slightly different direction in mind for their return home. Seumas' authority won and they proceeded through the forest. During one of their frequent rest stops Thomas found a separation in the bushes and slightly worn traces of the trail they had used earlier, about six meters to the east of their current course. Both paths were now covered by snow.

Six weary hunters emerged from the forest above the Gauls' huts to a heroes' welcome late that afternoon. Men came from all over to assume the load for the last few steps to the dressing yard. Free of their burden, Martin delivered Seumas to Ingrid, displaying his bloodied shoulder. After thanking their friend, Ingrid took her husband into their hut to tend to his injury. Peter volunteered to manage dressing the game; the remaining hunters wished him well and made their way to their own huts. Almost three inches of snow now covered the ground.

A Faerie cavie is a wonderful place, normally located deep below the leaves and rocks where men walk. Intricate entrances are often hidden within naturally occurring and obscure rock formations or at the base of an old tree. Normal forces of nature provide warmth in the cold winter and cooling in the hot summer. Faeries do not like cold weather. A heavy snowfall makes it impossible for them to fly and their small bodies do not produce enough heat to keep them warm. When the weather turns very cold the faerie population settles into their comfortable, life-sustaining cavie until warmer weather returns.

Outside the faerie cavie near *Ceo Dhachaidh* fine snow continued to fall for three days, accumulating over fourteen inches of frigid white blanket. Seumas called villagers into the lodge for common warmth and sharing their meager food supply. Fewer than half of the village residents heeded Seumas' call. Still, the lodge was crowded with bodies sitting or lying wherever room permitted. Smoke from the central fire rose through a small hole in the roof. The clay and straw building was dark with smells of unwashed men, women, and children mixing with day-old roasting meat creating a near toxic environment, but it was warm and dry. By the end of the third day many of the men were getting on one another's nerves and small fights broke out around the lodge. Seumas settled most of the disagreements by throwing both offenders out into the snow. While tossing Sean and one of his friends out, he was met by a surprise at the door.

As Seumas pulled the door open, a young woman carrying a bundle of rags fell into the lodge. Her face and exposed skin were bluish in colour and her eyes were blank. Several of the women grabbed the woman and carried her to the fire, but she would not relinquish her bundle. Warmed by the fire the young woman's skin lost its bluish color and her cheeks approached a rosy hue. Her arms began to relax and one of the women took the bundle, finding the still body of a newborn infant girl. Tending to the woman's needs, a midwife confirmed that she appeared to have recently been through childbirth.

Women asked questions softly while they cleaned the young woman and began feeding her. She offered no answers but after she was warmed, cleaned, and groomed, many of the men noticed how beautiful she was. Slender of build with long raven hair and clear of complexion, her inviting lips rested below a diminutive nose which made her amber eyes appear much larger than they actually were.

"It is getting late, who will care for her tonight?" Seumas asked, standing over the women.

"I will," Sean replied. "I will keep her very warm in my bed."

"Will somebody take him back to his hut and lock him inside?" Seumas requested, only partially in jest.

"We will care for her," Ingrid volunteered.

"Whit?" Seumas erupted. "Ye are going to bring this woman into our hut?"

"No," Ingrid replied softly. "We, the women of *Ceo Dhachaidh* will care for her. Here, in the lodge. Ye provide us enough wood and we will do the rest."

Seumas stood very still and looked down on the woman, then into the eyes of Ingrid. "All right. Men, bring in some wood for the ladies and return to yer own empty and cold huts."

When there was a substantial pile of wood easily accessible to the women, Seumas and Martin ran the men out of the lodge. Outside, knee-deep snow covered everything in sight; even at midnight the land shone with an uneasy iridescence. Sounds of livestock in a nearby *byre* slipped across the snow without echo, disappearing down the hillside.

Seumas stopped to pick up some wood that had been dropped outside. Dumping the logs on the pile inside the lodge he turned his head toward the woman. Catching her eyes, he saw a defiant hostile spirit, as though reflecting the entire world engulfed in flame. Remembering the black emptiness in the eyes of women in the other villages, Seumas left the lodge. Shaking the chill from his neck, the leader of *Ceo Dhachaidh* pushed his way through the snow to his own hut.

"Have ye women fixed any bread this morning?" Martin asked politely as he entered the lodge in search of warmth and food.

"NO!" Seumas bellowed in reply. "They have cared for one another but have done nothing for the village. Supper last night was cut short and now my stomach is growling to be filled." The huge man glared at the woman who arrived the previous night, his eyes laying all blame for his hunger on her.

Defiantly the woman stood and facing Seumas asked, "What stores do you have?"

"Over here," one of the village women replied. "We have some turnips, a few cabbages, but they are not very good. Over here are sacks of a few different grains and some meal."

"Did I have a bag and a bundle when you found me?" the woman asked as she looked around.

"Ye had a bundle," Ingrid replied. "And yeu found us. Whit is yer name?"

"I may have dropped my bag outside when I found your lodge. My name is Raven. Where is my bundle?"

"Several of us buried the child last night," Martin replied. "I felt we needed to protect her from the wolves and other beasts. She got as good a right as we can give in this weather."

"Thank you," Raven sighed, a tear rolling down her cheek. "She was without life when she was born but I could not leave her to the wolves. I feared I had lost her before I made it here."

"Raven. Like her hair. I like that," Sean offered, acting as close to a gentleman as he could.

"Sir, would you see if my bag can be found? Possibly outside between the forest and the door" Raven wiped the tear from her cheek and smiled at Sean, who melted into her request rushing out into the snow to look for her bag.

Without waiting, Raven grabbed a large pot and began mixing the grains and some meal. She enlisted the help of two men to carry the pot and place it over the fire. She then had them add a generous amount of water.

"Is this yer bag?" Sean asked as he hoisted a large cloth bag stuffed to capacity through the door.

"Yes, thank you, sir." Raven immediately began sifting through the bag retrieving a much smaller bag. Standing over the pot of grains she sprinkled a generous amount of something from the smaller bag. "It won't be long before your stomachs are satisfied."

Seumas looked at Raven and asked very bluntly, "Why were ye out in the snow if ye have just given birth?"

"My husband and I were on the way to my sister's home beyond the great mountains. He was killed when we were attacked and I tried to continue on my own. Fate brought me to your lodge."

"Would yer sister's name be Graclyn?" Seumas challenged, not sure he accepted her story.

"No," Raven replied with a quizzical expression. "Her name is Donella."

Seumas looked into Raven's amber eyes, trying to discern whether or not to trust her. She was a beautiful woman with a charming smile, yet a chill on the back of his neck told him to be wary. "Ye can't travel before the snow melts. Is there anyone here who can take Raven in?"

"I will," Sean volunteered immediately.

"Ye are no match for her, ye overgrown toad," Regina laughed. "Raven, ye can stay with me as long as ye feel the need."

Later that day the snow stopped and skies glistened crystal blue. Regina seized the opportunity to take Raven to her hut and began getting her settled. Several faeries from the local cavie took the opportunity to stretch their wings as well. Flying past the two ladies trudging through the snow, faeries were repulsed by foul air surrounding the women and returned to their forest.

***

Winter had begun that year in a very odd and unpredictable fashion. Two early snowfalls gave way to clear weather and unseasonably warm temperatures. Highlanders became wary of warm temperatures because they often turned frigid overnight bringing snows, which in turn quickly melted. Three months of strange weather left the ground soggy and difficult to traverse. Trails used for hunting were slippery and dangerous.

Covered with mud to his knees, Sean paid another of his frequent visits to Raven and Regina. "Good mornin', lassies. Is yer meat locker filled? Could ye do with a small pig or side of deer?"

"Mister Scorsby, it is closer to sunset than sunrise and our meat is fine, thank ye," Regina chastised Sean sternly.

"Do you not remember bringing us a side of deer just last week?" Raven smiled. "Perhaps you should not drink so much. With no one about to see to your needs you might find yourself in one of our unexpected snowbanks."

"I drink only to keep warm *bean-usual*.[25] If I had the warmth of a *bean an taighe* I know I would have no need of the mead."

Raven looked at Sean with a stern eye and lifted his hands in hers. Rolling them over she examined every part of them from the fingernails to the wrists. "You do not work, Mister Scorsby. How would you care for a wife?"

"By beating her, no doubt," Regina scoffed.

"My wife and child were killed by the Romans before we came to this forsaken land. I cared for her well enough!"

"Where were you when your family was killed?" Raven asked in a soothing voice.

"Standing at a peace gathering. Waiting to be attacked from our rear."

"Are you a farmer or a warrior?" Raven coaxed gently.

"I once farmed the land, until it oozed with the blood of our families. Then I became a warrior and a warrior I will die. This land is rocky and yields little but there will always be someone who wants to take it from ye."

"It would yield more if ye put yer back into it," Regina snipped.

Raven stroked Sean's shoulder and looked into his eyes. "I am sleeping on a mat in Regina's hut. She has two children and it is often crowded, especially when the night is cold. What can you offer me?"

"Oh, *bean-usual*, my hut is a hovel, but could be set right. My cot has fallen but could be repaired. Do ye care if chickens sleep nearby?"

---

[25] *bean-usual* - ben USAL - *Gaelic phrase for gentle-woman, pronounced ben-usal*

"I prefer the warmth of a strong man," Raven laughed out loud. "I will consider bedding in your hut for the duration of my stay in this village if you clean it to my satisfaction and repair the cot."

"Raven, ye are a fool," Regina scolded.

"Perhaps," Raven chuckled as Sean ran back to his hut, "but cleaning his hut will keep him out of our way for a time."

Sean worked for four days without bothering another person in *Ceo Dhachaidh*. Two days had been spent removing debris from his hut and then clearing the debris from outside his hut when Seumas and Martin complained. He spent the next day and a half building a cot large enough and strong enough to hold himself and one other. Several men of the village blocked his progress when he burned the contents of his sleeping sheaf and tried to get fresh straw from the community barn.

"Ye did nothing to bring this straw in and ye will not have one stem of it," they protested.

Sean said nothing but tried to push past the men to the pile of straw stored for the animals. Three men stopped the large man from his task and a fourth helped to lift and carry him out of the barn, where he was deposited in the center of the village.

"What seems to be the problem, Mister Scorsby?" Raven asked. She was holding a small basket of vegetables which she had just acquired from the larder in the lodge.

Sean quickly stood, then looking down at Raven replied, "I have cleaned my hut and made it as presentable to a *bean* such as yerself. A place ye might be comfortable in. And I have had only one draw of mead, even though my brothers offered me more. I have made the cot new and pulled the ropes tight enough that I do not touch the ground but the men will not let me have any straw so the ropes don't rub my back."

"Did you help to bring in the straw?" Raven asked, feigning innocence.

"No." Sean's reply was short but his breath afterward was long.

Raven smiled and took Sean's arm. Turning toward his hut she offered, "Let's see what you have that might soften those tight ropes."

After examining Sean's hut, Raven stepped outside. The sun approached the treetops as she called to Regina's son, "Michael, would you please fetch my bag from your mother's hut. I need it to prepare a proper supper."

That night it snowed unexpectedly, again. Neither Raven nor Sean were seen until snow began to melt, once again making the ground soft and soggy. But some say the sounds and voices coming across the snow were vile and warlike. Sean left the hut as soon as he could open the door, joining his friends for several tankards of mead. When he returned home, he complained of the foul odor that had permeated his hut. Raven tossed him out into the night where he could breathe "fresh air."

Women of the village kept a close eye on Raven, watching for bruises and still seeking to discover her purpose. When a small bruise appeared next to her eye, Raven tried to dismiss it, "Truly it is nothing. I fell against the table while picking up a bag of spices I had dropped." Sympathy abounded and Sean was scorned. With the sympathy, Raven noticed that suspicions about her faded. She made sure that a bruise appeared on her face or arm every week or so.

"They sound like the Andersons," Marian commented.

"Who are the Andersons?" Lillian asked, wiping her granddaughter's hair from her face.

"They live two doors down at home, but you can hear them fighting all over," Liam answered.

"Aye, well not everyone has a quiet marriage but who knows . . ." Angus sighed, apparently thinking of someone he knew. "We hae been going for quite a spell. How about we rest for the night and go for a walk in the starlight?"

Everyone stretched without objection. Angus casually led Lillian from the patio, through their garden and around to a hillside beside their home, the children stumbling behind.

"It has been a good day," Angus sighed looking across the treetops to the evening sky beyond. Lillian squeezed his hand.

Everyone busied themselves with different projects over the next three days. Lillian caught up on her washing and made a list for market day. Marian posted a letter to her parents. Alex and Liam played football (soccer) together and then went in chase of a young deer.

Returning from their "deer run" all hot and sweaty, Alex stumbled into Angus' study interrupting his grandfather's correspondence.

"Sure was a hot deer run!" Alex exclaimed, falling to the floor.

Smiling with pride and amusement, Angus asked, "Did ye catch it?"

"No - I never knew deer could run so fast!"

"We didn't stand a chance," Liam added as he entered with a glass of water. "That young deer was gone before we got started, but we ran in chase anyway. I sure wish you had a swimming pool!"

"A swimming pool?" Angus chortled. "We dinna need a pool, we have a loch."

Moments later all three men had swim trunks on and towels in hand. "Lillian, would yeu and Marian care for a dip in the loch?" Angus called into the kitchen.

"Nae, we women-folk are going to market," Lillian replied. Giving Angus a peck she added, "Be sure ta count yer toes."

Walking toward the loch, young Alex asked, "What did seanmhair mean 'count our toes'?"

"Oh, did ye not know? We have hungry gar in our loch. Great long eel-like fish with teeth like dinosaurs an' they love little boy toes," Angus teased.

Alex stopped in his tracks.

"Come on Alex," Liam prodded. "Seanair is just teasing."

"Aye, yer brother is half-right. We hae no seen gar in our cove in, oh, two or three years. 'Course, I hae not been swimming in the loch in longer than that, either."

After an hour of swimming during which Angus literally swam circles around both of his grandsons, they returned home. Reaching the top of the hill, near the pile of stones, Alex commented, "You swim pretty good for an old man who hasn't been swimming in years!"

"Oh I dinna say I hae not been swimming, just not in the loch. I swim fifty laps every week in the pool at the Y in town. I can wake ye if ye a mind to go with me next time," Angus replied with a laugh.

Alex and Liam looked at each other in total disbelief.

After a spirited dinner everyone settled into Angus' study for more reading from the book.

As night awakens into day and darkness increases then fades into soft light of dawn, so the winter wanes and early warmth of spring begins an annual transformation of the Highlands. Standing outside his hut, Seumas stretched out his arms and soaked in every bit of sunshine his old Celtic body could possibly absorb. He had just passed forty years of age and was one of the older men in the village. Not satisfied that he was getting what he needed he removed his shirt, thrusting his bare chest into the afternoon sun. It was warm. They had survived the winter, a winter of many snowfalls, not enough food, and a restless village pulling recovery out of hardship by pure force of will.

"Well, it doesn't look like ye lost too much weight over the winter," Ingrid laughed at her husband.

"Athair, ye look funny!" Leigh laughed at her father.

"Whit did ye call me?" Seumas turned quickly looking at his daughter with concern.

"Athair," Leigh repeated, shaking slightly from her father's expression. "It is whit the Gaelic children call thair fathers."

"ATHAIR," Seumas repeated. "I like that. Leigh, ye can call me 'athair' anytime." He reached out and lifted his daughter into his arms, giving her a huge hug.

"Seumas!" a faerie called to the big man. "It is time to search for the cavie. You gave us your word, as soon as the trees begin to bud."

"SEUMAS!" several younger men called in unison.

"DEER RUN!" one voice rang loudly.

"The snow is melting and it is a tradition to have a deer run as soon as the snow melts," Martin reminded him. "And we canna count yer snow white belly as a delay for the deer run."

Seumas sneered at Martin and turned to the assembled men. "We will have the deer run at next sunrise, so no baths for any of ye and do not get too close to yer wives or their sweet smells might rub onto ye and warn the deer we are coming. The female deer will be carrying and we need the young to replenish our forest. This will be an antlered run only; I will remind ye tomorrow. Before ye go to ready yerself for the run, I need five volunteers to join me on a journey to Benmost Bield to search for a lost faerie cavie. We will leave on the second sunrise and be gone nigh about six, maybe eight days. Those who wish to help our little brothers stay. The rest of ye smelly warts leave me in peace."

Martin, Peter and David stood fast after the others left. Seumas was about to address the meager group when he heard another voice a few feet away.

"Eric, what is this deer run?" Sarah asked softly.

"A tradition of *Ceo Dhachaidh*," Eric explained. "We hunt deer without weapons. When a deer is found, we give chase and must kill it without use of blade or any weapon except our hands." Sarah scrunched up her face. Eric continued "It sounds fierce but it gives the men a chance to stretch out and release energy not used during the cold winter. For the deer it is frightening but they have turned on the men, goring them with their antlers. Deer have the advantage in this hunt, so it is quite fair. Last year I had my first kill on the deer run and the deer presented me with its stone; the stone I wear about my neck."

"Eric, will ye be joining us on the journey to Benmost Bield?" Seumas called.

Eric thought for a moment and then looked into Sarah's eyes. "I need to help as I can," he confessed softly. When her eyes relaxed, he called out, "YES! I believe I will." He then kissed Sarah gently and joined the men and disgruntled faeries still gathered outside Seumas' hut.

Ceo Dhachaidh buzzed all afternoon and evening with talk of the coming deer run. Eric filled the evening with lilting melodies from his great pipes, inspiring all to reach out for tomorrow, to become more in the days ahead. Younger men filled with courage from the music boasted of how they would run over any young buck they saw. Older men and those of more experience listened quietly, smiling in their wisdom. All embraced the music of the pipes and peace of their hillside. Most of the runners retired before the sky was decorated with stars, but young braggarts continued their talks, bolstered with mead and bragging well into the night.

Eight men gathered at the lodge before any light shone on the horizon. Seumas looked around and spoke softly to the gathering, "Remember, do not run any deer unless ye can see antlers on their head. Ye should carry a dirk for protection but no blade may be drawn against any deer this day. Let's go."

As the men marched out of the north end of the village, Eric joined them, dressed in deerskin kilt and vest with leather leggings and arm wraps. "I see ye learned yer lesson last year," Martin laughed, welcoming Eric to the group.

"Aye," Eric chuckled. "Thorns will not pull this kilt from my waist and the wraps will stop them from tearing my skin as well. It is a shame Rachel is not with us, we made a good team last year."

Seumas set a fast pace for he wanted to reach the feeding grounds before sunlight bathed the hillsides and the animals bed down for the day. When they approached that glen where deer had been found at the beginning of winter, Matthew and Thomas grew uneasy. They thought only of the large hart who had defended his herd. Each of the young men placed a hand on the hilt of his dirk to be sure they were secure and available, but knowing weapons were not to be drawn against deer. Seumas continued through the glen to the top of the next hill where he squatted down and waited for light to reveal the glen below.

Eager men watched as darkness slowly evaporated. Some looked for shadows moving amongst the bushes; some looked for trails a deer might run to escape; some just looked. Eric was the first to launch into the bushes, running silently, trusting his leather clothing to protect him. Men on the hill watched in amazement as the young man wove his way down a deer path and sprang into the air off a fallen log. Seconds later Eric was seen being carried through the bush on the back of a four-point buck, struggling to twist the deer's antlers and bring him down. As quickly as he had appeared, he disappeared and the bushes shook violently. All went quiet and the men on the hill waited breathlessly. After a moment Eric stood amongst the bushes and silently raised one finger.

"Matthew, Thomas, go give Eric a hand, please," Seumas requested. His face was beaming with pride as though he had taken the first deer himself.

An hour passed, the sun emerging above the horizon without any more action in the glen. Eric's deer had been tied to a tree and bled. "It is the smell of death that has stopped all the life in this glen," Martin mused.

"Two of ye go to the right with Eric. Yeu three go left and circle around the glen," Seumas directed. "The rest of us will go up the middle, keep yer eyes open and yer dirks sheathed."

Quietly three groups began their stalking about the glen. Hunched over, attempting to hide from their prey, they stepped carefully without making a sound. Just before the center group emerged on the far side they stopped and listened. Behind them a large animal snorted. All three men turned slowly. A large hart sniffed the air around Matthew. "Don't move," Martin warned softly.

The hart did not understand Martin's words for he stepped closer to Matthew. "He smells the death from where ye helped to bleed Eric's deer," Seumas whispered. Matthew did not move even though the large deer challenged him.

Snorting, the deer lowered his head to the level of Matthew's head and brushed his rack near Matthew's face. Mustering all his courage the young man did as he had been told; he stood motionless. Again the hart challenged Matthew, however as the deer raised his head Thomas and Eric came out of nowhere, assailing the animal about its neck. Each of the young men held on with all their strength, every ounce of their energy feeding arms wrapped around the hart's neck. The deer rose on its hind legs and tried to shake the men off. Martin and Seumas acted as one when the animal reared, Martin grabbing the hind legs and

Seumas rising up under his belly. The deer and tangle of men crashed to the ground.

"LET HIM UP!" Matthew cried out.

Involuntarily, all four men released their grips. It took mere seconds for the animal to come back to his feet, whereupon Matthew grabbed an antler in each hand and stared at the animal, eye to eye. The hart struggled slightly to gain his release but Matthew held tightly, then gently released the deer when it became still again. Both the hart and Matthew postured briefly before the hart leapt over Matthew, vanishing into the forest beyond the clearing.

"WHIT ARE YE THINKING?" Seumas bellowed.

"I remembered whit yer cousin Iain said about the old deer," Matthew replied solemnly. "They are protecting thair forest and we should respect them. I remembered the show of force at the end of the last deer run. That old hart is protecting his forest, just like his brother, the one we killed at the beginning of the winter. If we kill off the old guardians, who will protect our Hielands?"

The other three hunters joined men in the bushes and all paid tribute to Matthew for his courage and wisdom. Mark teased his brother saying "Ye only let him go because there is no way ye could have turned that animal's neck back. I dinna know if the lot of us could have done it together."

Thomas and Eric were applauded for their flying attack and Seumas groaned, "Whit was I thinking coming underneath a brute like that?"

There were no deer-stones that night for this was Eric's second kill on a deer run. He professed his claim often "It was my deer stone that gave me the sight to see the deer and the strength to wrestle it." When Seumas retrieved the champion's deerstone which Iain had hung on the lodge post, Eric refused it, "I have my tribute and all know I am the champion. Leave it on the pole for this year as a tribute to Iain."

Others told and retold the story of the hart. The story grew with each telling until it took all eight men to hold the great hart back and Matthew subdued it with the touch of his hand.

"Seumas! You have had your run with the deer. Now you must find the cavie!" Fobothom screamed at Seumas as loudly as he could, but Seumas only rolled over in his cot and groaned. Flying out of the way as the big man moved, Fobothom refused to be ignored. Seumas now lay on his side with his left ear exposed. Carefully, Fobothom knelt down next to the ear and stretched across it, placing his hands as widely apart as he could on the opposite side to achieve a solid position. Seumas did not even feel the faerie as Fobothom drew a huge breath and screamed directly down the man's ear "SEUMAS! YOU ARE NEEDED!" Seumas brushed his hand across the side of his face, missing Fobothom and his ear completely.

As Fobothom rose from Seumas' ear, Seebtin poked his companion, pointing toward the fireplace. Fobothom followed Seebtin across the small hut, not at all sure what he wanted. Flying to the mantel over the fireplace, Seebtin began pushing a cup of spoons, forks and small knives, Ingrid's cooking utensils. Fobothom smiled and joined Seebtin in his task. Slowly the cup began to move then it stopped. The two faeries had moved the cup a couple inches, but not enough to push it over.

Aggravated by the situation Seebtin flew to the rafters above the cup and looked back. A wooden spoon rose above everything else in the cup. With the fury of a small storm Seebtin launched at the cup, flying with all the power he could muster. Grabbing the wooden spoon the determined faerie joined the cup and all of its contents crashing to the earthen floor. The dull clanging of utensils did not disturb Seumas but it did waken Ingrid.

Jumping from her cot and racing across the hut, Ingrid stopped quickly at the mess. Carefully she bent over and lifted Seebtin, "Wee faerie, are yeu all right?"

"I could not release the spoon," Seebtin cried in agony.

"Yes, that could be a bit of a problem. I suppose ye are trying to waken my husband?"

"He is to help us find the missing cavie today," Fobothom explained.

"I do remember his promise. Let me wake him for ye." Ingrid smiled and giggled a bit as she returned to her cot and began running her finger around Seumas' ear. The sleeping man swatted at her hand, but did not stir. "S e u m a s," Ingrid called, drawing out her husband's name. "S e u m a s, the faeries are preparing to attack."

"No, they are our friends," the sleeping man replied.

"They won't be if ye don't help them." Then, with a laugh she tugged on Seumas' beard until he hollered for her to stop.

"WOMAN! Whit ails ye this day?" Seumas growled, slapping her hands away.

"The faeries are waiting for ye to find thair missing cavie."

"Aye, I did promise them," Seumas conceded as he sat up on the cot. "Faeries, go wake the others. Martin, Eric, Peter, and . . . and David. Wake them and I will join ye at the lodge in a few minutes."

"Other faeries have already summoned them," Seebtin replied. "They should all be at the lodge when you arrive."

"Good. Yeu go join them!" Seumas growled. "I will be there in a minute." Standing, Seumas tried to stretch but found his muscles aching from the deer run.

While he dressed Ingrid gathered meat, bread, and cheese into a pouch. She then gave her husband a great hug and kiss, "Don't be gone too long, please."

"We should be back in eight days, maybe less." Looking in the loft where his daughter slept he called "Goodbye little one, take care of yer mother."

"Bye, Athair," Leigh replied as she climbed down to her mother. Seumas leaned over and kissed her on the head.

Slinging his food pouch over his shoulder and his broadsword over his back, Seumas crossed the village to the lodge. Martin joined him as he walked and they met David crossing as well. Eric, Peter, and faeries waited for their arrival.

"Seumas," Eric called. "Ye walk as though ye are in agony. Having a bit of a problem from that young deer yesterday?" Seumas stretched his back, rolling his shoulders, but said nothing.

"I could fix your back if you have a minute," Raven offered. She was returning to her hut with a bucket of fresh water which she had just drawn from the stream.

"No, thank ye," Seumas retorted. "I will stretch it out on the trail. Let's go; where are the gnats?"

"They were just here," Peter replied looking around. "They must have left already. I guess they are ready to solve this mystery."

"You have a mystery with gnats?" Raven queried.

"Nothing for ye to concern about," Seumas replied quickly. "Are ye planning to leave soon?"

"Not right away. My sister can wait a bit longer." Raven's gaze was stern and almost hostile toward Seumas.

Seumas simply turned and started walking without further discussion. Faeries joined the searchers as they approached the edge of the forest. With dark fading from the sky and great shadows of night becoming trees again, the search for the lost cavie commenced.

Conversation on the journey was light with many jabs thrown at Martin and Seumas for trying to lift a fully mature hart. Neither of the men responded beyond stretching their aching muscles. Seumas maintained a steady pace that was comfortable to both him and Martin but tired the younger men. Scanning across valleys, when they were visible, the older men took pleasure in seeing tender green shoots appearing on tips of otherwise bare skeletons. Scattered throughout the forest were early blooms on trees and a few lower bushes. Daylight was still short and dusk had settled on Blyth Brier before the men arrived.

Approaching the village the men heard unusual strains of music, from a harp. Smiling at the melody all five men pushed toward the center of the village but were stopped by three men of Blyth Brier, hidden sentries. A village elder called out from the shadows, "Seumas Gregor, Martin Albrecht, whit brings yeu men to our village this night?"

"We are traveling to Benmost Bield and had hopes for hospitality," Seumas replied as he and the elder greeted one another hand to elbow. "Is that Rachel I hear?"

"Aye, how did ye know?" the elder smiled. "Her music has been a delight since winter began to fade."

"How have ye fared this winter?"

The elder directed the travelers toward the lodge as he and Seumas continued talking. Martin was at Seumas' shoulder paying close attention to the conversation, but offered nothing. Hospitality included a hearty meal for the visitors. While they were eating, Rachel and Bryan joined them.

"I was going to invite ye to travel with us but I can see that might not be a good idea," Seumas laughed when Rachel stepped into the firelight. "How far are ye?"

"Almost six months," Rachel replied as she ran her hand over her enlarged belly. "I assume ye are going to Benmost Bield?"

"Aye, the gnats have reminded me of thair lost cavie. Bryan, would ye care to leave yer wife and join us for a week or so?"

"No, not this time. But would ye be interested in my uncle?" Bryan's eyes begged for a positive response.

Martin replied first, laughing, "I take it Bloigh Bryan is up to his tricks again?"

"Not really," Rachel sighed. "He won't keep his hands off my belly and wants to take credit for the fact that I am pregnant. I know he is proud of Bryan but sitting on a nettle would be less of a bother." Looking around the lodge, Rachel continued, "Where are yer faeries?"

"They said they were going to look for a bush," Peter replied. "They should be back soon. Why don't ye play some more music for us?"

"I believe we have suffered enough torture this evening. Playing that thing is not good for your child's ears," Bridg, the woman who had come to the village before winter, interrupted as she pushed into the conversation. "Did I hear you say you are going on a faerie hunt? Rachel, are you going on a journey with these men?"

"The answer to both questions is NO," Rachel replied with a sense of aggravation.

"Oh, my mistake. Seumas, you look as if you have injured your back. May I help?" Bridg moved toward Seumas.

"MY BACK IS FINE!" Seumas roared.

Rachel looked at him with alarm. Eric saw her concern and laughed softly as he explained, "Seumas and Martin tried to capture a mature hart on the deer run yesterday. The two of them tried to lift it."

"After yeu grabbed it about the neck," Martin chided.

Eric then proceeded to tell the story of the deer run to all who would listen, exaggerating minute details which made the old Celts look foolish and lauding Matthew's release of the animal.

"Enough of this," Seumas growled as he stood and made for the door. "I am going to speak with Bloigh Bryan. I hope this gathering will be much quieter when I return." Everyone laughed as he left.

After inviting Bryan's uncle to join the journey, Seumas strolled back toward the lodge. While looking at the stars he found his missing faeries. "Hello, gnats, where have ye been?"

"On our last visit we found a bush with the white blossoms on the edge of the village and wanted to see if there was any nectar," Seebtin smiled.

"Nectar? Ye mean like mead?" Seumas challenged.

"We don't like mead but nectar is very pleasing," Fobothom replied.

"Safe travels, Seumas Gregor," Bridg offered as she strolled toward Rachel and Bryan's hut. When she heard Rachel playing the harp she stopped and changed her course toward her own hut.

Seumas puzzled about what he saw, calling out to the faeries, "Seebtin, Fobothom. Tell me more about this bush." No faeries answered his question for they had flown high above the treetops. Rachel played the harp for only a few minutes, but it was enough to relax Seumas as he wondered about what had just happened.

*"How did Bridg know about Seumas' back? Was he hunched over?"
Liam asked, pondering his grandfather's story.*

*"Ah, that would be a question, now wouldn't it? But a question for
another day for I am a bit tired after our swim and am ready to call it
a day," Angus replied. He carefully marked his place in the book and
placed the volume on his desk. Picking up his pipe and tobacco pouch
he turned to Lillian, "Would ye care for a wee bit of night air before
bed?"*

*"I would love it," Lillian replied with a twinkle in her eye. Turning
to the children, still seated on the floor she told them, "yeu three get
ready for bed, now. We will be just outside and won't be too long."*

*Walking arm in arm with her husband she noticed he was a bit
unsteady. "Are yeu okay?"*

*Lighting his pipe, Angus replied with a soft laugh, "Aye, just a bit
tired. That swim with the boys wore me out!"*

*Angus' reading from his book had now become an evening treat.
After supper, Lillian would put dishes in the sink and join her
grandchildren on the patio or in Angus' study for an hour of ancient
history read by a master storyteller.*

"Bloigh Bryan, where did Rachel get her harp?" Seumas asked as
they left Blyth Brier before the sun climbed above the mountain ridges.

"Bryan carved it from a heavy oak tree, rather a branch from the
tree," Bloigh Bryan replied. "Where did she learn of this thing? This
'harp' ye called it?"

"The Roman spies were musicians. One of them took an interest in
Rachel and taught her to play. She learned quickly. I enjoyed hearing
it last night." Seumas mused.

"Young Bryan had the entire village working to figure out how to
make strings for that thing. Bridg showed us how to do it but she curses
every time Rachel plays; she says it is nauseating. I rather enjoy it, but
I think she needs better strings."

"I guess that would be something for us to work on," Seumas
agreed.

The trip continued for hours but seemed even longer as Bloigh
Bryan talked endlessly about nothing. One moment of silence was
granted as the travelers entered a glen where several deer were finishing
their morning grazing. "Look," Eric pointed out, "three of the does are

large. There will be fawn soon." Bloigh Bryan sighed slightly; his incessant chatter resumed with their steps. Faeries escaped the noise by flying ahead or off through the forests. "We are looking for bushes with the white flowers," they claimed. Everyone was relieved when they arrived in Benmost Bield well before the sun met the horizon.

The six travelers were met in the center of the village by two armed men and several elders. "Seumas, Martin, whit brings ye so far?" Sean, an old Celt, asked.

"Is Graclyn still in residence here?" Seumas asked, his expression expressing great concern.

"Aye," Sean replied. "She has become one of the community. Loved by most of the families. The wives even send thair husbands to her when she needs help."

"Whit about faeries; have ye seen any faeries about since we were here last?"

"Nae, I canna say that I have but then I never saw the ones yer cousin talked with either."

"Fobothom!" Seumas called. Immediately eight faeries gathered in front of Seumas and his companions. "Friends, we will get the locals to join us and begin the search at sunrise tomorrow. DO NOT venture into the forest on yer own. Stay in the lodge with us."

"Seumas have ye lost yer wits over the winter?" Thomas, another village elder asked.

"Nae. Good to see ye, Thomas," Seumas grasped the elder by the arm in a strong greeting. "I was speaking with some friends who are the reason we are here. Can ye assemble yer elders in a short while and put us up in yer lodge for a few days?"

"Yeu are always welcome in Benmost Bield, ye know that. Get settled in the lodge and I will gather the elders. Sean, would ye see if any are in the fields and ask them to join us?" Thomas turned away and moved toward a remote cluster of huts.

About an hour later Sean, Thomas, and four other elders joined the travelers sitting outside the lodge. "Ye must be tired after journeying from *Ceo Dhachaidh*," Thomas said as he sat on a log.

"The younger men are a bit weary but Martin and I trained under much more severe conditions than this," Seumas replied, as though stating an already known fact.

"We are actually getting rather lazy," Martin chuckled.

"So, why are ye here?" one of the elders asked.

Seumas took a deep breath and looked at the faeries clustered on a tree limb not far away. "When we were here last our faeries tried to find wee protectors around yer village. We have been working with the little ones for our common protection." Seeing smiles creep across his hosts' faces, Seumas raised his hands and the corners of his own lips. "Before ye start to laugh, I must tell ye that they do see and know things we cannae imagine. They were important in our victory over the Romans. But I stray. Our faeries found a deserted cavie with a warning that this village was no longer safe for them. We are supposed to find someone called . . . "

"Muestor," Truact reminded Seumas.

"Someone called Muestor," Seumas repeated. "Do ye know of a man . . . or a beast who goes by that name?"

The elders shook their heads but Sean spoke, "I have heard the children speak that name."

"Whit children?" Thomas asked.

"Yer grandson is one, the one called Thom and his friend, . . . let me think . . . Michael. I heard them speak of Muestor."

Thomas stood and looked around the village. "Ye men wait here. I will go ask my daughter to fetch Thom."

Thomas strode for his daughter's hut. The other men waited but Sean was growing more curious about the faeries. "Whit can these sprites do for us in this new war we are waiting to fight?"

Seumas looked at Sean and shook his head. "I dinna know. All I can tell ye is that the wee faerie called Vrenessbith told me that they would help us to win victory over the hags. But so far the gnats have been more of a bother than a help and I have seen no hags."

The Celtic leader paused, rolling his lips before voicing another concern. "Ye said that Graclyn has become part of the village? I thought she was to be leaving with the thaw."

"Surely, ye do not think Graclyn is with the hags!" an elder protested.

"I can only tell ye this, and Martin and the others will attest to it as well. Women without men arrived in four of our villages, including *Ceo Dhachaidh*. Each had a different story and each is beautiful and has become part of the village community. I would be more relaxed if they had warts and were packing up to leave tomorrow."

"Rest easy, old friend," Sean laughed, slapping Seumas on the back. "Graclyn has tended to our sick and has taught our women new ways to cook. Even our smallest warrior could strike her down with a single blow. She is no threat."

Before Seumas could ask more questions, Thomas returned with Thom. "I am sorry, Seumas, but young Thom here has not seen Muestor for many months."

"Thom, tell us about Muestor. Who or whit is he?" Martin asked seeking to give Seumas a rest.

"He is like a weasel but my father says he canna be a weasel," young Thom explained. "He once lived in the hollow of a big tree on the edge of the forest but Michael and I were there a few days ago and we dinna find a sign of him."

"Why did yer father say it was not a weasel?" David asked.

Thom thought for a moment then replied "The tree he lived in."

David smiled and returned, "He is a martryn. A cousin to the weasel but martryns live in pine trees and some eat berries."

"How do ye know this?" Eric asked.

"I have lived in these mountains far longer than any of you," David replied with confidence.

"So, we need to find a martryn who goes by the name Muestor," Seumas sighed. "Young Thom, will you and Michael join us in our search tomorrow morning?"

Thomas nodded and sent his grandson home.

"Good." Seumas smiled for the first time in two days. "Are there any other men of Benmost Bield who would like to join our search for Muestor and the missing faeries?"

Smiles covered every face in the invited group as well as many other men who had joined out of curiosity. "I would not miss this," laughed one of the men in the back of the group. "Our great Celts looking for a weasel and faeries."

Sean looked to Seumas and Martin with a bit of doubt and concern before turning to go to his own hut.

"Truact, Fobothom!" Seumas called. When all the faeries assembled in front of him, Seumas put forth a request. "Would ye please confirm where the cavie was and that the residents have not returned. And see if there is any sign of this martryn, Muestor."

"We have already, and there was no sign of this martryn they spoke of," Seebtin confirmed.

"So ye do know where we are to begin our search?" Seumas challenged.

"We do," Seebtin assured the old Celt.

Thomas brought food and drink for the visitors. Bloigh Bryan added his personal spice to the evening with stories of his own exploits. Locals and visitors relaxed, enjoying the rest of the evening. Seumas, however, ate very little and carried his tankard of mead outside, taking only occasional gulps. He sat alone where he could listen to the stillness of the Highlands and gaze at the heavens above.

"Is your back all right?" The question startled Seumas, pulling him back from his thoughts.

"I am fine," he said as he turned. Graclyn stood over him, smiling. "Whit makes ye think my back is not sound?"

"I overheard the men talking about how you lifted a large deer," she replied sitting next to Seumas.

"They are drinking and talking too much. Whit soreness was there is now gone. Thank ye for asking." Seumas stood and turned toward the lodge.

"I did not mean to impose on your solitude," Graclyn apologized.

"Ye did not, I was becoming exhausted with my thoughts. Now, I need sleep." Seumas began to walk away.

"May you sleep well, Seumas Gregor."

Seumas did not look back, he only walked slowly toward the lodge where the noise was subsiding for Bloigh Bryan was too drunk to continue. As Seumas bedded down near Martin he asked, "Martin, Bloigh Bryan was carrying on, but who spoke about our deer run? Who else might have been heard?"

"Ye don't speak over Bloigh Bryan," Martin chuckled. "Ye might join with him but not over him. I heard nothing about the deer run. Why do ye ask?"

"No reason. Sleep well my friend for tomorrow we have great game to capture."

<center>~~~~~~~~~~~~~~~~~~~~~~~~~~~~~~~</center>

Morning found the six visitors waking to the laughter of almost twice as many locals. Emerging from the lodge, Seumas looked around for his faerie companions. Not seeing them, he called out with aggravation, "GNATS!".

Growing laughter stopped as the faeries appeared, hovering in front of Seumas and Martin, their wings and bodies reflecting morning sunlight with an uncommon brilliance. "Are ye ready?" Martin asked of both Seumas and the faeries.

"Come, gnats, let us go find yer kin," Seumas sighed. He signaled with his hand to Sean, Thomas, and the two boys. "I hope ye don't get caught up with these old men, for they do not understand whit we are about this day." Both boys nodded and smiled.

Truact, Fobothom, Thom, and Michael all led the group of men to the same tree. David brushed the leaves away from the base of the tree, revealing a hole. "That is the old cavie," Fobothom explained.

David then examined the tree and found a burrow in the side, just over head height. "This must be where the martryn lived."

Other men crowded around to see the two holes. As they shifted all the leaves on the ground Seumas called for them to stop. "Can any of yeu men clearly read crushed animal signs in the forest?" Not one of the locals replied; all looked at Seumas as though he had lost his mind. "Good. Then I will ask all but Sean, Thomas, and the boys to go back to yer work. We will call ye if we need help but we do need to be able to read the signs yeu are walking on. Thank ye for helping but go. NOW!" The men grumbled about not being part of the expedition and laughed at those still searching, but they left.

"Bloigh Bryan, I want yeu to go over to that area and look for signs of a weasel or martryn." Seumas pointed to an area about twenty feet away. "Look for holes in the trees and at the base of trees." With Bloigh Bryan out of the way Seumas turned to the boys, "Where did ye see this martryn last?"

Michael and Thom looked at each other and thought out loud, "Was it over the hill or down by the stream?"

"It must have been by the stream. I do not know that we could have seen him on the hill."

"Where is the stream?" Martin asked softly.

"The only stream in this area is a bed that is mostly dry, barely enough to call it a stream," Sean offered. When everyone looked to him for direction he turned and began walking over a hill behind them, then down into a glen. After five minutes he stopped and kicked at the leaves with his foot, "It should be around here somewhere."

Up in the tree branches Truact poked Fobothom in his side and pointed to a tree on the hill a bit further beyond where the men were looking. "It is the beast!" Fobothom called out. All the faeries turned and looked where Truact was pointing. Fobothom flew down to Seumas and alerted him to look to a tree on the hill.

Perched on a low branch was a plumpish creature standing on its hind legs, reaching about sixteen inches. Its coat was dark brown with a lighter brown, almost golden collar and ears on a white triangular face. Seumas in turn alerted the other men. Everyone looked at the creature with awe and amazement; their mouths hung open in disbelief. As men pointed, the creature bobbed up and down several times before disappearing.

"If that is Muestor, the cavie must be nearby," Seumas called out. "Boys, see if ye can find Muestor. The rest of us look on the ground for a cavie. Fobothom, have all the faeries search for this cavie as well. At least ye know whit yeu are looking for."

Within seconds the hillside was covered with men kicking at the leaves and crawling around trees and rocks. When nothing was found, Seumas sent the boys back to fetch Bloigh Bryan. Together the eight men, two boys, and eight faeries searched the area for over two hours without finding the martryn or cavie. Frustrated, Seumas called an end to their search. "Sean, yeu, Martin, and I will return at first light tomorrow with our faeries. Maybe we will have better luck with fewer people. I ask all of ye, including ye two boys, to not speak of whit we did find today. When others ask, simply tell them we had no luck and will try again tomorrow with fewer men so the rest of ye can tend to yer work." Everyone agreed.

Later that afternoon while Seumas sat outside the lodge, he called David and Peter over. "Would the two of ye care to join me on another quest?" Neither man had any objections so Seumas began walking toward the forest above Benmost Bield. "Fobothom!" Seumas called. The faerie appeared before Seumas instantly. "Fobothom, take us to where that bush is that ye love so much."

"With the white flowers?" the faerie asked.

"Aye," Seumas nodded.

Fobothom led the three men just beyond the village to a small bush covered with waxy green leaves but was not yet in blossom or even budding. "David, Peter, see whit ye can learn about this bush," Seumas asked as he stood tall and looked around the area. He ceased his search when he saw the tree with the old cavie about thirty feet away. Turning back to the bush he asked, "Can either of ye see anything of use about this bush?"

Both men shook their heads. "Maybe later when it blossoms," Peter offered. As they returned to the lodge, Peter stopped and asked, "Seumas, as I recall we were to return to Doup Fell to investigate a bush there."

"Aye, I believe we were. Before we consider Doup Fell let us see if we can solve the mystery here," Seumas spoke softly, disturbed with the course the search for the cavie had taken so far. Everything the faeries had told him months before, which he had discounted, was proving out with a high degree of truth.

Seeking to settle his mind, Seumas spent the rest of the evening talking quietly about whatever folks wanted to discuss except the search for the martryn and the cavie. Bloigh Bryan again entertained any who would listen.

Martin, Seumas, and the faeries met Sean at the edge of the forest before dawn the next morning. They traveled silently to the hillside where they had seen the martryn the day before and in true Celtic fashion, waited. The three men sat quietly for more than an hour before the creature appeared on the same tree branch as before. Perching as he had, he stretched high and sat down, then stretched up and down. "Seebtin, take yer faeries and see if he will lead ye," Seamus called softly. The faeries disappeared immediately. The Celts waited.

Seumas looked around the forest where they sat. Leaf buds were just beginning to open, nearly a week behind those at *Ceo Dhachaidh*. The hillside rolled with rocks exposed by centuries of weather. Plants pushed through bits of snow remaining in crags of the rocks. With another week of warming weather flowers might appear on the ends of these resilient green stalks. When all else was quiet, sounds of a breeze gently pushing tree branches and rustling leaves on the ground provided a great settling effect on three warriors of a once great nation.

An hour went by before Truact and Fobothom returned to the Celts on the hillside. "We have found them! And their leaders are willing to meet with you!" Truact reported, his small voice vibrating with excitement.

Three Celtic warriors followed two faeries through the forest for fifteen minutes before arriving at a large rock outcropping. The faerie cavie rested safely in the midst of huge rocks locked into one another. Sitting above the cavie a martryn guarded its entrance and his friends. An elder of the cavie welcomed the warriors and introduced Muestor, their martryn. Sean reached out to Muestor who cautiously came to him and climbed up his arm.

Satisfied that they were safe, Seumas asked the elders, "Whenever we have found a cavie near a village of Hielanders, we have asked the cavie to help guard our village. Are ye willing to work with Sean and one other village elder to keep watch over Benmost Bield?"

"It is not safe for us in the man's village," the elder faerie replied.

"I have been told that is why ye moved yer cavie. Whit makes the village not safe for ye?"

"A demon of the mountains has come to live there and she kills members of our cavie."

"That is why I ask ye to join with Sean and Thomas; they are elders like yeu. We do not see these demons, but ye do. I believe the hag, or demon, in the village will be leaving soon and I need ye to warn our elders if another comes to live in this village."

Sean and Martin looked at Seumas with surprise. The elder of the cavie pondered Seumas' request before answering, "We will do that but we do not want people of your village to know where our cavie is hidden."

"I understand," Seumas replied. "I will ask Sean to bring one elder, Thomas, to meet ye. But he will wait for several days before he does this. Is this agreeable?"

"This is agreeable. Muestor, our protector likes Sean," the elder laughed. Muestor was busy crawling over Sean's arms, playing like a pup.

"Thank ye for watching over our people and our land. We must go now," Seumas nodded toward the elder and turned to leave. Eager to hear what Seumas had learned, Sean and Martin followed closely behind.

"Whit are ye not telling us?" Martin grabbed Seumas before they reached the village.

"If I were to say whit I was thinking, ye would be convinced I have lost my mind. I am not sure I believe it myself. Let me watch a while longer and then I will tell ye. Sean, trust in the faeries and wait three or four days before introducing Thomas. Remember to keep thair location hidden from everyone else. I suggest ye go to the cavie early in the morning before the village wakes." Seumas was earnest in his words.

Upon returning to the village, everyone gathered around the three Celts and waited for news. "We could find nothing of value," Seumas reported. "We did find the martryn and he is nothing but a creature of the forest who lives in a burrow of an old tree. My men and I will depart within the hour."

"Whit do ye expect from old warriors who chase faeries?" one of the local men said as he returned to his work, his voice overflowing with sarcasm.

"Vrenessbith?" Resbith called to the young faerie, who was too busy watching a nest of ants to reply. "VRENESSBITH!" the elder called, more forcibly this time.

Vrenessbith spun around and launched herself to the presence of her senior instructor at once. "Yes, Eldest?" she replied, her voice filled with innocence.

Shaking her head slowly and smiling, Resbith corrected the youngest faerie, "I am NOT the eldest, as they like to call me, I . . ."

"I apologize, but I heard the others . . . "

"I know what you heard the others call me. You will please refer to me as 'Comleidh,' as they should."

"'Comleidh?' What does this mean?" Vrenessbith asked as she sat next to Resbith.

"It is an old title given to me by our former Comleidh, the one who taught me. It means teacher, guide, instructor, counselor. It means I am the one charged with your upbringing and ensuring you are ready for your role in this world of ours." Resbith settled comfortably on the tree limb and looked out through the forest around their cavie hidden below. "Vrenessbith, tell me what you have learned since you came to us."

"The big men move very slowly and try to do things they should not. Many of the men try to be important to others when they cannot be."

"How did you learn this?" Resbith asked with concern.

"I have watched them and studied their faces. You can see much of a man's heart on his face," Vrenessbith explained.

"Yes, very good. Go on, what else?"

"Most men and women wear heavy garments that change shape and color. Children do not wear it at all."

"You can see this?"

"Only in the mornings, and sometimes in the evening, as the sun sets. These garments seem to be darker and heavier in the evening. And Seumas wears a different color than the others."

"You are observant. This is called *gleo*. Few faeries can see this. It is their burden of the struggle before them. What color is the one Seumas wears? I have not seen this."

"It was brown the others are grey. But since his trip to the villages it wants to be more red."

"Thank you for telling me this, I will watch him. What else have you learned?"

"Depost and Enstard and the others fly very fast when they are going on adventure and there are great beasts in the trees who are just like the man Seumas."

"What do you mean 'just like Seumas'?"

"I watched a great furry beast when his tree was torn apart by the wind. He snarled when I watched him but as I came closer he sat and looked at me. There was a sadness in his eyes. I think the sadness was because he lost his home. The man Seumas is big and loud and snarls like this beast did, but he has a very soft heart. His mate, Ingrid, is gentle inside and out . . . OH! The time of joining is very near. We are waiting for the flowers to bloom. Comleidh, when will the flowers bloom?"

"As the trees give birth to new leaves, bushes and smaller plants will present flowers. Flowers are rich in color and aroma which can take wee faeries out of their senses. When the forest is in full bloom, which will be very soon now, all of the animals and faeries will celebrate a new peace and awakening from the grey of winter. This is the time young faeries join together for their life journey." Resbith paused for a few seconds while she inhaled the aroma of her memories. "Vrenessbith, what does your heart tell you today?"

Vrenessbith thought carefully, casting her gaze through the forest, coming to rest in the direction of *Ceo Dhachaidh*. "There is a great unpeaceful growing in the villages."

"What do you mean 'a great unpeaceful'?"

"You just told me that a great peace should be filling the forest, and I can feel that; yet when I am in the village, especially near some of the people, they are not peaceful at all."

"You have described it well young faerie. You have described it well indeed." Resbith took a solemn breath casting her eyes toward the village. "It is my belief that the 'unpeaceful' you have felt is the reason for your birth. You must learn to work with these villagers so you can discover how to restore their peace."

Martin, Seumas, Eric, and Peter celebrated their return to Blyth Brier for they would now be free of Bloigh Bryan. Since leaving Benmost Bield the big man filled the forest with his incessant talking, complaining, and forecasting of dire events very unlikely to ever occur. Returning him to his home relieved the others of this unbearable burden. Rachel and Bryan spent the evening with the travelers catching up on developments from the search. Rachel was pleased with the resolution.

"Enough about the faeries," Seumas changed the subject. "How are ye and that wee bairn doing?"

"It was difficult at first, being sick most of the time. Now it just gets in the way, but in three short months I will hand him to his father and I will rest." Rachel smiled at Bryan.

"So ye want a son, young Bryan?" Martin laughed.

"I will take whitever my beautiful bride gives me," Bryan replied before anything else could be said.

Seumas changed the subject again, "Bryan, tell me about this woman Bridg. How is she involved in the village?"

"She has become quite the midwife, and more. She has potions and ointments for whitever ails any person."

"Rachel, have ye used her potions for yer bairn?" Seumas asked, crumpling his eyebrows.

"Noooo," Bryan answered quickly. "Bridg brought a potion to help with the early sickness but when Rachel put it to her nose the potion was thrown out the door. I was surprised it did not wash over Bridg as she left."

"Roslyn has helped me get through all my discomforts," Rachel smiled. "She may be my husband's mother but she is also the mother I never had."

"Good," Seumas nodded. "I am glad to hear of yer fortune. I do like Roslyn. Whit else can ye tell me of Bridg?"

"She is helpful, friendly, always has a nice word," Bryan replied, shaking his head with wonder. "Whit are ye looking for?"

"I wish I knew . . . truly, I wish I knew." Seumas then grew quiet.

"ERIC," Rachel called. "So ye did not lose yer wrap on the deer run! I am certain Sarah appreciates yeu protecting yerself."

"My bride does worry about me when I go off with these old warriors. She fears they love a good battle which might conflict with our love of a quiet evening together. These two passions are not a good partnership." Eric sighed and all grew quiet for a bit. "Rachel, do ye have yer deer-stone?"

"Yes. Like Iain, I wear it always."

"Aye, so do I. The great stone that Iain wore hangs on the pole in our lodge. We have the only other two that I know of."

"Eric, here, won Iain's stone this year but refused it," Martin added. "I believe ye have learned that yer run is the true prize. The energy that ye find within yerself. Yer ability to meet one of nature's most beautiful and powerful creatures in thair own world and do them honor. That is the prize. The stone is a gift in recognition of yer achievement."

"We have a hard journey ahead of us tomorrow," Seumas interjected. "I suggest we get some sleep."

"Where do ye go tomorrow? Not back to *Ceo Dhachaidh*?" Bryan asked.

"Doup Fell," Peter replied. "There was a question about the safety of thair cavie when the snows fell. Whit the elder of the cavie in Benmost Bield told us concerns me about whit we might find in Doup Fell."

Bryan helped Rachel to her feet where she gave a great hug to each of the four men of *Ceo Dhachaidh*. "Keep watch on each other, and thank ye for a few days of peace."

<hr>

Bird song provided music for the four men as they journeyed on well defined deer paths across the mountain to Doup Fell. None of the men spoke for they did not have energy to carry on conversation and negotiate the difficult terrain. Arriving in Doup Fell, they were surprised by a most unusual welcome. They were expected.

Seumas and Martin looked around for guards, but there were none. A village elder, an older man called Alastair, strode up to the men as they entered the village. "It is about time; we thought ye had forgotten about us!"

"Whit do ye mean?" Seumas asked, bewildered by the greeting. "How did ye know we were coming? We knew only two days ago."

Alastair blushed a bit, "We dinna know; only hoped. Young Ryan and a few of his friends were hunting and found thair way to *Ceo Dhachaidh*. They heard ye were out lookin' a faerie cavie and, well, I just hoped ye might find time to visit with Doup Fell as well."

"Yer welcome gave us a bit of surprise," Seumas laughed. "But tell me, was there anyone who might have suggested that we may be comin' this way?"

"Now that ye ask it, yes. The woman Brett was listenin' to young Ryan and suggested that maybe ye would be comin' here as well."

"And tell us, how is this woman Brett doin'?" Martin asked, now a bit suspicious.

"Oh, she is quite well, now. She had it tough at first but now is loved by all the bairn. And the women folk enjoy her company. She has made a most delightful addition to our wee village."

"And how is yer relation with the faerie cavie?" Seumas asked. "Do ye see them very often? Do they keep in touch with ye?"

"Nooo, I canna say at dey do. Come to think, I have not seen any of the wee folk since the thaw began."

"FOBOTHOM!" Seumas called. Within a few seconds, although it seemed too long for Seumas, the group of faeries presented themselves. "Good faeries, I need ye to check on the cavie. See that it is healthy." Immediately six faeries disappeared into the fading light of sunset.

Before another ray of sunlight disappeared, *Ceo Dhachaidh* faeries entered the Doup Fell cavie without reservation. As the last of the group got inside the entrance all rushed back out, gagging. "It is POISONED!" Stractor screamed. "To the treetops, quickly!" Flying was difficult as the faeries captured their breath through burning throats.

Seebtin directed everyone to a tree branch high above the forest floor, just below the top of the crown. Slowly, breathing became easier for each of them. "We must tell Seumas," Fobothom announced with concern.

Rising from the tree branch they found themselves surrounded by other faeries. "SEEBTIN," one of the faeries called. "Our guard saw you enter the cavie and came to get us. We did not know if you were friend or enemy!"

"Trastar, no faerie is your enemy!" Seebtin exclaimed. "What has happened here?"

"After you were here last time, many of our cavie disappeared. Then Vancint, one of our own, saw an old hag capture faeries. She smashed them about in a bag and killed some in her mouth. We began moving our cavie at once. When we returned to make sure all had left, we saw the old hag pouring something into our home. The air was foul and we could not breathe. We have always kept a guard near the old cavie in case missing family members return, as you did."

"We need one of your elders to bring this story to Seumas, our leader," Seebtin pleaded.

"Only if he will come to a place in our forest. It is not safe around the village for us."

"How is it not safe?" Stractor asked, his presence glowing as a dandelion, deepening into golden hue as his concern grew.

"The village has welcomed the old hag who hunts members of our cavie," Trastar replied, alarmed that his friends did not understand.

"Where do we meet you?" Fobothom asked, his voice filled with despair and determination.

Trastar pointed to a tree growing out of rock outcropping on top of the next hill. "Meet us at that tree at first light tomorrow. Is the man Martin with you?"

"Yes," Seebtin replied.

"He should come, too," Trastar replied as he and his family disappeared into the growing darkness.

Fobothom and his faeries flew as fast as they could back toward Doup Fell. When they came to the outer edge, a great stench halted their progress. Immediately the wee warriors flew back into the wood. Stopping to discuss their situation as soon as the air was breathable, the stench followed them. Looking toward the village they saw an old hag just five meters away staring at them. Without moving her eyes she uncorked a jug and drew a mouthful of liquid.

"FLY HIGH!" Seebtin cried.

The hag spewed liquid at the faeries; only five escaped the acrid spray. Stractor was bathed in a full stream and fell writhing to the ground. After several seconds his small body lay still. A glow filled with every colour of the rainbow appeared. When the glow faded Stractor was gone.

"We must get to Seumas," Fobothom cried, terror choking his small voice.

Flying above the trees faeries watched the village below for their men of *Ceo Dhachaidh*. Martin, Peter, and Eric were talking with villagers but Seumas was not to be found. Flying lower Fobothom was assaulted by another stench, not as powerful as the previous but still more than he could stand. Rising to find cleaner air he caught a glimpse of Seumas walking across the village common. Quickly he called the other four faeries; each positioned themselves in a beam of moonlight. Slowly the wee group danced back and forth reflecting the moonlight trying to capture Seumas' attention.

After several minutes Eric noticed the odd lights. "Seumas," Eric called softly. When Seumas looked at Eric, the younger man pointed toward the dancing lights. Without hesitation Seumas ran to the edge of the village and nearly one hundred meters beyond. The faeries joined him in the shadows where they would not be seen.

"One of ye is missing," Seumas observed.

"Stractor has been killed by an old hag," Seebtin replied, sobbing. "The cavie was attacked but they had already moved to a new location. The elders of the cavie will meet with ye and Martin. No one else."

"How was Stractor killed?" Seumas asked, ready to draw his sword.

"As we were returning to tell you of the meeting, an old hag was near the bush. She sprayed us with drink from her jug. It burned Stractor and he fell."

"Was this hag wearing a blue apron?" Seumas questioned.

"No, her clothes were all tattered. There was no apron at all."

Seumas thought for a moment, looking into the village. Brett was walking toward her hut; she was wearing a blue apron. "You faeries go to the tops of the trees over the village and wait there. I will call if I need ye, but Martin and I will meet ye at the other side of the village at daybreak." Seumas watched his friends disappear into the grey night sky before going in search of Martin.

Martin sat outside the lodge with Peter and Eric. Alastair was entertaining them with local lore. "Alastair," Seumas interrupted, "how many women have come to yer village since the battle?"

"Brett," Alastair replied with a cock of his head. "Brett is the only one. Why? Ye seem troubled."

"I am. One of our companions has been killed by a hag in YEUR village and the faeries will not come near Doup Fell for fear of being killed themselves. I ask ye again, how many women, men, children, or even dogs have come to Doup Fell since the battle?"

"Again, I tell ye only Brett. If it would please ye I will call together our council and ye can ask all of them."

"Gather them all here. Now!" Seumas watched as Alastair slunk across the village common in search of other members of their council. When Alastair was gone Seumas turned to Martin, "Yeu and I must meet with elders of the cavie at first light tomorrow. Nobody else is to know. Eric, yeu and Peter will guard our backs. If anyone tries to follow us, ye are to stop them." All nodded agreement for they could see that Seumas was not in a mood to discuss any changes.

Six members of the Doup Fell council, including Alastair, arrived after many minutes. Alastair took the lead addressing the men, "Our friend Seumas is concerned about visitors to our village. It seems there has been a mishap this evening and he is looking for the person responsible." After looking each council member in their eyes, Alastair continued. "Since the time of our return from the great battle, have ye seen any visitors in our village? Other than Brett?"

Four of the men shook their heads indicating that they had not seen anyone. One man looked pensive, then replied, "Aye. I do recall seeing an older woman that I did not recognize leaving Brett's hut. I did not think anything of it at the time."

"When was this?" Seumas asked.

"I remember thinking that it was good that the snow had melted so it must have been seven to ten days back."

"Have ye seen her before or since that time?"

"Nooo, I don't believe I have."

"Whit time of day was this?" Martin asked.

"Ohhh, it was dark but let me think. I often walk late at night and sometimes early in the morn, before daybreak. It was before daybreak I believe. Yes, for I remember how odd it was to be leaving a hut at that time."

"Should we ask Brett who her visitor was?" Alastair asked, eager for an excuse to visit the attractive younger woman.

"No," Seumas replied coldly. "She would only lie about it. I warn ye men that at this moment we are at war, at war with an enemy we do not know. One of our own has been killed this night so we know the enemy is near. If ye see anyone in the village ye do not know, ye MUST hold them and send a runner to *Ceo Dhachaidh* at once. As soon as we can identify our enemy we will be able to protect our villages from them. Please do not speak of this meeting to anyone not on council, not yer wives, not yer children. Ye are guardians of Doup Fell and at this time yer only weapons of defense are yer eyes and yer silence."

After the village reclaimed a sense of peace, Martin took Seumas away from Eric and Peter and questioned him. "Seumas, whit are ye not saying?"

Seumas looked at Martin and confided in his friend, "These women are somehow our enemy. I do not know how, but I am certain now that they are with our enemy. Yet, if I try to run them out of our villages, other women and families, and many of the men, would beat me. They have woven themselves into our lives. I would cut them out with my sword if I could, but I swore an oath to never harm any child or woman. If they were hags, as the one who waged war against us, I could strike them down in an instant. But, if I lay a hand to any of these women I would be scourged."

"Ye may be right, my friend. Ye may be right," Martin sympathetically agreed. "But for now let us get some sleep. I would like to return to my Sophia tomorrow, and I know Ingrid waits for yeu."

～～～～～～～～～～～～～

Seumas tossed restlessly most of the night. After many hours of rolling back and forth he rose and went to a bench outside the lodge. Sitting on the bench he could see any creature that moved in the village common. He laid his sword across his legs in case he needed it. His head was weary and not clear so he did not realize that he had a small companion on his shoulder singing a soft melody and soothing his restless soul. Not long after taking his watch he was sleeping soundly.

Before dawn approached Doup Fell, Martin removed Seumas' sword and shook him gently. Instinctively the warrior grabbed for his weapon but found his friend's hand. "Martin! Thank ye. I could not sleep but once I took this watch I could not keep my eyes open."

"It is time to meet elders of the cavie. Our faeries are waiting." Martin offered Seumas a hand, lifting him from the bench. They walked toward the forest together. Eric and Peter stood guard watching for other movement.

The moon had disappeared from the sky taking away all light. Travel through a strange forest in the dark is difficult but the Celtic warriors were well trained and made the first part of their journey with only minor mishaps.

"Seumas, Martin, welcome to our forest," Trastar called to the men. "We must hurry before our enemy sees us."

Without a word, the men followed the barely visible faeries through the dark. During the day these wee creatures were filled with reflected light but in the predawn darkness they were mere shadows, visible only because of their movements. Trastar was accompanied by four other faeries from his cavie and there were five from *Ceo Dhachaidh*. Locals led the way and visitors kept the men going the right direction. After traveling for nearly thirty minutes their course changed and they headed directly into the light of the rising sun. After another thirty minutes they stopped and waited.

All of the visitors stood in silence on a rock outcropping near the top of a hill. They had excellent visibility of other hilltops and glens in between. Watching the day arrive, they could see no other faeries or creatures moving anywhere in the forest. The experience was mesmerizing to both Celtic warriors. Overcome by a peace neither had experienced, both men witnessed the waking of a hidden world that surrounded them, the domain of woodland faeries. Mist silently filled glens below and around them, creating a haunting uneasiness in both men.

"Seumas, Martin, it is good to see you again," welcomed the elder who had met with the council of Doup Fell months before. "I am sorry to have you waiting so long but we had to wait for all of our groups to arrive with their news."

"All of yer groups?" Martin questioned.

"Trastar and his group led you in a very winding path, then we had three other groups behind you to make sure you were not followed."

Seumas smiled, "Aye, I understand. We left two of our companions watching the village as we left."

"I must apologize to you for we cannot honor our agreement. The village has become unsafe for us and it is dangerous for our kind to even approach your people," the elder explained.

"I understand, elder," Seumas agreed. "But I still ask for yer help. Yeu see whit we cannot and we need to know when our enemy approaches. Would it be possible for yer cavie to fly among the tops of the trees and watch over Doup Fell? If ye see anything we should know about, send two of yer faeries to the cavie in *Ceo Dhachaidh*, for they talk with us."

"We will do this for you but I must warn you that this village has many hags moving through it."

"Whit do ye mean?" Seumas asked with a puzzled look on his face.

"On nights when there is no moon in the sky hags move up and down the hillside where the village sits. I have seen myself how they can walk past a man as though he were asleep and never disturb his thoughts."

"My friend, how do we fight an enemy we cannot see?" Seumas sighed.

"We must find a way to teach you to see them," the elder faerie smiled. "I do not know how to do this now, but we will try to find a way."

"Thank ye for yer help, my friend," Seumas smiled and nodded his head with respect toward the elder.

"Together we can make our forest secure again. Be safe in your travels," the elder replied. He then disappeared into the morning mist.

When the men approached Doup Fell, Fobothom stopped them, "THE BUSH! This is the bush that had the white flowers!"

Martin pushed the bush over with his foot and cut it loose with a single strike of his broadsword. He then carried the bush back to the lodge where he gave it to one of the villagers. "Burn this bush, please. Burn it completely." The man looked at Martin with concern but seeing the intensity in the old Celt's eyes, he took the bush to be burned.

Alastair met the men at the lodge shortly after. "Did ye men sleep well?"

"Not really," Seumas replied with a moan. "We need to be off, but I have a request of yer council. Would ye please assemble them?"

Alastair looked around the common. Seeing all five elders, he called to each of them. The council assembled within minutes. "My friends, I have an unusual request of yeu. It is very important that ye do as I am about to ask. On any night when there is no moon in the sky, whether by clouds or without, ye must post guards in yer village common. Build four fires, one at each corner and keep the fires going all night. Four men must be alert and watchful on these nights."

"Whit will we be watching for?" asked one of the council.

"Hags, old women, creatures that should not be traveling in the dark," Seumas replied.

"And how long will we be watching through the night with our fires?" a councilman asked.

Seumas thought for a moment before replying. "Until we are certain that there are no more of these creatures in our Hielands." When he looked beyond the council his eyes locked on Brett whose expression was cold and stern. Seumas could see she was breathing heavily. He smiled as he called to his fellow travelers, "Let us return to our wives and families."

<hr>

Everyone kept silent on the journey back to *Ceo Dhachaidh*. Seumas was filled with concerns for what he did not know and how to fight a war where swords would be useless. His thoughts bounced from the hags' travels to the loss of a comrade to the simple comfort of Ingrid's arms. Thoughts bouncing quickly and without focus. Martin watched the land for anything that was not right, shadows out of place, leaves blowing without wind, echos without a source. Peter and Eric struggled to keep pace with the others. Faeries flew just above their friends, keeping watch for the men's safety as well as their own. The loss of Stractor weighed heavily on all minds and hearts.

Long shadows crept across the land as travelers reached their homes and arms of their loved ones. Raven appeared as the men talked with villagers. Keeping a short distance from the gathering, she glared at Seumas with the same expression which Brett had worn earlier that morning. Seumas refused to acknowledge Raven's discontent.

As shadows of night were replaced by first lights of dawn, Seumas awoke refreshed with Ingrid sleeping on his shoulder. His mind however, was still filled with the problems he had acquired on the journey. Softly he slipped Ingrid's head from his shoulder and sitting beside his sleeping wife, the large man cast his eyes around their small hut hoping to see faeries. His senses were filled with the quiet of the village. After several minutes of contemplation he dressed and left the peace of his hut. Again he searched for a faerie but found none. Raven walked by with her water pail glaring at Seumas, the accepted leader of the Highlanders. Seumas refused to acknowledge her presence.

Frustrated by what he knew yet did not understand, Seumas went to the forest where he had seen faeries come and go. After waiting several minutes the large man called out names he could remember, "Seebtin! Fobothom! Vrenessbith!" He waited in silence. "Are there any wee faeries about today?" A gentle breeze stirred the leaves and Seumas listened.

"Seumas?"

Seumas looked around but in the dim light of dawn could not see the source of the reply. "Faerie?" he called softly.

"It is me . . . Vrenessbith," the wee faerie called as she cautiously approached Seumas.

"Vrenessbith," Seumas sighed with relief. "Thank ye for coming. I need yer help and the advice of yer wisest elder."

Vrenessbith did not hesitate but immediately flew toward her cavie, calling back "Wait there; I will return!"

Seconds streamed into minutes as Seumas waited. His eyes scoured the forests watching for movement, alert for trouble. A martryn climbing down a tree in search of breakfast caught Seumas' eye. Instinctively the Celtic warrior reached for his broadsword but it was not there. He was going to visit a faerie, a friend, and had not picked up his battle gear. Wringing his hands impatiently, Seumas took a deep breath and let it out slowly, closing his eyes as he did so.

Resbith gasped as she approached Seumas, his *gleo* was thick and clung to his body like battle armor. What disturbed her most was the dark red hue. Collecting herself she called soothingly, "You are very worried. How can I help you?"

Seumas slowly opened his eyes and saw, just in front of him, a very old and very round faerie floating next to Vrenessbith. "I am Seumas Gregor and I have been charged with leading the Hielanders into tomorrow. But to do this I must learn to do something I do not understand."

"I am Resbith, Comleidh of our cavie. What can I do for you?"

Seumas thought for several seconds without speaking.

"She is my teacher and guide," Vrenessbith offered with great confidence. "She is the oldest and wisest of all the cavie in the mountains."

Seumas smiled and explained his problem. "My good Comleidh, I have been told that I must learn to see whit is beyond whit my eyes tell me is there. How can I do this?"

"Man sees with his conscious mind. He sees only what he is aware of, only what life has presented before him. When a man carries too many thoughts, others can manipulate his thoughts and change what he sees. You must open your mind to what your life has not yet revealed to you and accept the world as it truly is. View the world with your inner mind, clear of problems and troublesome thoughts."

"How is this possible?"

"You must shed the weights you carry in your mind: your problems, your worries, your concerns. Let your heart guide your mind and what you see. The man Iain learned to do this and he was much happier because of it. Remember, your life is shaped by what you see. What do you wish to see?"

"How do I do this?" Seumas asked, struggling to understand.

"When we approached, you had your eyes closed and were breathing slowly. This is a good first step. Learn to focus on only one thought at a time; too many thoughts create a storm which blocks much of the true world. Listen to your heart; it will tell you what thoughts need your attention. It will take time, but you can do this and you, too, will be happier when you do."

"I will try, Comleidh. I have one other request which I make for yer protection."

"What is your request?" Resbith asked patiently. As she waited for his reply, she watched him breathe more slowly, wrestling with and trying to control his thoughts and emotions. Seumas was trying to do as she had instructed.

"The hags have planted bushes that have a white blossom. These blossoms are intoxicating and dangerous, poison to faeries. It is my understanding that Seebtin and Fobothom, and possibly others, know the location of these bushes. I need them to show two of my companions where these bushes are so we can destroy them."

Resbith nodded and replied, "It will be done. Vrenessbith, go wake the rascals and tell them to help Seumas."

Vrenessbith glowed as though thrilled by a bit of mischief, then disappeared in a blink.

"Thank ye, Comleidh Resbith. I will try to do as ye have told me," Seumas nodded in respect to the teacher.

Resbith took hope seeing the leader's *gleo* was not so heavy nor so red as when she arrived. "Count your steps as you return, and do not step forward until you are certain where your foot will land," she called to Seumas as she disappeared into the dawn sky.

∿∿∿∿∿∿∿∿∿∿∿∿∿∿∿

Seumas returned to the village slowly, contemplating all he had just been told and counting his steps as he went. He even looked to the road frequently, a road he had traveled countless times, to see where his foot was landing. He saw a road that was well worn by thousands of steps yet still had many small stones which might cause a foot to slip and several which could twist an ankle. As though his feet had eyes of their own they stepped around the rocks and debris finding firm placement. The big man smiled when he saw a small field mouse scurrying across his path, presumably heading home after a night of foraging.

Approaching the common lodge, Seumas saw David talking with Peter about their recent excursion. "Peter, David," Seumas called softly as he came near. "I have asked the faeries to show us where the bushes with the white blossoms are growing. Would the two of ye accompany them and destroy every bush?"

Before they could answer a small voice responded, "This way! There are two this way!"

"May I go get an axe to cut the bushes with?" Peter chuckled as Seebtin and Fobothom tried to lead the way.

"We will wait by the big tree on the trail above the village," Fobothom announced as he and Seebtin quickly flew away.

"YE ARE A FOUL WENCH AND I WANT YE OUT OF MY HUT!" A man's loud voice yelled, disturbing the quiet morning. Seumas looked quickly and for an instant, a brief second, saw a hag standing in the door of Sean's hut. Startled, Seumas blinked and looked again. The second time he saw Raven and Sean arguing. The big man had been drinking again and was trying to throw Raven out of his hut.

"YOU INVITED ME INTO THIS HOVEL AND PROMISED ME A HOME!" Raven screeched. "WHERE IS MY HOME?"

Seumas tried to clear his mind so he could see what was happening but their noise overpowered his senses. Stomping to Sean's hut Seumas interrupted the scene, "Will the two of ye please quiet down. Raven, this is Sean's hut and ye are his guest. If he does not want ye in his company any longer then I suggest ye move out - AT ONCE!"

"WHERE am I to go?" Raven wailed back at Seumas and villagers gathering behind him.

"Why don't ye resume yer journey to yer sister's village?" Seumas challenged.

"NO! She can move back to my hut," Regina offered, pushing past Seumas and Sean. "Raven has become a valuable part of our village and ye should not be so quick to throw her out."

Raven snickered at Seumas and pushed Sean aside as she entered his hut to retrieve her meager belongings. "I will have all of ye hags out of our villages," Seumas growled under his breath.

"She's not so bad when I was dry," Sean offered. "But then she would not warm my bed and I took back to drinking. She is foul when I have been drinking. She is hideous to look at and a powerful stench; even the air about her tastes bad!"

Seumas thought about what Sean said; there was a truth there that he could not quite grasp. Stepping off toward his own hut Seumas gave in to the current situation, "Nobody likes a drunk, Sean."

As the women gathered Raven's bags and clothes, Peter and David marched toward the back of *Ceo Dhachaidh*.

"Quickly, we must go quickly," Seebtin called to the men.

Both men worked hard to keep up with the spry faeries, who led them through briars and thickets with no respect nor regard for any lack of trails or pathways through the dense forest. Working throughout the morning the men uprooted and collected a total of five bushes known, or believed to be those they sought. Having circled the village they carried the broken bushes back and tossed them into a village fire. The bushes burst into flame giving off an unusual green glow as fire consumed them. Everyone stopped their work, staring breathlessly at the uncommon blaze.

<hr>

Martin frequently tried to talk with Seumas regarding his suspicions about the women who had appeared in the villages, but Seumas refused to discuss the matter. On a quiet day when there was no one else around

Seumas did confide, "Martin, I know there is something foul about these women. Yeu, too, have seen this in Doup Fell. But I cannot strike against them until I know whit I am striking at. Please, be patient with me and be ready to stand at my side when the time comes."

Seumas tried constantly to focus his mind, as Resbith instructed, but the slightest distraction or noise defeated him. Confiding his torment to Ingrid, he explained, "I am a Celtic warrior. I can slay an army with my sword, I can lead a hundred men into battle but I canna hold but one thought in my mind. How did my cousin do it so easily? What was his power? I fear if I canna do as the faerie told me. This new war will explode around us and I will be powerless to fight in it." Ingrid could only hold her frustrated husband for she had no idea what he was talking about.

When the season filled the trees with a lush green, the faeries sponsored a great *ceilidh*. This grand celebration not only welcomed spring but united faerie couples as life partners. Villagers of *Ceo Dhachaidh* joined the magical celebration for the first time. Eric provided music on his bagpipes. Faeries came from cavies all over the mountains to a meadow next to the great loch near *Ceo Dhachaidh*. Resbith allowed the celebration to swell to a point where wildlife was disquieted and then called all young faeries seeking to be joined to the edge of the waters. Among the couples that pledged their futures to one another were Seebtin and Estavery, and Fobothom and Brianne.

Floating over the loch, Resbith charged each of the couples. "You will find many challenges in your lives together and just as many opportunities for happiness. The way of the faeries is to welcome challenges and celebrate opportunities as one by always putting the safety and happiness of your mate above your own. You must always be the strength of one another and never allow a breath of harm to fall upon either of you. This is your charge, one to another, from this moment until the end of days." When she finished each couple joined hands and facing one another twirled into the night sky as one, one single light reflecting all of nature. The sounds of countless wings filled the night with a magical swelling of music, a melody of enchantment, a song carrying all spectators and participants into tomorrow with a sense of purpose and awe. Just before the couples disappeared, Resbith called to Eric, "Play us a RANT!"

Seebtin and Fobothom pulled their mates close as they began twirling in Eric's pipes. They found that the closer they held their love the faster they would spin. Both Brianne and Estavery became sick with the spinning and had to sit on a tree limb to recover. Filled with the vigor of the evening, Seebtin and Fobothom resumed their twirling. After a time Eric realized that Sarah and Chris were tired and lowered his pipes, "I believe the time has come for the pipes to rest and for me to take my bride and bairn back to our bed." They were the last of the village to leave the magical gathering.

Brianne flew to Fobothom who was unable to fly after leaving Eric's drones. Seebtin wavered dizzily, unable to control his direction, as he tried to make his way back to his bride. Estavery rose from the tree limb to join to her new husband but as she did she was grabbed from behind by a large gnarly fist. Quickly, a hag grabbed at other faeries nearby, all too intoxicated from the evening to sense her approach.

"Gosnarl exbtracken en rubren!" she snarled, then released the faeries she had captured. As more than forty beautiful young faeries escaped the hag's open clutches each changed into a beetle of the night, glowing red as they ascended into the sky. The horror confounded other faeries, many of whom like Seebtin had just lost their loved one. The hag slipped away, cackling as she went.

A great frenzy filled the faerie population, all except Vrenessbith. Calmly the young faerie rose into the night sky, boldly reciting words she knew but did not understand, words that came from her birth in the stars. When she finished her words, a streak of lightning shot through the trees followed by a screech of pain.

Seebtin, and a number of other faeries who had watched their mates transformed into glowing creatures of the night, gave chase after the horde of night-flies. Fobothom and Brianne grabbed their friend, trying to hold him back.

"She is gone Seebtin!" Fobothom exclaimed. "She is lost to our world."

"NO! If an old hag can change her then our love can change her back. SHE IS MY LIFE PARTNER! I must find her and bring her home!" The desperate young faerie wrenched away from the grip of his best friend, disappearing into a dark and dismal search.

Springtime is not only a time of rebirth and celebration it is also a time for planting new crops, harvesting winter crops and refilling stores emptied during cold months finally passed. This early spring harvest was meager throughout all Highland villages because there had been no time to prepare the land in late autumn. Summer crept up on villagers as they toiled every day to feed their families and fill their larders. Slowly the land began to yield crops. Threats of a new war seemed distant, except to those men haunted by the loss of faerie companions.

In the village of Blyth Brier women gave great attention to a warrior about to become a mother. Rachel was reaching the end of her term. Every woman of the village had advice on how to prepare for the imminent event. Bridgett had more advice than others and insisted on being present for the birth, offering a special blessing that would ensure a prosperous future. Bryan and Roslyn politely asked her to stay away. Rachel bluntly advised Bridgett "If ye come within two meters of my child ye will meet the warrior I am known to be and ye will hobble out of our village." Other women of the village chastised Rachel for her attitude, consoling Bridgett.

There were no faeries near Blyth Brier but as Rachel began her labor a wave of excitement swept through the forest. Resbith and Vrenessbith picked up on the message at the same instant. "Rachel is a special friend of the faerie realm; go protect her child," Resbith instructed. Vrenessbith left immediately, arriving at Rachel and Bryan's hut as a new life drew its first breath.

A baby's first cry will shatter any silence. As the sun crested the trees and began to warm the village of Blyth Brier, the son of Rachel and Bryan stopped all activities of the village with his first Highland wail. Roslyn received her grandson and immediately lay him on his mother's belly. Another woman of the village assisted Roslyn in tending Rachel and the baby. Outside, a throng of women gathered at the door. Nearby, men surrounded Bryan slapping him on his back and declaring good wishes. "A cry like that means a great warrior is born!" someone decreed.

Vrenessbith hovered in the rafters watching the event with both joy and great concern. As Roslyn wrapped the infant in a blanket, Vrenessbith sensed a great trouble approaching. Quickly, she raced to Bryan, who was waiting eagerly outside his hut.

Bridgett grabbed a small bag she had prepared for the birth of Rachel's baby and rushed to the hut to give her congratulations. Seeing the gathered women she pulled and pushed them aside until she reached the doorway. Squeezing her bag of herbs in anger she witnessed Bryan laying Rachel's deerstone about young Robert's neck.

"Never remove this talisman," Vrenessbith warned. Then, gagging as Bridgett appeared, Vrenessbith disappeared into the forest above the hut.

As Angus closed the book a bolt of lightning lit the sky behind his desk. "Well, this ends part four of our great adventure, and at a good time, too." Looking at faces filled with questions, he added, "Good thing we dinna hae sheep and coos. With a storm approaching, we would hae to move them to safe pasture."

"Why don't you have sheep and cows?" Liam asked.

Marian turned to her grandmother, asking "Seanmhair, did Rachel have a baby?"

"Aye, wee one, a wee baby boy. And they named him Robert," Lillian replied smiling joyfully at her granddaughter.

"And an evil hag tried to steal him," Alex teased.

Seeing Marian's look of horror, Lillian consoled her, "It will be alright, ye will see."

"What about the sheep, Seanair?" Liam persisted.

"We hae not had sheep since I was about Alex's age. Sheep take a lot of land to graze and we were using a neighbor's land. Then my seanair got into a tussle with the owner of the land, he wanted to sell it and Seanair tried to stop him. Well, we lost grazing rights so Seanair just stopped keeping sheep. Then stopped the coos, too, a few years later. It was a lot of work and me father was not interested in continuing. Each generation must find their own way."

"Like Mom?" Liam asked, somewhat concerned about what he might have lost.

"Oh, it is not that yer mother dinna want to stay here. Yer father took a job in the states. But as long as we, yer seanmhair and myself, are here ye are all welcome to come." Looking squarely at Liam, Angus added, "I might even get yeu to help me work the last few diaries if ye hae a mind to."

Liam's eyes grew twice their normal size just as a bolt of lightning and clap of thunder shook the house.

A New Life

Supper on Tuesday evening was disturbed by a loud knocking at the door. Seeing her husband put another bite of lamb into his mouth, Lillian volunteered, "Would ye like me to see who that is?"

"No," Angus replied, swallowing prematurely. "I believe I know who it is and whit they want. I will take care of it" He then wiped his mouth with a linen napkin and excused himself from the table.

Opening the door, Angus looked at the face before him. Stepping outside he asked, "Whit is it, Jock? I was enjoying a bit of supper."

"I know Angus, and I am truly sorry," a man about Angus' age replied. He held his cap, a balmoral, curled nervously in his hands. "A special meeting of the village council has been called for ten tomorrow morning."

"Ye could have called on the telephone. Ye dinna hae to come in person," Angus replied with a heavy sigh.

"Aye, I did. A few of us got hold of the plans they wish to discuss in the morning. I wanted ye to see it before thair great 'unveiling'." Jock then handed Angus a large, page-sized envelope.

Angus looked at the package his lifelong friend was offering, hesitating before accepting it. "Okay, I will look at it later this evening. Ten o'clock ye say?"

"Aye, ten o'clock."

"Why so early? Council does not usually meet until three o'clock."

"I am not sure, but rumor says they want to drive up on the hill to sell thair project."

Angus looked at dark clouds filling the dusky sky. "It is likely to be wet. We shall see." He then paused silently. "Well, I thank ye for yer trouble and this information. I guess I will see ye at ten tomorrow morning. Please give my best to Merin."

"Aye, I will. Tomorrow, then."

Angus delivered the envelope to his desk before returning to supper.

"Well?" Lillian asked.

"Council meeting. Tomorrow, ten o'clock," Angus replied as he sat in his chair, rolling his shoulders as though trying to remove a discomfort.

"Why so early?" Lillian asked with growing concern.

"They want to 'drive out on the hill'. We shall see. Do we have any sweets? I could use something before we return to The Book."

"Aye, but not until ye finish yer supper."

All three children giggled and quickly cleaned their own plates.

Seebtin stood before Resbith, his eyes clear but his soul heavy with burden. Resbith looked at the young faerie, her heart weeping with his loss yet proud of his determination to recover the life and happiness which had been stolen from him.

"Young Seebtin, you have searched our mountains for Estavery for five years. Where do you venture now?" Comleidh Resbith asked.

"My heart tells me that my life partner has left our mountains and has wandered beyond. I must now venture where my heart calls me to go," Seebtin replied.

"Brother, you have been gone for five seasons," Fobothom interrupted. "What of those here who love you?"

"Fobothom, my dear brother since birth. Four of us were born on the same gust of wind, born of our parents' love. Thirty cycles of seasons passed as we grew together, learned together, grew bold and foolish together. You have Brianne as your life partner and together you are becoming parents of our next generation. Estavery was born with the three of us and she is my life partner yet we cannot become parents until I can bring her safely home to our cavie. Comleidh Resbith has asked where I venture now. Every winter since Estavery was stolen from me I have returned to our home for the cold months. I fear that my new direction will not allow me to come home until I can bring Estavery back with me. I go over the mountains, a distance too far to return simply to rest."

"Seebtin," Resbith acknowledged. "You have not only returned to rest, you have also returned to us seventeen of the twenty-nine souls lost to the hag's attack. In the one hundred forty three seasons of my knowledge I have not witnessed a loyalty and strength such as yours. I fear I will not be Comleidh when you next return, but know that your friends will always recognize you and welcome you home."

Seebtin looked away from the face of the great faerie who had trained him when he was young and given him charge when he joined with Estavery. Looking into the eyes of his birth mates, Fobothom and Brianne, he closed his eyes slowly and launched himself into the dawn sky. When he felt he was high enough to be alone he opened his eyes and turned toward the peaks of distant mountains. A young friend who had not been with the cavie when he left waited amongh the clouds for him.

"Guard your heart kind Seebtin," Vrenessbith whispered. "Do not let it become weak from searching for it is your strength and it holds the magic you will need when you find your partner. I will miss your presence this season but I know I will see you and Estavery together again."

Seebtin closed his eyes once more, but not in time to prevent an escaping tear from falling. He disappeared into the dawn sky.

Seumas looked down to the path as he emerged from the forest above *Ceo Dhachaidh*. Four much younger men discretely followed his footsteps for they observed how he had become increasingly aware of how his feet were placed on the earth. Since his talk with Resbith, the eldest faerie, Seumas would talk to himself on journeys. Traveling companions, actually most of the village had heard him mumble to himself, "Be aware of where yer foot is placed. Count yer steps. Be aware. . . . " Many thought he was losing his mind but everyone respected the change in him and the calm that Seumas tried to keep at all times.

Today's hunt yielded a small stag which Seumas carried on his shoulders, having accepted the challenge of his hunting partners that he was too old to carry such a load the distance back to the village. Seumas breathed easily and stepped quickly, making certain each footstep was sure. As he placed his second step beyond the edge of the forest, his eyes rose to the village which was about to surround him. The sun had just passed its peak, women were preparing the evening meal and children were running and playing. For the first time he saw grey cloaks hanging about the shoulders of many men and women. Before he could wonder about these peculiar wraps, his eyes found a sight that warmed his heart. His wife Ingrid and their daughter, Leigh, peeled turnips and carrots at his hut. Ingrid had no grey cloak about her shoulders. Comforted by the sight of his wife, Seumas looked up, beyond their village. Mountains were changing from winter grey to the tender green of early spring. Tops of distant mountains were still capped with lingering traces of white.

Suddenly Seumas let out a war cry, pulling his broadsword as he threw the stag from his shoulders. Every eye in the village turned toward the huge man racing across the common area, his sword held in both hands ready to strike. Before him four hags taunted and tormented Erial, the three-year-old daughter of Eric and Sarah.

Seumas could hear their words clearly in his mind as they argued, "You remove the talisman! It will burn your hand but then we can take the child."

"I have tried! I cannot get my hand around the child's neck. You have more experience with these people, you have lived among them for many years . . . why can't you remove this enchantment?"

Seumas brought his broadsword down with killing force, slicing the hag whose back was to him from her neck to her waist; it was Raven. The villagers witnessed the horror as the woman who had claimed to be Raven's sister and her two traveling companions cast off their cloaks of deception, focusing all their powers, both physical and mental, on Seumas. Raven's sister screamed an enchantment as the others drew knives hidden in their dresses, plunging them into the man who had been trying for five years to reveal their true identities. As the great Celt fell, he wielded his sword one final time dividing the body of a second hag.

Raven's sister reached for the talisman around Erial's neck. Eric picked up Seumas' sword and while it was incredibly heavy to his hands, ripped it through the hag's body. The fourth hag disappeared in the melee that swelled as Seumas fell.

Villagers of *Ceo Dhachaidh* turned their heads as Seumas cried out but not one, save Eric, could move. Hearts had ceased to beat when the blood curdling scream filled the air and not a breath was drawn until the attack was over. It took twice the time of the event for most villagers to comprehend what had just happened. Overcome by absolute disbelief and terror, villagers slowly stood and turned toward the spot of battle. One by one they ran toward their fallen leader as a brutal reality replaced their disbelief.

"RUNNERS!" Martin cried, supporting himself with a wooden stave, his voice mixed with the wave of awakening. No one responded for this call had not been heard in more than five years. "I NEED TWO RUNNERS!" Two men appeared before the old Celt. Martin looked at the two men, both breathing deeply, "To the villages at once! They are to bind every woman who has come to thair village since the battle on the hill. EVERY WOMAN! Bind them and bring them here at once. Tell them also that Seumas has fallen and we will hold a wake in eight days - they must be represented. Run quickly for our future relies on yer swiftness."

"Whit are ye thinking?" Newlyn, one of the last remaining Celts, asked as he approached Martin.

"We all thought Seumas was mad because he constantly challenged the women who visited our villages. These women were pleasant to all except Seumas. He knew who they were but we, all of us, would not let him run them out of our homes. When he attacked them today, I believe he could see them clearly for who, or whit, they truly were. One day, a long while back, he asked me to be ready to act when he would have need of me. I am acting now! The hags have finally revealed themselves! The war Seumas learned of many years ago has been struck. When we hold the wake for our fallen brother, we will also hold a council and prepare ourselves to fight these hags who hide among us."

"But whit of these women ye would have brought here? Do ye plan to kill them when they arrive?" Newlyn asked with grave concern.

"If Seumas was right in whit he has told me, all the hags have already left thair villages. Someone should mark this time and day; we will compare it with the leaders of the other villages when they arrive. We should clean up from this battle now and see to Ingrid and Leigh."

When the gathered men and women turned to Seumas, Ingrid was holding him, her tears bathing his face. A faerie rested on Seumas' right shoulder and another on Ingrid's left shoulder. Sarah held Leigh. Eric held Erial safely in his arms as he placed Seumas' sword in the fallen Celt's hands, resting across his chest. Bodies of the hags had melted into the ground. All of *Ceo Dhachaidh* stood in shock at the horror of recent minutes. A horror that instantly and drastically changed their lives, revealing the uncertainty which lay ahead.

Angus looked at the faces in front of him. Lillian was crying, tears running unabated down her cheeks. Marian, Alex, and Liam sat wide-eyed in disbelief. Angus shifted the book and drew a breath so he could continue.

"If Angus is dead, who will lead the battle against the hags?" Liam asked softly. "Nobody else believes there is a war, only Seumas could see these old witches."

"Aye," Angus agreed, "an they are 'hags' not 'witches.' A wee difference to be sure but an important one ye will come to understand. Now, consider this. While everyone thought Seumas to be a bit strange because he knew, now all know."

Looking at the faces of each of his grandchildren, Angus could see each was trying to understand what he had told them. Alex, the oldest, was becoming disturbed which showed he did grasp some significance of what had happened. Satisfied it was okay to proceed, Angus resumed his tale.

Seumas' body was burned to ashes at sunset on the day after his death. Ingrid and Leigh sat on the stone chairs at the top of the hill as his funeral pyre blazed nearby.

"May I speak with you?" a small voice called softly.

"Vrenessbith, I always welcome yer visits," Ingrid replied.

"I was not present when Seumas was killed," Vrenessbith began, "but I have listened to what many others who were there have said. I wanted to tell you that I think Seumas became who he wanted to be."

"Whit do ye mean?" Ingrid asked, concern filling her voice and face.

"Five, maybe six years ago he asked Comleidh Resbith for help. He wanted to be able to see the hags for what they truly were. I talked with him often as his ability to see the hags grew stronger, but he could never see them for more than a brief time. He saw them clearly yesterday as he struck them down."

"Vrenessbith, why did he strike them down at that moment? Whit were they doing that made him so violently angry?"

"The child Erial is one of two children protected by the power of these mountains. The hags fear this power and were trying to kill the child. I believe Seumas heard their threats in his heart as he saw thair actions with his eyes."

Ingrid thought about what Vrenessbith told her before asking "Why did no one else see the threat of Raven and the others?"

"The hags hide their true nature from you and others of your villages. Seumas recognized this and many of your friends thought he was . . . he was . . . 'out of his mind' I believe someone said. As Seumas learned to control his thoughts the hags lost their control over him."

"He tried to speak with me about this once. I could not understand whit he was talking about," Ingrid confessed as a tear rolled down her cheek.

"That is why he asked the faeries to help him," Vrenessbith sighed. "We have long seen these women as a danger to our own, but as you accepted them we could do nothing but avoid them."

"Whit are we to do now? How do we fight an enemy we cannot see?" Ingrid appealed, her voice flooding with despair.

"That is the very question that tormented Seumas," Vrenessbith replied. "You must trust in your heart and the power of the mountains. Learn how to let your heart draw strength from the land that you love."

"Wee faerie, ye make it sound so easy," Ingrid sighed as she turned her eyes back to the fire that consumed the body of her husband. Vrenessbith cried as she witnessed a massive wrap of gleo swelling about Ingrid's shoulders.

<center>~~~~~~~~~~~~~~~~~~~~~~~~~</center>

Families began to arrive to remember Seumas at noon on the seventh day after his death. Cullet Cavie arrived first, followed soon by Doup Fell. Martin expected a small representation from each village. Instead, the field below the stone chairs filled with Highlanders, wives, and children. Even dogs arrived to pay tribute to their fallen leader. This was the first great gathering since the wedding of Rachel and Bryan and Sarah and Eric, which was only weeks after the battle on the hill, more than five years past.

Martin assumed leadership of the gathering, walking calmly with the aid of his heavy stave, visiting with friends as they filled the hillside. Even though his mood was somber, he welcomed fellow Celts warmly and with muted joy. Eric and Peter greeted warriors they had helped to train when this same hillside swelled in preparation for battle with the Romans. It was a heartwarming gathering for a somber event.

Benmost Bield arrived late on the seventh day. Rachel and Bryan stayed with members of their village even though many from *Ceo Dhachaidh* invited them to more comfortable bedding in huts. Tristan, once the wee infant with incredible lungs, now ran through the gathering ahead of his parents. The deer stone which his parents had laid around his neck at his birth swinging wildly as he ran. Rachel carried Arland, their thirteen-month-old son, in her arms as she and Bryan renewed acquaintances which had lingered in the background in recent years.

Families from Stag's Byre and Haugh Mailen arrived before noon on the eighth day with villagers from Heigh Fell and Benmost Bield arriving a few hours later. Martin welcomed leaders from each of the villages, asking them to join him for a council meeting at the lodge as soon as they could get there. Making his way back up the hill, moving toward the heart of *Ceo Dhachaidh,* Martin invited leaders of the other five villages to the same meeting. He managed a smile for the children and stroked their heads as he went.

"David!" Martin called out when he reached the *Ceo Dhachaidh* common. "Do ye have any more of that skin or writing material ye use?"

"Aye, whit do ye need?" David replied quickly. He had been keeping a log of the village since the time the Gauls had arrived. Earlier journals were lost when the Romans raided his own village.

"I need ye to write something down, so we can look at it," Martin replied. David immediately left to retrieve his skins and charcoal sticks.

"Martin, whit have ye done to yer leg? Ye look like ye are gettin' old," Alastair from Doup Fell taunted.

"I may be gettin' old, but I can still put ye on yer behind with this stick," Martin retorted.

"Oh I did not mean to challenge my elder, I only meant to ask whit happened to yer leg."

"Last Autumn, Seumas and I were lookin' at the change in colours across the mountain. Suddenly a stack of wood rolled down on us; a log bounced on my leg. I whittled it down to make this stave." Martin raised his stave so others could see the elaborate art carved into his walking stick. "Tell me, Alastair, how goes the hags' roadway through Doup Fell?"

"Ye know, yeu and Seumas told us to watch our village at night until we were told it was not needed any longer. Neither of ye came back to tell us we could go back to bed, and that was a good thing. Near every month, as the moon rises full, we find hags sneakin' through our village. We challenge them and they run back up the hill into the forest from where they came. Until last full moon, that is. Last full moon there was six of 'em . . . "

"Seven!" another man from Doup Fell interrupted.

"Yes, seven of them came through. When we challenged 'em they came at us. Screechin' and wavin' big knives. Two of my men suffered mighty cuts and are still ill from 'em. We cut one of the hags down and she melted into the earth, left a black spot on the ground! Ye can only see it under the light of the moon."

"Whit of the other hags?" Martin asked.

"We canna tell. They fled, in all directions," Alastair concluded.

David joined the gathering of leaders and tried to hand the writing tools to Martin who replied, "David, I need yeu and Robert to record whit I am about to ask. I fear it will be important." Then looking to the gathering he addressed the leaders of the eight villages. "Thank ye for coming to this council meeting. Seumas confided many of his suspicions to me over the past year. He knew in his heart the vile nature of the women who had come to live among us but I saw none of them brought in today. Did ye forget to bring captives?"

"Brett disappeared. When we got news from yer runner we went to her hut and she was gone. My wife told me that she had walked away from a gatherin' of the women and has not been seen since," Alastair reported.

"When did she disappear?" Martin pursued.

"The women usually gather about midday, when the sun is high. Then they go back to thair own huts."

"Midday. Whit day?" Martin asked.

"Umm," Alastair thought, "I guess it was eight days back. The day Seumas was killed."

"The rest of ye have similar stories?" Martin looked around at puzzled faces surrounding him.

"Aye, that would be 'bout right," another leader agreed.

"Yes, Seumas, I am a believer," Martin said softly, then returned to the leaders, "When I walked through yer camps I noticed many of the younger children had marks on them: lazy eyes, half ears, torn lips, and other physical marks spoiling otherwise beautiful children. I want each of ye to tell David and Robert whit children have been born in yer villages since the battle on the hill and whit marks they bear."

While David and Robert collected the information from the many leaders, Martin spoke with others. He asked about the women who had come to visit for such a long time, other women who might have joined them for a spell, and anything that struck the leaders odd about them. Martin also asked after the health and help of the faeries. Every report included many events and visitors, events that had gone unreported over the years. One report which Martin had not expected disturbed him; faeries would never be in the same area as the women or hags. If faeries were about and the female visitor appeared, the faeries would vanish into the treetops. Realizing the connection, Martin called Peter, "See if ye can find one of our faeries, possibly Vrenessbith; she had been helping Seumas. Ask them to bring thair elder to our council."

When David and Robert completed their task, they told Martin what they had found. He called the council to order and repeated the information. "Forty-three children have been born in five years; twenty-nine have marks on them and twelve have younger siblings who have no marks. Only two of the older children do not have marks; Tristan, the son of Rachel and Bryan, and Erial, the daughter of Eric and Sarah but she has an older brother born after the battle."

"Aye," Eric replied, "but Chris is the son of Sarah's first husband and he was born only days after the battle. Chris bears no mark."

"Erial and Tristan are protected by their parent's connection to the mountains," replied a small voice that was heard by all.

"Ye are the elder of the faeries?" Martin asked.

"Yes, I am Comleidh Resbith. I heard your call and will lend what I can to your council."

"Thank ye for coming, Comleidh Resbith," Martin acknowledged. "How are we to address ye?"

"As a friend; please call me Resbith. We are all the same here."

"Thank ye, Resbith. How are Erial and Tristan protected and what are these marks?"

"Both Tristan and Erial have a parent who showed thair respect for the mountains and in turn was given a tribute, a heart stone. I believe you call it a 'deerstone.' Vrenessbith wisely told each parent to hang this tribute about their infant's neck when they were born. The hags cannot touch these infants, therefore these children may be important to your future. As for the marks on the other children, we believe them to be marks of the hags. Each mark is meant to cause disgrace and pain in the bearer's soul. Other children and adults will tease marked children because they are different and the child will become less than they should be."

Members of the council murmured to each other and tempers began to rise.

"The hags' evil is working against this council," Resbith continued. "They came into your communities and were welcomed, even cared for. You gave them every opportunity to do as they wished, even protected them against Seumas' rants. This is how they have begun their war against you, by causing distrust and seeding a great sickness in each village. Once you discovered their presence they left. You must now come back together and find the courage and community to fight them. If you do not, you will all live miserably in fear and your spirits will die before your lives end. The hags seek to control all that you do through your fears, preventing the pleasures life can offer."

Resbith stopped and waited for Martin, who thoughtfully continued, "Hielanders, ye have heard the story of our enemy. As Resbith has warned us we must now lift up those children of the mark. Honor them and do not let any other defile their nature. We must encourage them to become whole inside. I fear my next piece of information will cause great concern for this council. Seumas long suspected that the hags had a way of telling each other what they knew. They all shared a common knowledge. I thought Seumas was out of his mind when he told me this but as ye have all told us that the hags left yer villages at the moment of Seumas' death, I must acknowledge that he was correct. I called ye together to form a plan of defense which might lead us to a way to push these hags out of our mountains. Right now we need to find leaders among us; leaders who can move through the Hielands and support our villages. But before I ask, I would like to ask Resbith for her guidance."

"I wish I had guidance to give," Resbith replied soulfully. "These 'hags', as you call them, are spirits of the dark. They move through our mountains silently. Each of you must be on your watch as they might invade your villages or attack you on a trail. They are not of our realm so I do not know for sure what they might do nor how to defeat them."

There was an intense and uneasy quiet when Resbith finished speaking. Martin saw everyone growing restless so he concluded the meeting, "Hielanders, we are a council of elders. Let our age and experience guide us into this war we are now facing. Do not quarrel about whit has already happened for that would help the hags defeat us by defeating ourselves. I join Iain and Seumas in thair call; draw yer strength from these mountains that surround us and our mountains will defend us. Let us now honor our brother who gave his life to expose our enemy."

The sun had barely touched the tops of distant trees when Eric raised his pipes. His music began with a slow rhythm, like the heartbeat of someone sleeping. Activity on the hillside stopped as melodies drifted down, caressing every ear and touching every heart. Finishing his first tribute, Eric nodded to a young man about seventeen years old who was waiting with his own set of pipes, a set he had made with Eric's help. Raising his pipes, Perth joined Eric playing rhythms which pulled at everyone to get to their feet in celebration of Seumas Gregor. The two pipers took turns keeping the wake, a celebration of life, lively and filled with joy. Sean helped Farrell, the local brew master, tap three kegs of mead for all to enjoy.

Rachel approached Ingrid, who was sitting at the top of the hill in the stone chairs with Leigh at her side. "I believe Seumas is enjoying his *ceilidh*."

"Aye, he would that," Ingrid sighed, filled with loneliness. "But I would prefer that he were with me in body, not just spirit." Ingrid accepted a warm and loving hug from Rachel, neither truly willing to let go of the other.

When the moon began to slide toward the mountains, Martin hobbled up the hill toward his hut. He had been enjoying the mead and was struggling to make it to his bed. Stopping at the top of the hill he called back, "Alastair, let us see the black marks Seumas made of the hags!"

Newlyn and two younger men joined Alastair and Martin as they stumbled toward the village common where Seumas had been killed. Indeed, the moonlight revealed three black marks on the ground, a mark where each of the hags was killed. "Whit makes these marks that we can see only in the light of the moon?" one of the men asked.

"Dinna know," Alastair replied. "But if those hags think on using Doup Fell as thair roadway agin, we will make a black mark the length of our village with thair dark souls!"

Suddenly Fobothom flew into the middle of the men, crying loudly, "HAGS ARE COMING!"

It took several seconds for the message to register with the men who, like Martin, had been drinking mead. Alastair and Newlyn were the first to draw their swords as they met four hags descending upon their small gathering. Both swords greeted hags with immediate contact, adding to the black marks. Two others attacked Martin, who fell before he had a chance to defend himself. In a rush to escape these two hags ran directly into younger men who carried staves. With the speed of young warriors the hags toppled the men, doing as much damage as they could without lingering to fight. One hag pushed over a young man, stepping on his leg and fracturing it as he fell. The second hag trampled her victim pushing him down backwards across a log, injuring his back. Having done their damage, the hags vanished into the darkness as quickly as they had appeared.

Martin's body was cremated at the next sunset with all the villagers of the Highlands again watching in silent disbelief. They had come for one wake and now also attended a solemn fear-filled funeral. Resbith looked on as the sun cast its last rays across the hillside. Every man and woman struggled to stand under the weight of expanding gleo. The Highlander's struggle to survive had taken a darker complexion. Without a leader to direct them, Highlanders left the hillside the following day unaware as they left that each group was watched by a flight of eight faerie guardians.

Traveling with families is much slower than warriors on the march. "You should stop here, before it gets dark," a small voice advised an old Celt leading the procession toward northern villages.

"Whit?" the startled Celt stopped and looked around. "Ah, wee faerie. We canna stop here, we are but half way to Blyth Brier. It will be late, but we can make the village before we rest."

"It will be dark soon," the faerie repeated. "You must form a circle before the sun fades away, protection from the hags."

Thinking deeply the old Celt agreed and formed the four villages into groups which he, and others, could easily watch over. Men of each village stood guard by fires throughout the night. When replacements woke to relieve them, their first duty was to walk the perimeter of the camp before the past watch could retire. Younger men were uneasy and talked. Older men and experienced Celts stood silently, straining to watch bushes through rising mist.

Morning haze hung heavy with the day struggling to dawn as travelers resumed their journey homeward. Families of Doup Fell quietly parted from the group when they reached the first split in the road. Villagers of Benmost Bield and Heigh Fell stayed in the safety of Blyth Brier for a night; some with smaller children stayed two nights.

Highlanders returning to villages of the eastern mountain made it to Cullet Cavie the first night and rested. When they approached Stag's Byre on the evening of the second day, many from Haugh Mailen decided to push on saying "We have the advantage of a bright moon." Four of the faeries who had been watching the villagers of Stag's Byre joined with Haugh Mailen folk as they pushed on toward home.

When the nighttime travelers were about an hour from home, faeries sounded alerts from every direction. Men quickly pushed women and children to ground in the center of group and greeted attacking hags as warriors prepared for battle. Hags emerged from the shadows running at the men, striking them with long staves and disappearing back into the dark depths of the forest. Steadfast Highlanders easily defended themselves but did not have time to strike back as their attackers quickly disappeared. Short strikes repeated every few minutes for nearly an hour before the air cleared of the hags' stench. Highlanders then resumed their journey homeward, ever watchful of changing shadows. Only one man was injured, a broken arm, but all the hags escaped.

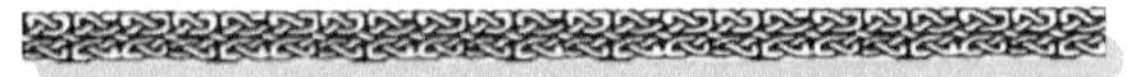

Resbith looked to the young faeries forming a circle around her, each holding a flower bud waiting to bloom. "Faeries should not cause anything to happen that would not happen without them," the patient Comleidh began. "We can guide a breeze but we cannot create a wind. We can lift a mist from the loch but we cannot make it rain. The mountains are filled with incredible power waiting to be used; you need only learn to call it to your purpose. Today we will bring the energy of the mountains into your hands. You must begin by releasing all the energy you are now holding within you. Breathe deeply and let your breath out slowly. As you breathe out, release those thoughts, good and mischief, that are floating around in your minds."

Nearly all the faeries, each nine seasons or older, plus Vrenessbith who was only in her sixth season, followed their Comleidh's instructions. A great peace settled over the gathering until Resbith felt a wave of mischief. "Brendon! Vrenessbith! Let your thoughts go. Do not try to send them to one another," the Comleidh chastised without turning to the two mischievous faeries. Calm restored to the circle, Comleidh continued, "Feel the energy of the mountain rise in your heart. Gently guide this energy to your hands. Do not be alarmed at its warmth; just let it flow as a rivulet of energy. If you feel your heart begin to beat faster, take a deep breath and release it slowly. Watch flowers in your hands take this energy from you."

One by one buds opened into delicate white flowers. Two faeries grew very frustrated as their blossoms did not open. Vrenessbith's flower bud opened delicately, as most others, but then continued to grow and change colours. Her bud produced a stem, roots and other blossoms, each a different colour: delicate pink, soft blue, luscious lilac, and gentle white. The original blossom doubled in size and reflected all colours of the rainbow, beginning with a deep red in the center and reaching a rich blue around the edge. Vrenessbith gently placed the plant on the ground in front of her where its roots dug into the mountain and more limbs and blossoms began to appear.

"VRENESSBITH! RELEASE IT!" Resbith called out excitedly.

Vrenessbith moved her hands away from the small bush in front of her and stepped back, admiring what her small bud had become.

With a deep sigh the Comleidh dismissed her faeries from their lesson, "Young ones. We are guardians of the mountains and all that dwell here, plants and animals. It is not our place to change the energy we are given, only to direct it where it is needed. Your buds had been taken from the plants that would have fed them the energy they needed to bloom. You provided that energy. Do not seek to change the nature of our world; we are here to protect and guide it. Btorgh and Gister, come see me later and we will try again. The rest of you enjoy your day. Vrenessbith, please wait with me."

Immediately young faeries flew off in different directions, most of them pleased with what they had done. Resbith hovered next to Vrenessbith and with another deep sigh asked the young faerie, "What did you do?"

"I did as you instructed, Comleidh," Vrenessbith replied innocently. "I felt the energy of the mountain swell up in my heart and I directed it toward my hands. Then my mind saw these beautiful colours and I felt the energy increase. It flowed through me like a stream of rain rushing down the mountain."

"Have you ever felt this stream of energy before?"

"Yes, two times."

"When were those two times, young one?"

"One time I was watching the martryn in the glen. A great bird knocked the martryn from the top of his tree and he began falling. In my mind I saw the young martryn stop falling and safely land at his hole on the other side of the tree. A great energy raced through me as I watched and suddenly the martryn was safely inside his nest."

"Where were you when this happened?" Resbith asked with great concern.

"I was hovering near the middle of the glen," Vrenessbith stated calmly.

"And the other time you felt this energy?"

"The first time was when the hag attacked the faeries and turned them into night creatures."

"It was you who produced the lightning that struck the hag?" Resbith smiled.

"I guess I did, but I felt sick after it happened. I was very weak and had to lie down in the grass. I woke the next morning not knowing all that had happened."

"Where were you when the lightning appeared?"

"I was sitting at the top of the old tree, above Estavery and the others. I was angered by the hag and then fell from the tree when the lightning appeared. I was too weak to fly so I rested in the grass."

"Vrenessbith, it troubles me to tell you," the Comleidh responded, "but I do not have the powers that you do for I was born of a faerie's love. You were born of a different miracle. I do not know what power is within you. I cannot summon lightning as you have, but I can raise a mist on the loch so that neither man nor hag can see. Abilities such as these should not be used foolishly for they can weaken your soul. Make certain you are strong enough to bear the events you create. You must learn to control and direct your abilities in a proper way. Saving the martryn from the hawk was good, but the lightning is not natural. Nor was the bush which you created today. I fear that if you use your strength unwisely it will call the hags to our quiet places and give them control over us. Do not change the nature of the energy of our mountains. Guide it gently. Now, while your bush is quite beautiful, you will please remove it!"

Smiling at her Comleidh, Vrenessbith reached out and held the multicolored flower at the top of the unusual plant in both hands. Immediately the bush began to fade until it was once again only a flower bud waiting to blossom.

<hr>

"A 'right, lassie and laddies, I must stop now for I hae other reading I must do before tomorrow." Looking at his book, Angus continued, "I see we will be returning to Doup Fell."

As Angus lay the silk ribbon across the page, Marian asked, "Do you think we can make a flower bud open in our hands?"

"I dinna know," Lillian replied with a broad smile. "Perhaps tomorrow ye can give it a try."

"I would rather make lightning," Alex inserted with a burst of energy.

"Lightning?" Liam chortled. "You would most likely burn your hands off!"

"Aye, lightning can be a bit hot to handle," Angus agreed. "First, try the flower buds."

Lillian rose in time to get a kiss from Angus as he shifted to his desk. After laying the book down he plopped into his desk chair and lifted the envelope left by Jock. Holding it in his hands he sighed and shook his head slightly before peeling the closure open.

Angus pulled a glossy brochure from the envelope. Several separate sheets were attached with a paper clip. A map on one of the sheets caught his eye, it was their cove and the hillside where the stone chairs once rested. A two-lane road was drawn across the hillside with an overlook where the remains of the seats rested. This road continued across the page to what was now virgin forest. Outlines of buildings destroyed the serenity of nature. Turning to the brochure, Angus found images of the loch, photographs taken from where the new development was to rest. These photographs had either been enhanced or taken on an uncommonly clear day. Artist's concept drawings of a new village to be constructed filled other pages along with flowery phrases constructed to entice buyers. Another sheet of paper contained a chart of costs, what it would cost to buy into this village. "I hae not seen that much money at one time in all my life," Angus mumbled under his breath. The last sheet of paper distressed the old Highlander even further. It was a timetable. According to this plan heavy equipment would be brought in within three weeks and first residents would move in by early spring of next year.

Angus began to fall deeper into depression, his shoulders sagging under an extreme weight, but a crack of thunder caught his attention. Only then did he hear rain falling against the window behind him. A meager smile crossed his lips as he looked upward and softly prayed, "Thank yeu, Lord." His shoulders lifted, just a bit lighter.

~~~~~~~~~~~~~~~~~~~~~~~~~~~~~~~~~~~~

The Council Chamber was already full when Angus and Lillian arrived. As they shook rain from their coats, men and women standing in the doorway parted to allow their entry. Smiling with gratitude Angus and Lillian walked to the front of the room, briefly greeting other villagers as they proceeded. They sat on the front row in the last two empty chairs which had been saved for them.

A man seated center of the head table nodded at Angus as he lifted a gavel. Angus acknowledged his welcome. Mayor Bryce Munro then banged his gavel on a wooden plate calling, "Seeing that we have no more seats, I call this special council meeting to order. This meeting has been called to hear a request from Bradshear Enterprises. Do they have an officer present and ready to present their request?"

"Yes, sir, your honor," a man about thirty years old replied as he stood from his seat across the aisle from Angus.

Bryce looked to Angus again, then to the young man as he asked officially, "Whit is yer request?"

Taking a deep breath, the young man began his request with a distinctively American accent. "Gentlemen of the council, Bradshear Enterprises has acquired rights to a large tract of land on the northern banks of your lake, excuse me, 'loch.' Before executing these rights, we
~~~~~~~~~~~~~~~~~~~~~~~~~~~~~~~~~~~~

ask for two things. First, the blessing of not only this council but this community as well. Our development will, in essence, create a new community that will significantly increase the wealth of your village. But, in order to reach our land we need permission to cross lands held by Mister Angus Gregson and his family. He has been reluctant to discuss this with us so we appeal to the community for help."

All eyes turned to Angus. Bryce called upon Angus to respond, "Angus, whit say ye?"

Angus faced the young man as he stood, then turned to the council table before replying. "Permission is not mine to give. As I explained to this young man before, I am only the caretaker of this land. Permission must come from Clan Gregor. We have a gathering this year, the first weekend in October. I can present yer request at that time."

"Mister Gregson, are you not 'Laird' of this land? And as such don't you have authority to make decisions such as this?" the American asked, trying to flatter Angus.

"'Laird,' now there is a title I hae not heard in a very long time," Angus replied with a smile. "Aye, I do hold the title of 'Laird,' but that is all it is." Angus paused briefly, then continued. "Nae, it is more than that, it is a responsibility. It is a responsibility to care for and protect this land and these people who live on it. But I hae no authority other than to advise. As I said, I will be glad to bring yer request to our Clan Chiefs in October."

"Your honor," the American responded quickly. "I was aware the Clan Gregor meets every three years but did not realize they were to meet this year. However, anticipating this response, our attorneys contacted each of the governors, excuse me 'Chiefs' of Clan Gregor, and have signed statements from them regarding their permission to cross this hillside." Reaching back to an associate, the spokesman took a folder of papers and offered them to the council. "One chief gave permission, only two denied permission, and nine others left the decision to Mister Gregson. We now appeal to Mister Gregson for a decision."

Angus took a deep breath and turned to members of the village crowded into the small council chamber. Looking down at Lillian he took strength from her smile, turned back to the American, and began his reply. "Sir, I hae seen yer plans for yer community and I challenge yer statement that this will bring wealth to our village. Yer plans include all the shops ye would need to support yer own village. Oh, yes, we might get a pound or two from tourist trade, but we hae that already, and it has nae made any difference in our wealth. A few of our younger men might find work building yer grand structures, but again, this would be insignificant over time. According to yer schedule, they would be out of work again in little more than a year. Nae, I canna personally support yer community, but I will leave that to the village to decide.

"Before I ask my neighbors to vote their conscience I offer one other comment. Ye not only wish to build a highway across sacred Hieland soil but to construct a tourist stop at the very spot that gave birth to these Hielands. Nae, I will nae vote to defile our heritage."

The American quickly took advantage of Angus taking a breath, not caring whether or not he had finished. "Sir, you speak of a pile of crumbling rocks as though it were a holy shrine. I have heard these legends and they are nothing more than that, legends to attract tourists, just like . . ."

"LEGENDS!" Angus roared. "Ye may call them legends, just as ye call our Hielands 'hills' and 'trees.' Nae, young man, it is not legend, it is OUR HERITAGE, and there is a vast difference between the two."

"Fine, you placed the decision with the village," the American replied. "We have most, if not all of your village here right now. I ask for a vote. Mayor, will you please call for a vote from those present? May we have access to our land by crossing the hillside of Mister Gregson?"

Bryce banged his gavel several times as he stood. "A vote has been called. All opposed to the proposal of Bradshear Enterprises move to my left, behind Angus. All in favor move to the right behind the American."

It took five minutes for everyone to get resettled on their choice side of the room. The room was lopsided in that those behind Angus were older, long time residents of this village. Those on the other side were younger, new land owners who had inherited or purchased old family estates. Bryce stood and called, "Bailiff, yeu count those in favor. Clerk, yeu count those against. Members of the council, take yer sides as well, it looks close." Five members of council shifted with three moving toward Angus and two moving toward the American.

When the vote was tallied on both sides, the clerk and bailiff wrote their numbers down and handed them to Mayor Munro, who stood beside Angus. "We have thirty-six against and thirty-nine in favor. Permission to cross the hillside and develop thair tract of land is hereby granted by community vote."

Filled with victory the American turned to Angus announcing, "Mister Gregor, our survey crew will begin marking the road tomorrow morning. I trust there will be no problem."

"Nae, ye canna begin tomorrow," Angus replied calmly.

"Why, your neighbors have just given us permission!"

"Aye, but the land won't. It is too wet. Yer equipment will destroy the hillside. Ye must wait till the land drys a bit."

"Okay," the American agreed tentatively, "how long?"

"Four days, that is four days without rain. Ye have gained permission to cross but nae destroy. I will be there to supervise and if ye touch one tree or stone off the roadway, I will end it then and there. An there will be no tourist station on the hillside!"

"Yes, sir," the American agreed between clenched teeth.

The children had no idea how long their grandparents were to be gone and all three were restless with curiosity about what this meeting was all about. When the rain stopped and a wee bit of blue shone through grey clouds, about quarter past eleven, Marian cried out, "I'm going to see Belinda!"

"What?" Liam called with disbelief. He was not excited about running out into wet grass.

"Why do you want to visit Belinda?" Alex asked. Being the oldest he was to make the decision to go out or not.

"Flowers! I want to make a flower bloom like the faeries!" Marian cried, convincingly.

Alex and Liam looked at one another for several seconds, then all three bolted for the door.

Angus and Lillian arrived home to an empty house. "I'll check the hillside," Angus volunteered.

Both grandparents arrived at the top of the hill in time to hear Marian laugh with pure delight. Looking to the faeries' oak tree they saw their granddaughter holding a stem with a wild rose blooming in her hand. The boys both struggled with buds that refused to open.

Throughout lunch Marian giggled as she looked at her rose, now resting in a vase in the center of the table. Both boys grumbled about flowers being a "girl thing."

"No, it was just like Seanair read in the book. Belinda told me to clear my mind and reach into the ground, to pull energy from the mountain," Belinda explained.

"Yea, Belinda reached into the mountain for you!" Liam pouted.

"Enough. It is a beautiful rose and it bloomed in Marian's hands," Lillian interrupted. "I hae lived on this hill for nigh on thirty-nine years and I never even dreamt of doing such a thing. You are a beautiful spirit wee girl. Now, finish yer lunch."

As all finished their sandwiches, Angus invited them back to the story.

Alastair stood watch in the center of the village of Doup Fell. After searching dark shadows for signs of what should not be, he looked across to their guard. Robert stood near the lodge. Michael, a young man of seventeen and new to the guard, kept watch at the lower end of the village. All was peaceful so the elder walked over to a pile of hot coals where he lit a small stick which he used to light his pipe. As smoke billowed about his head, he marveled at the beauty of the star-filled heavens peeking through a hole in the tree canopy. Wearily he gazed around the village, looking at the shadows once more.

"THREE HAGS ARE COMING! THREE HAGS!" a wee faerie called to Alastair.

Without a word Alastair snuffed the fire in his pipe with his thumb and slipped the pipe into his vest pocket, saving the herb he enjoyed puffing which was seasonal and difficult to find. Quickly he scoured the edge of the forest searching for signs of movement. Not seeing any, the leader of Doup Fell turned to signal the alarm to the other two men on watch.

Michael and Robert saw the hag at the same instant, just above the center of the village. Without hesitation both men ran toward the intruder, Michael pulling his dirk from his belt as he ran. This lethal short sword was a gift from his father acknowledging Michael's coming of age.

High above the village the faerie who sounded the alarm looked back. Realizing that something was wrong the faerie called to other faeries hiding around the village, then summoning all his courage, he dove toward Robert. Befuddled by the interference of the faerie Robert ceased his attack on the hag but Michael continued to charge. Four other faeries raced toward Alastair, but Michael got there first, plunging his dirk deep into the hags bowels before she made a move to defend herself.

Filled with rage five wee faeries stopped their breathing as they charged toward three hags standing in the shadows at the edge of the village. One of the faeries signaled the others to attack only the hag on the right. As they swarmed about her head, the other two hags moved, breaking their concentration. The one hag under attack swatted at the bothersome faeries, catching and crushing two. Another hag crushed a third faerie warrior.

Seeing the hags at the edge of the forest, Robert charged after them. Distracted by faeries, the hags did not see the Highlander's approach. With a thrust strengthened by rage Robert drove his stave into the chest of the center hag. As she melted into the ground the other two fled.

Seeing his dirk protruding from the belly of Alastair, Michael froze in his killing motion, a ripping turn of the blade. He had driven his blade into a hag, yet it was Alastair, the leader of his village who now suffered its horrible effect. Relaxing his hand Michael gently turned the weapon backwards, drawing it out slowly. Alastair looked into his eyes with astonishment and disbelief. "We saw ye as a hag," Michael sobbed, tears flowing down his cheeks. "We saw ye as a hag."

Alastair's eyes relaxed and closed.

Robert stood over Michael, placing a hand on his shoulder speaking softly, "There were three at the edge of the forest, but only two lived to flee."

Robert quickly alerted other members of the Doup Fell council of elders who were outraged at the murder of their leader. Their anger and shouts woke the rest of the small village who demanded immediate action against Michael. Robert tried to calm them but he too came under attack.

"STOP!" came a wee voice hovering above the village elders. "STOP! We lost three brave faeries tonight as you have lost your leader."

"WHIT?" Gregory, a village elder, challenged abruptly, then turned on the villagers. "BE QUIET! All of ye!" As soon as everyone became quiet, Gregory turned to the faerie floating in front of him. "Faerie?"

"We lost three brave souls tonight as you have lost your leader. Our guards tried to attack the hags who changed your leader's appearance. Three of our family gave their lives trying to save yours. These men did nothing wrong! They were trying to protect your village."

"Thank ye for stopping us from making another grave mistake, elder faerie," Gregory said softly, his rage changing to confusion. "Whit do ye mean they changed Alastair's appearance?"

"Three hags hid at the edge of the forest. They must have known a faerie would alert your leader to their presence. All three cast their energies toward your leader causing the others to see him as one of them."

"Again, thank ye for yer protection, elder faerie. Will ye join us for Alastair's funeral pyre at next sunset? We will include yer fallen heros as well," Gregory offered.

"We will be here with you, but our warriors will be laid with flowers at sunrise." The faeries then returned to their cavie, all but five who continued to stand guard over the village.

Faeries of Doup Fell gathered in a glen near their cavie as the darkest hour of night gave way to dawn. Three broken spirits lay side by side on a soft clump of moss surrounded by flowers of the forest. Slowly the shadows of night gave way to the light of a new day revealing friends and family of the fallen standing silently, waiting. Highland myst grew heavy at dawn, then began to lift, allowing first rays of sunlight to strike the clump of moss. An unusual scent filled the air, unlike any produced by a single flower. The air bordered on sweet, relaxing all senses and lifting minds to total awareness. Bathed in this richness of the mountains three small warriors slipped from this world into the realm that had nourished them. Immediately, flowers closest to the moss took on a new brilliance. Their robust colour and the unusual aroma spread across the glen before fading like the myst.

In Doup Fell, younger men built a funeral pyre while elders and others argued about what had happened. Some did not believe the words of the faerie and blamed Michael for being drunk while on watch. Gregory came to his defense, "Michael was not drunk. I looked into his eyes; he dinna know how he killed Alastair. He dinna know! And I dinna know whit we should do about this new threat. We canna trust whit we see, but I do know that we must warn the other villages or we will have mass slaughter by our own hands. We could send runners, but I dinna see that as an answer to this problem."

Men continued to mumble and complain about the current war until sunset. With the last rays of sunlight fading, Alastair was laid upon the funeral pyre which was lit at the close of the day.

Once the body of Alastair had been consumed, Gregory called remaining elders together. "I will take Michael and two others to *Ceo Dhachaidh* in the morning. As we travel to the south two runners need to go north and explain this new threat to those villages. The two who travel with me will go to the eastern villages and warn them. They can then join us in *Ceo Dhachaidh*."

Several of the men, including those who were not on council, grumbled angrily about Gregory's solution but nobody offered a better plan.

〰〰〰〰〰〰〰〰〰〰〰〰

Alastair's pyre was still a bed of hot coals when six men of Doup Fell departed at sunrise. Gregory wrestled with an awakening realization all the way to *Ceo Dhachaidh*. When one of his fellow travelers asked a question, they would have to repeat the question only to receive a very short answer from their leader. His attention remained focused on his inner struggle.

Arriving at *Ceo Dhachaidh,* Gregory called their council together and explained his dilemma to all who gathered. "First, Seumas was killed and Martin stood up as a leader. In no time at all Martin was targeted. Alastair told me about the attack after Seumas' wake. Those hags were after Martin. Now Alastair, the leader of Doup Fell has been attacked. They are killing our leaders and doing thair best to create doubt and mistrust among the rest of us. They don't have to kill us. They will create so much confusion that we kill ourselves!"

Men and women of *Ceo Dhachaidh* stood silently as Gregory presented his story. Not one man offered an argument. Not one man offered a solution.

"Leaders stand out from the others," Newlyn finally replied. "Each village must learn to lead and protect themselves. If any leader is seen in the village, the hags will cut them down. We must have no leaders."

"No, Newlyn, we must *recognize* no leaders," Gregory corrected. "Whenever a decision is to be made, make it as a group. Everyone must have a say in the decision and then decide as a group. I do not know that they will try to kill a group, especially if they think the group is struggling with answers. But I do agree, we canna count on *Ceo Dhachaidh* for protection any longer. Each village must provide thair own protection and defense." There was an uncomfortable quiet choking all men and women at this gathering. Gregory broke the overwhelming silence with another problem, "And whit of nae being able to trust whit we see?"

"Trust the faeries," Eric called out. "They have sworn to help us and they need us as we need them. Ask elders of the faeries to see that each guard has a faerie on his shoulder. The faerie can alert him when something is wrong and if a guard sees a hag, the faerie can say if it is real before they fly to higher safety."

"When my runners arrive we will return to Doup Fell and I will send news to the northern villages," Gregory agreed. "But we need *Ceo Dhachaidh* to send runners to the eastern villages."

"It will be done," Newlyn offered. "Will two runners stay and talk with the council? The rest of ye go home and hug yer children."

Two runners left *Ceo Dhachaidh* at next sunrise. Villagers in Cullet Cavie and Stag's Byre welcomed them, and after brief counsel sought faeries within their village. Elders of the villages met quickly with elders of their local cavie. Villagers of Haugh Mailen were unhappy with this new strategy for there was no faerie cavie near their village. "We have no wee folk in our forests!" an elder cried out to the runner who brought the news.

"But we did have the faeries travel with us after Seumas' wake," a woman offered.

"Aye, but they were of *Ceo Dhachaidh* and Stag's Byre," the elder rejected.

"But Stag's Byre is nae so far away. Could some of thair wee folk move to Haugh Mailen?" a woman asked.

The elder looked around, "So, as it is yer suggestion, ye and yer husband and my wife and I will travel to Stag's Byre tomorrow. It will look like a family outing and not leaders desperately seeking help."

<center>~~~~~~~~~~~~~~~~~~~~</center>

Faeries from Stag's Byre did establish a new cavie in the forest outside Haugh Mailen. As faeries and Highlanders worked together, the hags' trickery began to fail. Nearly every trick and deception devised by the hags was foiled by faeries revealing truth to Highlanders, who were then able to defend themselves, often killing the hags. But this partnership was not without cost, for hags began actively hunting faeries, seeking to crush each cavie. Several cavies found it safer to move into the villages and live in the rafters of huts.

Faeries and Highlanders grew stronger together as they learned the ways of the hags. No longer did they fear the moonlight or shadows around their fields. Several times hags attacked at dusk as weary Highlanders returned from their fields but they found that farm tools also make effective weapons in the hands of angry farmers.

As Highlanders found new ways to defend themselves, their spirits rose and their confidence returned. With the help of faeries, Highlanders learned that hags would muddle minds of men before attacking. They also discovered that a weary mind or one too alert is easily confused, but a calm mind could not be attacked. Highlanders took advantage of this discovery by carrying a jug of mead or ale to the fields with them. When faeries were not around, two sometimes three men would drink of the jug as the sun began to reach the treetops. Just enough to ease their minds a wee bit. When hags would hex the men, those warriors of the jugs could see the truth and sound an alarm. This defense did have its drawbacks as most of the men wanted to be drinkers and now night guards often drank too much, falling asleep on their watch.

When the cold of winter returned attacks of hags ceased. Snow and ice quickly turned to slush before fresh snow began falling. Highlanders found it difficult to visit other villages to get news. When groups did make it between villages, each community rejoiced at the calm in the war. Rejoicing, however, changed to complacency before the fresh green of spring arrived. Pain and fear are difficult to endure but are easily ignored in favor of more pleasant pursuits. Conversations and activities turned toward planting new crops and thoughts of fearsome hags continued to fade. Few highlanders felt the weight of gleo as their life was now more pleasant.

Quietly life returned to normal as crops were planted, nurtured and harvested. With prospects of full storage bins, threats of hags were forgotten. In the evening after the first spring harvest Rachel brought her harp into the village common at Blyth Brier. Her music warmed everyone's hearts. Men and women danced to lilting sounds and voices joined melodies. In *Ceo Dhachaidh,* Eric and Perth took to the hill with their pipes. Together they played rants and aires as faeries swirled in their drones. Every one of the eight villages had their own celebration with mead, ale, and song.

Early the next morning women in each village went to their storage bins to get grain for bread and found the stores spoilt, rotted as though soaked with rancid water. Once the spoilt grain and vegetables were removed less than half the supply was usable. As men returned to their fields to plant summer crops they found the crops would not prosper. Highlanders carefully tended their seedlings by day and guarded storage bins by night. After many weeks nurtured crops began to thrive. Men of every village continued their vigils.

New problems appeared; rodents were found in food bins even though they had been watched. Crops would be thriving one day and lying in the field the next. Men and women traveling between villages found similar stories in each community, though not one person in all the Highlands could report seeing a hag since the beginning of the past winter. Once more morale of the Highlanders faltered and there was not enough food, or understanding, to strengthen their failing spirits.

Newlyn had spent many sleepless nights talking with faeries and watching over summer crops. The big man was exhausted as he watched fields nearing harvest. Late one afternoon he and several others walked through the rows. Wearing a broad smile Newlyn asked, "Tomorrow we will harvest and then store the food in many bins around the village. Who will sit with me one more night and watch over our bounty that will provide meals for the coming months?"

Six men sat with Newlyn; two brought full casks of ale which were emptied before the stars had reached their splendor. Weary from labor and lack of rest, the intoxicated guards slipped into a deep sleep. When the seven men awoke and surveyed their crops, every plant had withered and lay on hard dry ground as though there had not been rainfall for sixty days.

"FAERIES!" Newlyn called with all his voice.

Almost immediately six faeries hovered in front of the angry Celt. "I heard once that there is a meadow with a white bush where hags dance under the moonlight. Can ye take me to this meadow?"

"Fobothom knows of this meadow. I will fetch him," one faerie called out as he disappeared into the dawning sky.

"Robert!" Newlyn called out.

It took some time for Robert to arrive, "Newlyn, whit happened to the crops? I thought we were going to harvest today."

"A year ago, ye harvested bushes with the white flowers. I need ye to help find one more."

"That was Peter and David who cut the bushes. I will ask them to join us."

When word spread that Newlyn was seeking the bushes of the hags, many were frightened but warriors of *Ceo Dhachaidh* grabbed their staves and swords, joining Newlyn at the fields. Fobothom arrived as men gathered; he was accompanied by Truact, Depost and Frenzy.

"MEN!" Newlyn called out to the gathered warriors, the power of his voice quieting their chatter. "Men of *Ceo Dhachaidh*, I am not going to battle this day. I am only seeking the hiding place of these hags who are trying to starve us by destroying our food. We have only four faeries to guide us so only four of us can travel in safety. Peter, yeu and David know these plants. Robert, ye are welcome to help. The rest of ye stand guard over our homes. These hags cannot hide forever!"

A faerie sat on the shoulder of each of the four men as they left *Ceo Dhachaidh* in search of the now infamous bush with white flowers. Fobothom disappeared frequently over the treetops to confirm their direction. It had been several years since he looked for this bush and he had been flying above the treetops at that time. Guiding men walking trails and deer paths of the highlands was slow travel for an anxious faerie. The sun was cresting when the small group pushed through brush into the meadow they had been seeking.

The edge of this meadow was well defined by lush green grass. Robert, Peter and David were stunned by its richness. Newlyn drew his broadsword from the sheath on his back as he marched across the grass to the far side and a large bush located left of center. This bush stood alone, solitary, now more than three meters high and just as broad. There were no flowers.

"Is this the bush of the white flowers?" Newlyn called to the others.

"This is where the small bush with the small white flowers was growing," Truact reported.

"Newlyn, look at the change in the grass," Robert called out.

"Whit change?"

"Look around the bush, this grass is much finer and not as lush," Robert observed. "It looks as though the grass in this section is new growth, not as sturdy as the rest of the meadow. If the hags did have a ceremony here, they have not been back this season."

"Peter, David, is this the same kind of bush ye once harvested around *Ceo Dhachaidh*?" Newlyn asked, standing next to the bush with his sword in hand.

"That was a year ago but I would say it is the same kind of bush," David replied. "Much larger than whit we cut and burned."

Pulling a stone from a bag he kept on his shoulder, Newlyn knelt down. Sparks flew from his sword as he struck it with the stone. After several strikes the bush began to burn with a green flame. Robert gasped at the color of the flame, Peter and David opened their eyes wide for it was more intense than the bushes they had burned. Newlyn smiled with satisfaction, commanding "See if ye can find anything of the hags around this meadow. Faeries, would ye please help?"

Four men and four faeries searched all parts of the field but found nothing beyond a few yellow and blue flowers. When fire had fully consumed the bush, men and faeries found what they had been seeking.

Three etched stones lay on the ground beneath the blackened skeleton. Newlyn and Robert collected the strange objects, each the size of a man's palm. They also found a great many shards of stone.

"These stones, they are tools of the hags," Fobothom told Newlyn. "We saw hags hang them in the bush while they danced."

After collecting the talismans, Newlyn dropped them into his bag and stood staring at the burned branches. Nervously holding his sword, loosely rocking it from side to side with both hands, Newlyn called out, "Faeries! Fobothom! Do ye sense any hags in the area?"

"Not at this time but this meadow is very uncomfortable to all of us," Depost replied. "Something about this meadow robs us of our senses."

"Aye, fly high and look around the forest. Escape the evil of this meadow and let yer senses work as they should."

With hesitation all four faeries flew above the trees and looked down. The forest crown was filled with different colors of green, light and dark, showing new growth and different types of trees. Each faerie flew in a different direction, returning a moment later to Newlyn. In turn each gave the same report, "Hags are in the region but none are near this meadow."

"How many hags?"

"Far too many to count; the forest reeks of their presence," Truact explained.

"Well done friends," Newlyn smiled with anticipation. "Now we return home and assemble a Celtic war party. We have found thair lair!"

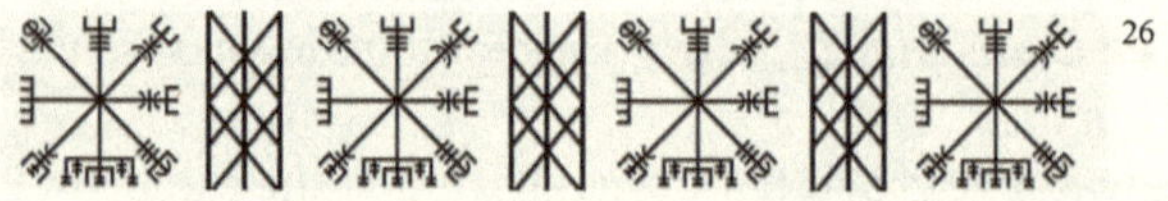 [26]

More than three hundred and fifty years before *Ceo Dhachaidh* encountered the hags, ancestors of the Celts sailed from frigid waters of the high north seas in a great fleet of ships. Rowing around floating mountains of ice and snow, the last surviving members of a once great civilization took temporary refuge in the fjords of Norway. Their plan was to take on supplies, by force if necessary, and continue their journey to a warmer, more hospitable climate. These refugees encountered Vikings, warring Norsemen who not only defended their

---

[26] This section break is a combination of two Norse symbols - the Vegvesir which "shows the way" and the Web of Wyrd which includes all Norse runes and represents fate.

villages but recognized within their visitors an aggressive kinship. At each village Celts suffered a brief battle followed by a welcoming of kindred attitude, like two rams butting heads to say hello. Few lives were lost and many friendships were forged. But the men and women escaping the frozen north would not stay in the small Norse villages. Rather than settle so close to the realm they were fleeing, these travelers recruited men and women who shared their wanderlust and proceeded south, leaving behind members of their own community who were unwilling or unable to continue.

Agrald, a man with a pregnant wife and six children, decided to stay in Norway with his growing family. After watching the fleet of ships carrying his friends sail south, he wasted no time sinking roots into the frozen Norwegian soil and becoming part of his new community. Agrald quickly rose to a position of power in his village, but was filled with great sorrow as the birth of his seventh child, a son named Vidar, took the life of his wife. Vidar was suckled by women of the village and as he grew showed a character unlike any man known before him.

Attentive to the moods of nature, Vidar knew rain was coming before clouds gathered. He could discern the second heartbeat in a pregnant doe and spare two lives. He could detect a pack of wolves before they picked up the scent of his village, and he could hear the oars of an enemy dipping into the water as it left the raging ocean entering the peaceful waters leading to his home. When confronted with battle for his home, Vidar stood against his enemies with conviction and unstoppable power. He seemed to draw energy from the earth itself, conquering all who stood against him, whether man or beast.

As a young man with his own growing family, Vidar refused his father's mantle of leadership when Agrald died an old man. "I can better serve if I tell you what I learn from the earth rather than lead you into the next sunset," Vidar explained.

Vidar's gift passed from generation to generation, some showing only a trace of the gift, others showing nearly as great a gift as Vidar himself. At the time when *Ceo Dhachaidh* was mourning her heroes lost in battle against the Romans, a boy was born to the lineage of Vidar, a seventh child whose birth took the life of his mother. The infant was suckled by women of the village and knowing his family history and ancient legends of his village, the boy's father named him Vidar.

"Wait, this is not about the hillside!" Alex protested.

"Aye, ye would be right," Angus replied with a smile. "Ye see, one of our heros, one who helped to save our Hielands, dinna come from our hills but from a distant land. This would be his story."

"Does he talk with the faeries?" Marian asked with a twinkle in her eye.

"Ye will just have to wait until he arrives to learn about him," Lillian replied, tweaking her granddaughter's nose.

"An he will not arrive at all if we dinna continue," Angus coughed, impatient to proceed.

Seeing everyone had settled back once more, the gentle grandfather resumed his reading.

Four Celts stood silently outside the lodge of *Ceo Dhachaidh*, listening to a dozen farmers-turned-warriors argue that they should attack the hags' lairs before dusk.

"We canna find the hags in the light of day," Newlyn cried out to the band of warriors gathered in front of him. "We have found the forest of thair lairs, but canna see the lairs themselves in the light of day. We found no hags only the area where they sleep. These unnatural beasts hide from the sun. We must be at thair lairs at dusk and slay them as fading light reveals them."

"But we do not want to be in the forest after dark!" a warrior protested.

"Aye, but this night we have the help of faeries," Newlyn replied confidently. "They have promised me that they will watch over us and warn us when hags approach. If ye fear the darkness then stand guard by the fires here in *Ceo Dhachaidh* and prepare to welcome us home in victory!"

Many men mumbled to one another until one asked, "Can we wait until we get help from the other villages?"

"How much grain and food do ye have in yer larder?" Newlyn challenged. "I dinna have enough to feed my family for three days. Where are we to get food to keep us for six days while we wait for others to join us? We must strike before any more of our stores are spoiled."

Again the men mumbled one to another but no one spoke up.

"Good, then. All who will help us attack our tormentors be here when the sun is half way across the sky."

Forty-nine families called *Ceo Dhachaidh* home, but only four Celts and six farmers joined Newlyn at midday as he marched into the forest toward the distant meadow of the white bush. Faeries flew in front of them and above them, twelve wee guardians watching over these men consumed with an intense purpose. When they reached the meadow, Newlyn called out to Fobothom, "Good Faerie, send yer troops out and see if the hags are still in thair lair." Immediately a dozen small sets of wings reflected the fading light as they disappeared into the forest.

Moments later Fobothom returned to report, "As before, the signs are there but we can find no hags."

Newlyn looked at the faces of the men surrounding him, searching the eyes of his fellow Celts. "We will wait until dusk falls!"

Ten men waiting with Newlyn grew increasingly uneasy watching daylight fade. Newlyn moved to the center of the hags' meadow and watched dusk swallow the land. Darkness surrounded the small band of Highland warriors but no hag approached them. "Fobothom!" Newlyn called out softly. When the faerie appeared in the darkness Newlyn made a strange request, "Wee warrior of our Hielands, have yer brave band go into the forest a distance of about ten paces and then fly straight up until ye can see one another above the tops of the trees. Wait there for a minute or so and then come back to me." Before any man could draw another breath, twelve faeries went into the forest as requested, each in a different direction. Newlyn watched the treetops and saw five of the faeries appear in the light of the rising moon. While Newlyn searched treetops for the others, men joined him in the center of the field, swords drawn in anticipation of battle.

Newlyn's eyes continued to follow every line of the treetops watching for any glint of his companions or his foes. With every pounding beat of his heart he became more tense, more keyed to strike when suddenly twelve faeries appeared before him. "We can find nothing but the lingering stench of hags. They are not around this meadow."

Before his heart beat another pulse, Newlyn called out, "BACK TO *CEO DHACHAIDH* AT ONCE!" Every man began to run and every faerie zigzagged in front of them and around them watching for hags to appear.

Emerging from the forest above the field of *Ceo Dhachaidh*, the war party stopped to catch their breath. Every eye focused first on the village and then scanned the hillside and field for any sign of hags. A nearly full moon had changed from orange to brilliant yellow, lighting the fields, making it easy to see. Yet the only creature anyone saw was a deer grazing at the edge of the forest below the field of wilted crops.

Silently, men spread out to achieve greater maneuverability in the event they were attacked. Suddenly a young man spotted a hag among them and brought his stave down on the shoulder of his enemy. Rearing for a second blow against the now crumpled figure, the young man found his stave arrested by an older Celt. Each man looked around and saw that several hags stood among them, ready to do battle. Every man and hag immediately moved to protect themselves. Panic began to fill their hearts, how had these hags slipped in among them?

"Look to yer opponent's shoulders and head," an older Celt advised his warriors. "See the wee faerie reflecting the moonlight? The faeries will not rest near a hag! That hag ye see is yer brother!" Each of the men looked around the field excitedly and saw a faerie hovering beside or above each of the hags standing in their number. The men exhaled with relief but not trusting what they saw, maintained their readiness.

Seeing no true hags in the field, the old Celt asked, "Faerie, where are the hags?"

"I see five groups along the edge of the field," the faerie on the Celt's shoulder informed him.

"Good. I need a faerie to guide each of us Celts to a cluster of hags. Ye other men split up and follow; be ready to strike at a true enemy."

Each of the Celts consulted their faerie then like mad men began to run across the field, gaining speed and power with every step, each heading toward a different location. Bewildered but willing, other men joined the run behind crazed Celts. Before Highlanders reached the edge of the forest hags came out of the darkness. Bathed in moonlight, men of *Ceo Dhachaidh* and hags lashed out at one another. Armed with short knives and crooked sticks the hags swung and stabbed, chanting strange words. Faeries flew at the eyes of hags, seeking to distract them as men struck out with dirk, sword, and stave.

Highlanders cried out in pain as hags beat on them with tremendous force, breaking arms and legs. Their screams alerted villagers and in the midst of a battle begun by eleven brave Highlanders more than thirty men and women ran from their beds with staves, knives, swords, spades, whatever they could grab. Vanquished hags melted into the field, each leaving a cursed dark spot spreading in the moonlight. Even as the field darkened, more hags came out of the forest.

Five hags circled Newlyn, jabbing him and beating on him with crippling blows. Filled with pain and anger the Celt swung his sword repeatedly, dismembering his attackers. Two more hags came up to Newlyn from behind and drove their sticks into his back. Another wave of hags came from the forest, this time met by a series of lightning bolts coming from the center of the field. Three . . . four . . . five times lightning struck across the hags, melting the unnatural beings into the earth. Sisters who could, turned and fled.

Vrenessbith, exhausted and unable to breathe or call for help, fell from her position over the center of the field. Ingrid, the widow of Seumas, lifted her skirt, catching the wee warrior as she fell. "FAERIE!" Ingrid cried out to passing wings reflecting moonlight, "Go get yer elder! Vrenessbith needs yer help!"

Before the passing faerie could depart, Resbith arrived and advised Ingrid, "She has suffered a tremendous loss of life energy. Do you have a safe place where she can rest and get the warmth of sunlight in the morning?"

"I do," Ingrid replied.

"Good. Then see that she is in the sunlight when it first graces our land. I will see you later but now I must see to other injuries," Resbith instructed and then was gone.

Highlanders helped one another up the hill to their huts, caring for wounded by splinting broken bones and bandaging cuts. Two Celts and four farmer-warriors were carried off by solemn brothers who began mourning their loss. Newlyn was carried off on a stretcher but would live to see another sunrise. Moonlight flooded the field after all departed revealing countless blotches in the rich soil.

<hr>

At sunrise, bodies of two faeries joined the essence of their mountains. Tears fell from Resbith's eyes forming reflective streams in the sunshine.

Ingrid had placed Vrenessbith on a pillow next to her fire overnight and now carried her gently to the stone chairs above the hillside. Placing her pillow in the early morning sunshine, Ingrid sat with the wee faerie until Vrenessbith awoke, three hours later. Groggy and weak, Vrenessbith sat beside Ingrid and waited for Resbith who arrived shortly after noon.

"The shrouds have grown. Some people are no longer visible," Vrenessbith told her Comleidh upon her arrival.

"Yes, little one, this attack has increased their struggle to survive," Resbith agreed, her voice straining with despair. "Many villagers are ready to give up."

"Whit shrouds?" Ingrid asked, confused by the faeries' conversation. "Whit struggle?"

"We can see your struggle to survive as a dark shroud which weighs on your spirit," Resbith replied. "This morning these shrouds have grown substantially, nearly overpowering all your people."

"I feel no weight," Ingrid responded honestly.

"No, you are one of the precious few who always looks forward to each new day, yet even your shoulders bear the gleo at this time," Resbith told Vrenessbith's caretaker.

"Whit are we to do?" Ingrid asked, seeking a way to save her village.

Resbith extended her hand to Vrenessbith while looking at Ingrid, offering, "Welcome each new day with a smile and the hope it deserves." The two faeries then returned to their cavie.

According to custom six pyres were constructed to honor the six Highlanders who had fallen. "Wait," Ingrid called out as she left the stone chairs. "Consider whit ye are doing."

"Whit do ye mean?" one of the men building the pyres asked.

"Six fires lighting the sky at dusk," Ingrid replied soulfully. "Yeu will be calling the hags back to our hillside."

"But how are we to honor our dead if not on the pyre?" another man asked. "It is whit we do."

"Yes, it is whit we have always done but can we endanger our village and do it now?" Ingrid challenged.

There was a long and very discomforting quiet among the men and women working on the pyres. "We are men of the earth," one young man offered. "Hielanders should be always at one with the mountains. We should commit thair bodies to these mountains."

"They do that in many cultures; we saw it as we traveled in years past," an old Celt remarked.

"But where?" another asked, trying to comprehend a new tradition.

"There is the thorny glen beyond the village," the old Celt offered. "We canna use it and the animals dinna go there either."

"Collect yer swords and spades, men; we must bury our kin this evening at dusk," another man said with resignation as he turned toward the thorny glen.

Before digging six graves, weary Highlanders cut thorns along the edge of the wide glen with their swords. While younger men dug, an older man, Liam, wandered among the bushes on the opposite side of the glen examining a plant growing beneath the thorns. He collected grain from these small plants which grew close to the ground. After carefully rolling the grain between his fingers he put a kernel between his teeth, biting down on it. Hard on the outside, the grain was chewy in its center. Smiling, he collected a large bundle of the plant.

Dusk rolled over the hillside as the bodies of six warriors were carried beyond the village to the glen. Six holes waited, each over two meters in length, a meter wide and just as deep. Deceased men were laid in the holes respectfully just as they would have been laid on the pyre.

As Celts' swords were laid across their chests, a young girl approached the grave of her father. Gently laying a doll her father had made for her in his arms she told her mother, "So he won't be alone or forget me." Eric piped soulfully, honoring each of the fallen warriors as others ran back to their huts to retrieve remembrances to accompany their loved ones. Finally a cloth was laid across each of the departed Highlanders to protect them from the dirt that would follow.

Eric and Perth took turns piping as men buried friends in their final resting places. When the last mound of dirt had been put down the music ceased and quiet greeted a star-filled sky.

Men and women of *Ceo Dhachaidh* wrestled with mixed and confused emotions as they awakened the next morning. Fear of their enemy had forced them to change how they honored their dead. Even though most understood the reason for the change it was difficult to accept. On top of this confusion was an intense sense of loss. Six men lost their lives and another, Newlyn, lay in a sleeping death. *Ceo Dhachaidh* was no stranger to death but it had been many years since such a loss was suffered so close to home.

Sunlight warmed huts as screams erupted throughout the village. Each time a woman opened a grain store hidden in her hut she found smelly decaying bodies of rodents where the night before clean grain had been stored. The big larder in the lodge had suffered the same loss. Every store of food in the village was spoilt with decaying rodent bodies.

Filled with rage and frustration, women and men gathered in the village common. Every mouth demanding attention and screaming for relief, yet not a single ear could hear. Slowly Liam wandered into the fray carrying a small sack. Quietly he opened the sack and pulled a few grains out. As he put the grains into his mouth, he offered small bits of grain from his sack to each of the women and then the men. Men quickly spit the seeds out in disgust, offended by their bitterness, but the women chewed and looked at one another.

"It grows in the meadow of the glen above the village, beneath the bushes of thorns," Liam smiled. "Easy to collect and separate from the chaff."

Men, women, and children worked through the morning collecting the brown and grey rice-like grain. "We can use this chaff for thatching the roof," one woman called as she bound a bundle together.

"A wee bit short for thatching but I suppose it could be used for repairs," a man replied.

Several men worked together gathering a large number of plants so they could be replanted in the field below the village away from the thorny bushes. Arriving at the field they dropped their treasures and stared dumbfounded. This field used for planting and growing was the same field where the battle with the hags had been fought. Every place where a hag had been killed was now marked with a healthy briar bush. Thick stalks and branches bore briar thorns large enough to go through a man's arm. Each bush was nearly two meters in diameter and a meter high. "It is the richness of the soil," a man offered, his shoulders falling yet his jaw set firmly and a bit of tear forming in the corner of his left eye. "We have nurtured this field for years and now it is wasted on these thorny hag bushes."

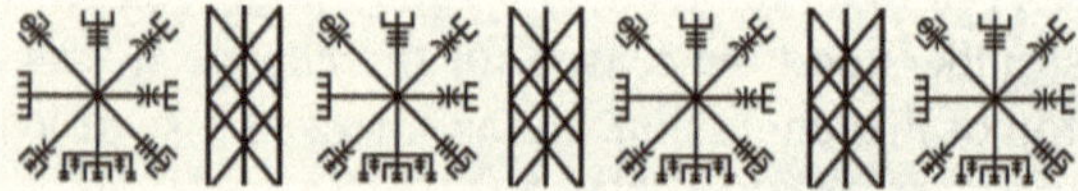

In a small insignificant village on the northwestern coast of Norway a young boy approaching his eighth year stopped his play and listened to the wind. A sound was rising but nobody else seemed to hear it. Vidar looked around his village. Men were working, women preparing evening meals, children running after one another or a dog. Vidar closed his eyes and listened again.

"Father," Vidar called out.

"Not now, boy, I need to finish laying this log," his father replied breathlessly as he heaved a log over his head where another man took it and placed it on a wall of timbers. "Let's lift another," the father directed men working with him. "Darkness is coming and we need to have these walls finished."

Vidar looked around, nothing had changed. Again he closed his eyes and listened, but this time he heard nothing. Feeling a chill down his back Vidar left the everyday commotion of his village. Crossing a small bridge he heard the sound again, this time very distinctly. Listening, the young boy counted out loud, "One, two. Two? No THREE!" Turning he ran as hard as he could back to where his father and other men were working. "THREE BOATS ARE COMING UP THE FJORD!"

"What are you saying, Vidar?" one of the men asked.

"Three boats are coming up the fjord. Two boats landed beyond the point. The third still glides slowly. It barely ripples the water . . . why so slowly?"

Every man went white in the face and the village erupted into chaos. Throm, Vidar's father, barked orders as he ran to his hut to retrieve his own weapons. Mothers grabbed their children; older children grabbed younger brothers and sisters; young men and boys old enough to start a beard grabbed tools they might use for defense. As men returned to where Throm waited, he turned and began running up a path through the forest. The men followed.

Emerging from the forest at the edge of a marsh the men stopped and spread out. "We are too late; they have reached the levee," Throm moaned. Looking to the fjord he saw the stern of the third ship disappearing behind the trees, toward the village. "MEN IN BACK - RETURN TO THE VILLAGE AND DEFEND THE DOCK! DO NOT LET THEM INTO OUR VILLAGE!" Staring ahead, Throm watched as warriors of unknown origin or allegiance raced across the levee constructed to protect the village from northern invaders. Two images stood out on shields carried by the invaders, a sea lion and a flaming tree. Throm knew these were not men of the sea lion for they visited often and were friends; a friend would never try to sneak into their village. The flaming tree was not a familiar icon. Taking a deep breath Throm charged ahead, toward the levee, toward the invaders, toward almost certain death.

Leading their charge with his shield Throm pushed into the line of men as they came off the levee, driving them off dry land and into the waters and mire of the marsh. Six men fell into the water before one stood against Throm's drive. Without hesitation Throm struck with his sword, struck as hard as he could, but not hard enough. The invader was ready and shoved his sword into Throm then pushed him into the marsh. Stepping closer to firmer ground, the invader killed another villager as he had Throm. Few invaders made it all the way across the levee; most were pushed into the marsh where it was impossible to stand or fight, or they met death trying to advance. Nobody had an advantage on the levee, not the invaders and not the villagers, but all fought and many lost their lives.

Villagers lost no time defending their dock. Stronger men immediately began throwing torches into the ship before it reached the landing. Villagers gained the end of the pier and lowered great poles against the hull of the ship, keeping it far enough away that invaders could not reach safety. Many men jumped from their burning ship into the water; weighted by their heavy battle-gear and with no bottom to walk on, invaders drowned. The few who dropped their weapons met the weapons of villagers as they tried to climb onto land.

Flames from the ship could be seen from the levee, frightening invaders at the rear of the attack. Experiencing a fierce defense and seeing destruction of a ship, attackers turned and ran back to their own ships. Intruders on the levee still trying to reach firm land had no support from their rear and soon fell to the aggressive defense tactics of villagers.

No prisoners were taken and no chase was given in pursuit of fleeing invaders. Wounded intruders were beheaded where they lay or stood mired in the marsh unable to flee. The dead and wounded of the village were taken back to their homes. A barge would have to be built for their funeral.

Vidar watched the entire event from the place where he had alerted his father of the coming ships. Chaos surrounding him, he simply stood and watched. When bodies of the dead were carried past him, Vidar saw his father and an older brother. His oldest brother was carried back with the wounded; he had lost a leg at the knee. Eleven men of the village had been killed. Sixteen had been wounded, some severely.

Most of the able men of the village spent the next day building a funeral barge, a raft with a great bow. Grass soaked with oil was laid across the bottom. Sixteen men who gave their lives defending the village lay on that grass side by side with honor and respect as dusk approached. Fading light veiled the ship as it was pushed away from the dock, toward the stars. Two men threw burning torches onto the ship of lost men. It burst into flame. A nearly full moon changed from orange to brilliant yellow as flames sank into waters of a mournful fjord.

Vidar's three sisters and two brothers turned from the fjord and were taken in by families of the village. Vidar, the youngest of his now broken family stood at the edge of the water alone, watching the moon climb higher into the sky. He could still hear steam rising from the burning ship which carried his father and brother into Valhalla, their next world.

══════

" 'Valhalla,' that is where the Vikings go when they die," Liam called out.

"Aye, it is," Angus agreed.

"And this 'Vidar,' he is a seventh son like the other 'Vidar'," Alex observed. "Were they related? Grandfather and grandson?"

"Related? Aye, I believe he was but not so closely as yeu and I are. This young Vidar was the seventh son possibly seven generations from a seventh son," Angus replied thoughtfully. "But I have a big day tomorrow and should get some rest. We will read some more when the clouds roll away."

"Clouds?" Marian asked. "Is it raining?"

"Nay, sweet lassie," Angus mused closing the book. "A different cloud and possibly far more dangerous than those we have seen of recent."

He then placed the book on his desk and looked out the window and beyond for a few seconds before turning back to help Lillian shoo the children off to bed.

Highland Myst hung heavy on the hillside as Angus trudged past the old stones toward the oak tree. Standing at the edge of its ancient branches the old man called, "Comleidh Belinda, they are coming." His kilt swished slightly from a breeze rising lazily from the loch.

Within seconds a beautiful faerie of advanced age hovered in front of Angus. "Thank you for telling me, Angus. All is as it should be and has always been. I have asked the cavie to stay well out of sight but the young ones are eager to see these men and their machines. Do not worry; the Highlands will protect themselves."

Angus nodded with a tip of his cap and turned to walk across the hillside. Passing the remains of the once great stone seats he unconsciously heaved a heavy sigh. Continuing past where straw and mud huts once stood, he came to a broad patch of briars. Leaning against his walking stave, he paused to look to his right where unmarked graves were now hidden beneath centuries of growth. Adjusting his balmoral he resumed his journey. After walking nearly *thirty minutes he arrived at the end of a road that stopped abruptly at the crest of a hill.*

"Angus, pleased to see ye here in yer official capacity," a friend said as he extended a hand to the Laird of the Hillside.

"I am told the Spirit of the Hielands has all well in hand, but she appreciates a show of support from those she has given life to these long years. Ye should be in tartan and not those traitorous Levis." Angus was in traditional Highland dress with kilt, hose, skein dubh, tweed jacket, and fly plaid. Most men wore blue jeans and t-shirts; only two others were kilted.

"Does anyone know whit time thay're coming?" one man in jeans asked.

"They are here now. I hear thair engines choking the peace of our hillside," Angus replied, straightening his posture to greet the unwelcome intruders.

Within a minute six vehicles roared up the road, stopping in a line at its end. Two motorcycles zipped past sounding like bothersome bees then spun in the dirt as they turned around. Angus sighed and addressed the American from Bradshear Enterprises. "I would ask that ye bring only one vehicle across the hillside, initially. It can be any one ye choose, but only one until a path has been agreed upon."

The American looked to the mayor, who stood beside him on his left. Mayor Munro shrugged his shoulders. Turning back to Angus, the American nodded and whispered instructions to a driver at his right. This driver called to another vehicle using a hand-held radio. Within seconds a beast of American ingenuity crunched bushes beside the road as this off-road vehicle pulled out of the line of cars and rumbled to where the men waited. The American climbed into the open back of this vehicle and with a self-satisfied smirk told Angus, "Lead on, Laird."

Angus turned and extending his stave began to stroll back the way he had come. Mayor Munro raced to catch up and walk beside Angus, amazed to find a sly grin on Angus' face. Without a word Angus marched on in his official capacity. Coming to a hilltop before the ancient briar patch, he paused briefly. Recognizing the glint of Belinda and other faeries in the tree tops he drew a deep breath of fresh air and resumed his journey, with a slightly brighter smile.

The American had his driver turn victorious music up loud enough to announce their arrival to a sleeping kingdom. The great land-crusher roared as it climbed the hill behind Angus. Confident of his victory over legends and superstition the American also drew in a deep breath of highland air. Cresting the hill before an ancient briar patch the engine of the vehicle died and the music stopped. "What is the problem? Why have we stopped?" he bellowed in anger.

"I don't know, sir. It just died!" the driver replied with surprise.

"Well, get it started and let's get going!"

"I am trying, sir. It won't turn over."

"Give me the radio!"

The driver handed a two-way radio to his boss who called immediately, "Bring the bikes up. Make it fast!"

Within seconds two motorcycles roared up the hill, one on either side of the big off-road truck. Their speed launched them into the air as they crested the hill and their engines died while in flight. Landing in highland grass both riders kicked their starters furiously, trying to get their engines roaring again. Neither motorcycle started.

"OKAY, GREGSON, WHAT HAVE YOU DONE?!" the angry American bellowed. "You men search the woods for some device he put out to stop us!"

Angus turned and smiled politely as he replied, "There is no device, only the Spirits of the Hielands. These hillsides hae seen and felt the torture of countless lives given that they might survive, but they hae never felt any machine tear up their soil nor plunder their beauty." He winked at Belinda whose delight cast a rainbow across the tree tops.

"You have access to the loch from your hillside?" the American growled.

"Aye, we do," Angus replied humbly.

Determined to not be outdone, the American screamed into his radio, "Bring the boat to the cove. We can get to our site by water!" He then climbed down from his vehicle and stomped past Angus.

Angus and the others reached the top of the hillside as a sporty motorboat roared up the loch. The American stomped down the hill toward the cove just as the motor on the boat went quiet. Hearing unsuccessful attempts to restart the engine the American turned and stormed to Angus.

"THE LAKE, TOO?!" he screamed.

Angus shrugged his shoulders then replied, "I suppose ye will hae to use the lane on the other side of the mountain if ye still want to reach yer property."

"That will take five times longer and cost that much more!" the American screamed.

Frustrated beyond belief he reared his leg back to kick a stone resting in a pile of debris. Before his foot reached its target, Angus *stuck his stave out blocking the kick and landing the American on his backside.*

Angus stared down at the fallen American. Speaking without compassion but with absolute authority, he told the intruder, "Ye will not disturb one stone of this sacred hillside. Now, if ye are finished with yer business I will ask ye to leave and never set foot here again."

Mayor Munro stared at Angus in disbelief then ran to catch up with the Americans. Angus stood patiently on the hillside, looking across the loch, until Belinda joined him. "We are safe for now, Comleidh. But I dinna believe they are gone."

"Trust in the Highlands," Belinda told him and flew back to her cavie.

Moments later Angus heard the roar of engines starting and then fading down the distant hillside. Men in the boat paddled back into the main loch where they restarted their engines and they, too, disappeared. With a joyous but heavy heart, Angus turned. He had taken only a few steps when Lillian and the children appeared to escort him home.

<center>~~~~~~~~~~~~~~~~~~~~~~~~~~~~~~</center>

"Okay, where were we?" Angus asked as he opened the large book to resume reading.

"They had just had a great battle with hags on the hillside," Liam reported.

"And thorns have appeared in the growing field," Alex added.

"And they found rice under the briars where they buried their friends," Marian concluded.

"Aye, so now we continue with struggles made more difficult by the hags . . ." Angus looked down to his book and resumed its story.

In *Ceo Dhachaidh* days of mourning those who fell to the hags gave way to weeks of toil. Aches from constant labor rolled unnoticeably into months of anguish as Highlanders struggled to survive seasonal challenges of nature and an ever-present threat of hags.

Newlyn awoke from his death sleep after forty-seven days. Nine days later he charged into the thicket of hag thorns screaming and thrashing out wildly with his great broadsword. No one had attempted to remove the growing thorny mass and on this day they learned that the thorns were not only sharp but carried a lethal poison. Newlyn died fighting the hags of his memories. Men of the village, many close friends of Newlyn, dug a hole at the edge of the meadow above *Ceo*

Dhachaidh at sunrise the following day. He was laid to rest with his broadsword and tokens of love early that afternoon. Eric piped as mourners bade farewell and by sunset all Highlanders were safe in their huts.

Few Celts who settled this great land remained to guide those who had come to their villages. Weary from battles they could not win, suffering injuries that festered without fully healing, these great men worked beside their neighbors during daylight hours, retreating to the safety of their own huts before sunset. Hags ruled the dark hours of night, stealing away any traveler or Highlander who happened to be away from their bed when darkness swallowed the mountains. Even though hags were seldom seen during daylight their fearsome power and control over men and women of the Highlands stretched through all hours of every day.

Guardians of Doup Fell maintained their nighttime vigils, staying close to one another as they huddled around great fires. The parade of hags marching through their village eventually waned. One night, more than a year after the great battle at *Ceo Dhachaidh*, men appointed to watching for hags found themselves weary of searching for purpose around watch fires and elected to end this watch. Nights were meant to be spent close to their loved ones in their own beds.

Rob, the last of the fighting Celts in Doup Fell, felt weariness and defeat growing in his neighbors before they abandoned their night watch. Concerned for the next generation of Highlanders, he resumed an old tradition not long after the watch ended. With the help of two men trained to fight the Romans, Rob taught young men techniques of hand-to-hand combat and how to use traditional weapons of sword, dirk, and spear.

Feeling confident with their new abilities after three weeks of training, two young men ventured a great distance from Doup Fell on a hunting trip. They were an hour away on their return home when the sun slipped below the horizon leaving them in dark woods. Friends discovered they were missing early the next day and formed a search party to find the young men. The search party found a hand of one of the missing hunters at the far edge of the meadow below Doup Fell, still clasping the hilt of his sword. Fear once more ruled the night.

In the thorny meadow above *Ceo Dhachaidh* darkness slowly began to release its hold on the night, yielding to dawn. Vrenessbith sailed silently over a thicket of briars finding grain available for today's harvest was less than would be required. Hovering over the field she chanted a soft melody of growth. Finishing her song, the small faerie wavered slightly then flew to a nearby tree where she rested.

"A very commendable deed, young faerie," complimented a familiar voice.

Summoning all her remaining strength Vrenessbith replied, "Thank you, Comleidh. I only call the mountain to give what it has stored in its ground."

"How often do you make this request of the mountain?" Resbith asked.

"The plants can produce healthy grain for only a few days, three sometimes four days. I assist the plants when their yield is small; on the third, sometimes fourth sunrise," Vrenessbith replied, her strength beginning to return with warming sunshine. "The people would find little to eat if I did not help these struggling plants."

"Maybe we can get help from other faeries," Resbith offered. "I can see how weak you are after your song."

Vrenessbith smiled softly as she nodded to her teacher and guide. The two faeries sat quietly and waited for Vrenessbith to recover more strength. With daylight, men and women of the village carried baskets into the thicket. Weighed down by growing burdens of gleo they harvested grain that waited for them each morning, unaware of the enormous contribution from a wee faerie.

"Comleidh," Vrenessbith asked as she stretched her arms and wings into the sunshine, "why can we not protect their hidden stores?"

"We are creatures of the earth, sweet one. While we can call forth energy from the mountain we cannot transfer that energy to something once it is removed from the earth." Resbith looked to her student. Seeing she was ready to fly again asked, "Shall we return to our cavie?"

Sighing, Vrenessbith looked across the meadow where villagers had begun to talk while they filled their baskets with grain and daylight brightened the sky. An older woman collapsed under the weight of her gleo shroud. Resbith dried her tears as others helped the woman back to her feet and shared their own grain with her.

Knowing their day had just begun, two faeries flew silently to their own labors.

When times become desperate enemies might unite for strength, however a haughty and cruel spirit can emerge, even between friends. Hag marks subtly left on infants grew more prominent as these children grew older, leading to torment by others their age and even some adults. Children without the hags' kiss who had played side by side with marked children became bitter tormentors with the onset of adolescence. Girls who matured with great beauty, except for their mark, were hit and abused without mercy, both physically and emotionally. Boys, who could till the soil as well as any man were ostracized and forced to start their own fields when they became able young men. Some elder villagers came to their aid but were unable to overcome this darker side of mankind. While open persecution may have made tormentors feel powerful for a moment, even momentarily replacing fears, these actions ate away at the already eroded morale of Highland villages.

Two young people of Blyth Brier suffered their oppression silently for seventeen years, finding strength in one another. Struan's left eye drooped severely, drawing the attention of unfamiliar onlookers to an unseemly flap of skin which appeared as though a dog had chewed his ear off. He let his hair grow long covering his malformed ear but nothing could hide his eye. Eve suffered a badly malformed lip, making it nearly impossible for her to speak words but her eyes gave Struan the strength to till a small field away from the village and build his own hut beside it.

When Struan's first crop stood tall in the field and he saw promise of a fruitful harvest he went to Eve's parents to ask for her hand in marriage. Eve's father knew Struan's strength of character and body, and wrapped his arms around the young man welcoming him into the family. Hearing the news elders of Blyth Brier announced that all the villages of the Highlands would be invited to the wedding. Indeed, a celebration was needed and a wedding was a great opportunity to put prejudice of the hags' mark and their war aside, even if for a brief period. Every village did send representatives and as the sun crested its journey on the longest day of the year, Struan and Eve exchanged vows. Their wedding kiss was so filled with promise and passion that the hearts of those who had tormented the couple ached with envy.

Eric brought out his pipes and his music blended with the strains of Rachel's harp as kegs of mead flowed freely. These two memorable

Highlanders who had once run down a deer together now stood side by side providing enjoyable music. Music which lifted the morale of Highlanders to a level it had not reached in many years.

In the midst of this great celebration two young people encountered each other for the first time as young adults. Eric's daughter, Erial, smiled at Tristan, Rachel's oldest son. They had played together as small children but had not seen one another for many years. After sharing innocent yet flirtatious smiles they were both wrapped in an intense bond of infatuation throughout the celebration of Struan and Eve's wedding. Sharon, a young lady whom Tristan had been courting tried to intervene but could not separate her sweetheart from his uncommon entanglement with Erial.

Slowly the sun began its slide toward the ridge of mountains surrounding Blyth Brier and with kegs of mead running dry the celebration waned. Many wedding guests found space in huts with friends or in the great lodge. Others had to find a comfortable spot on the ground near the center of the village. Fires were built and guards posted, for surely this was too great a festival to be ignored by hags.

Bryan volunteered himself and Tristan for first watch. Silently Tristan walked Erial to Rachel's hut where she would sleep as a guest. Their fingers entwined, Tristan stopped and leaned over to kiss this bewitching young lady. Erial's heart raced with desire yet she cautiously tilted her head, accepting his kiss. Softly their lips met and the gentle caress exploded into an instant separation. No longer were their lips together, nor their hands, nor were their bodies touching in any fashion. Each stared into the eyes of the other and without reservation both simultaneously burst into laughter.

"I believe we will always have a very special friendship," Tristan smiled.

"Yes . . . very special," Erial replied as she wrapped her arms around Tristan for the greatest of hugs two very special friends could possibly share.

<hr>

Struan looked deeply into the eyes of his new bride. Alone in their own hut, away from the noise of the village, time moved more slowly. Each newlywed filled with a unique sense of their other. But even time such as this can be interrupted. When Struan was half-dressed he stopped. Wheeling around he grabbed an old broadsword he had cleaned, sharpened, and now kept ready by the door. Confidently he stepped outside and brought his ancient sword hard across two hags holding one of several young men who had come to the hut to heckle the wedding couple. Before the hags could melt into the ground Struan wheeled and slashed again and again. Each blow fatal to another hag. Filled with absolute terror, young men who had come to taunt and tease the newly wed couple fled back to their own huts. Two hags disappeared into their own dark world. Struan stood ready, listening, sensing the world that had returned to quiet around him.

Slowly, Struan relaxed. Lowering his sword, he continued to listen to the still night around him. After a moment, feeling Eve's disquiet, he returned the sword to its place by the door and joined the longing arms of his bride.

Men of the village could not wait for the bridal couple to awaken the next morning, yet they yielded to pressure from Bryan and Eric to do just that. When the sun was half way to its peak, a gathering of men stood restlessly outside the hut of Struan and Eve. Filled with anger and suspicion they called Struan to come out. It took several minutes for the young groom to dress and appear before the impatient and growing crowd. The young bride lingered before dressing and preparing a breakfast for her new husband.

Fourteen men, including the three who had come to heckle the couple in the night, stood impatiently wanting to speak with Struan. Twelve faeries hovered above their heads. "We are told ye killed a number of hags last night," an elder challenged, not believing this feat to be possible.

Struan stood silently.

"We are told that every blow of yer sword killed an enemy!" another accused, fueling the suspicions of a crowd consumed by mistrust of these children *kissed* by hags.

Struan stood silently.

Bryan joined the group, politely walking up to the bride-groom. "Struan, three young men sought to follow tradition by taunting yeu and yer bride on yer wedding night. These three boys say they were attacked by hags and that yeu killed all of them without any aid. Is this so?"

Struan looked at the growing crowd of people and acknowledged Bryan's question. "Aye. I was preparing for bed when I heard a commotion outside. I grabbed my sword and stepped out. I dealt my sword to every shadow I saw. I did not look to see whether it was man or hag."

"That is not true," one of the young men called out. "He burst out of his hut and immediately began killing hags. He never came near one of us, only the hags. He knew right where they were with every swing of that great sword of his!"

Struan stood silently.

"It appears," an elder faerie offered, "that when the hags marked your children they also left a bit of themselves within these marks. Young Struan, and possibly others who bear this curse, may have the power to sense a hags' presence. I believe this could be good for your communities, not something to be reviled."

"Husband, yer breakfast is ready," Eve called from inside.

"Good day to ye all and thank ye for such a glorious wedding yesterday. My bride has breakfast for me." Struan smiled and returned to his hut. The others returned to the village, shaking their heads and talking among themselves.

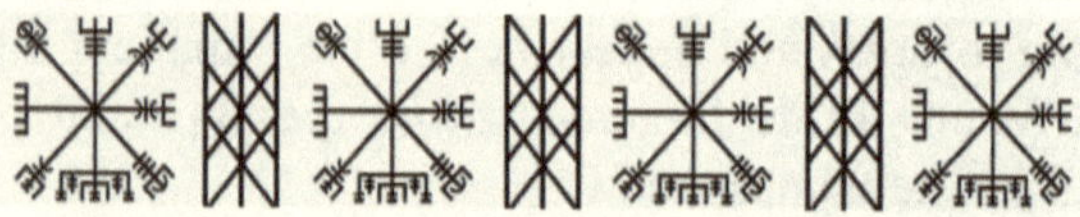

As Doup Fell celebrated a wedding, a small village in Norway struggled to survive. Vidar stood silently watching men of his village march eastward in search of game. Knowing the village to be desperate for food, Vidar shook his head and went hunting in a southerly direction. Throughout the day this unusual young man listened to the wind, deciphering the many scents it carried. Methodically he worked his way across the marshes and rivers and then stopped . . . and waited. His wait was short and well rewarded for he killed two rabbits and a small deer. After tying the rabbits to his belt the hunter hoisted the deer to his shoulders and proceeded directly home. Darkness was wrapping around the village when he delivered the deer to his village council. Agarn, a young man Vidar's age who had led the larger hunting party, scowled at Vidar for his group had returned without a kill. Barely large enough to feed the village, the single deer would keep starvation from claiming any lives that night.

Vidar left the village common as his deer was being skinned and delivered one of his two rabbits to Alicia, a young lady whom both he and Agarn favored. The second rabbit he cooked for himself, but had to share with Bjorn and Jock when his only friends dropped by for a visit.

"Agarn wandered aimlessly all day," Bjorn laughed. "Tomorrow we will hunt with you and feed the village."

Vidar did not reply but smiled as he handed his friends portions of roasted rabbit.

Before sunrise the next day Agarn again led a small band of young men eastward in search of food. An hour after sunrise Vidar and his two friends left the village on a southerly path. Vidar went directly to where he had found game the day before. When they reached the site, Vidar stood and listened, breathing in scents carried on a gentle breeze. He then walked east for a mile and waited. When Bjorn began to chuckle at his friend's odd method of hunting, Vidar looked at him sternly. All colour washed from Bjorn's face. Minutes later a herd of deer entered the field near where the three waited. Carried on a whisper, two arrows flew through the air; two large bucks fell to the ground. Feeling good about their success the three hunters approached their kill, but before they took many steps Agarn's group launched an attack against them.

Drawing uncommon strength and agility from the earth Vidar warded off his Agarn's much larger party, maiming two of the young men. Bjorn and Jock were taken hostage and released only after Vidar agreed to let the interlopers take the two deer lying on the ground. Realizing his friends' safety was in the balance Vidar shrugged his shoulders and announced, "Take them. We will find more." Vidar turned and led his friends south, away from their village to resume their hunt.

Vidar, Bjorn, and Jock returned to their village with only seven rabbits. Walking quietly to the center of the village, they found themselves surrounded by an armed guard led by Agarn's father. "My son says you attacked his party and tried to steal their kill! Two of his men will not be able to hunt for many weeks thanks to your sword."

"NO!" Jock cried out, but before he could continue Vidar grabbed his arm, his eyes warning Jock to be still.

Vidar looked at the guard, many with swords drawn, then cast his eyes around the village. "To the boats," he whispered to his friends. Locking eyes with his accuser, Vidar waited for him to move. The wait was short for Agarn's father was an impatient warrior and impatient warriors make mistakes. He turned his head to bark a command and as he did so Vidar burst through the circle of guards, wheeled around to his right and vaulted down the pier toward the boats. Bjorn and Jock followed his moves with stumbling steps. Reaching the boats Vidar slashed the ropes of the boat closest to the ocean, launching the craft as his friends leapt aboard. They were under sail and heading into dark waters of nightfall before the circle of guards regained their senses and made their way down the pier.

"Where are we going?" Bjorn asked.

"We have seven rabbits and a good wind; does it matter where we land?" Vidar laughed.

Eric and the other men of *Ceo Dhachaidh* gathered their families, preparing to leave Blyth Brier. "Come," Eric called, "we have a long day of sunshine, but we also have a long way to travel." Tristan gave Erial a great hug; both laughed as they gazed into one another's eyes.

As soon as Erial stepped away, Sharon reasserted her claim on Tristan. One month later Eric and Erial returned to Blyth Brier for the wedding of Tristan and Sharon. While visiting the village Eric asked Struan if he had any more experiences with hags. "No, but I do have to cut down thorn bushes outside my hut every week. I guess I am thankful that my field is not as fertile as the field of yer village or I would have to move my hut."

Eric shook his head, laughing with Struan.

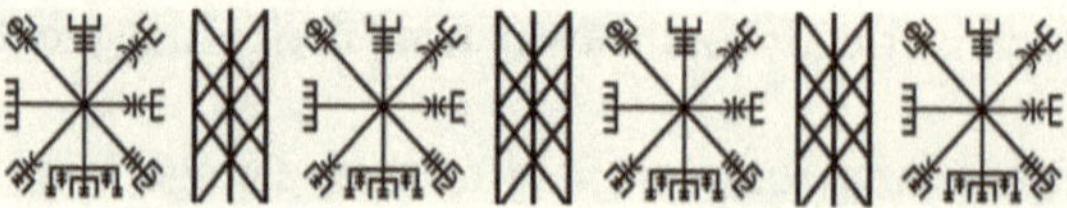

Vidar steered his small boat into a protected cove and lowered its sail. The moon was waning, partially concealed by passing clouds. Three young escapees sat quietly and waited to see if they had been followed. After nearly an hour Vidar looked to his friends, "Let's cook some rabbit!"

It took only a few minutes to beach their boat and build a fire. While the rabbits roasted Vidar instructed his friends, "I believe there is a stream feeding the cove just over the mound there. Why don't you freshen our water skins?" Jock and Bjorn retrieved the skins they carried while hunting and collected water.

"Just once I want to visit a land where Vidar does not know what is over the next rise," Jock laughed.

While they ate, each devouring an entire rabbit, the skies cleared.

"It is the short night tonight," Vidar proclaimed, "we should get going before the men of the village wake up and come in pursuit." They scattered their fire, put the extra rabbits in their boat, and set sail for destination unknown.

Bjorn and Jock suggested it would be best if they followed the shoreline, "That way we can find food and water when we need it." They traveled south along the coast of Norway for seven days until they found a large settlement where the coastline turned east. While Jock and Bjorn acquired enough food for a voyage of several days, Vidar spoke with a local sailor.

"On to Denmark!" Jock called out thinking they were continuing south but Vidar turned the boat west. Good fortune was with them as the sea was relatively calm and wind was favorable. After three days of seeing only open water Bjorn spotted land on the horizon.

Reaching land was initially disappointing for there was no place to beach their small boat. The coastline was rough, rocky, and unapproachable. Vidar kept sailing west until they found a broad beach covered with small rocks which made for easy landing. Not seeing any sign of a village, the escapees slept with their boat one last night.

Vidar woke his companions early the next morning. He already had his hunting gear on and was ready to move. Complaining of hunger, Bjorn and Jock grabbed their gear and meager supplies from the boat. They began to march inland in a south-west direction. Not long after entering a forest, about one kilometer from the coast, they killed two rabbits and settled themselves for breakfast. Vidar cast his eyes toward mountains ahead of them.

They did not march through the forests, these three travelers, for they had no destination in mind. Rather they simply walked on through forest and glade, hour by hour, day by day until they reached the top of a mountain. It was not an especially impressive mountain but it provided a view which extended across an unpopulated region. Looking across the wide expanse Vidar listened with all of his senses. The air was fresh and clean, carrying a scent of pine. No sound was heard coming from the forest and all of Vidar's senses strained to hear the gentle wind that fell across their shoulders. Smooth rolling hillsides of lush green stretched as far as they could see. A large lake, a long finger of blue water, filled the narrow valley below. One end was hidden by trees, the other end fading into forests of the mountain beyond. A hawk broke the silence as he dove after a smaller bird.

"This land may be nice to the eyes," Jock called out, "but these pesky bugs are killers." Vidar grabbed Jock's arm as he tried to clap his hands on the pest in front of his face.

"That is not a bug! It is a small pixie with wings," Vidar laughed. "We have found a land of enchantment!"

Suddenly another creature arrived and tugged on the first. Vidar could barely hear its small voice, "Fobothom, come! Estavery will seek another mate if you are not at her side when your child arrives." Just as suddenly as the creature appeared, both disappeared in a north-westerly direction.

"Jock, Bjorn," Vidar called out. "We have about four more hours before sunset. Let us see if we can get down to that great finger of water before nightfall."

Faeries come into this earthly realm in several different ways. Vrenessbith was born of the last loving tear from a broken heart as it fell on a frozen heather blossom. Other faeries are born of spring lightning striking a faerie stone. Sparks from the stone climb back up the lightning path and steal its energy. On rare occasions these sparks turn this energy into life, becoming faeries with many magical powers. Then there are those born of the love between two faeries, such as Estavery and Fobothom. If the couple lives by themselves, the birth is much like that of any other creature, painful and hazardous to both newborn and mother. But, if a faerie is a member of a cavie where another faerie imbued with magical powers lives, then the birth is a special event celebrating the full meaning and purpose of all life.

Resbith called to those gathered around her, "Brothers and sisters of the cavie, we have three young faeries who wish to give birth to new faerie spirits this day. Estavery, Thistlebon, Rosetip . . . I see that you are all ready and that you have your partners with you . . . no, Fobothom is missing?"

"He went to get a lavender blossom," Estavery replied meekly. "They are still blooming at the top of the mountain."

Resbith took a deep breath, appreciating who she was waiting for. "Vrenessbith, will you please stand with Estavery until the father arrives?" Resbith paused, looking at the large community surrounding the three couples, especially the three very pregnant faeries about to become mothers. "Community, please form a circle around these parents. Come now, one big circle around all of them. Each of us must now clear our mind and reach out to the forest that makes us strong. See the flowers of spring, colours of autumn, the quiet of winter, and fullness of summer. Breathe in each of these elements and focus them on our mothers. Mothers, release your concerns and hold the hands of your partner in life, both hands. Vrenessbith, will you sing with the elders please?"

Six elder faeries stood side to side forming an arch behind Resbith and began to chant, not just words but melody. Their words and melody surrounded the mothers, making them glow. Slowly each mother floated at shoulder height with her life partner who also had a bit of glow about him. Vrenessbith followed the elders' music, which continued for several minutes, until it was suddenly interrupted by Fobothom's arrival.

"I need to talk with Eric and the village elders," he whispered to Vrenessbith.

"You need to take Estavery's hands and clear your mind of everything except the arrival of your child," Vrenessbith chided Fobothom, slowly sliding Estavery's hands into his. As the exchange was made Estavery's glow slipped and she dropped, just a bit. Vrenessbith rejoined the chanting with a stronger sense. Estavery's glow returned, exceeding the other two for a brief instant.

The musical chant fell into a soft hum and only the wombs of the mothers glowed. Three new spirits then added a melody of their own, arriving almost simultaneously. Gently, fathers lifted the newborn from their mother's stomach as the mother returned to a standing position. Each father, in turn, announced the names of his newborn.

"Liptin, a girl!"

"Stronach, a son!"

"Evalin, our daughter!" Fobothom called out proudly.

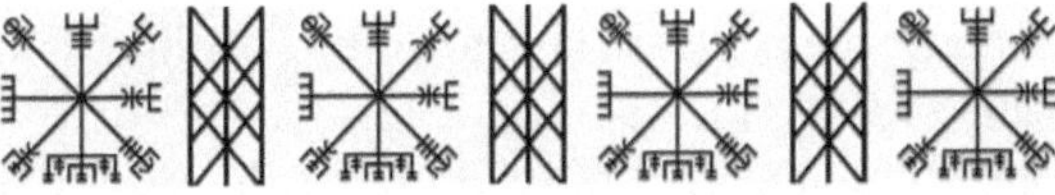

Tripping down the western slope of a richly forested mountain amidst late afternoon shadows, Jock and Bjorn worked to keep up with Vidar who was sure-footed and agile even in the steepest descent. The two followers began laughing at their own clumsiness when Vidar held up his hand and signaled them to be quiet. Slowly Vidar removed the bow from his shoulder and notched an arrow, pulling it back as far as he could reach. A twig snapped in the distance just as the arrow flew. "Supper, boys," Vidar announced, as he bounced across leveling ground to the destination of his arrow. A small deer lay camouflaged beside a thicket of bushes.

"Why don't the two of you refresh our water skins while I start a fire and skin this beautiful contributor to our health and well-being." Jock and Bjorn looked at Vidar with question in their eyes. Vidar removed his water skin and tossed it to his companions, "Oh, a lake is just beyond this thicket. I would go around it, rather than through it."

"We have never been in this land before and still he knows what it has to offer," Bjorn mumbled as he and Jock trekked around the thicket.

"Would you rather journey with Agarn who cannot find his way out of the village?" Jock laughed.

Once they returned with replenished skins, both young men collected wood and built up Vidar's fire. Heavy darkness replaced sunset before the venison was ready to eat and three hungry men could feast.

"This water is as sweet as spring wine; did you get it from a bee hive?" Vidar asked, taking yet another gulp.

"That lake," Bjorn replied, "is sweet like you say, and cold as well. I cannot remember being as refreshed as when I washed my face in it."

"It is sweet because it is fed by the nectar of these hills," offered a woman's voice filled with smooth and sensual tones.

All three men instinctively grabbed for their swords before seeing three women standing before them. Bjorn and Jock smiled admiringly, lowering their weapons. Vidar increased his guard, his muscles tightening.

"Please forgive our intrusion," the first woman offered, "but we saw your fire and smelled your meat. Do you have enough to share?"

"Oh, Yes!" Jock announced, falling over himself to cut slices of venison for their guests. "Please sit and enjoy." Neither Bjorn nor Jock could take their eyes off the visitors.

Each of the women settled next to one of the men. One, who had light brown hair and a slim face leading to a slender seductive body, settled next to Bjorn. Jock's temptress had auburn hair, a round face with luscious white complexion, and a plumpish figure. The woman who had been speaking for the three sat next to Vidar. She was raven-haired and of moderate build, but Vidar was not taken in by her appearance. His senses were tingling and he reinforced his guard, watching every move these women made.

Soon each of the women produced a flask and enticed their host to enjoy the sweet liqueur it contained. Vidar pushed it aside, keeping his defenses up. Then, as if on cue, each of the women tried to embrace their host. Jock and Bjorn put up no resistance but Vidar moved away slightly and sat silently, wary of the proceedings.

Simultaneously, each of the vixens bent down as though to caress their partner. Vidar caught a glint of something shiny as the raven haired woman tried to lean toward him. Rolling away from his pursuer, Vidar stood, sweeping his sword across her neck; she held a blade in her hand. Leaping over the raven vixen, toward his companions, Vidar dispatched Bjorn's seducer but her knife had already sliced him from ribs to navel. The auburn seductress disappeared before Vidar could get to her but she left Jock in the same manner as Bjorn; their insides exposed and their life blood running unabated across the ground.

Sword in hand Vidar turned back to the two women he had killed but they were gone. Firelight revealed two great black spots covering the ground where they had been. Vidar stood silently looking at his friends. A cold dark weight of loneliness and an empty forest wrapped around him.

"Peter, how many of our children were marked by the hags?" Eric asked as he and Peter stood at the great stone chairs. Both looked over the hillside to the sky beyond which turned crimson in a setting sun.

Peter began naming children of *Ceo Dhachaidh*. Together Peter and Eric counted eighteen children who carried the hags' kiss. All were now young adults, sixteen to eighteen years old. Nineteen families of the community had children from infants to young adults, sixty-seven children in all.

"We need to talk with them," Eric mused, thinking about Struan. "We should gather them here tomorrow . . . about this time." The two men admired the fading sunset a moment longer before returning to their huts.

News of the gathering spread through the village as the sun rose the next day. As news went from person to person questions about the reason for the gathering proliferated.

"They are grown; why look at them now?"

"Haven't they suffered enough?"

"Our warriors are all dead; would they now make these children our protectors?"

"Whit right do they have to call our young people together at sunset?"

"Sunset? Would they not rather meet at midday?"

Sixteen young people bearing different marks of the hags gathered around the stone chairs long before the sun touched the horizon. Each also bore a mark on their jaw which was called the "hags' kiss," a mark which the whiskers of the young men would not cover. Other members of their families and the village assembled as well.

When Eric and Peter arrived, nearly every person who lived in *Ceo Dhachaidh* had come to their meeting. Neither of the men had ever really looked at the hags' marks before. One lass had a lip that curled to the side of her nose, another had a drooping eyelid. One lad had a deformed ear, much like Struan, and another had no ears at all. Some folks considered the loss of ears devastating, however as Michael grew up he learned to hear sounds no one else could dream of hearing - a deer stepping on a twig or a beetle chirping on the far side of the village. Two young men had webbing between their fingers and one young woman had no toes, the bones were there but the toes were all one. Two children who bore the hags' kiss were missing; Ian Blackstone and Shawn Murphy went hunting at sunrise and had not yet returned.

"Everyone except the young people with the marks of the hags please move back," Eric called. Peter, Mark, and others helped move the villagers away from the stone chairs. Eric then softened his voice, speaking with the young people who remained. "We learned recently that yer marks may give ye an ability to know when hags are near. I dinna know if this is true or how it works, but my question to yeu who bear the mark of hags is, do ye have any unusual sensation when these foul women are close-by?"

The young people looked at one another, talking amongst themselves in whispered tones. Finally a young man named Matthew spoke up, "This mark ye call the 'hags' kiss' aches when a hag is near. But I can see her, why do I need my jaw to ache?"

"Does it ever ache when ye do not see a hag?" Peter asked.

"Yes, a few times," Matthew replied hesitantly.

"Yes! That is whit we are trying to learn about," Eric assured the young man. "Are there any others?"

Many of the young people shifted their weight from one foot to another, as though they wanted to say something but were afraid. When Peter saw everyone looking to the distant mountains, he turned his head; the sun was beginning to set. "It is near time we should all be in our huts," Peter asserted. "But if any of ye young people have had an experience similar to Matthew, please come talk to Eric or me. Dinna be afraid!"

"Ye better be afraid!" a voice called from the road into the forest.

"Shawn, how was yer hunting?" Peter called.

"Hunting was not good but there is a group of hags heading this way! Eight or more," Ian added.

"How do ye know this?" Eric asked. "Where did ye see them?"

"We dinna see them; we feel thair presence," Ian replied.

"How close are they?" Peter asked, excitement building in his voice.

"Look to the thorns! They should be coming out any time now," Shawn answered.

"Everyone! Return to yer huts!" Peter called to the crowd.

"Shawn, Ian! Will ye please wait with Peter and me just for a moment?" Eric called.

Shawn and Ian grew more uneasy for their sense of hags' arrival was growing more intense. Shawn offered a reply, "We can talk while we walk. I believe there will be more than eight arriving very shortly."

"We can talk later!" Peter consented. "I do not care to do battle today."

Within seconds the sun dipped behind a distant mountain and the forest around *Ceo Dhachaidh* shrieked. Eight hags swept up the road behind Shawn and Ian, five more charged around the hag thorns below the hillside, seven appeared from the forests behind the lodge. Most of the villagers made it back to their huts safely, but not one returned to assist these four men trapped at the top of the hillside.

Before these men could defend themselves, hags swept down on them, knocking them to the ground, pounding them with sticks, assaulting and escaping in one movement. Eric stumbled to his feet, preparing to defend himself with his stave as Ian lunged with his dirk into a hag approaching from Eric's rear. Shawn began striking at the air with his stave, connecting each time with a hag. The attacks slowed and Shawn used the delay to notch an arrow and fire into the field, narrowly missing a hag. As the men continued to fight, attacks became more severe, hags were now using knives.

"FORTRYLLAIS!" an unexpected stranger screamed as he plunged his sword into an auburn haired hag. Turning, he drew his sword through another hag and spun immediately into a third. The stranger's attack afforded the four men of *Ceo Dhachaidh* time to orient themselves and organize an effective defense against their attackers. Without instruction or call, the four men formed a circle with their backs to one another giving them full vision in all directions. When a group of hags attacked their formation, the visitor joined their circle, fighting his way into their defensive position. As hags disappeared in one quarter the man looking in that direction would turn and join the man beside him, keeping watch to his unguarded side. Black spots began to cover the ground near the stone chairs. Suddenly, the attackers disappeared back into the dark of the forest.

Finding no more hags, the four men turned their attention to their unexpected defender.

"Whit was that ye called out?" Ian asked the visitor. "Was it a spell?"

"No. 'Fortryllais,' it is word of my people," the young man smiled. "I know little of your language. It is not spell, it is magic . . . no . . . one who does evil magic, dark magic."

"Bana-bhustraich . . . a witch," Eric offered.

The young man shrugged his shoulders and smiled. "I am Vidar, son of Agrald of Norge. This fortryllais, she kill my friend yesterday."

"We are certainly glad she did not kill yeu," Peter chuckled with a sigh. "We should be getting to our huts. Vidar, would ye care to rest in my hut tonight?" Vidar nodded and followed his host.

〰〰〰〰〰〰〰〰〰〰

"Angus, it is gettin' late and these wee ones have to catch a plane tomorrow," Lillian advised.

"Aye, it has been a grand summer having the three of ye bairn with us," Angus said with a smile. Sighing heavily, he placed the ribbon back in his book which closed on his lap.

"But what about the story?" Liam cried out. "When will you finish reading the story?"

"Well," Angus replied thoughtfully, "we are about half way through, I believe. I still have two journals yet to include. No, three. Will ye be coming back again next summer?"

"YES!!" all three children screamed at once.

"Good, then," Lillian said with a laugh. "Ye all need to get washed up. We can pack yer bags in the morning, after breakfast."

Lillian then began herding children upstairs. Angus placed the book on his desk, squarely on top of the Bradshear Enterprises brochure.

"Seanair . . .," Alex called to Angus with a question.

"Aye, lad?" Angus replied, turning to face his oldest grandson.

"Are those men on the hillside gone? They won't destroy the stones, will they?"

"Gone? I doubt it. They have invested quite a sum of money in our hielands. But, they will nae touch a single stone on our hillside while I am alive!"

"Good. Next summer, could you teach me to read the old journals and scrolls?"

"Aye, laddie, that I can. In fact, I will save the last scroll for ye to do while ye are here. I can show ye how with one, then ye can take over. My Seanair taught me, I will teach yeu. How does that sound?"

Beaming with delight, the eleven-year-old scholar wrapped his arms around his grandfather, and thanked him. "I would really like that!"

The legends of *Ceo Dhachaidh*, the Highlanders, and Vrenessbith continues in "Vrenessbith - Catharrachd."

Cast of Key Characters

Family on the hillside
Alex - eleven-year-old grandson
Angus Gregson - seanair, grandfather
Belinda - current Comleidh of the cavie in the oak tree
Liam - an eight-year-old grandson
Lillian - wife of Angus
Marian - ten-year-old granddaughter

Highlanders (alphabetical order) - their village
Alistaire - Doup Fell - Celt, elder / leader of village
Bloigh Bryan - Blyth Brier - noisy braggart, uncle to Bryan
Bryan - Blyth Brier - young warrior enlisted to train Highlanders
Chris - Ceo Dhachaidh - son of Sarah by first husband, brother to Erial
Elizabeth - Ceo Dhachaidh - wife of Iain
Erial - Ceo Dhachaidh - first born daughter of Eric and Sarah
Eric (first generation) - Ceo Dhachaidh - young farmer, piper, deer runner
Iain - Ceo Dhachaidh - Celtic leader, brought families to mountains
Ian - Ceo Dhachaidh - first-born son with hags' kiss
Inger - Ceo Dhachaidh - wife of Seumas
Martin - Ceo Dhachaidh - Celt, elder / leader of village, trainer
Peter - Ceo Dhachaidh - younger leader of village, trainer
Rachel (first generation) - Ceo Dhachaidh - red haired orphan, desired
    and feared by all men, deer runner, warrior, trainer
Roslyn - Blyth Brier - Bryan's mother
Sarah - Ceo Dhachaidh - wife of Eric, mother of Chris and Erial
Sean - Benmost Bield - Celt, protector of faerie cavie
Seumas - Ceo Dhachaidh - cousin to Iain, second in command
Shawn - Ceo Dhachaidh - first-born son with hags' kiss
Struan - Blyth Brier - first-born son with hags' kiss
Tristan - Blyth Brier - first-born son of Rachel and Bryan
Vidar - seventh son refugee from Norge (Norway)

Important Critters
Muestor - martryn, guardian of faerie cavie
Thimpkin - son of the martryn Muestor

<u>**Key Faeries**</u> - many faeries float through our story, here are the names of the steadfast key faeries who help to carry us along.
Brianne
Estavery
Fobothom
Resbith - Comleidh
Seebtin
Vrenessbith - our guide and Guardian of the Highlands

For other books by author
E Gale Buck
Please visit
www.woodsmanstories.com

www.ingramcontent.com/pod-product-compliance
Lightning Source LLC
Chambersburg PA
CBHW050233110726

47898CB00007B/2137